Anya gest _____ the mark
of the Horned Viper. Did you see him do that?"

Virgil nodded. *"Damndest thing. He drew on the floor
with his finger, and it glowed, bright as coke in a steel mill."*

The spirit was messing with her, or he'd lost his grip
on reality over the years, or . . . her logical mind refused
to contemplate what the alternative meant, if he told the
truth. She crossed her arms over her chest. "He didn't have
a torch or welding equipment?"

*"No, ma'am. He came in here with empty hands. He set
that mark on the floor, and then . . . this wave of fire rolled
up from the floor. It was like looking at the ocean, only red,
the way it moved . . ."* Virgil made curving shapes with his
hands. *"It was beautiful,"* he admitted.

"Thank you, Virgil. I appreciate your help."

Virgil tipped his hat and melted into the wall. *"It's a
pleasure, Miss Anya. Good luck."*

Anya turned to look at Brian. "Did you get any of
that?"

Brian showed her a voice recorder. "We'll see. I take it
from your end of the conversation that he positively ID'd
your suspect?"

"Yeah. But it's not exactly the kind of evidence that will
stand up in court. I can't put a ghost on the stand."

Brian surveyed the wreckage of the basement. "Somehow, I think that's going to be the least of your problems."

Embers is also available as an eBook

Embers

LAURA BICKLE

POCKET BOOKS

New York   London   Toronto   Sydney

Pocket Books
A Division of Simon & Schuster, Inc.
1230 Avenue of the Americas
New York, NY 10020

This book is a work of fiction. Names, characters, places, and incidents either are products of the author's imagination or are used fictitiously. Any resemblance to actual events or locales or persons, living or dead, is entirely coincidental.

First Juno Books/Pocket Books paperback edition April 2010

JUNO BOOKS and colophon are trademarks of Wildside Press LLC used under license by Simon & Schuster, Inc., the publisher of this work.

POCKET and colophon are registered trademarks of Simon & Schuster, Inc.

For information about special discounts for bulk purchases, please contact Simon & Schuster Special Sales at 1-866-506-1949 or business@simonandschuster.com.

The Simon & Schuster Speakers Bureau can bring authors to your live event. For more information or to book an event, contact the Simon & Schuster Speakers Bureau at 1-866-248-3049 or visit our website at www.simonspeakers.com.

Designed by Jacquelynne Hudson
Cover design by John Vairo Jr., illustration by Chris McGrath

Manufactured in the United States of America

10   9   8   7   6   5   4   3   2   1

ISBN 978-1-4391-6765-6
ISBN 978-1-4391-6767-0 (ebook)

Dedicated to my infinitely patient husband.

ACKNOWLEDGMENTS

THANKS TO MY WRITING GROUP, the Ohio Writers Network: Linda, Michelle, Melissa, Rachel, Emily, Tracy, and Faith.

Thank you to my editor, Paula Guran, for teaching as you work.

CHAPTER ONE

TRUTH BURNED.

It always burned, even in the dark, cold hours of the morning when nearly everything slept.

Anya stood on the doorstep of the haunted house, hands jammed into her pockets, stifling a yawn. She'd taken a cab, not wanting her license plates to be seen and recorded in the vicinity. The cab had peeled away, red lights receding down the gray street. The two-story brown brick house before her looked like every other house on the block, windows and doors ribboned in iron bars. Cables from the beat-up panel van parked curbside snaked under the front door, but no light shined inside. Empty plastic bags drifted over the cracked sidewalk until trapped by a low iron fence.

She poked the doorbell. Inside, she heard the echo of the chime, the responding scrape of movement. Anya wiped her feet on the doormat duct-taped to the painted stoop, waiting.

A lamp clicked on inside the house, and the door

opened a crack. "Thanks for coming," the masculine voice behind the door said.

"It's not like I could say no."

That was the truth; it was not as if she could turn down what they asked, even if she wanted to. She held back a larger truth that scalded her throat: *And I wish you would stop calling. I wish you would stop asking me to do this.*

Anya stepped over the cords into the circle of yellow light cast by a lamp with a barrel-shaped shade in the living room. The shade's wire skeleton cast dark spokes on the ceiling, illuminating a water stain that had been carefully painted over. But the water had still seeped through, yellowing the popcorn ceiling. A wooden console television sat dark and silent as a giant bug in the corner, rabbit-ear antennae turned north and east, listening for a dead signal. A shabby plaid couch dominated the room, covered with out-of-place pieces of tech equipment: electromagnetic field readers, digital voice recorders, compact video cameras. Laptop computers were propped up on TV-tray tables, casting rectangles of blue light on the walls.

Anya's gaze drifted to the video cameras, then shied away. "I don't want to be recorded."

"We know."

Jules, the leader of the Detroit Area Ghost Researchers, leaned against the wall, nursing a cup of coffee. No one would ever suspect Jules to be so deeply interested in the paranormal that he would lead a group of ghost hunters. He was the epitome of an ordinary guy: early forties, slight paunch covered by a blue polo shirt, well-worn jeans. A tattoo of a cross peeked out underneath his sleeve. Exhaustion creased the mahogany face underneath the Detroit Tigers baseball cap. Judging by the amount of equipment and the rolled-up sleeping bags in the corners, DAGR had spent a number of nights here.

Anya perched on the edge of the couch and rubbed her amber-colored eyes. "What's the story?"

Jules took a swig of his coffee, creamer clinging to his dark moustache. "We first took the case two weeks ago . . . the little old lady that lives in the house was convinced that her dead husband was coming back to haunt her. She described lights turning off of their own accord, dark shapes in the mirrors."

"Did she come to you or did you find her?"

"I found her." Jules worked as gas meter reader in his day job. He had a knack for easy conversation, and people instinctively trusted him. Anya suspected he might have some latent psychic talent in getting a feel for places and people. He had an affinity for most people, anyway. Jules seemed wary of Anya. She didn't think he liked her much or thought very highly of her methods. But she got the job done when Jules couldn't.

"She's got a basement meter and was afraid to go down there all by herself. Neighbor lady who used to do her laundry won't do it anymore . . . said a lightbulb exploded while she was loading the washer." Jules took a sip of his coffee.

"What evidence have you found?" Anya asked.

Brian, DAGR's tech specialist, peered over one of his computer screens and took off a pair of headphones. "Come see."

Anya sat beside him on the sagging couch, which smelled like lavender. Brian scrolled through some digital video; she assumed it had come from a fixed-camera shot of the basement stairs. A flashlight beam washed down the steps, green in the contrasting false color tones of night-vision footage. The glow from the screen highlighted the planes and angles of Brian's face. Anya noted the circles under his blue eyes and his mussed brown hair. She thought she smelled the mint of the caffeinated shower soap he favored still clinging to him.

Anya never asked where Brian got all his techno-toys. She knew that most of DAGR's clients had little money and that donations were few and far between. DAGR was more likely to be paid with an apple pie than cash. She suspected that Brian borrowed much of it from his day job at the university. Apparently, the eggheads in the IT department never seemed to notice that things kept disappearing into Brian's van.

The footage paused, fell dark green once more. In the well of jade darkness under the stairs, something moved. The shape of a hand clawed up over one of the upper steps, then receded.

"Weird," Anya breathed, resting her heart-shaped face in her hand. "What else have you got?"

"This." Brian handed her his headphones, still warm from his ears. Anya fitted them over her head, listened to a static hum of low-level white noise that barely vibrated an on-screen noise meter.

"I don't—"

"Wait for it."

There. A hiss shivered the line on the meter. Then a voice—reedy and snarling—ripped the volume line to the top of the meter: *"Mine."*

Anya frowned. "Can I hear it again?"

Brian backed the tape up. Static hummed, something hissed, and the voice repeated: *"Mine."*

Anya pulled the headphones off, disentangling them from her sleep-tousled chestnut hair. Her hair caught on the copper salamander torque she wore around her neck, and she gently unsnarled it. The salamander gripped its tail in its front feet, the tail sinuously curling down to disappear between Anya's breasts. The metal, as always, felt warm to the touch. "Did you guys provoke it?"

"Of course. We told it that it was ugly and that its transvestite mama dresses it funny." The youngest member of the group, Max, grinned at her, megawatt smile splitting his brown face. He'd been exiled to the floor, hands wound in his warm-up jacket, his sneakers and long legs tucked under one of Brian's TV tables.

Jules smacked him on the back of the head. "Max got too mouthy with it. Started in on the 'your mama' jokes while I was reading the Scriptures to it."

Max ducked. He was still on probation and was very close to getting booted from the group. Anya hoped the kid would stay, that he would eventually fill the spot on

DAGR's roster from which she was trying to extricate herself. Though no one could do exactly what she could do, it would be good for them to have someone new to focus on.

"So . . . what is it, exactly?" Anya asked, redirecting the conversation from Max's punishment to the matter at hand.

"We don't think it's the old lady's husband." Katie's hushed voice came from the darkened kitchen as she pushed Ciro's wheelchair across the wrinkled olive-colored carpet. Katie was DAGR's witch. She was dressed in jeans and a patchwork blouse, her blond hair curled over her back, tied with black velvet ribbons. A silver pentacle hung just below her throat, gleaming in the dim light. "It feels like an impostor, something toying with her."

Ciro folded his gnarled ebony hands over the blanket in his lap. The light from Brian's computers washed over his small-framed glasses, and he smiled at Anya. "Hello, Anya."

"Hi, Ciro." Anya crossed to the old man and gave him a hug. He felt more fragile than the last time she'd seen him. It had to be a serious event for Ciro to be here . . . he was the group's on-call demonologist. And he was the one who had brought them all together, over Jules's objections. Ciro understood, more than anyone else, what it cost Anya to be here with them.

Anya put her hand on Ciro's thin shoulder. "Is it a demon, then?"

Ciro shook his head. "I don't think so. I think it's one pissed-off malevolent spirit that's moved in. The woman's grief opened the door . . . but it's a tough bastard."

"You tried to drive it out already?"

Katie nodded. "Salt, bells . . . we even brought in a priest. It's rooted here and we can't dig it out." From the corner of her eye, Anya watched Jules frown at Katie. He didn't think much of Katie's methods, either. Jules preferred to put the fear of God—or at least his version of it—into ghosts to scare them out the windows, but that seemed to be working less and less. Anya observed the carbon stains worked into Katie's fingernails. The witch had been trying hard, but all her spells and incantations had also failed to drive it away. This had been happening more and more often in recent months: recalcitrant, restless spirits that just wouldn't let go. Once a spirit had chosen to hang on, after all efforts to convince it otherwise, there was no choice but to remove it by force.

"The old lady wants it gone?" Anya asked, just to be certain. There was always the possibility that the old woman's attachment prevented it from leaving. Perhaps, in her loneliness, she'd taken in a spiritual boarder. Anya understood how isolation could cause a person to unwittingly do things contrary to one's best interests. An empty, silent house left a lot of room for ruminations, for regrets. And, sometimes, sinister things could move into those spaces.

"She wants it out. She wants to sell the house and move to Florida." Ciro smiled. "I'm jealous."

"Will you do it?" Jules's expression was pinched. "Will you get rid of it?"

Get rid of it . . . that sounded so tidy. So clean. Like taking out the garbage. Ciro glanced sidelong at her, the only one with an inkling of what this cost her over and over again.

"Okay." Anya shrugged off her coat. "Take me to it."

Anya's step creaked on the basement stairs. Her boots crunched on the eggshell fragments of broken glass . . . the remains of the overhead lightbulb, she guessed. She smelled the cinnamon tang of Katie's crushed magick rotting in the dark. Behind her, the basement door closed off the dim light from the kitchen, leaving Anya in darkness.

Anya clicked on her flashlight, then swept it down the stairs. Shadows shrank, pulling back behind the washer and dryer. She smelled moldering potatoes and onions, dampness on the dirt floor . . . and pickles. Her brow wrinkled. Dozens of canning jars were arranged on a wooden shelf, most of them shattered, some cracked and still drizzling glass and vinegar to the now-filthy concrete floor. *A waste of perfectly good pickles*, Anya thought, stomach grumbling.

Overhead, a flexible dryer duct threaded through the unfinished ceiling. Boxes of Christmas decorations lined the walls. Old dresses, carefully encased in plastic bags, were neatly hung from lengths of overhead pipe. A scarred workbench, which must have belonged to the old man, stood in the corner, its tools stilled. This place was the vault of the old woman's memories; no wonder the malevolent spirit had found a home here, in all the dust and emotion of years. Fertile ground for a wandering spirit.

"Another witch?" Something giggled from beneath the stairs.

"No, not another witch." Anya's salamander torque burned her neck, causing prickling sweat. The heat uncurled away from the torque around her throat, spiraled down her arm, and leaped lightly to the steps. A fire spirit, a salamander, was unleashed from the necklace. He shimmered with semitransparent amber light, large as a Rottweiler. Sparky took the shape of the massive speckled salamanders found in mountain streams, the monsters that folks called hellbenders. His size and shape were as mutable as flame. The hellbender was one of his favorite forms, although Sparky modified even that shape to suit his needs or fancy. Head as large as a shovel, body as thick as a tree, Sparky's tail sizzled around Anya's knee, his tongue flicking into the darkness. Sparky was invisible to most people, although Katie could sense him and Brian could read the temperature changes he invoked on his instruments. But Sparky was not invisible to the thing under the stairs.

The spirit hissed. *"Elemental."*

"This is your last chance," Anya said. "Get out now. Or I will destroy you."

The spirit snarled: *"Mine."*

Anya sighed. Just once, she wanted one to go out easy. One spirit that hadn't been aggravated and goaded beyond all reason, one spirit to just go away when she told it to. Nice and quiet, for a change.

She strode down the steps, Sparky flowing before her. Under the steps, the spirit thumped against the risers as she walked, trying to intimidate her. Anya ignored it, descending with an even stride. She would not give it the satisfaction of rattling her.

A board splintered, then broke. Anya stumbled, tripping over the shards of wood. Sparky flung himself across the foot of the stairs, breaking her fall. Her flashlight bounced down the stairs, went dark, and rolled away in the darkness. She landed in a tangle of hot salamander skin and her own boots on the cold concrete floor, unhurt in the glass and pickle juice, but irritated. The only light remaining was Sparky's glow, dimmer and more diffuse than the flashlight.

The thing under the stairs snickered.

The doorknob at the top of the stairs rattled, but wouldn't open. The sound of something heavy striking the door echoed like a gunshot. Jules's voice filtered down through the door. "Anya? You okay?"

"I'm fine," she answered, picking herself off the floor and brushing glass from her hands and jeans. "Leave us be."

Sparky orbited around her, a curling mass of light. He hissed, a sound that rippled the loose, mottled skin on his body. Fernlike gills on the sides of his head fanned out, primitive and fearsome. He cast enough light for her to see by, a soft gold light of distant fire.

The basement spirit was stronger than she'd thought. She imagined the owner of the house facing this thing alone, and bristled at its arrogance. Power like that could have crippled or killed the old woman.

As for what it had done to the pickles . . . blasphemy.

Anya rounded the corner to peer under the stairs and her breath snagged in her throat. The knot of darkness under the steps radiated cold, smacking her as if she'd just opened a door and stepped outside into winter. Her warm breath steamed as she exhaled, and she put her hands on her hips, staring at the old-fashioned soda pop machine underneath the stairs. It was scarred and dented, painted with a picture of a perky woman in sunglasses and a head scarf holding a glass bottle. Flowing white script exhorted customers to "Drink up!" The coin slot stated that pop was ten cents. This forgotten antique would have been worth a fortune at auction, but it also made a very nice home for a malevolent spirit.

Anya kicked the picture of the smiling woman. "You. Get the hell out of there." She was tired, smelled like pickles, and was beginning to get pissed. She had an early shift in the morning and should be safely in dreamland, not beating up on a pop machine.

The machine spat out a glass soda bottle. It exploded against the floor like a small grenade. Anya jumped back. Cold, sticky fluid splashed over her boot.

Within the machine, she could hear more glass bottles ratcheting into position. Sparky shoved her behind the workbench as a volley of glass shattered against the cinder-block wall and the raw wood surface of the bench. Bolts and screws clattered off the table in a metallic rain, plinking as they dripped to the floor. Sparky's head peeped over a drill press, tail lashing.

Anya growled, "Enough of these tantrums."

When the machine clicked empty, Anya and Sparky leaped from behind the workbench to charge the machine.

The machine rattled, rocking back and forth. From the corner of her eye, Anya could see that it wasn't plugged in—the cord lay coiled on the floor. Sparky snapped at the cord that slithered to life, curling across the cement.

Anya slapped her left hand to the cold surface of the machine, pressed her right to her heart. She felt a familiar heat swell in her chest, felt it burn in her throat. She breathed it in, allowing it to rise and suffuse her, feeling it crackle in her hands as the unearthly glow washed over her. Her amber aura expanded, winged out like a cloak, and a hole opened above her heart. The flame inside her roared, reaching for the pathetic, pickle-smashing ghost.

She could feel the cold spirit in the soda machine, cool and slippery as liquid. Ghost-fire flickered at her fingertips and she could feel the small, petulant shape of the spirit in the dark. Anya drew the ghost into her chest with an inhalation, feeling it icy against her throat. Like swallowing an ice cube whole, she felt it stick, melt, and glide down into her empty chest. Devouring it, she allowed the fire in her heart to immolate it, burning it to ash.

She stepped back, breathing deep. Her body steamed in the chill, and she smelled burnt things. Her incandescing aura settled around her like a second skin, then dwindled. Sparky, victorious over the limp electrical cord on the floor, slithered to Anya's side. He faded to a fine golden mist, curling up over her arm and solidifying around her neck once again. Shivering, Anya was grateful for his warmth.

Anya was the rarest type of medium: a Lantern. Spirits were inexorably drawn to her, moths to the flame. That was common enough among most types of mediums. Ordinary mediums could allow spirits to wear their skins at will; to use their voices, their hands; to surrender their bodies to another spirit. Anya shuddered to imagine allowing a spirit that kind of control.

But Lanterns were unusual. She had never met another Lantern. She only knew the term from her conversations with Ciro. It was not a role she relished playing. Katie had said that Anya had the blessing of fire upon her. Like a human bug zapper, she took spirits into her inner elemental light and devoured them, incinerating them. She hated the cold touch of spirits in her throat; they tasted hard and metallic, like water with too much iron. After devouring one, it seemed that days would pass before she could feel truly warm again.

"Couldn't go easy, could you?" Anya bent to retrieve her flashlight, then viciously kicked the winking woman on the soda machine. Her boot left a scuff mark on the woman's chin.

The front of the machine sprang open like a refrigerator door, startling her. Skin prickling, she shined her flashlight into the metal void, swallowing hard.

At first, she thought it was a doll stuffed inside the machine, curled in the fetal position. But she was not to be that lucky tonight. Blood pounded in her ears. Closer inspection showed the desiccated corpse of a child, dry as a milkweed husk. Tattered lace at the hem of a dress moved, disturbed by Anya's breath. Plastic barrettes clasped braids in the child's black hair. Leather sneakers the size of Anya's hand were curled up against the wall of the machine. The girl had clearly been here for decades, missing and forgotten. Perhaps a game of hide-and-seek gone wrong. Perhaps a homicide. There was no way to know now.

Anya wiped her fingerprints from the front of the door with her sleeve, watching her arm shake. She didn't want the police to know she'd been here. It would raise too many questions. DAGR would have to notify the police. They had better cover for her, not reveal that she had been here. She worried about what the shock of this discovery would do to the old pickle woman who was afraid to do her laundry in the basement . . . assuming she was innocent of putting the girl in the pop machine.

Dimly, she still heard pounding on the door above. Finally it splintered away, and footsteps thundered down the broken stairs.

"Watch the step!" she called, too late. Max jammed his foot in the breach and fell half through the stairs. Jules tried to reel him in, reaming him out for going first.

Anya stared at her feet. She reeked of pickles. Her hands were sticky with decades-old cola, and her hair was peppered with glass.

And now a dead child. Not a good night.

She stared, blinking at the ceiling, vowing to stop answering DAGR's calls. DAGR's calls always led to strange truths, and she was tired of digging for them.

CHAPTER TWO

"I TOLD JULES NOT TO CALL," Brian said. He stared through the van's windshield at the deserted streets. He didn't look at Anya, just focused straight ahead. He'd insisted on taking Anya home, over her protestations that she could call a cab.

Anya glanced at his profile. It was a handsome profile, one that she'd known better once upon a time: strong jaw, aquiline nose, sensuous mouth. That was before Brian had gotten too close. And she didn't want him to get burned. Anya kept to her side of the van seat, fingers wrapped around a hot chocolate in a Styrofoam cup.

"Oh," she said.

Brian shook his head. "I didn't mean it like that. I meant . . ." He blew out his breath, fogging the glass. "I meant that you seemed to want your distance. From DAGR. From all of us."

Anya stared into her hot chocolate. "Look, I'm just going through some stuff at work right now."

"Those arsons?"

"Yeah." Anya sank into her seat, rubbed the bridge of her nose. She worked as an investigator for the Detroit Fire Department during the day. "The chief's been on us to get those solved. We're on number three."

"Are you sure it's the same guy?"

"Has to be. Same MO . . . no traces of accelerant. Whoever is doing this has time to case the buildings. He knows when they're going to be unwatched for a long period of time, to let the buildings burn." She shook her head. "It's only a matter of time until someone gets seriously hurt."

Anya stared out the window at the city, which was still covered by the velvet blanket of night before the sun rose. At this early hour, buses had just begun to run, creeping along in the bus lanes like caterpillars chewing along the veins of leaves. The shift had begun to change at the auto plant on the border between Detroit and Hamtramck. Workers trickled from the parking lot to the massive gray building behind razor wire. Anya wondered how deeply those men and women felt the tension that crept over the city in recent years: the increase in unemployment, the crime. These visible and invisible unrests fed an undercurrent of spiritual unease. The psychiatric hospitals were full, as were the church pews. DAGR was going out nearly every night to answer pleas for help from people whose homes and businesses had been invaded by phantoms.

Brian turned past the massive Catholic church at the heart of Hamtramck. St. Florian's spires reached taller than any other building for blocks. Incorporated by Polish immigrants in 1921, this part of the Detroit area was

Anya's backyard. She'd grown up in the shadow of the church, and she remained within sight of the steeple, even though she'd never passed through its doors as an adult. In its shadow, there seemed to be a bit less decay than elsewhere.

Brian shut off the engine before a modest story-and-a-half white-sided house, identical to every other white vinyl-sided house on the street, only the shutters on this one were green. A crabapple tree grew in the yard, shading curling roof shingles. The blinds inside were drawn tight against the sun.

"I found something in the pickle lady's house. Something I thought you'd want to hear." Brian reached over her knees. Anya flinched. He pretended to ignore her reaction, unhurriedly opening the glove box. He pulled out a voice recorder. "I got something on tape while you were tussling with the pop machine."

Her cheeks flamed in anger. "I told you not to record me. That's a deal-breaker and you know it."

"I wasn't. I just watched on the webcam."

Anya crossed her arms. She didn't like the idea of being watched. Even though she knew there was nothing for ordinary eyes to see, eyes that couldn't see sprits, she wouldn't allow it. And Brian was well aware of her stance.

"Look, I just wanted to make sure you were okay." He blew out his breath. "After all the thumping . . . never mind." He waved his hand. "This recorder was in the pickle lady's bedroom. It picked up some sound right about the time you opened up the pop machine." He clicked it on.

The faintest whisper blew across a background of white noise: *"Sirrush is coming."*

Anya blinked. It was amazing that he heard it. Damn it, but Brian was a thorough researcher. She couldn't hide from the facts he uncovered.

Brian shut the recorder off. "Does that mean anything to you?"

She looked down at her hot chocolate. Her thoughts churned and she could feel the weight of his gaze on her. "I don't know."

He remained silent, watching her. Finally, he gave up, piercing the uncomfortable silence. "Look. If you need anything . . ."

Anya listened to the engine tick, then lifted her chin. "I'm fine, Brian." She tried to smile. "Thanks." Her fingers brushed the door latch.

"Anya."

She turned to face him, and the seat squeaked under her jeans, still damp with cola and pickle juice. "Brian, please. I just . . . devoured the soul of a child. A child haunting the pickle lady's house." She rubbed her hand over her amber eyes. The sting of vinegar in the pickle juice blurred her vision and her voice caught. "I just want . . . a shower and a couple of hours of sleep. Can we talk about this later?"

Brian, looking as if she'd punched him, jammed the key in the ignition. "Okay. Just . . . be careful."

Anya often wondered where the souls she devoured went. Did they receive a free-parking permit to some sunlit place of spiritual enlightenment? Did they simply cease existing, snuffed out in darkness? She hoped that they moved on or, at the very least, stopped suffering. Whatever happened, she hoped that they didn't become food, a spiritual nourishment for the vacuum in her heart.

That vacuum had grown in the last several months. She could feel its numbness, its isolation growing larger, like a black hole. Ever hungry, the hole devoured everything that fell within the reach of her terrible gravity. It seemed to spin faster with each breath, reaching for more. The more spirits she collected, the larger and denser and heavier the hole grew. She was afraid of what else might fall into its event horizon, if she let others get too close.

Anya closed her front door and leaned against it. The taking of the child-spirit disturbed her. She'd expected that the force haunting the pickle lady's house would have been a run-of-the-mill spirit, turned malevolent by the weight of time and boredom. A mischievous imp, one she could snuff out without her conscience troubling her sleep. But this incident would haunt her for a long time. She could feel the weight of regret dragging at her as she kicked off her boots and threw her coat on the faded couch.

Her stocking feet scraped up static electricity on the rust-colored shag carpeting in the living room. She'd decorated the room plainly, with garage-sale finds: a captain's trunk standing in as a coffee table, a pair of mismatched ginger jar lamps, a mirror in an antiqued brass frame over a velveteen sofa. Anya had handled each of the items carefully before buying them—she didn't want to deal with anything harboring negative imprints or spirits of the previous owners. If Anya could've afforded it, she'd have bought new furniture.

Katie had helped Anya choose many of these objects that held no residue of anything that came before. The witch had blessed the house and said it had a happy history, which was a small comfort. There were too few houses like that in Detroit nowadays. The house smelled of lemon juice and sage, scrubbed clean of any spiritual or physical dirt. Anya kept her gear from the fire department in the car, reluctant to bring the debris and contamination into the oasis of her home.

She didn't bother to turn on the lights. All the appliances in the house were unplugged, and the outlets were covered with child-safe plastic plugs. Sparky had an abnormal interest in all things electrical, and Anya couldn't trust him not to taste the electrical juice and blow a fuse. Lacking opposable thumbs, Sparky had not yet figured out how to pry the plugs from the walls. Last week, she'd bought a microwave. As far as Sparky was concerned, this was the best kitchen gadget, *ever*. It sat, back in its box, on the kitchen table, the white enamel finish charred black and the window cracked. Anya figured the odds of returning it were low, but she'd give it a try.

She stepped into the bathroom and clicked on the overhead light. The black-and-white retro tile gleamed. A collection of rubber duckies lined a shelf on one wall, grinning down at her with cartoon smiles. Anya turned the bathtub tap as hot as it would go, then dropped a fistful of bath salts into the water. She plucked her favorite duck, a jaunty pirate with a plastic eye patch, from the collection and dropped him in the water. He spun in lazy circles under the faucet.

She peeled off her sticky, pickle-stained clothes and stuffed them in the washing machine in the bathroom closet. The chill rippled over her body as she measured detergent into the basin and set the water temperature to hot. When she'd moved in, Anya had the foresight to install an extra-large water heater. As a fire investigator, her work always got her filthy and she didn't deny herself the luxury of as much hot water as she needed.

She paused, catching sight of her reflection in the mirror. Her light chestnut hair swung over her milky-pale shoulder, which was studded with a constellation of beauty marks. Her fingers fluttered across her chest. Below the salamander collar that housed Sparky, a black char mark was burned into the flesh over her left breast. The wound didn't hurt. She knew it would eventually fade, like all the other exorcism burns, but it was a lingering reminder of the soul she'd devoured.

She stepped into the bath, wiggling her toes, feeling the warmth begin to radiate up her legs. She sank up to her neck in the water, massaging the hot water through her hair. The pirate duck bumped against her toes. She reached for a loofah and began to scrub hard, as if she could scrub the memory of the dead child away from her skin.

The sepulchral voice captured on the recorder buzzed in the back of her head, and her thoughts nipped at it:

"Sirrush is coming."

Her brow wrinkled. She'd never heard the name spoken aloud, only read it in books. Sirrush was an old term used for firedrakes and salamanders, a name used only in witches' ceremonial magick to draw down the element of fire. But the spirit's message seemed to be aimed at her and she chewed on it, tasting it for any flavor of a threat.

As the water cooled, Anya climbed out of the bath. She smelled no pickles or ash as she pulled the drain plug, just soap and a hint of jasmine from the bath salts. The pirate duck spiraled around the drain.

Anya toweled off and pulled on her robe, which was decorated in a pattern of yellow cartoon ducks. Wet footprints on the shag rug in the hall trailed behind her. She paused in the hallway to turn up the thermostat, looking forward to the warmth of her bed. A simple futon piled high with blankets dominated the small bedroom. Anya couldn't bring herself to buy a secondhand bed. All beds were stained too much with the dreams of their prior owners.

Anya climbed under the blankets, sighing. She'd be able to get a couple of hours of sleep before her shift began. As she drowsed, the salamander collar warmed around her neck. Sparky unpeeled himself, slipped down to the floor. He padded across the floor to a large flannel dog bed placed against the wall. Resting in the bed was his favorite toy: a Glowworm. The stuffed toy was a flashlight ingeniously disguised in a cherubic plastic head and a caterpillar body. Since it ran on batteries, there was little electrical damage that Sparky could do to it that would result in a hazardous situation—unlike the microwave.

Sparky placed his foot on the Gloworm. It lit up. He removed his paw, and the light winked out. He cocked his head, watching it, then patted it again.

On.

Off.

On.

Anya scrunched her eyes shut against the blinking light. As much as he enjoyed biting ghosts and other ghoulies on the spiritual plane, Sparky could only directly affect two things in the physical world: energy and Anya. The toy had brought him many hours of delight. She'd placed it in the dog bed that he never used, hoping that Sparky could eventually be persuaded to sleep on his own in his own bed.

A whine emanated from the side of Anya's bed.

Anya opened one eye. Sparky's head peered over the mountain of covers. Anya groaned. She was too tired to try to Ferberize the salamander tonight.

She climbed out of bed, grabbed the Gloworm, and tossed it into her bed. Sparky climbed in with her and rooted under the blankets. He made himself comfortable, draped over one of Anya's hips. He cradled the Gloworm between his feet. Anya idly stroked his loose speckled skin and Sparky began to purr, a low vibration in the back of his ribs.

Sometimes, Anya wondered what it would have been like to have had Brian's warmth next to her. She'd seriously contemplated it in the past. But she didn't know how to explain sharing a bed with a familiar elemental spirit. While it was true that humans couldn't see Sparky, his presence could be sensed: fluctuations in temperature, static electricity, a sense of being watched. When Anya had taken lovers before, Sparky had not taken well to them. It was distracting to be in the act of making love to a man with a five-foot salamander sitting at the foot of the bed, head cocked, slapping his tail on the blankets. Sparky manifested at will, unpredictably. But he could always be trusted to make an appearance whenever Anya was in the presence of spirits . . . or when the possibility for intimacy with a man presented itself.

The copper salamander collar had been her mother's. Though her mother had never spoken of it, Anya assumed that Sparky had been bound to the collar as long as it had existed . . . however long that had been. When her mother had recognized Anya's budding gift of mediumship, she had given her Sparky for protection. Anya had never known her father, but Anya's mother had obviously managed—at least once—to surmount the obstacle of romance with an elemental chaperone. But Anya's mother was gone, and there was no one else to ask how to train a salamander to sleep in his own bed.

But then again, maybe sex was overrated. Sparky's warm tail coiled around her ankles and he snored softly. At least Sparky had good manners: he didn't fart, scratch himself, or have morning breath. He was rather like sleeping with an electric blanket . . . which was probably the best Anya could hope for at the present.

Curled in the warm embrace of the salamander cuddling his toy, Anya drifted to sleep.

She dreamed of ice.

Anya turned on her heel in a vaulted chamber, ice crunching under her feet and covering the walls in a wet sheen of gray and glitter. The only illumination emanated from Sparky, incandescing as he wound about her heels. The ceiling stretched stories above her, beyond the limits of her sight. Chill radiated from the walls. Striations of earth striped the ice in broad brushstrokes, as if this place had been carved from centuries of glacial sediment.

Large as a canyon, the chamber yawned into darkness ahead. Sparky's light couldn't penetrate it; it was too far. But something shifted and moved in that black distance. Sparky's tongue flicked in and out, tasting the darkness. She could sense it, too . . . something massive turning over in its sleep.

Beside her stood the child from the pop machine: a little girl dressed in a yellow dress, white pinafore, and white sneakers. Plastic multicolored barrettes tied her hair back in neatly braided cornrows. She looked up at Anya with beautiful brown eyes framed with thick eyelashes.

Sparky cocked his head at the girl, then bent down to nibble at one of her untied shoelaces. The girl made no move to discourage him.

Anya's eyes stung with tears, seeing this child as whole as she had been in life. She knelt before the little girl. She couldn't imagine what the weight of time had done to the child to warp her into the malevolent spirit she'd met in the pickle lady's basement. "Sweetie, I'm sorry. I didn't know you were in there."

The girl regarded her with her solemn, unblinking eyes. She pointed into the pitch-black nothingness: *"Sirrush is coming."*

Like a marionette on a string, Anya was drawn toward the darkness. She walked farther into the ice cathedral. The walls now glistened with dampness and she could feel warmth on her skin. Heat shimmered, casting glimmering illusions from Sparky's luminescence on the walls, like a candle behind an ice cube.

Something was there. She could hear it breathing. She smelled something burning, could taste carbon and ozone in the air. She inhaled the warmth deep in her lungs, and it seemed that breath filled up the cold void, the bottomless black hole that devoured the spirits she touched.

For the first time, that hole in her chest was full. Warm.

The thing in the cave bellowed with a roar that shook ice fragments from the ceiling and cracked the ice underfoot. Anya clamped her hands over her ears to block the terrible howl that sounded like the end of the world. . .

. . . and the howl dissipated into the ringing of a phone.

Anya rolled over, disentangling herself from Sparky's webbed foot in her mouth, and snatched the phone on her nightstand.

"Hello."

"Lieutenant Kalinczyk? It's Captain Marsh."

Anya stared blearily at her clock. It was still an hour before she had to get up. It was not a good thing for Marsh to be calling her at home.

"What's up?"

"We've got another burn site for you to look at. We're cooling it down now."

"How bad is it?" She cradled the phone on her shoulder, scrabbled for a pen. Sparky snagged the phone cord and gnawed on it. Anya shoved him away and he retreated under the covers, sulking. The Gloworm blinked under the covers like a neon sign in the red light district.

Marsh paused. "One of our guys got hurt. Beam fell on him."

"Who is it?" Her heart thumped under her ribs. It might be someone she knew.

"It was Neuman from Ladder Company Eight. He's at the burn unit at Detroit Receiving Hospital now."

Anya blew out her breath. It was no one she knew personally. But now that the fire had taken blood, blood from the Department, all resources would be brought to bear on the offender. "Got any firebugs in custody?"

"We're holding a security guard for you to question."

Anya scribbled down the address. The address was a warehouse a few blocks from the river, south of Vernor Avenue. The area was industrial, likely to be deserted in the early hours of the morning—a perfect target.

She hung up and flipped the covers back.

"Sparky. Up."

Sparky yawned, plodded up her arm, and dangled around her neck like a sloth before he shrank and melted into her collar.

Anya pulled on a pair of black dress pants and a black turtleneck. As an arson investigator, she was rarely required to wear a uniform, but there was no point in owning dry-clean-only clothes or clothes that showed stains in her profession. Her closet had dwindled to a sea of black, brown, and gray pants, sweaters, and jackets. It suited her well; she disliked being the center of attention.

Anya tied up her long hair in a knot at the nape of her neck, then checked her reflection in the bathroom mirror. She swiped on a bit of copper-colored lipstick—the only concession to a professional appearance she had time for—snatched her coat, and bolted out the door into the cold gray dawn, dreading what she might find at the scene.

The damage had been worse than she'd thought.

The entire block had been cordoned off with police tape. Wending her green 1972 Dodge Dart through the clotted fire trucks, police cars, and utility company vehicles to the scene was like attempting to find parking for a tank at a theme park on a summer weekend. The street was wet from leaking fire hoses and the smell of chemical foam and char was sharp in the air.

Under the pink light of dawn, Anya rounded the corner to the target building. It had formerly been a warehouse, probably constructed just after the turn of the century, blackened brick pierced with sixteen-pane

windows. Decades of ever-widening roads had en-
croached upon the property; the facade sat nearly on the
sidewalk, the front door only steps from the street. Anya
noted that there should have been four high stories, but the
top two had collapsed in. The mass of blackened cinders
that had been a roof hung suspended like dark feathers in
a nest. The street-level windows had been boarded up with
plywood, and those had burned quickly. The tentacles of
fire hoses reached in and out of the building. The firefighters were, no doubt, trying to keep the ash down and keep
the building from flaring again, never mind what other
particulates were likely to be in the air: asbestos, burnt
plastic, rubber.

Anya shut off the ignition and opened the trunk of the
Dart with her keys. The Dart had no fancy features, except
for power steering and a radio. Even the transmission was
manual. For Anya, the lower tech, the better. Once upon
a time, she'd owned a compact car with a power sunroof
and door locks, automatic transmission, even a back
window wiper blade. That had lasted all of three months
with Sparky's poking and prodding of the gadgets. She'd
bought the Dart, a low-mileage cream puff without a spot
of rust, for next to nothing at an auction from a collector
who was going bankrupt—not an uncommon occurrence
in Detroit these days. With the Dart, Sparky found very
little to tear up inside such a battleship of a car. She still
had to replace the battery more often than she thought she
should, but she rarely caught him under the hood, gnaw-
ing at the terminals like a dog with a rawhide. As a bonus,

the leather seats wiped clean of fire scene carbon and other nasty debris from her investigations. The only drawback was the gas mileage. That, and the two-door model was called the Swinger, a fact which random car enthusiasts would tell her when she was minding her own business loading groceries in the parking lot.

Her tools were neatly arranged in a pair of heavy duffel bags in the trunk. She pulled off her coat and shoes, donned protective coveralls, then, balancing against the car bumper, stepped into a white hazmat suit. No matter what size she ordered, the suits were always too big and made her feel like a walking marshmallow. She slipped her firefighters' boots on over the plastic feet of the hazmat suit, then shrugged into her yellow firefighters' coat. The white letters of her name reached from armpit to armpit. For good measure, she slipped a respirator mask over her neck. Parking her firefighter's helmet on her head, she grabbed her bags and made for the incident command post.

It had been three years since Anya had ridden on fire trucks in full uniform, feeling the adrenaline jolt of the sirens. That part of the job had its allure, as well as its challenges. There were fewer women in the Department than men and she had worked hard to distinguish herself as a capable and reliable firefighter. She'd been promoted quickly and her superiors relied upon her to work quietly, efficiently, and without drama.

That lack of drama handicapped her at times with her colleagues. Firefighters were, by nature, a close-knit family. If she was honest with herself, that was part of the reason why Anya had joined—she wanted to feel some of that sense of belonging. In earlier years, she'd spent her share of twenty-four-hour shifts at the station house. Anya had found it difficult to live in a fishbowl. Though she'd had many opportunities, she'd turned down the men who'd tried to date her. She was usually the only woman on shift and had the good fortune to be able to sleep in a room alone, where no one would sense Sparky kicking the covers.

Sparky had loved the firehouses. There were always things to get into, to root about in, things that smelled of delicious fire. In one firehouse, Sparky had developed an interest in licking the light switches and electrical panels. The captain there had been convinced the station was wired badly enough to warrant entirely new wiring. When Sparky had developed a taste for one of the firemen's neon beer signs, he'd nearly burned the station down. A bored salamander with nothing to do was a dangerous thing.

When the investigator position opened, Anya was ready to transfer to a position that would allow her to sleep in her own bed and keep Sparky from tasting the machinery. Anya had found the investigative work to be more satisfying. Working behind the scenes, she unraveled the puzzles of forensic and behavioral science that pointed to a myriad of reasons for setting fires: to cover up crimes, for insurance money, for revenge, for pathological plea- sure . . . the exact reason for each fire was unique, just as unique as the patterns of flame and smoke damage.

But transferring to the investigative division took her out of the fishbowl; now she was on the outside looking in. Investigators worked regular shifts, then went home to be with their families. There was little of the camaraderie that existed at the firehouse. Anya's isolation from her colleagues widened as time passed.

Anya clomped to the command post for the scene, identifiable by a knot of firefighters and utility personnel poking at blueprints. She spied a familiar bear of a figure in a hazmat suit and helmet scribbling on a clipboard: Captain Marsh. He towered over the utility workers, his respirator dangling from his neck. The hazmat suit was a bit too short in the sleeves for him. His chestnut brow gleamed with sweat, his graying hair clipped closely to his skull. He wore the scar creasing his forehead as a badge of honor, making no attempt to hide the wound he'd received years ago when he'd been on a ladder truck and a building exploded. Marsh was matter-of-fact and didn't believe in sugarcoating the truth.

"Captain," she greeted him. "What's the story?"

Marsh looked up from his clipboard. "Kalinczyk. What we've got is a warehouse partitioned up for storage. It's been sliced and diced up with all manner of walls that weren't up to code." It annoyed Marsh when people didn't follow code and something bad happened.

"Any luck contacting the owner?"

"Not yet. So we don't know what was in there. So far, we've got furniture, office supplies, document storage, what looks like personal storage . . . who knows what else. All of it was highly flammable, crammed into small spaces." Marsh flipped pages in his clipboard. "Fire was reported at oh-four-twenty by a security guard at the car lot a half block away." He stabbed his thumb at a man sitting in the back of a patrol car. "That's him."

"Does he have a record?"

"No. DPD ran his background and got nothing."

Anya's eyes roved over the EMT vehicles still at the scene and a charred, human-shaped form half covered with a blanket. Her brow knitted. "You said that one of our guys got hurt."

"Yeah." Marsh blew out his breath. "Rather than spring for security, the owners posed a mannequin in one of the second-floor windows. Tried to make it look like someone was there, working." He gestured to the prone form. "First ladder company on the scene mistook it for a person, broke into the window to get him. Neuman got burned pulling the mannequin out. Kid got burned bad." Anger twitched Marsh's mouth. She knew Marsh worked part-time at the training academy and knew most of the young firefighters.

"I'm sorry, Captain."

"Yeah, well, me, too."

Anya nodded. "I'll get to work."

Anya turned her attention to the only witness. The security guard, a Hispanic man in his early twenties with buzzed hair, sat in the back of a police car. She noted he was an unarmed guard and that his brown-and-white uniform was new enough to still have the factory creases pressed in it.

Anya opened the door and slid into the seat beside him. "Hi. I'm Lieutenant Kalinczyk, DFD."

The young man looked up at her. She noticed that he had a backpack under his arm. "Am I in trouble?"

Anya shook her head, taking out her notebook. "No. The back of the car is just the safest place right now, since we don't know what crud might be in the air from that burning building. Your name, please?"

"John Sandoval."

"John, why don't you tell me about what happened?"

"I work over at the car lot, night security. It's a sweet gig. I go to school during the day and there's usually nothing happening on the lot. They've got a tall fence with razor wire, good alarm system . . . not sure why they need a guard. Not that I'm complaining. It's good money." His words fell all over each other. His eyes slid sheepishly to his backpack. "I was studying for an exam, when I noticed some light across the street."

"What kind of light? Headlights? Flashlight?"

He shook his head. "I don't think it was either one of those. It was a kind of soft light. Yellow. I noticed it disappearing around the corner of the building."

"It was on the outside of the building?"

"Yeah. In the alley. I didn't think much of it until about an hour later, when I smelled smoke. I got up to check and saw the first floor was on fire. I called 911." He spread his hands. Anya noticed that they were clean, no visible evidence of accelerant under his nails or on his palms. "That's all I saw and what I told the cops."

"Did you see anyone hanging around? Kids, cars, anything out of the ordinary?"

He shook his head. "I didn't see anything. I was sitting in the security van in the south edge of the car lot. No traffic."

"Any strange smells? Gas, chemicals?"

"No. Everything seemed pretty normal." John's face clouded. "Um . . . are you going to tell my boss I was studying on the job?"

"No." Anya shook her head. She gave him a half smile as she capped her pen. "I wouldn't want to mess up your sweet gig."

John grinned in relief. "Thanks, ma'am. Um . . . can I go now? My exam's at eight thirty."

"Sure." She handed him her card. "I'll be in touch. Give me a call if you remember anything else."

"Sure thing." John swung his backpack over his shoulder and scrambled out of the patrol car.

Anya climbed out of the cruiser and fished her camera out of her equipment. She paced around the perimeter of the building, camera clicking. She took note of the front and back doors from which leaking fire hoses snaked. These heavy metal doors bore the scratches of the tools the firefighters had used to enter. The ladder was still extended up to the broken second-floor window that had held the mannequin, clearly sketching the scene where the young firefighter had gotten into trouble.

But how had the firebug gotten in? The extent of the structural damage suggested to Anya that the fire had been set from inside. Without fuel for the fire, a blaze set in the alley or against an exterior wall would have burned itself out in short order. Her practiced eye roved over the boarded-over windows on the lower level, the upper windows with the glass broken out by the heat and pressure of the fire. Her firebug hadn't gotten in up there. He would have found a way in at ground level.

She frowned. Fires set for insurance purposes usually occurred at the roofline. Fires always traveled upward. Roof-set fires caused minimal damage to the actual contents, but made spectacular blazes that compromised the structure enough to ensure a payout and airtime on the evening news. A fire set at ground level or below was a fire set to burn everything inside. The person who set this one knew about fire.

Anya paced around the foundation and basement windows. Most were covered with steel grates still solid to the kick. The glass behind them was embedded with chicken wire and would have deterred most attempts to enter.

Still. This was an old building, a building that wasn't patrolled, a building that had no working alarms . . . otherwise the fire department would have been summoned automatically by the alarm company, not called by a student security guard when the flames grew too large to miss from across the street. Maintenance was not at the forefront of the owner's mind. There would have to be a way to get in.

There. She kicked away a section of metal bars. This window was hidden in the shadow of the alley, away from view of the street. The charred grate had been screwed into the brick at one time, but the rusted screws had loosened. Anya could imagine her firebug crouched here in anonymity, working on the grate until he could pry it free. He'd also put it back into place when he left, suggesting he hadn't panicked, that he wanted to cover his tracks. He was careful and methodical. Not a good sign.

The glass beneath had been ripped out, the tatters of chicken wire cut cleanly. Anya photographed the edges carefully. Wire cutters or tin snips would have made short work of this. She made a mental note to get the evidence technicians here to check for prints.

But now, she wanted to see what the firebug saw, what he'd done when he'd set fire to the building. Anya circled back around to the main entrance, stepping over the tentacles of fire hoses.

She clicked on her flashlight and peered into the damp blackness. The first floor was a ruin. The weight of the second and third floors groaned heavily on the remaining walls, trailing charred beams through holes open all the way up to the ruined roof. Structures of this era used wood extensively, not as much steel as modern ones. Anya could see where the fire had raced along the scarred wooden floors, fed by decades of old varnish and debris. Pieces of drywall were cracked open on the floor like bits of eggshell, shattered by the weight of walls falling. Anya expected that those bits of wall had been built much later, as Marsh had said, to accommodate rented storage space. The debris strewn above and around her was a jumble of junk: broken file cabinets, soggy black cardboard boxes, melted trash bags trailing from the ceiling like ghosts. Pieces of waterlogged furniture were stacked in massive piles, standing in ashy puddles. Water dripped down on her from above, drops suspending filthy ash in a black rain. She saw no evidence of sprinklers overhead as she picked her way through the rubble. Anya expected that this space would simply need to be bulldozed. She could see nothing salvageable.

She swept her light before her, searching for the way into the basement. She found a stairwell door beside an elevator. The elevator was old-fashioned, with a cage door now disintegrating on hinges that had melted from the heat. Patterns of smoke and carbon swirled inside the shaft, and she imagined the flames roaring up from the basement. She looked up and saw the ruins of the car dangling somewhere on the second floor. This open elevator shaft would have been a perfect conductor for the oxygen that the fire needed to move throughout the building.

The stairwell door was blocked by a mass of blackened crates. She shoved them aside, feeling the surface of the ruined wood shatter in her gloved hands. The firebug likely hadn't made it to the first floor; he'd done his work in the basement and left. If he'd taken the elevator back down, the car would have remained in the basement.

Why hadn't the firebug been curious about what was in the warehouse? Wouldn't he have wanted to take a look around, see if there was anything worth stealing? He had plenty of time and opportunity—no alarm, no one watching—but apparently no motivation for theft.

Anya opened the metal door and it grated against the warped doorframe. Her flashlight picked out steps above and below, ruined and disintegrating in the fire. There was nothing left above her that would hold the weight of a person. Below her, only a decorative metal handrail remained.

She snagged a short ladder from one of the trucks and dragged it through the maze of debris. She shoved it into the doorway, braced it on the doorframe, and clambered down into the mouth of the basement. Her last step landed her in a puddle that sloshed coldly around her ankles.

This deep in the building, she was insulated from the street noise. All she could hear was her breath hissing against the respirator, the tap of water working through the structure into the puddles underfoot, and an occasional worrisome creak from the ruins above.

The blackened walls confirmed her suspicion that the basement was the source of the blaze. Only metal items remained, covered by a thick film of carbon black. Everything else had been destroyed in the heat. Her flashlight illuminated a strange collection of mechanical parts. Some looked like pieces of great clocks, gears and twisted hands in melted cases. Others were identifiable pieces of vacuum cleaners, the snouts of hoses burned away, but the metal shells and handles remaining like the carapaces of giant black beetles. A massive boiler dominated the center of the room, reaching iron tentacles up to the ceiling. She opened the door and peered into its belly, poking at its contents. Just charcoal—and very old charcoal at that. This wasn't her ignition source: the boiler had more serious scorch marks outside than in.

Arson scenes were notoriously difficult to investigate: so much evidence could be destroyed by attempts to put out the fire that any lead was a treasure. This scene was proving to be no different; she wondered what the water swirling around her feet obscured.

Her brow knitted. With this much heat, there should be some evidence of what had started the fire. There was no obvious place where the flames had originated, no V-shaped carbon plume where the fire would have begun and spread up a wall. All the timbers above her were equally blackened with carbon, surfaces cracked like alligator skin. She took an ice pick from her tool kit and randomly stabbed the beams, trying to see how far the char went. The char would be heaviest in the area where the blaze began . . . but the char went just as deeply into the beams in the center of the room as it did at the fringes. It was physically impossible for the fire to have begun everywhere at once.

Anya picked through the rubble on the floor, finding no remains of gas cans, no evidence of flammable substances. She lifted her respirator for a moment, smelled no natural gas, no residue of gasoline. From her bag, she pulled out a portable hydrocarbon detector. The palm-sized machine could sniff out virtually any common volatile compound in the air that could have been used as an accelerant. She swept the machine twice through the perimeter of the basement, and the machine frustratingly yielded no results.

She scraped pieces of the carbon film coating the walls and beams into a sample container for analysis. Perhaps the lab would be able to identify some chemical trace that might tell her what began this fire, but the etiology of it troubled her. It seemed to ignite evenly, rising up from the ground. Yet the witness had not described an explosion, and Anya could see no signs of the outward pressurization of an explosive blast: the metal pipes and the boiler were structurally intact, and the bricks remained mortared in place. It didn't make sense. Fire just didn't act this way. It behaved in a predictable manner, with one or more ignition points that spread fire unevenly, in response to obstacles, wind, and oxygen. There was logic behind it. But this place had been baked as inexplicably evenly as a cake in an oven.

She wished she could say that she hadn't seen it before, but seeing it before hadn't improved her understanding. She suspected this was the work of the serial arsonist she'd been tracking. This same peculiarly even heat had incinerated three other buildings in the past month. The blazes had all begun in a basement, all in unoccupied buildings within city limits. At all the other sites, the firebug had left a calling card. No evidence, but just one inscrutable clue. She shined her light on the murky water of the floor, then dropped on her hands and knees to sift through the rubble. The light bounced off the surface of the water, casting moving tongues of light on the ceiling. She pulled a piece of debris from the floor drain and the dingy water began to slowly sluice away from the concrete floor. She hoped it wasn't here, but if it was, she needed to find it.

Anya paced out the size of the basement, estimating where the center lay. She paused, squinting, scraping sludge away in the receding water. Her breath caught in her throat as she cleared the ash to reveal a symbol etched in the concrete, right where she hoped it wouldn't be, in the exact center of the floor.

A curving, serpentine shape, like a wave, had been dug into the concrete. The end of the shape was capped with a pair of curved horns. Anya took off her gloves, felt the mark. The edges were perfectly smooth; she could think of no tool that would not leave a mark in hardened concrete. Like a huge brand, the black mark stretched for three feet on the floor.

Her arsonist had been here. This was his work.

She could feel heat radiating from the mark through the fingertips of her gloves. Hesitantly, she stripped them off, let her fingers run over the sinuous line. It tingled when she touched it . . . not unlike the feeling she'd had in her hands when she touched the Coke machine inhabited by the little girl.

Around her neck, she felt her necklace warm as Sparky shifted in his sleep. She felt a tentative salamander toe on her collarbone.

"Not now," she whispered.

Sparky withdrew and curled back up, but she heard a growl reverberating through his chest.

"That'll be fifteen dollars, miss."

She turned to the source of the thin, whistling voice, tripping in the ashy muck. The ghostly outline of an old man bent over the metal canister of a vacuum cleaner. The hose had melted away, and the shape was barely recognizable under the char. But the old man bent over it with a screwdriver and looked right at her.

"It just needed a new filter. It got gummed up on the filth down here."

Sparky uncurled, draping himself around her shoulders. She could feel him breathing, but he didn't seem alarmed enough to rouse himself to greet the spirit or to assume his full, threatening size.

Anya approached the old man cautiously. "Thank you very much."

He tipped his hat. *"You're welcome, miss."* Anya could see that he wore a repairman's uniform. *"I haven't gotten much business down here, until lately."*

"I see that." Anya smiled at him. "How long have you been down here?"

The spirit looked at his watch, rubbing his beard. *"Twenty-three years. Seven more until retirement."*

"That's a long time."

The spirit shrugged. *"I keep busy, tinkering with my junk."* He gestured around him at the broken parts and gears littering the floor. He began to whistle, and he turned back to his work. *"Soon it'll be lawnmower season. Business will pick up then."*

"Did you have . . . a customer last night?"

He stopped whistling, and his brow wrinkled. *"Yes.*

There was a man." He continued fussing over the vacuum canister. *"A tall man with eyes like burning coals."*

"Do you know what he wanted?"

The spirit stood up, and rubbed the back of his head. *"No. I laid low. After-hours customers are always trouble."*

"Are you all alone here?"

"It's just me. Nice and quiet here." He looked around at the devastation. *"Until recently."*

She edged closer to him. "Why are you all alone? Why haven't you left?"

His face froze, and a twinge of fear lanced across his leathery face. *"I'm afraid of elevators."* The spirit turned away, faded into the wall.

She shivered, wondering if that had been how the repairman had died—in an accident with the rickety elevator.

Anya didn't like her day job and her night work to intersect. She liked these things to be in two separate boxes in her head, not touching. But the buzzing feeling in her fingertips remained as her camera flashed over and over, illuminating the strangely beautiful shape in the floor, the shape she'd seen at the three other arson sites. She vowed to unravel its meaning, even if it meant crossing that intellectual line into her nocturnal work.

CHAPTER THREE

IN THE FAIRY TALES ANYA had read as a child, witches stuffed screaming children into ovens and ate them without bothering to peel them. In those stories, witches did not run their own bakeries specializing in wedding cakes and novelty pastries. Nor did they advertise the use of organic flours and cruelty-free eggs.

As dawn reddened the horizon, Anya parked in front of Wicked Confections, a bakery tucked in a tidy row of shops in suburban Ferndale. This early in the morning, parking was easy to find; only the delivery trucks were parked at the curbs, parking lights flashing. She fed the meter, then peered inside the front plate-glass window displaying an orgy of cakes. Fondant icing as smooth as skin, sugar leaves, and frosted vines covered tiers of pastry balanced on vintage glass cake stands. The cake featured in the center was a meticulously decorated white vintage Ford Thunderbird, complete with fins. A miniature "Just Married" sign leaned in the back window of the car, and tiny gumdrop cans were tied to the bumper with ribbons of licorice. Inside the car, a marzipan bride and groom made their getaway, the bride waving to an unseen audience like a beauty queen. Anya's stomach rumbled. She knew that the cakes in the window were merely frosted Styrofoam, for display purposes only, but . . . damn, did they look good enough to try.

When she opened the door to the shop, a bell jingled overhead. Inside, stainless-steel counters were strewn with books of sample cake designs. A glass case behind the counter was full of pirogis, pinwheel pastries, paczkis, and cookies.

Katie came from the back room, her apron dusted with flour. Her hat was primly perched atop her head, no tendrils of blonde hair leaking from it. "Anya. Welcome back to my den of culinary wickedness." She made a flourish that puffed flour from her apron and nearly knocked the hat from her head. "Can I get you some breakfast?"

Anya grinned as she climbed onto one of the retro red stools before the counter. "I need some chocolate. Hit me."

Katie pulled a white cardboard box from under the counter. "Just for you." She pulled the lid aside to reveal a writhing mass of marzipan people, contorted and bent. "They didn't set up properly. The grooms are all dipped in dark chocolate. The brides are white chocolate."

Anya peered into the box of tangled bodies. She plucked up a groom and delicately bit his feet off. "Yum. I feel like Godzilla grazing on a mosh pit."

Katie broke the head off a blonde bride and

thoughtfully crunched her skull. "Yeah, this one was a bitch. I've had to do them over a half-dozen times because the bride says they don't look enough like them."

Anya rolled her eyes. "Did you get them finished?"

"Yeah. I just threw out their engagement photograph and worked from a Disney animation cel of Cinderella and Prince Charming. She thinks it's perfect now." Katie smirked. "I did make her butt a bit bigger for revenge, though."

Anya snorted. "I love your sense of spite."

"Hey, don't mess with the woman who's preparing your food." Katie put her chin in her hand. "So . . . what brings you here at the ass-crack of dawn?"

Anya looked away. "Work calls. My day job, I mean." She'd been reluctant to spend time even with Katie, for fear that disentangling herself from DAGR would grow even more complicated. She hadn't found a good way to explain that while she yearned for a connection with the group, the use of her powers as a Lantern made her feel even more of an outsider. She was a freakish tool in DAGR's arsenal, something to be used when what Jules considered "conventional methods" failed.

Katie reached out and touched Anya's sleeve. "Look, I'm worried about you."

Anya's eyebrow quirked upward and she savagely twisted an arm from her groom. She set the limb down beside the dismembered figure. "I'm just . . . I'm just a bit burnt out right now."

Katie nodded sympathetically. "Do you want to come

by my house later for some energy work? I could do a Reiki adjustment for you, if you want."

Anya's collar twitched under her turtleneck. Sparky loved having his energy realigned. It was the equivalent of a massage for the scrappy little elemental. She smiled, relenting. "I appreciate it . . . and Sparky would, too."

"I'll mix up some extra incense for Sparks." Katie couldn't see Sparky, but she could usually sense him when he was on the prowl. Sparky loved Katie's cats. They would race up and down the halls, chasing each other until they wore themselves out.

"But I'm actually here in connection with work. I need your help with something." Anya pulled a photo out of her pocket and slid it across the counter. The photo showed the symbol on the floor of the ruined warehouse. "I've been running across this symbol on a regular basis. Any idea what it means? I thought maybe it could be a rune or something."

Katie looked at the photo, turned it this way and that. "Hmm. It's not a Norse rune that I recognize. And it's not an alchemical symbol. I'd be happy to do some research on it, though, and tell you what I find out."

"Great, thanks."

"If I can't figure it out, do you want me to check with Ciro and see if he knows?"

Anya paused. "Sure." She would be happy to have Ciro's advice, but she didn't want to necessarily get sucked back into DAGR's activities. The more she was on their radar, the more likely they would be to call her for spiritual garbage duty. And she felt guilty for avoiding them, especially Ciro. He would understand why she was trying to leave and he would let her, but she would feel terrible for leaving when the old man was so frail.

"Why don't you come by for dinner?" Katie suggested. "Bring Sparky and he can have a playdate with Fay and Vern. We'll scrub your aura and I'll have a chance to look up your mysterious symbol. Sound good?"

Anya's stomach rumbled. "What're you making?"

Katie grinned. "Matzo ball soup."

"'Nuff said. I'm there." Anya slid off the stool, looking longingly into the pastry box. "Can I have a groom for the road?"

Katie fished one out. "Take him. I got frustrated with the texture and modeled him after Munch's *The Scream*."

Anya held the melted figure in her palm. The figure's hands were pressed to his head, his openmouthed face contorted in an expression of culinary agony. Across his chest, the words "Eat me" were scrawled in icing.

That was something she could do. Anya devoured him in three bites. For once, devouring someone gave her a warm, satisfied feeling.

Certain places were always haunted.

Some locations held a magnetic pull for the dead. It was a good bet that there would be a restless spirit or two hanging around a museum of any substantial size: the spirits of artists could sometimes attach to their creative works, and, of course, there were burial urns and bones of the dead. When she was a child on a field trip, Anya was convinced the spirit of a dinosaur was roaming the halls of the Smithsonian. Jails and prisons were another favorite for spirits: there were always inmates who were murdered or killed themselves, and they tended to linger, imprisoned in death as surely as they were in life. Nursing homes invariably harbored a collection of spirits still attending their daily activities and staring at the television, as if nothing much had changed. Those spirits seemed stuck in a never-ending tape loop—more often than not, living residents played bingo beside the dead. Anya doubted that many of them knew they had died.

Hospitals, though, were the most haunted. Anya avoided them whenever possible. The fluorescent lights burning twenty-four hours a day, the smell of bleach, the hurried movement of the living . . . these things did nothing to scour away the souls of the confused who wandered the corridors in search of a restroom or their rides home.

Anya steeled herself, gripping the steering wheel of her car in the parking garage of Detroit Receiving Hospital. She never took a spirit unless there was no other choice. But in these places, the spirits could behave badly. She would have to ignore the trouble they caused, trying to catch her attention.

She stepped out of the Dart and slammed the door. The solid sound echoed across the cavernous garage like a summons and she swore she could hear rustling somewhere below her. The salamander collar on her throat warmed. She felt Sparky stir, his ear-gills perking up. The familiar spirit would be riding shotgun on this one; there was no way she could imagine Sparky wouldn't feel compelled to sniff at the strange spirits and gnaw on expensive electronic equipment.

He unfurled from her throat, sliding down her back, and took shape on the floor of the parking garage. He looked up at her, tongue flicking.

"Be good, Sparky," she murmured. "I'm at work, so keep a low profile."

Anya turned to walk toward the parking garage elevators. Sparky kept pace with her, his hips swishing side to side as he came to heel. He was trying very hard to be well-behaved. She'd see how long this would last.

She stepped into the elevator and punched the button for the ground floor. Sparky reached up and licked the grimy button. The light behind the button dimmed.

"*Sparky,*" she hissed.

His feathery ear-fronds laid back, Sparky put his head down between his front feet, chastened.

The doors opened to the ER lobby, and Anya groaned inwardly. The lobby was full of living patients perched in chairs and wheelchairs, with doctors and nurses milling calmly around them. A young woman with needle tracks on her arm was retching in a trashcan. A mother yelled at her son for sticking a marble up his nose, threatening to slap it out of him. A man wearing a business suit stared blankly at the soaps on the television in the waiting area. He was restrained to a gurney, and his hands were bound with heavy gauze mittens.

These things didn't disturb her nearly as much as the translucent spirit of the elderly lady with the bowl of Jell-O on her head. She screamed at Anya from the information desk, shaking her fragile fists in wrath. She wore pink fuzzy socks and a hospital gown open in the back to expose buttocks sliding down toward the backs of her knees.

She pointed her finger at Anya and howled, *"That's the one! That's the nurse who stole my cigarettes!"*

Anya inwardly resolved not to react to the woman. She strode deliberately to the information desk and spoke quietly to the clerk. "I'm here to see Steve Neuman, please."

"I'm sorry," the clerk answered, paging through her clipboard. "He's in the burn unit, and no visitors are allowed. Are you family?"

Anya flipped out her badge. "I'm with DFD. I promise that I'll be brief."

"Hold on . . ." The clerk punched the buttons on her phone.

"She stole my cigarettes! Bitch!"

Anya steadfastly tried to ignore the brittle old woman, who was leaning across the desk at her, craning her neck to stare up at her with beady bird eyes.

"Give 'em back!"

Sparky bellied up to the old woman and bit her foot. The old woman jerked back, falling in a sprawl of twisted limbs. The hem of her hospital gown flipped up over her head and she screeched incoherently. Out of the corner of her eye, Anya saw Sparky scamper away with a pink sock in his mouth. Her mouth hardened and she willed herself not to turn around. She leaned forward on the counter, shielding her eyes from the old woman's ectoplasmic nudity with one hand. The old lady's screaming was drawing the attention of other apparitions; the phantom of a teenage kid with a chest full of gunshot wounds walked through a wall and gave Anya the once-over.

"Hey, princess."

Anya ignored him, focused intently on the clerk talking into the phone. The clerk was wearing incredibly long, intricately airbrushed false fingernails. Anya wondered how she could type with those pink daggers glued to her hands.

"You stuck-up or somethin'?"

Anya continued to contemplate the clerk's nails, wishing she'd hurry the hell up.

"Hey, I'm talking to you." The spirit tried, unsuccessfully, to grasp her arm, and she felt a draft of cold air.

She turned to him, glowering.

"You need to smile, baby. Pretty girl like you should smile." The kid grinned, showing her his custom-made golden grill. He leaned on the countertop beside her, his sagging jeans showing entirely too much skin. Anya rolled her eyes. If he'd been alive, she'd have told him to get his ass back to school. Now there was no point. His destiny was to hang out in the ER, hitting on chicks. She wondered if there were any ghost girls here his age or whether his only company was the crazy Jell-O lady.

"You can go back now," the clerk told Anya, mercifully. "He's in room 7-A . . . it's the tank in the back. You can't miss it."

"Thank you so much."

In her periphery, she could see the teenager sauntering over to hit on the girl throwing up in the trash can. The girl would have no idea he was there, but the kid needed all the practice he could get talking to women in the afterlife.

Anya slunk down the hall. She didn't know where Sparky had run off to, but she hoped he wasn't pulling the plug on somebody's grandfather.

"Sparky," she snarled.

A woman in a wheelchair turned around to stare at her and Anya tried to cover the snarl with a cough. Whose idea was it to have an uncontrollable familiar? This didn't happen in books. Every witch and warlock in popular culture had familiars who did their bidding. She resolved—again—to try to introduce this concept to Sparky.

The giant salamander poked his head out from beneath a biohazard bin.

"Ew. Sparky, get out of there." She didn't know if salamanders could pick up communicable diseases, but that was certainly a good way to find out.

Sulking, the salamander waddled back to her side and looked up at her with eyes as unrepentant as marbles. The crazy ghost lady's sock was gone. She could only assume that he'd eaten it.

Resolutely, Anya followed the signs to the burn unit. This wing's atmosphere felt palpably heavier than the rest of the hospital, as if an enforced curtain of silence had been drawn around it. Even the spirits here were quieter:

she glimpsed one staring out a window; another lay in an unoccupied bed, staring up at the ceiling, lips melted shut. The ghost of a woman holding an infant walked down the hallway, humming a soft lullaby.

Anya turned away. Long ago, she'd promised herself that she wouldn't interfere with spirits who weren't disturbing humans. But she felt sorry for the ones that seemed trapped in loops of time, reliving painful hours for years without end.

She rounded the corner to what might have been a renovated neonatal unit, windows looking into a glass fishbowl full of technologically arcane equipment studded with lights and dials. Medical personnel swam around the obstacles in masks and green scrubs. Inside, in a bed covered by an oxygen tent, she saw a body swathed in gauze. The figure's eyes were taped shut, a tube extending from its mouth. It looked like a scene from an alien autopsy show, all shiny and sterile and raw.

Anya pressed her fingers to the glass. Neuman was clearly in no condition to talk . . . if he ever would be. She saw no trace of a spirit lurking around the plastic tent. That meant Neuman's spirit had either moved on or was still locked away in his body.

"They're keeping him sedated . . . on paralytics, anticonvulsants, opiates, benzos . . . you name it. They don't want him to feel anything, and they don't want him to remember any pain if he does manage to wake." Captain Marsh stood in the hallway, arms crossed over his chest. On the chair behind him, Anya could see two empty coffee cups and a rumpled newspaper. Marsh had been keeping watch. It was Marsh's day off, as well as Anya's, but his jeans were pressed with military-sharp creases. From the time she started as an investigator, she'd learned there were really no days off when working a major case—any good investigator's sleep would be too troubled by a case to truly be able to relax until it was resolved. But no matter how much overtime Anya worked, she never managed to compete with Marsh's record of the most unpaid overtime worked in the Department. She suspected his conscience bothered him even more than hers did.

She gestured to Neuman through the glass. "That doesn't look too good."

"The initial burns were complicated by that damn mannequin melting all over him." Marsh shook his head. "You know. Plastic burns and keeps burning. The fumes got into his lungs."

"He's not breathing on his own?"

"No." Marsh's dark eyes peered through his reflection to the man in the bed. "They aren't acting like he's going to, either."

Anya frowned. "Where's his family?"

"The kid's parents are out of state. Snowbirds—spent their whole lives in Detroit. They retired and moved to Florida last year to get away from the crime." Marsh's mouth twisted downward. "They're flying in now."

Anya was glad she'd missed that. She knew she had to come, though there would be nothing useful gained in the investigation through her presence. As the lead investigator, it was her duty to see all the results of the arson, to see the truth from all its devastating angles.

She looked down to see Sparky snaking around her feet. He seemed a bit sobered by the burn unit. Perhaps, being impervious to fire himself, he was fascinated by what he could never experience. His obsidian eyes peeped up over the window glass, working back and forth as he seemed to take in all the glittering machinery.

"Did the lab analyze those prints you found?" Marsh asked.

"Yeah. There were several sets of prints, but no hits in AFIS. Our guy hasn't been in prison, the military, or the police."

Marsh rubbed his head. "Damn. We have to get this solved. Yesterday."

"I know." Anya knew that Marsh was running a good deal of interference for her from the chief, trying to give her space to work. But she could feel the administrative net tightening.

"If Neuman dies . . ." She could see that Marsh was having a hard time articulating the words, as if voicing them might give the thought shape and make it true. "Then it's a homicide. The case will be turned over to Detroit PD."

The fire chief would give the best sound bite he could and the press would be all over the idea of a fireman killed in the line of duty by a serial arsonist, like ants after an egg sandwich. Anya wouldn't turn down the idea of extra help, but she didn't relish tripping over investigators unfamiliar with the case, who would need extensive debriefing and who could easily shut her out. She'd had some negative experiences before and would rather not repeat them.

"So . . . what do you have for me? Anything?"

"Lab's analyzing the gaseous evidence from the carbon scrapings. The smoke patterns are too regular to identify a single point of ignition. The best lead I have is this." Anya pulled her pictures out of her purse, showed him the symbol on the floor of the warehouse basement. "This has been found on the floor of every scene. I took a cast of it. The techs are looking for any corresponding tool marks."

"What the hell is it?"

"I've got an expert working on it." Anya's mouth thinned. "But I think we need to seriously consider the idea that our firebug isn't a usual one. He's not after money. He's not trying to cover up another crime. My sense is that this is ritualistic, an occult crime."

"Damn." Marsh rubbed the scar on his head. "Halloween's coming up, and all the crazies are out early."

"Devil's Night is just over two weeks away."

Detroit was notorious for the night before Halloween, Devil's Night. The criminal element appeared in full force to commit all manner of mischief and property damage; entire city blocks had burned in the seventies. The fires had waned in the late nineties, but the economic crises of recent years had created sufficient psychological fuel to reignite the blazes: unemployment, despair, and anger. Last year alone had seen more than thirty houses, several dozen cars, a post office, and a shopping mall burned to the ground.

Marsh frowned. "I hope this isn't the firebug's idea of practice."

Anya stared through the glass. There was no sign that the firebug was interested in stopping himself. She would have to stop him before the burn unit got more crowded.

Anya wondered what Katie's neighbors would have thought if they'd known that a witch lived in their little piece of suburbia. Small brick ranch houses lined Katie's quiet street. Streetlamps and yard and porch lights revealed concrete yard ornaments standing guard over mulched flowerbeds and postage-stamp-sized yards. But this chunk of the middle-class American dream seemed to be slipping away, as Anya could see more and more FOR SALE signs cropping up like dandelions. On Katie's street alone, there were five signs with paper flyers stacked in clear plastic sleeves, touting improvements to a market that didn't exist. The grass was beginning to grow tall around those signs.

The witch in their midst was standing her ground, however. Katie's porch light cheerily illuminated marigolds around the front step going to seed. Her door was decorated for Halloween with a wreath wrapped in orange and black ribbons. From the maple tree in the front yard, she'd hung bats and tiny ghosts. Anya was surprised that the neighborhood kids hadn't run off with them, but perhaps the kids had moved away with their parents.

Katie appeared at the front door, and Anya could smell something delicious through the screen. She'd given up her baker's uniform for an ankle-length tiered skirt and tank top, her long hair tied back in a ponytail. Her bare toes curled over the doorframe.

"C'mon in. Soup's on."

The instant Anya crossed the threshold of the witch's domain, Sparky shivered with excitement. He peeled himself off Anya's neck and leaped lightly to the floor. His spade-shaped head twisted right and left, peering intently under the fringed velvet couch, around the floor cushions, into the fireplace overhung with drying herbs smelling of lavender and rosemary.

Shining eyes peered from the hallway. Named after Vernors ginger ale and Faygo pop, both Katie's cats were fully carbonated—shake 'em up, and they went off like rockets. And they were primed and ready for Sparky's arrival.

Vern took the offensive. The gray-striped tabby circled behind the couch, stalking Sparky's irresistibly lashing tail. Fay, a round calico cat, stealthily crept across the wooden floor in slow motion as Sparky nosed in the fireplace.

And all hell broke loose. Sparky's head whipped around in delight as he caught sight of Fay. Fay scrambled backward on the slippery hardwood floor and skidded down the hallway. Sparky gave chase, short legs churning in the air. Vern leaped from behind the couch, startling Sparky. Sparky rolled, Vern pounced on his tail, and the two tumbled down the hall in a series of trills and snorts.

"I wish I could see Sparky like the cats do," Katie remarked, padding into the kitchen. Her silver bracelets and earrings jingled musically when she walked.

Anya followed, stomach rumbling. "Trust me, he's more of a pain in the ass than you know." She perched at Katie's scarred butcher-block kitchen bar. Katie bustled around the kitchen bristling with low-tech culinary items: wooden spoons, glass decanters, copper pots, wire whisks. Katie was an old-school chef and proud of it. Above the sink, a kitchen witch figurine spun slowly, keeping watch over the herbs growing on the windowsill. As Katie ladled the soup into the bowls, Anya told her about Sparky's adventures in the hospital.

Katie grinned. "You know, witches have been known to keep nearly any kind of creature—seen and unseen—as familiars. I've met witches who have parakeets and witches who have naiads."

"What are naiads?"

"Water spirits. But there's a reason a witch won't take a salamander as a familiar."

"That reason being?" Anya was pretty sure she already knew the answer.

"They're entirely unpredictable and uncontrollable . . . destructive, like fire." Katie shrugged, placing a steaming bowl of soup and slices of fresh-baked bread before her. "They're also said to have very little in common with humans, so their goals and our goals don't intersect much."

A crash echoed from down the hall. Anya covered her

eyes with her hand. "Sorry." There were few electronic items in the witch's house that Sparky could destroy. Katie kept the number of electronic gadgets in her house to a minimum, as electrical fields interfered with her magick work. But Sparky and the cats could still find many breakable nonelectronic objects.

"No worries." Katie perched on a bar stool beside her, her bare toes splayed on the wooden rails of the stool. "Elementals will be elementals."

"I wish mine were a bit less elemental. Can you cook up some magickal sedatives for him or something? Something to chill him out?"

Katie shook her head. "Nope. Sparky is what he is. You're stuck with him, until and unless he decides to serve someone else. And since he seems pretty attached to you, I don't see that happening."

"I just wish that he came with an off switch."

"Didn't you get a user manual when you summoned him?"

Anya snorted. "I never summoned him. My mom gave him to me before she died."

An aggrieved yowl sounded from the bedroom. Fay trotted into the kitchen and parked herself under Katie's chair. The cat mewed plaintively. Katie stared down at her. "Well, if he plays too rough, bite him back."

The cat slunk back across the kitchen linoleum to the hallway, tail kinked.

Katie smiled over her soup spoon. "It's a good thing I don't have kids. I'd let them eat each other and the victor would be one badass homicidal freak. There would be no point in summoning a salamander to protect the winner."

"Sparky's a very good protector, I'll hand him that. Better than any Rottweiler."

Katie gave her an arch look. "He protects you from all the things that go bump in the night, does he? Even the things you *want* to bump you in the night?"

Anya made a face. "Something like that." She stuffed her mouth with a hot matzo ball to keep from having to elaborate.

Katie plunged in anyway. "Look, Brian knows about Sparky, right? What's the big deal?"

"Issss complimifacated," Anya muttered around the matzo ball scalding her tongue.

Katie rolled her eyes. "It's only as complicated as you make it, you know. Brian's a good guy. And he cares about you."

Anya continued to chew.

"And he's hot, in a geeky sort of way," Katie continued.

Anya kept chewing. "Gnnnew subject, pllllshhh."

"Okay." Katie lifted her hands and backed away from the topic, silver bracelets jingling. "Let's talk about your symbol."

Anya swallowed her matzo ball. "Did you find something?"

"Check this out." Katie pulled a book across the counter, bookmarked with Anya's arson scene photograph. The title was *Egyptian Divination*, and featured a fearsome picture of a man with the head of a jackal on the cover.

She flipped it open, and pointed to a page of symbols. The page depicted a sketched symbol of a wavy, serpentine line, with a curving upturned arc for the head. "It's called the Horned Viper, in Egyptian hieratic script. The serpentine ideographic meaning is clear, but it's phonetically equivalent to the letter *F* in our language."

Anya placed the picture beside it. The figures were the same. Now she could see the sinuous curve of the serpent's spine, that the curve of the horns indicated a head. "That backs up my suspicion that it was a ritualistic crime. Do you know of any uses this might have in ceremonial magick?"

Katie shook her head. "Egyptian magickal systems aren't my specialty, but I've never heard of this particular symbol being in common use. Its purpose would depend upon the other objects in the environment and the specifics of the ritual."

"If there were any other items used, most of them would have been obliterated." Anya frowned. "I asked the lab to take a casting of the symbol, to see if they can find any tool marks. I want to know how this mark got impressed in the concrete."

Katie turned the photograph around in her hands. "The viper's head," she said suddenly. "Do you remember what direction it faced? The direction the viper was crawling?"

Anya ran through the building's orientation in her mind, remembered the sun rising over the building. She thought a moment more. "South. It pointed south."

"That's the cardinal direction associated with fire."

Anya cupped her chin in her hand. "I'm going to have a hell of a time trying to explain this to my superiors. Magick and forensic science don't play well together."

"It doesn't have to be that way," said Katie. "Those things don't sit neatly behind their lines, never touching."

But I need them to be, Anya thought. *I need the balance between the known and unknown worlds. And the unknown is leaking too far over.*

"Deep breath."

Anya lay on the floor in Katie's spare bedroom, surrounded by books and the saffron glow of candles. An exhausted Sparky was curled around Anya's feet, tail spilling over to one side. She could feel his warmth on her bare feet, and she wiggled her toes. Vern lazily licked his tail, while Fay had fallen asleep with her paws around one of Sparky's gill-fronds. The familiars enjoyed Katie's Reiki treatments as much as Anya did. Though the goal of the treatments was to balance and smooth the wrinkles out of Anya's energy, the critters enjoyed lapping at the edges.

Anya closed her eyes. She felt Katie press her fingers lightly over her face, the heels of her hands resting on Anya's brow. Katie's slow, regular breathing, the crackle-pop of the candle flames, and the occasional contented sigh from a familiar were the only sounds in the room. She was conscious of a warm buzz in Katie's hands.

Anya let her mind drift, drinking it in. She was tempted to let herself fall asleep while Katie worked. Usually, she was able to stay awake, but she felt herself pulled slowly down, down into the warm darkness of the dream she'd abandoned this morning.

Heat shimmered from the floor of the ice cave, moving in lazy transparent curtains from one side of the ice cave to the other. Anya could feel the heat washing over her skin, drawing sweat from her pores. Beside her, Sparky paced. His tongue probed the darkness, tasting. It seemed that, in this warmth, he moved even more fluidly. Amber light played over the speckles of his skin in a hypnotic swirl.

Anya looked down to see the Horned Viper sigil she'd seen at the arson scenes engraved on the slick floor. Her eyes picked out another . . . and another. Dozens peppered her path. Like an army of snakes, they were sketched in the ice, horns pointing toward the blackness. In the seething light, they seemed to squirm, to undulate in the haze.

The little girl from the pickle lady's pop machine faced Anya. She tipped her head to one side, and a barrette grazed the shoulder of her dress. She pointed to the darkness.

"Sirrush is coming."

Anya knelt down on the slippery floor before the girl. "Sweetie, I don't know what that means. Who is Sirrush?"

The girl stared at her with glassy eyes. "Sirrush is fire."

CHAPTER FOUR

ANYA AWOKE WITH A GASP and hissing from the cats and salamander at her feet. The cats, disturbed by her movement, scrambled away. Sparky lifted his head, skin on his back rippling.

Katie froze, her hands resting on Anya's collarbones in a V-shaped position. "What did you say?"

Anya swallowed. Her mouth tasted scorched. "I didn't say anything. I was dreaming . . . I think."

Katie narrowed her eyes. "You said, 'Sirrush is coming.'"

Anya sighed. "I've been hearing that a lot lately."

Katie finished the Reiki session in silence, pressing her hands over her heart, solar plexus, waist, and knees. Anya turned over, dislodging Sparky, so that Katie could work the Reiki hand positions on her back. Sparky uncurled himself, his tail spiraling, and yawned. He padded away in search of the cats. Katie finished sitting at Anya's feet, holding her bare feet in her hands with her head bowed over them. Anya's skin prickled and buzzed. The sensation ebbed away when Katie let go.

"I'll bring you some water," Katie told her. "Relax now."

Anya turned over and stretched. She stared at the ceiling. The dream felt close, still roiling in her chest. Katie's energy work usually left her feeling calm and energized, but she couldn't help but feel that the dream had interrupted the process, leaving a metallic taste in her mouth and a sense of unease in its wake.

Katie returned with a glass of water and sat cross-legged beside her. "Tell me about this dream." Her freckled face was carefully blank, but Anya could see the agitation in her hands as she fingered her bracelets.

Anya sat up and drank the cool water. In between sips, she told Katie about the dreams. The telling and the water seemed to rinse the taste of iron from her mouth. Katie listened carefully, stroking the edge of a bracelet.

When Anya had finished, the witch frowned. "When I was aligning your energy, I felt something shift. It flared for a second."

Anya blinked quizzically at her.

"Well . . . everyone's energy patterns are unique. When I do energy work for myself, I visualize my aura as being a curtain of blue light, like a stage curtain at a theater production. I imagine pulling the wrinkles out of it and brushing the dust off." Katie passed her hands in front of her body. "I think of your particular aura as like the surface of the sun. Dark spots, like sunspots, occasionally bubble up and I try to use Reiki to even them out. But what I felt in this last session was like . . . a solar flare. Your aura twitched and receded."

"Um . . . so what does that mean?"

"I don't know for sure. But, if I had to guess, I'd say it was a reflexive reaction to stress or something you felt was invading your space. It felt angry, hostile."

"So that was the spiritual equivalent of kicking the doctor when he hits your knee with the little hammer?" Anya winced. "Sorry."

Katie's blue eyes were serious and Anya's joking tone faded. "You mentioned Sirrush."

"He's the king of the salamanders, right? Like Sparky." Anya envisioned a salamander wearing a crown, chewing on a light-up scepter more impressive than Sparky's Glo-worm.

Katie shook her head. "Not like Sparky. Sparky's a fire elemental, sure. But there are different levels of elementals, a hierarchy. I'll show you." Katie stood up, rummaged through her bookshelves. The shelves lining the walls were in no discernible classification order, stained country cookbooks intermingled with paperback gardening books and handwritten spell notes. Muttering to herself, Katie plucked a tome from the shelf and flipped through the index.

"There are five levels of salamander. It's analogous to the hierarchy of angels: seraphim, cherubim, archangels . . . you get the drift." Katie handed the book to Anya, open to a page depicting a drawing of a creature that resembled a tadpole. With a long tail, no arms, and big black eyes, it looked like it could star in its own cartoon and have its own line of trading cards. "At the bottom of the list are the efts. Efts are the elemental forces behind candle flames, pilot lights . . . they're the littlest fish and the most numerous. Paracelsus described them as being like fireflies."

"He's cute."

"Yeah, well they get progressively less cute the further you go up."

Katie flipped the page. Embedded in the text, a small lizard stood on two legs. Its arms were short, holding a tiny ember like a squirrel holding a nut. "These are newts. Newts are common in home hearths and bonfires. They're usually the spirits or guardians of houses and they're almost always tied to places."

"Still cute."

"Keep going." Next was a larger creature with familiar proportions: long body, short legs, and loose, speckled skin. "These are the firedrakes, like Sparky. They're also called hellbenders in some places. They're evolved enough to have free will, but they don't speak. They're drawn to large fires . . . burning buildings, that kind of thing."

"Okay, I'll admit it. Sparky is slightly less adorable than the newts."

"More powerful than firedrakes are the basilisks." Katie turned the page. The creature depicted on the page was much less cute than Sparky. It stood on two legs, dusted in soot. It reminded Anya of Godzilla, covered in bumpy scales and a ridge running down its back. "They're said to be rare, as large as men, with the power of speech. There are only few dozen of these known to exist and they're said to spend their free time snorkeling in volcanoes."

"Good thing for us."

"Most definitely. And this is their daddy." Katie flipped over the last page. "Sirrush. A dragon." The image of a dragon churned over two pages, wings outstretched. Its fearsome horned snout leaked fire and its claws raked the air. For scale, a man was drawn the size of a house cat at his feet. Anya didn't think the man at his feet had much of a chance against the fearsome creature.

"Shit," Anya said.

"No kidding. There used to be dozens of other dragons throughout history in this category. Fables tell of them going underground, but the most prevalent theory is that Sirrush ate most of them around the time of ancient Babylon. The good thing for us is that he's supposed to hibernate underground and pay humanity little mind."

"I'm confused. I thought witches invoked Sirrush in ceremonial magick?"

"We do, but it's really just a courtesy. Kind of like when you send your nasty great-uncle Mort who you haven't seen in ten years an invitation to your wedding. You don't really want him to show up, but he'll be pretty pissed if you don't show him the respect of asking. The vast majority of the time, he just drops a check in the mail and doesn't show up to family events."

"And . . . what happens on the rare occasions when he does show up?" Anya wasn't sure she wanted to know.

Katie pursed her lips. "Then, he gets totally wasted and wrecks your party. He gropes the bridesmaids, yells obscenities into the microphone, and falls into your wedding cake."

Anya stared down at the page. "Um. He looks more fearsome than any of my relatives."

"Yeah, well, Sirrush, like the other elementals, isn't good nor is he evil . . . like many of our extended family members. Sirrush is like a hurricane, or an earthquake. He's a force of nature. He can be terribly destructive, but it's nothing personal."

"Shit." Anya wrapped her hands around her knees. "If my firebug is trying to summon Sirrush through ritual magick, what are the odds that he'll succeed? How likely is the cranky dragon to show up to the party?"

Katie spread her hands in a helpless gesture. "No way of knowing. I'd say that the fires he's setting are definitely getting the spirit world's attention. Rather than sending Sirrush an invite in the mail, he's pounding on the door."

"If Sirrush takes him up on it, what then?"

"Then nothing. You can't stop a hurricane." She leaned forward. "Your best bet is to keep this idiot from waking Sirrush up. If Sirrush shows up to the party, there's no bouncer in the world big or bad enough to keep him off the dance floor."

The news media ran the arson as the lead story. Neuman's photo was plastered on the front page of the papers. The little girl found mummified in the pop machine was buried in the back of the metro section and received less than thirty seconds' attention on the evening news.

Anya watched the local news broadcasts in half-time on her desk computer. Elbows planted on her scarred desk, she had to remind herself to blink in between frames. Headphones covered her ears, blotting out the sounds of ringing phones and office foot traffic outside her door. The transom above the glass and wood door had jammed open years ago, and sound infiltrated the space as easily as smoke.

Her office was a hodgepodge of scavenged steel furniture and files stacked neatly in cardboard bankers' boxes. She'd put in a request when she'd gotten the job for a file cabinet, but none ever materialized. A map of the city was taped to the dingy yellow wall. The locations of the four arson sites were indicated by red pushpins. No discernible geographic tie had emerged: besides the warehouse fire, the arsonist had hit two abandoned houses on opposite ends of town and a beauty salon. But that didn't keep Anya from scribbling around them with markers, from tying strings around the pins and trying to determine a pattern or common entry and escape route.

Now she focused her attention on combing the media footage of the crime scenes for suspicious bystanders. An arsonist could rarely stay away from his own work. More often than not, he was compelled to stand back and admire what his hands had wrought, his power. And it was almost always a he. The only female arsonist Anya had ever investigated was a woman who torched the apartment her husband had rented for his mistress. In the majority of cases of arson involving single perpetrators—excluding those that were lit for revenge or monetary gain—the motive was sexual. Anya had caught her fair share of pyromaniacs masturbating at the scene of the crime, but she sensed that the ritualistic motive overshadowed any sexual thrills to be gained from watching buildings burn.

But that didn't mean that he wouldn't return to the scene. If the arsonist had any ego at all, he would drive by to see what he'd created. Just seeing it on the evening news wouldn't be enough. He'd have to be there, touch it, smell it. Who knew? Perhaps the idea of summoning up Sirrush turned his crank.

And so she watched, head in hand, inching through the footage. She'd asked the news stations for any footage they'd shot on the previous fires. No images had been televised and those fires had only warranted small blurbs in the metro section. They hadn't even bothered to cover one of the house fires at all. The warehouse fire had gotten a good deal of airtime, owing to the firefighter's injury, but the previous two fires hadn't been shown. There had been more than enough bad news to overshadow these events; they'd represented little more than ordinary days in Detroit. Those arsons were like the perfunctory mention of the little girl in the paper—business as usual.

She ignored the newscasters blathering in the foreground and watched the crowds behind them, the cars inching behind the crime scene tape. She watched for someone who didn't belong, someone who was trying too hard to be inconspicuous, someone who couldn't tear his eyes away from the moment.

On the screen, a reporter drank a diet soda through a

straw, unwilling to smear her makeup. She seemed young, fresh out of college; Anya supposed that she was an intern. The assignment was likely her opportunity to practice on a story that wouldn't see the light of day: this feed from the beauty shop fire had never been broadcast. It had been recorded on the sidewalk across the street after the scene had been released by DFD. The beauty shop owner stood, crying, behind the barricade. Neighbors clotted on the sidewalk behind her, watching the fire crews clear out. The reporter bent over to put the soda on the pavement and Anya squinted.

That guy. Something struck her as unusual about him. He walked by the edge of the knot of people, his hands jammed into his pockets. He was tall, wearing a black overcoat, walking with a limp. Long, dark, glossy hair was pulled back behind the nape of his neck. She couldn't tell where he was looking; sunglasses covered his eyes. He looked too corporate for the crowd of bystanders on their way to blue-collar jobs—the dark wool among the flannel and denim just didn't fit. He wasn't doing anything suspicious, just walking down the sidewalk. He could be a business owner or private individual come to check out the damage to a neighboring property. Maybe.

But there was something about him that prickled the base of her neck, caused her to fish through the DVDs from two weeks ago. She switched discs and her computer grumbled as it digested the new one. She drummed her fingers on the scarred desk, waiting as it summoned up clips of the house fire from two weeks ago.

This had been a suburban fire, in Redford Township, just outside of city limits. The site had been an empty house that had been vacated due to the owner's bankruptcy. Redford FD had called DFD for help, since the blaze had spread to a detached garage and threatened a school. Once it became apparent the fire was an arson, the township had punted the case to DFD's crime lab. Anya had toured the site once the arsonist's hallmark had been discovered. But she hadn't had the opportunity to see the scene when it had been fresh.

This footage was taken the following afternoon, the newscaster standing in the street before the schoolyard, with school buses parked in view. Parents were picking up their children, milling in the background. She slowed the speed, scanning the crowd . . . and spied a familiar figure walking down the sidewalk. A pale face with a straight jaw turned in three-quarter profile, belonging to a man dressed in a nondescript gray jogging suit. He wasn't doing anything unusual, but as before, he stood a bit too far apart from the others. Too isolated. Even in these casual clothes, there was something indefinably . . . aloof . . . about his stance. It wasn't just the limp. He just didn't blend in. And he entered and exited the shot without a child.

"Gotcha," she breathed. It was the same guy from the beauty shop scene. And he would have no reason to be at both places, even though both the shots had been taken long after the fires had burned out.

The phone on her desk chirped. She snatched the receiver. "Kalinczyk."

"This is Jenna from the crime lab. We've got some new results from your arson scene you'll want to see."

"Be right there."

Anya snagged her jacket and keys. Banging the door behind her, she wound her way out of the basement of the Detroit Fire Department headquarters. Like much of Detroit's downtown, it had been built in the construction boom of the 1920s. Renovations had touched the upper floors, but had forgotten the basement. Black-and-white tile checkerboard still covered the floors. She waved at the guard on the first floor, the echo of her footsteps clicking against the vaulted ceilings.

She'd parked across the street at Cobo Hall, a squared-off concrete building that stood in sharp contrast to the arches and brick exterior of Fire HQ. There had always seemed to be a tension between the old and the new in downtown: the glass and steel tower of the Ren Cen jarred architecturally with the Italian Art Deco styles of the lower brick buildings built in the twenties. Some of the newer buildings, like Comerica Park where the Detroit Tigers played, had attempted to blend into the existing architecture by incorporating brick and sculpture into the design. Still, it always seemed to Anya that the past held more sway here than more recent eras.

Police HQ was no exception. Just blocks south of Greektown, the low brick shops and restaurants with brightly colored awnings gave way to the stately gray Art Nouveau building. Anya found an open parking space, then climbed the short flight of steps to the arched entry.

Decorative metalwork on the lower windows cast geometric patterns of sunshine on the tiled floors. She punched the elevator button and waited.

Detroit's forensic laboratory had a rocky history. After a string of false findings that resulted in overturned cases, the laboratory had been closed. It had recently reopened, as the state crime lab had been unable to take on the massive backlog that Detroit had generated in recent years. The entire department had been restructured and reformed, begun from scratch with a series of grants from the feds. Though accreditation had been reinstated, it would take many years for faith to be rebuilt.

Within the decorative outer facade of the building, technology hummed. The elevator doors opened onto a room with drop ceilings and fluorescent light—the central evidence area. Yellow steel cabinets lined the walls and stood in islands; computers perched beside glassed-in cabinets. Black stone countertops held microscopes and paper evidence bags. On one table, Anya glimpsed the pair of shoes that had belonged to the little girl in the pop machine being carefully examined by a lab-coated woman holding a pair of tweezers. Anya's gaze lingered on the shoes. One of the laces was broken, and the woman was picking apart the knot.

"Sad, aren't they?"

Anya started, turning at the voice. Jenna Bentham, the forensic department's trace evidence specialist, stood beside her. She shook her head, clucking at the technician plucking fibers from the small shoes as carefully as a farmer would pluck a chicken. Her long brown braids moved against the shoulder of her lab coat, beads clicking against her earrings.

"Who do those belong to?" Anya genuinely wanted to know. The news reports had indicated that the girl's identity was unknown.

"A little girl that some monster-hunters found in a Coke machine." Jenna sighed.

"Found dead?"

"Yeah. Found dead from a long time ago. The ME thinks that she's been dead for thirty years. No evidence of foul play—yet. But we're looking to see if we can compile a description to run against any missing little girls from that time."

Anya wanted to say: *She's about three feet tall. Brown eyes, round face. Eyelashes as thick as a doll's.* But her voice remained stuck in her throat.

"C'mon. I've got some preliminary findings on your case." Jenna gestured for Anya to follow her to a desk shoved in a corner. She opened a manila file folder and paged through it. "We ran your chip samples through the gas chromatograph, checked for light, medium, and heavy accelerants. We didn't find any conventional or unconventional accelerants—no lighter fluid, gasoline, mineral spirits, kerosene . . . hell, we even checked for jet fuel. Twice." Jenna handed Anya the page of printed test results.

Anya believed her, but she understood the tech's impulse to check and double-check; the lab was under too much scrutiny from all sides for anyone to trust them at their word. Anya trusted Jenna, though, and handed the page back. "I wonder if it burned up," she mused.

"I went ahead and sent them to the mass spectrometer at the state lab," Jenna said. "The only thing of interest they were able to find was traces of sulfur."

"Sulfur?" Anya echoed.

She felt Sparky brushing against her pant leg. She looked down to see the salamander creeping across the tile floor, stalking a microscope perched on a table. Anya stepped on his tail, pinning him to the floor. Sparky glared up at her in irritation, straining forward with his legs churning in futile slow motion against the tile.

"Sulfur can melt . . . and when it does, it releases hydrogen sulfide gas," Jenna continued, oblivious. "It's toxic and flammable. There wasn't much there, but it's something that just doesn't belong at that kind of scene . . . unless someone's chemistry set burned."

Anya frowned. "Wouldn't we have smelled it at the scene?"

"Depends. The amounts we found in your samples were pretty small traces. It would depend how close one was when the compounds were released. By the time you got there, the smell might have been mistaken for the mercaptan smell added to commercial natural gas lines, or it could have dispersed to the point that it was virtually undetectable. The handheld sniffer that you all carry isn't programmed to pick up trace amounts of sulfur dioxide."

Sparky switched directions, circling around to get a better look at an unattended slide projector that had attracted his attention. Anya adjusted her stance to remain on his tail, trying to look nonchalant—not like she had to pee.

"What else have you got for me?" Anya asked.

"I saved the best for last." Jenna picked up the cast of the mark from the concrete floor. "Your symbol here has no tool marks."

"It *has* to have tool marks," Anya blurted. "It was carved into the concrete floor." She immediately regretted her words. She didn't want to doubt the lab's competence, but . . .

Jenna held up a finger. "It wasn't carved. It was melted."

"But concrete melts at . . ."

" . . . around four thousand degrees for silica-based concrete," Jenna finished. "Under the microscope, we could see drip marks and stretches in the material."

Anya sat back. "Christ. So this guy is running around with . . . what? A blowtorch?"

"An acetylene torch isn't hot enough. You'd need something like an arc welder . . . something hot enough to melt steel. That's a huge machine needed to generate enough electricity to get the job done . . . and not something that your firebug can throw in a backpack and trot off with."

"How in the hell could that happen?" Anya muttered, fingering the edges of the cast. She felt none of the shimmer of heat in the cast that she had felt in the concrete floor.

"Beats me," Jenna shrugged. "But don't take my word for it. I'm just the lab rat."

———

Since she'd succeeded in pissing the forensic lab off, Anya was looking forward to spending the evening alone with her take-out Chinese food. Her solitary ambitions were dashed when she saw Brian's battered van parked at the curb in front of her house. Brian sat on the front stoop, hands jammed into his pockets, listening to music on headphones. She had the urge to keep driving, but she knew Brian had already seen her.

Great. Another opportunity to offend.

Anya bumped the car door shut with her hip, juggling her keys and the take-out bag. "Hey, Brian."

"Hey," he answered noncommittally. Anya sat down beside him. He looked like hell. A shiner blackened one eye.

Instinctively, Anya reached out to touch the bruise. "What happened to you?" He ducked self-consciously away from her.

"Rough night." He didn't elaborate.

Anya stared down at her hands. "Do you want to come in?"

"No. I came to tell you about Ciro."

Dread prickled through her, quickening her pulse. "Is he all right?"

"Not really. The old man's sick. Really sick. He doesn't want anyone to know, but he went to the ER last night for chest pains."

Anya jumped to her feet. "Let's go see him—"

Brian waved her down. "He's home now, sleeping. I just came from his house. Max is staying with him."

Anya sank down to the stoop. "It's his heart?"

"Yeah. They think he's got a weak valve. He didn't have a full-blown heart attack, but the scans they did showed some previous damage." Brian looked away, fidgeting with the cord of his headphones. "Jules sent me to ask you something."

Anya's eyebrow lifted.

"Jules wants you to come out with us tomorrow night. With Ciro out of commission, we're a man down." Brian shrugged. "I think that we're fine. Max is coming along well."

Anya's face froze. She knew Brian could see it.

Brian nodded. "I'll tell him you said no. No big deal." He stood to leave. "I'll keep you posted on Ciro—"

Anya reached up and grasped his sleeve. "Wait."

He paused, looking down at her.

Her phone rang. She swore under her breath. "Hold that thought," she told him, as she released his arm and dug into her purse for her cell phone. "Kalinczyk," she muttered into it.

"It's Marsh. I've got bad news."

Anya rubbed her brow. This was the day for it. "About . . . ?"

"Neuman. He's dead."

"I'm sorry, Captain."

"Yeah, well . . . the case is going over to DPD. Chief's forming a task force to work on these arsons. Meet with DPD's detective bureau in the morning and fill them in."

"Understood." She snapped the phone shut, grimacing. With Neuman's death, the arson was now a homicide and control of the case would belong to DPD in the morning.

But tonight the case was still hers.

She looked up at Brian. "I'll go out with DAGR tomorrow night. But you have to do a favor for me tonight."

CHAPTER FIVE

"THIS PLACE IS LIKE THE Batcave."

Anya emitted a low whistle as Brian turned on the light. Fluorescent lights fizzled on, one panel after another, reaching far back down a corridor stacked floor to ceiling with computer monitors, cords dangling from cabinets, and discarded circuit boards. A half-dozen wall-sized server racks stood silent sentinel, fans whirring, green lights blinking. Anya would never have thought that this hub of technology was here—the next door down in the bowels of the university services building had been a janitorial closet.

"Welcome to my lair." Brian crossed behind a black glass desk covered with the largest computer monitor Anya had ever seen—it was larger than the HDTV displays at the electronic stores. Brian opened a drawer and began rummaging.

Anya felt Sparky stirring against her neck. She flipped the collar with her middle finger, and he settled back down. She didn't want the salamander running amok in

Brian's toys. Unlike the microwave Sparky ate last week, these were very expensive items. Anya was certain that her entire lifetime salary wouldn't begin to touch the cost of some of these pieces of equipment.

She plucked a pair of goggles from the top of a cabinet. They looked like a prop from a science-fiction film, wrapped in wires and dark plastic. She peered through them and saw shapes outlined in green and blue, the servers outlined in yellow. Brian's red form glowed from the opposite side of the room, reflecting body heat against the metal cabinets behind him. Infrared goggles. "What the hell is it exactly that you do here, anyway?"

"Stuff for contract R&D," he said vaguely, as he sorted parts on the top of his desk.

Anya put the goggles down and stared up at a map of cell towers taped to the wall. The bubbles surrounding them covered the entire Detroit metro area, the wireless carriers neatly labeled with Brian's precise capitals-only lettering.

"What kind of 'stuff'?" she persisted. The investigator in her wanted to know what exactly he did. The woman in her wanted still to know who he was; she hadn't gotten close enough to him to find out.

His blue eyes flickered up. "You know those facial recognition systems that the feds tried to implement after 9/11?"

"You mean those cameras they wanted to install on street corners that would pick out terrorists' faces?"

"Yeah. That stuff."

"You work on that?" Anya's jaw dropped. All this time, she'd thought he did tech support for the undergraduate computer labs, resetting passwords and filtering for porn.

"I invented that." A trace of smugness quirked the corner of his mouth. "Among other things."

"You are one scary dude, Brian."

"It's a living." He dumped a seemingly unrelated group of mismatched plastic parts from a cardboard box onto his desk and began plugging them together. He blew dust off a lens and scrubbed it across his T-shirt. "The scariness is just one bonus that really enhances my personal life."

Anya swallowed. "That's not it."

"What's not what?" Brian didn't look at her. He screwed the lens into a black plastic tube.

"You. Me. Your scariness. That's not why there's not . . . you and me."

He snorted. "Are we having the 'It's not you, it's me' discussion? We don't have to do that, you know. I get it."

She bit her lip. "That's not it. It's my scariness."

Brian set the parts down. "Your 'scariness.'" He made air quotation marks around the word.

She stared down at her hands. "Look, you know what I do isn't exactly normal."

"This is not news."

"And . . . I've got an elemental familiar who likes to play chaperone," she finished lamely, wishing she could shut the hell up before she started going on about her fear of intimacy.

"I know about Sparky. I've picked up his temperature disturbances on my instruments. I get that he's always around."

"I mean . . . he's *always* around."

"So?" Brian shook his head. "I live in an old apartment building. There are probably a couple of spirits who get a kick out of watching me do my Hendrix impression in the shower." He sat on the edge of the desk. "If that's an issue for you, okay, I get it. You're shy around Sparky. But I'm not."

"But . . ."

He caught up her hand, kissed her palm. Anya's breath snagged in her throat. The kiss thrilled up her arm. "I'm more interested in the flesh and blood world than the spirit world," he murmured around her fingers.

Anya rocked forward on her toes. She wanted so much to leave the spirit world behind, to feel grounded in the physical world. The more the spirit world impinged on her life, she had to admit, the more she craved the stability of something . . . wholly human. She lifted her head toward him and his mouth brushed hers, then melted against her lips.

She drank him in, the taste of him, the feeling of his hands winding in her hair. She could feel his heart beating against her chest as her arms slid around his waist. He felt real, his breath rising and falling against her palms. He smelled real, like soap and coffee, and she clung to that, to him.

His mouth brushed her jaw, behind her ear. She stiffened, feeling Sparky stir against her throat. She focused her attention on the feeling of Brian's lips against the pulse behind her ear, and lifted her hands around his neck. His arms wrapped around her waist, and she leaned back against the server cabinet. She could feel the warm breath of the server's heat sink fan against the small of her back, tickling the hem of her shirt.

He pursued her, kissing her among the litter of computer parts. Something rolled off the desk and smashed on the floor; he ignored it. She wrapped her leg around the outside of his knee, feeling the length of his body pressing against her. She felt wanted, desired . . . and that was a new sensation for her, one she wanted to taste in all its delicious gravity.

She felt Sparky's heat sliding off her neck, down her back. She ignored him, feeling him peel away from her skin and scrabble among the circuit boards. She ignored him, wrapped up in Brian's arms and the feel of his mouth on her skin. . .

Right up until Sparky took a bite out of one of the servers. A blue flash of light arced over the server panel, and the fluorescent lights overhead flickered.

"Sparky!" she snarled. Anya passed her hand over her eyes. "I'm sorry. He just ate your computer . . ."

Brian pushed himself back on his palms, twisting to stare at the server. He couldn't see Sparky standing beside the server, licking the access panel as if he were a child with an ice cream cone.

"No big deal. I've got protection—surge suppression and a backup generator." His hair fell over one eye, and he grinned.

Anya leaned her head on his shoulder. "This is what I mean. He . . ."

"Hey." He lifted her chin, kissed her forehead. "Don't worry about it, okay?"

She nodded, but her cheeks flamed. Her hands fell to her sides, and Brian pulled back. Anya circled around the desk to chase Sparky from the servers.

Brian cleared his throat. "You said you wanted to do some surveillance. What are you looking for?"

Anya dug into her purse. She unfolded printouts of the picture of the man from both the arson scenes, then handed them to him. "This guy showed up at two of the previous arson scenes. I want to know if he's going to turn back up at the warehouse fire site."

Brian smoothed the grainy photos out on his desk. "I don't think that the resolution is good enough on these to do facial recognition." He looked up at her. "But I can rig something up so that you can watch your sites, see if he comes back."

Anya smiled. "Thank you, Brian."

He shrugged. "Hey, it's what I do. It's the evil-genius gig."

Without the scurry of EMTs, fire trucks, and police buzzing around it, the warehouse felt entirely too still, like a hosed-down hive abandoned by its bees. In the evening dimness, it had finally begun to cool. Lacking light and movement, the hulk was plunged in darkness. Yellow hazard tape cordoned off the scene from the sidewalk and a makeshift fence of orange plastic netting had been stretched around posts at the perimeter. No Trespassing signs were stationed at regular intervals along the edges.

Anya drove around the northeast corner of the building, where her witness had seen the light. She parked in the alley. Brian grabbed a box of his gear from the backseat, and she switched on her flashlight to lead the way to the building. Footing was treacherous, and they were forced to pick their way through the rubble. She pulled aside a corner of the makeshift fence, and they ducked inside.

"Where do you want to set up?" Brian asked.

"If we can, I'd like to set up a wide-angle at the front door, and one in the basement. Our firebug seems to have spent the most time there. I would think that if he's coming back, he'd want to see that again."

Brian set down his bag and fished out a wireless camera the size of his fist. The lens was the size of a silver dollar, and two iridescent black wings spread from its housing, like a black satellite. He pointed to the ruined lintel above the door. "Up there?"

"Yeah. I want to see who's walking by."

Brian stepped onto the hood of the car, reaching up toward the top of the door. Like a malevolent black canary, the camera stared down at the ground with an obsidian eye. It was unobtrusive enough to be mistaken for a piece of rubble, the black housing blending in with the char. Unlike most webcams Anya had seen, this one displayed no lights to show that it was online. Brian opened his laptop on the hood of the car, then turned it around to show Anya. "Does this work for you?"

In shades of green night vision, Anya could see herself and Brian huddled over the laptop. The angle of view stretched from one edge of the building to the other.

"Nice," she said. "But how long will the batteries last?" Electric and gas had not been restored to the site and might not ever be.

"About forty-eight hours, give or take. The transmitter has a solar backup, so it should recharge during the day. But if you have a cloudy day, it's going to be dead by the next nightfall."

"I didn't know they made those," Anya remarked.

Brian grinned. "I'm considering this to be a field test."

She leaned against the car, watching him fiddle with the screen resolution. "I get the feeling that you 'field test' a lot of gadgets with DAGR."

"Sure. It's a chance to work on surveillance in a wide variety of conditions . . . and the things we measure are very subtle. Gives me the chance to test-drive the equipment before I put together final prototypes."

"You got another one of those birdies for the basement?"

"I like that . . . you just gave me a code name for these little guys. Blackbirds." Brian pulled another one out of his bag. "Where do you want this one to perch?"

"Follow me." Anya stepped around the corner of the building, to the window she knew the arsonist had entered through. The camera at the main entrance would catch him if he was casually walking by; the camera in the basement would capture his image if he decided to come play some more.

Anya pulled back a piece of plywood covering the window. Forensics had taken the grating and the glass in their unsuccessful attempt to lift prints. All that remained was a gaping black hole, leading to darkness. Gripping the edge of the window frame, she lowered herself down into the basement. Landing in a puddle, she reached up for Brian's bag. Brian followed, clambering down beside her.

Anya's flashlight beam swept the basement. She saw no sign of the handyman spirit. "You might catch some ghost footage on camera, too." She told him about the repairman with the vacuum cleaner who'd witnessed the arson.

"I wouldn't get my hopes up too much with this camera," Brian told her, affixing the camera to a blackened beam facing the window. "Since sunlight won't penetrate down here, you're likely to get twelve hours on batteries, max, before it needs to be switched out."

Anya felt the collar around her neck warm, felt Sparky's head lift from her shoulder and look backward.

"That's a pretty fancy gadget."

Anya turned, seeing the outline of the repairman's ghost standing over Brian, peering up at the camera perched in the support beam.

"Brian," she said, "our ghost is here." She doubted that Brian would be able to see or hear him, but she didn't want him to think that she'd gone off the beam, talking to the walls.

Anya addressed the ghost. "Hello, again."

"Hello, miss. May I ask what that geegaw is?" He held his hands behind his back, looking into the fish-eye lens. She wondered if he could see his own reflection in it.

"It's a camera. We're hoping that the man who set fire to the warehouse will come back, and we want to try to identify him."

"Son of a gun." The spirit passed his hand back and forth over the lens, fascinated. *"That's neat."* He looked back at Anya. *"The only people who have been down here have been the firemen. I talked to them, but I was pretty sure they didn't hear me, like you do."*

A good sign. That suggested that the firebug hadn't been back to the scene yet.

"Would you mind if I asked you a couple of questions about the other night?" Anya asked, treading carefully with the ghost. She didn't want to frighten him off. But, for now, he was her best witness. "I'm Anya, by the way. And this is Brian." She gestured to Brian, who had discreetly backed into a corner, fiddling with a digital recorder. Christ, she thought. Did he have a utility belt full of surveillance equipment, too?

The repairman tipped his hat. *"I'm Virgil. Pleased to make your acquaintance."*

Anya felt Sparky twining down her arm. After taking shape on the floor, he walked up to Virgil and sniffed his pant leg. Virgil knelt before him and offered his hand for Sparky to smell. *"And who is this?"*

"This is Sparky."

"I've never seen a dog like that. Is he named after Sparky Anderson?"

"Yeah, I'm a baseball fan. He's, um, sort of a mutt."

Anya left it alone. She didn't want to get into a discussion about elemental familiars and what she did for a part-time job. The spirit would be less inclined to talk if he knew she could eat him as easily as if he were a cookie. She unfolded the printouts of her suspect's image from the news tape and shone her flashlight on them. "Could you please tell me if this is the man who came in here the other night?"

Virgil peered at the pieces of paper. He brushed them with his fingertips, and his hand passed through. *"Yes. That was the man."*

"He came alone?"

"Yes. But I didn't talk to him."

"Why not?"

Virgil paused. *"I was afraid that he would eat me."*

Anya's brow wrinkled. "Why were you afraid of that?"

"He seemed very hungry. Like you, but not like you." He cocked his head. *"I don't believe that you'd eat a spirit without good reason, Miss Anya."*

Anya's thoughts churned. Had another Lantern been here? Or was the old spirit just fooling with her? Spirits, especially if left to rot for decades, could be unreliable pranksters. Still . . .

She gestured to the symbol on the floor, the mark of the Horned Viper. "Did you see him do that?"

Virgil nodded. *"Damndest thing. He drew on the floor with his finger, and it glowed, bright as coke in a steel mill."*

Now she knew the spirit was bullshitting her. She crossed her arms over her chest. "He didn't have a torch or welding equipment?"

"No, ma'am. He came in here with empty hands. He set that mark on the floor, and then . . . this wave of fire rolled up from the floor. It was like looking at the ocean, only red, the way it moved . . ." Virgil made curving shapes with his hands. *"It was beautiful,"* he admitted.

Anya frowned. The spirit was messing with her, or he'd lost his grip on reality over the years, or . . . her logical mind refused to contemplate what the alternative meant, if he was telling the truth. "Did he get out?"

"Right back the way you came in. The fire didn't seem to bother him much."

"Thank you, Virgil. I appreciate your help."

Virgil tipped his hat and melted into the wall. *"It's a pleasure, Miss Anya. Good luck."*

Anya turned to look at Brian, who was staring intently into a fistful of gadgets. "Did you get any of that?"

Brian showed her a voice recorder. "We'll see. I take it from your end of the conversation that he positively ID'd your suspect?"

"Yeah. But it's not exactly the kind of evidence that will stand up in court. I can't put a ghost up on the stand."

Brian surveyed the wreckage of the basement. "Somehow, I think that's going to be the least of your problems."

"Did you pass your exam?"

Anya sat in the showroom of the used-car dealership

across the street from the warehouse. A fully restored 1969 Ford Mach 1 sat in the floor, gray and white paint gleaming under years of wax. Anya had to restrain herself from asking if she could sit in it. Beside her, Brian had set up the laptop on a salesman's desk, fiddling with the video feed. The place had a snack machine and bathrooms; it was warm and quiet . . . best location for a stakeout Anya had ever had.

John Sandoval sat at a conference table, books stacked around him. The young security guard grinned and gave Anya a fist-bump. "Ninety-six percent. I rocked that test."

"What are you studying?"

"Premed."

"No kidding?" Anya stared over her coffee cup at him. She'd decided to avail herself of the coffee John had brewed in the salesmen's lounge; she couldn't quite look at a pop machine yet without wincing. "What area do you want to go into?"

"Epidemiology." The kid put his chin in his hand, and Anya could very nearly see the shapes of his daydreams. "If I go to work for CDC in Atlanta, they have some great research programs . . . and some sweet loan forgiveness."

It was a shame that a bright kid like that dreamed of fleeing the city. But Anya couldn't really blame him. Unemployment was over 25 percent in the city, and the crime . . . a government research fellowship looked undeniably better than an inner-city life guarding a rich man's Mach 1. Anya wished him well, but also wished that there was something in the city to keep good kids like him around. But Detroit had nothing to offer him.

She lifted her cup. "To the future doctor. Salut."

"Cheers."

From the next desk, Brian called out, "Hey, you might want to take a look at this."

Her heart quickened, and she rose to bend over his shoulder. Brian pointed out a twinge of movement on the periphery of the dark screen. "I think we have a visitor."

Anya sprinted past the Mach 1 and out the door. The fluorescent brightness of the showroom receded into the darkness of the street. It took a moment for her eyes to adjust, and she scanned the ruined façade of the warehouse. Around her neck, she felt Sparky churn to life. He slithered over her hip, landing on the sidewalk in full hellbender shape. His feathery gills strained forward, tail lashing in agitation. He was in full agreement with Brian's instruments that something was out there, but she couldn't see where . . .

There. She spied movement behind the fence, around the corner of the building where the firebug had entered. Her heart hammered in her chest and she reached into her jacket for her gun and flashlight. In all the time she'd been an arson investigator, she'd never had cause to draw the little .38 revolver. More than anything, it had been just an extra piece of heavy junk to lug around, like a watch or cell phone, that she carried only because she was expected to. Now, in the pursuit of this criminal, she was glad to have it. The metal felt cool and foreign in her hand.

She jogged across the street, her steps light and nearly soundless on the cracked macadam. Sparky surged soundlessly beside her. She paused at the fence line, listening. Hearing nothing, she ducked under the open edge of the fence, then crept through the rubble to the basement window. She could see a light moving in the basement, pale yellow as a firefly. It bobbed and weaved from one edge of the basement to the other, as if searching. But the light was not bright enough to be a flashlight; it was pale as Sparky's Gloworm. She kept to the right of the window, knowing if she stood directly before it, the intruder would see her shadow against the paler blackness of night.

She aimed her gun into the dark, then clicked her flashlight on in the other fist. "Come out with your hands up." It sounded like a line from an old movie, but she couldn't come up with any clearer instructions.

The light in the basement stilled, then extinguished itself. From the darkness below, she heard Virgil's voice: *"Be careful, Miss Anya. He's got a . . ."*

She heard a crash of something metallic being kicked over. She sensed Virgil's cold, ghostly presence beyond the wall. Then . . . he simply fizzled away in an amber flash, as if he'd been sucked into a black hole. That rushing of strange gravity felt so familiar to Anya that she rocked back on her heels. It felt like when she devoured a spirit.

"Virgil?" she whispered.

No one answered. She couldn't sense him beyond the charred black of the wall. In the sick pit of her stomach, she knew that he was gone.

A brilliant red light erupted from the basement window. Anya flung her arm up to shield her eyes. The shape of a man burst from the window frame, climbing up to the ground level as easily as fire driven by wind. She smelled a whiff of sulfur and her stomach churned.

Sparky lunged at him. The salamander tackled him, growling. Instead of passing right through him, Sparky made contact, rolling with the flaming man on the ground. Anya stood over him with her gun trained on the figure's head. Sparky did his best impression of a pit bull, snarling and biting at the man in flames. The heat roared up, driving Anya back. Somewhere in the back of her mind it registered: for Sparky to be able to get his jaws around him, this flaming man must be magick.

The flaming figure's head turned, looked at her. The fire dimmed for an instant and she could make out his face. It was the same face from the videotape, but in person his eyes burned with such terrible heat that Anya nearly gasped.

"Freeze," she snarled at him, though it seemed a useless order.

The arsonist rolled over, flinging Sparky away. The salamander skidded across the narrow alleyway on his back, legs churning. The man climbed to his feet and made to run.

"I said, 'Freeze.'" She squeezed off a round from the short-barreled revolver that flung her arms up over her head with the recoil. The shot struck him in the shoulder. The flaming man spun around, gazing at her with burning wrath. He lowered his head and she had the sense of a bull getting ready to charge her. Where the bullet had struck, the fire seemed to drain away. Over his body, the fire guttered, twitching. She'd broken his concentration, and she'd break a hell of a lot more if he didn't stand down. He limped two running steps forward, flaming hands reaching toward her. She felt her hair crack and sizzle, turned her chin away, and flexed her finger on the trigger.

A black blur rocketed across the alley, knocking the burning man ass over teakettle. In the singe of motion that crashed both figures against a dumpster, Anya yelled.

"Brian!"

The fiery figure peeled away, away from Brian's prone form on the alley floor. Anya reeled in rage, firing at the receding man. As he ran down the alley, favoring his right leg, the flames flickered, and he melted into the darkness.

Anya knelt over Brian, hands shaking. He smelled like char. She shook him. "Brian!"

Brian struggled to sit up. She could see that the zipper on the front of his jacket was melted. She ran her fingers over his exposed skin, his hands, his face, coming away with just bits of ash. The skin was reddened, but not blistering. He'd been lucky.

"I'm okay. I'm okay." He repeated it like a mantra as she ran her hands over him. He finally took her hands in his and stilled them.

"What the hell do you think you were doing?"

"Trying to keep you from being barbecue."

Sparky limped up to her side and put his head in her lap. She stroked the salamander's back, and he groaned. Sparky rarely got into fights—the only things that he could directly touch were Anya and spirits . . . and that thing, whatever it was. The salamander wasn't used to being slung around like a sack of potatoes.

She looked back down the alley where the arsonist had disappeared. Whatever he was, he wasn't going to get far with a gunshot wound. She pulled her radio out of the belt to summon DPD and the squad.

"What the hell was that thing?" Brian muttered.

She peered down into the basement window. What had the burning man wanted down there? This felt like more than simple voyeurism, more than wanting to revisit the scene out of pride. The burning man had gone down there with a purpose.

Something glowed red in the darkness below. Casting a backward glance at Brian and Sparky, she asked, "Will you be okay for a minute?"

Brian waved her on. "I'm good."

Anya shimmied down the rabbit hole. Shining her light into the black she called, "Virgil? Virgil, are you here?"

There was no answer. Anya picked her way over to the heap of vacuum cleaner parts, touched the blackened vacuum canister that the repairman's ghost had been working on. She felt no chill of a spirit within it. She sat back on her heels, feeling sick.

Whatever the burning man-creature was, it had eaten Virgil.

She cast her light over the basement, searching for the source of the red glow. Initially, she'd feared that the arsonist had tried to reset the fire, to destroy what little was left.

But, no. The glow emanated from the floor of the basement, beside the symbol of the Horned Viper. The number *14* had been slashed into the concrete, the number still glowing dull red from the intense heat.

Fourteen. Fourteen *what?* The puzzle rattled in her head. Fourteen fires?

The realization chilled over her slowly.

Fourteen days.

Fourteen days until Devil's Night.

CHAPTER SIX

THIS WOULD BE A TOUGH room to sell the truth to.

Anya stood beside Captain Marsh in the DFD headquarters conference room, hands laced tightly behind her back. With Neuman's death in the fire classified as a homicide, the police department would be taking over the lead on the case. DPD had sent over three detectives from their Major Crimes Division, and none of them looked too pleased to be there. The three men sat in the back of the room, lounging back in their chairs. Only one of them had brought a notebook. Their division commander had ordered them to work on an arson task force with DFD, and it was clear they resented not having full authority over the case. One of them had asked Anya to make some coffee. She'd sweetly directed him to the vending machine down the hall.

Detective Vross made faces as he drank his vending-machine brew. Evidently, he'd had some difficulty operating the machine, as creamer dribbled down the side of the cup. He was a short, pudgy, pasty, balding crank of a man. In her occasional dealings with him, Anya had suspected the only reason he hadn't retired was because he enjoyed being unpleasant. In his current position, he was allowed to be unpleasant to the public at large. If he had to go back to being a civilian, that sort of behavior just wouldn't be tolerated. Some hapless fast-food worker who was sick of his rants would poke his eye out with a spork.

"So you screwed up your case. And you want the big dogs to bat cleanup." He slurped his coffee.

"Actually, the term you're looking for is *collaboration*," Marsh responded with a glare that would have frozen Vross's coffee.

"Fine. We'll use big words. We'll *collaborate*." Vross's mouth twisted around the word, as if it tasted bad. "What do you have for us to *collaborate* on?"

"Four arson sites, all with similar MOs." Anya handed out photocopies of a map with each location starred. "No common relationship in terms of structure, use, or owner-ship: two houses, a beauty shop, and a warehouse. The lab's detected no use of conventional accelerants or explosive residue and the heat damage is far too even for a single igni-tion point." She passed out pictures from the scenes.

"And you trust the lab on this?" Vross flipped the picture back. "They need to do this over. They missed something."

Anya gritted her teeth and continued. "The lab also found that these marks, which were discovered on the concrete floors on the lowest levels of the structures, were caused as a result of high-temperature melting." She showed a picture of the Horned Viper symbol. "The arsonist created the first symbol at the time of each arson. It's an Egyptian hieratic character called the Horned Viper. He returned to the scene of the warehouse fire last night and carved the number 14 beside it.

"My analysis is that the crime is ritualistic in nature and I think the number is a countdown to Devil's Night. I went back to the previous scenes of the other crimes, and found that similar numbers had been burned into the concrete: 24, 21, 19, 14." She fanned her photographs on the table. "He seems to return to the scene within two days, after the scene has been released and the site is quiet."

Vross kicked back in his chair. "I got a report from the patrol bureau that you saw this guy last night."

The two detectives behind him looked up. Hume she knew to be a yes-man, who would always go along with whatever Vross did. The other one, Millner, was new. He was the one who brought a notebook. He was scribbling furiously, hand pressed to his forehead. Perhaps there was hope for him. If there was, Anya had no doubt that he'd transfer to another area.

"Yeah. I staked out the scene."

"From what I understand, you got a civilian burned, shot at the guy, and didn't hit him."

Anya wouldn't allow him to bait her. She responded in a cool voice, though one hand was balled behind her back, ready to punch Vross. "I hit him in the shoulder. The local emergency rooms have been alerted. If this guy shows up with a gunshot wound, we'll know about it."

"You need to leave the cop stuff to the cops."

"Lieutenant Kalincyzk is authorized to use force when the situation warrants it." Marsh leaned over the table. "The use of force investigation by DFD will back me up on that."

Vross leaned forward. "How exactly did you feel threatened enough to use force, Kalinczyk? Did the guy throw a cigarette at you?"

Anya's eyes narrowed. "No. He tried to set me on fire. He burned a civilian."

"With what? A book of matches? A flamethrower?"

"I'm guessing it was some kind of combustible material. He was covered in it."

"You guess? Aren't you supposed to be the expert, dragon lady?"

"Enough." Marsh slapped his hand down on the desk. The blow shook the faux mahogany with the force of a gunshot. When he spoke, it was in a very low voice, barely above the pitch of a growl. "I will not tolerate backbiting. Are we clear?"

Vross stared back at him, nonplussed.

Marsh leaned forward. "If you can't play nicely with the other kids on the playground, Vross, I have no problem asking your division commander to reassign someone else to the task force. One of ours got killed in the last arson and I want people to get to work."

Vross glared, but said nothing.

"Lieutenant Kalinczyk has a composite of the arsonist." Marsh gestured to Anya.

Anya held up a sketch compiled by a police artist from

her recollections and two stills from the news broadcast. "The firebug is approximately six foot two, two hundred pounds, medium build. He's Caucasian, dark brown or black hair, shoulder length, unknown eye color. His prints aren't in AFIS, so no priors. He's got a gunshot wound to the right shoulder and walks with a limp."

Vross glanced at the photo and waved dismissively at it. "If that's him, we'll pick him up in hours. You guys can go back to playing with your fire extinguishers."

"Then," Marsh said, "I suggest that you put out an APB on him and get started on some of that much-vaunted police work."

In Vross's view, police work was a game for the boys. They took Anya's marbles and went back to their fort to play with her evidence and set their plastic soldiers out on the street to hunt for the villain she'd described to them.

Anya had spent the largest part of the afternoon copying her case files and boxing them up for Vross and his men . . . not that they would bother to open them. Vross would likely order the boxes tossed in the Dumpster, if anyone even bothered to pick them up.

She decided to go where she was wanted, instead.

"Hey, Ciro. How are you feeling?"

Anya sat on the edge of the chenille bedspread and took the old man's hand. It felt cold under her palm and she rubbed Ciro's bony fingers. Ciro lay tucked in bed, pillows propping up his frail shoulders. But he smiled when he saw her, and her heart warmed to see it.

At least *someone* was happy to see her today.

"Better, child, better. They're telling me that my ticker's a bit temperamental. But that happens to everyone. Take my advice, though: don't get old."

Anya smiled at him. "The alternative's not very good."

Ciro chuckled, then coughed. She handed him a glass of water, and the old man sipped at it gingerly. "How's the little salamander?" he asked.

Anya looked down at the foot of his bed, where Sparky lolled. "Keeping you company, by the looks of it." Her familiar had been quite clingy since last night. He seemed a bit stiff and sore from the experience, but not much worse for wear. She'd let him take a hot shower with her and allowed him to sleep with his Gloworm on the bed.

Ciro stretched his hand out toward Sparky. Sparky's tongue curled over his fingers. The old man closed his eyes. "Ah. He feels warm."

Anya smiled. Ciro always tried to interact with Sparky in his limited human way. And she thought that Sparky appreciated the attention. Poor fellow was too used to being ignored . . . no wonder he was so dependent on Anya. Sparky fell over on his side and cuddled up to the old man, like a heating pad.

"I hear that you and Brian ran into some trouble last night."

Anya frowned. She didn't want to disturb the old man with the details of her investigation. But things were rapidly moving out of her depth, and there was no one else to ask: *How can a man burn marks in concrete? How can he be consumed in flame and not scream?*

Reluctantly, she told him about the marks on the floor, about the arsonist returning to the scene. She told him about the yellow light bobbing in the darkness of the basement that flowered into a full-bodied apparition of flame.

"The paramedics treated Brian at the scene and released him . . . said the burns were first-degree," she told him, guiltily. Brian had gotten hurt and it had been her fault. She looked down at her hands.

Ciro touched her face. She noticed that his fingers shook. "Child. It's not your fault. He'll be okay. I saw him just this morning. Boy's got a bad sunburn, that's all."

"But it could have been much worse," she said in a small, tight voice.

"He cares about you. Don't push him away."

Anya stared down at the bedspread, fingering a tuft of yellow chenille. "Ciro, I've got a long history of people close to me getting hurt—hurt bad."

She could feel the weight of Ciro's gaze upon her. Her words came out stilted, as if she were confessing to a priest. She took a long time to finish, but Ciro waited, listening through all of her blank pauses and trailing words as she took off part of her armor and showed him what roiled beneath her skull.

"My dad wasn't around, so it was just me and Mom. And Sparky. He's been with us ever since I can remember. It took me years to realize that no one else could see Sparky but Mom and me . . . my teachers at school insisted

I was making up imaginary friends. They sent notes home to Mom about my overactive imagination." She shook her head. "If they only knew . . . instead of a lamb following me to school, I had a hellbender.

"My mom was very cautious. She was the kind of mom who took all of my Halloween candy to be X-rayed for razor blades, made me wear an extra sweater, and insisted that I take extra vitamin C. My bedtime was seven o'clock until I was in the fifth grade. I remember her always with a worry mark right here." Anya pointed to the space between her brows. "And I never really knew what she was afraid of. Everything. Nothing. I could never tell. I felt bad that whatever I did, whether it was walking to the park or staying too late at the library . . . I was always scaring her.

"I think that's when my mother gave me Sparky. Perhaps she had summoned him, somehow, to protect me even before I was born. I feel that she struck some sort of a bargain, somewhere in the past. I don't remember her being a witch or a magician . . . we went to church twice a week. When I asked her about Sparky, she would tell me that he was my guardian angel. Which was true enough, I guess. But the little statue in the church of St. George slaying the dragon really bothered me. I wondered: what saint would hurt someone like Sparky? My mother told me that the dragon St. George was slaying wasn't like Sparky, that he was an evil dragon. But I still felt really bad for him.

"We lived in a row house in Hamtramck. It was there that I swallowed my first spirit . . . it was the ghost of a woman who died in the 1950s . . . she was dressed in a polka-dot dress and sat beside the upstairs window. Her hair was perfectly coiffed and her lips were rouged red. She never spoke, just watched the street, as if she was expecting someone. I remember feeling so sorry for her that I threw my arms around her. I felt . . . I felt a hole open up in my chest . . . then she was filling it. And then she was gone. I never saw her again.

"I asked my mother what happened. She went very pale. I remember her kneeling down before me and telling me never to do that again." Anya rubbed her arms. "She shook me so hard that I thought my teeth would rattle out of my head, but she seemed very afraid that something bad would happen.

"So . . . I did my best to ignore the spirits after that. I ignored the spirit of the librarian at the library when she asked me what I wanted to read. I didn't speak to the ghost of the guy singing on the street corner for money. I trained myself to look down whenever we drove past the graveyard, so I wouldn't see who was walking in between the stones.

"I know my mother saw them, too. I remember being at church and the ghost of a young priest sat beside us. He watched her and she stared straight ahead, anywhere but at him. I didn't understand how she could do that, but I think I do, now. She was afraid. Afraid of acknowledging these spirits all around us, afraid that they would come to dominate our lives.

"She kept things pretty normal, though. My mom used

to put up a Christmas tree every year . . . that was my favorite part of the year. My mom always insisted that the lights be unplugged every night when we went to sleep, though. I thought she was being her usual neurotic self.

"At the ripe old age of twelve, and knowing better than my mother, I sneaked down the stairs and plugged the Christmas tree in. Sparky and I stretched out before the tree, watching it snow through the living room window. It was truly a magical experience . . . I remember the pulse of the lights behind my eyelids, Sparky snoring next to me.

"I woke up, feeling Sparky jerking on my nightgown collar with his teeth. The smoke alarms were going off. The Christmas tree was on fire and he was trying to drag me out of the house. I screamed for my mom, but there was too much fire and smoke; I couldn't see up the stairs.

"I remember firefighters breaking the door, being carried out into the snow. The snow was so very peaceful, falling gently on the massive blaze that I used to live in."

Tears dripped down her nose. Ciro handed her a tissue.

"They found that the fire had been caused by faulty wiring in the Christmas lights. Mom had been right. They found her, dead of smoke inhalation, at the top of the stairs." Anya's fingers fluttered up to the collar around her neck. "CPS sent me to live with my aunt and uncle a few blocks away. Sparky came with me, but I never told them about him. They just . . . wouldn't have understood."

She lapsed into silence. Talking about it had reopened the wounds, made them too fresh and raw. Ciro's fingers brushed her elbow.

"It wasn't your fault."

She made a face. "Of course it was my fault. I . . ." She looked down at Sparky. Sparky was damn well near indestructible. She could allow herself to love him. Sparky had always been there . . . but other people just seemed too fragile. And seeing Ciro, thin and weak like this, just made her even more wary to get too close, for fear she'd break someone. Everyone seemed to get broken sooner or later, and she didn't want to be to blame for any more of it.

"It wasn't," Ciro told her with stern certainty. He grabbed her hand fiercely. "You were a child. It was an accident."

Anya looked at the ceiling, blinking back tears. She didn't know why all this had come rushing out now, to Ciro, but she wanted to slam on the brakes. "Can we—can we talk about the arsons? About that man—that thing—we saw?"

Ciro nodded. "If you want." He leaned forward in bed. "But please know that you have no blame in any of this. Don't do penance for a crime that isn't yours—you'll be doing it forever."

Anya swallowed. She didn't want to imagine *forever*—what it would be like when she finally died. Would she be a spirit, denied a resting place, wandering the streets of Detroit with Sparky at her side?

And how would that be different, at all, from now? she wondered.

The demonologist knotted his gnarled hands. "Your burning man . . . he must be human, since you've recorded his image clearly on camera. Brian can see him. He's real."

"But the fire!" she protested. "He can walk in fire and not be burned. He was able to melt concrete, to create a massive fire without accelerants. That's not human."

"True, there's an element of the Other about him. Sparky can interact with him. He's developed mastery over the element of fire. He sees spirits. Indeed, it seems as if he devoured the spirit of the repairman."

"Do you think . . . ," she asked in a very small, frightened voice, dreading to articulate the thought. "Do you think that he could be like me?"

"A Lantern? Perhaps. He could be a Lantern who's more in touch with his elemental nature than you. He sounds as if he's an accomplished magick worker." Ciro smoothed imaginary wrinkles from his bedspread. "He would have to be to try and summon Sirrush. As Katie has told you, that's a very dangerous endeavor. Once summoned, Sirrush can't be controlled by mortal means."

Anya wrapped her hands around her elbows, suddenly cold. She thought she'd been the only one, the only Lantern. Unique. But now that there was the possibility of another, she wanted to know more. "He doesn't have a familiar."

"He may not have had a mother who loved him enough to conjure one for him." Ciro's smile was gentle, but his voice was hard. "I cannot imagine what it would have been like to grow up without a protector, to be at the mercy of every spirit he encountered."

Anya's brown knitted. She hadn't thought of that. Would she have been as fearless of the casual spirits moving through the world without Sparky at her side? No matter what happened, she knew that Sparky would fight for her. She reached down to rub the loose skin under his neck. He made an amphibian face of pleasure and rolled over on his back.

"It's no wonder that he became a destroyer," Ciro speculated. "Regardless, he must be stopped."

"How do I do that?" She spread open her empty hands, feeling helpless as the thoughts and theories slipped through them.

"You'll need to bind him, my dear. That's the only way to cage elemental energy." Ciro shook his head. "I'll need to research how this might be done." He looked at her with rheumy eyes. "But you will need to capture him in the human world, first, before you can hope to bind his magickal power."

Anya descended the stairs of Ciro's apartment to the main floor. The old demonologist kept an apartment above the site of his primary occupation: the running of the Devil's Bathtub. Outside, a neon sign sketched out a blue bathtub with red horns and a pointed tail emerging from the rim. Back in the Prohibition era, Ciro's place had a speakeasy in the basement. Now, the bar ran on the first floor and DAGR gathered in the basement. When Ciro had taken possession of the run-down brownstone decades ago, he'd had all the original bar fixtures hauled up from the basement. A scarred, deeply waxed bar gleamed from one end of the room to the other. Wooden cabinets lined the walls, cleverly designed to look like bookshelves. They held bottles of gleaming liquors, outlined in the shimmer of mirrored glass behind them.

The centerpiece of the bar was a turn-of-the-century bathtub, once used for making gin. It now sat in the center of the floor, filled with pennies. Like children casting coins into fountains, the bar patrons made wishes on the devil's bathtub. Anya didn't know how many of those wishes came true, but it didn't stop Ciro's patrons from trying. She tossed a dime into the bathtub, sending a wish for good luck for the old man.

"How's he doing?"

A sultry whisper emanated from the bathtub. A long, feminine leg reached out from the edge of the tub and two heavily kohled eyes emerged from the rim. The ghost of a flapper shimmered into view, her stylishly feathered hat cocked over one ear. She played nervously with her beads.

Anya pulled a chair up close to the bathtub of coins. "Hi, Renee." Sparky coiled up under the chair, nonchalant. He was used to Renee; Anya thought he especially liked her because she always smelled like smoke and the fringe at the edge of her dress was fun to bat at.

Renee had been a singer in the speakeasy, before a bust by federal agents went terribly wrong. Her experiences hadn't marred her zest for the afterlife. She'd kept Ciro company in the bar for decades. Ciro could have exorcised her years before, but kept her around after Renee had tearfully pled for him not to kick her out on the street of the hereafter. The old man didn't mind her pranks, and she didn't mind playing them. From the corner of her eye, Anya could see the glassware stacked upside down behind the bar and wondered if that was Renee's way of trying to cheer the old man up.

Renee's dark eyes flickered under a thick fringe of lashes. *"I don't want Ciro to go. I'd be very lonely without him."* Her cupid's bow mouth quivered.

Anya felt vaguely absurd, reassuring a ghost. "He's resting, Renee."

Renee bowed her head. *"I'll sing something for him to-night. That might make him feel better."*

"It always does." Anya thought she detected something more than simple concern for the old man. "What is it?"

The ghost of the flapper fidgeted with her beads. *"I'm hearing things from the other spirits."*

Anya suspected that many of the more sociable spirits found ways to communicate with others. Renee had been a social butterfly in life; she would be no less in death. "What did you hear?"

"That something very bad is coming." Renee sank up to her nose in coins. *"Someone is eating ghosts, without cause or justification."*

"What do you mean?"

Renee gestured to Anya with a marcasite-ringed finger. *"You only take spirits that are harmful. Evil. Ones that aren't welcome among the living. There's someone out there who's taking spirits who are minding their own business, ones who aren't hurting anyone."*

Anya's brow wrinkled. The other Lantern. "Why?"

"No one knows."

"Where are the other spirits disappearing?" Perhaps she could glean a clue about the other Lantern's haunts.

"All over. He supposedly ate all the ghosts in the library downtown in an afternoon." Renee's eyes were wide. *"That's the rumor."*

Anya ruminated on it. Her arsonist was drawn not only to fire, but to eat spirits . . . just like he'd taken Virgil. Why?

"Don't worry, Renee," Anya said sincerely. "Ciro is a powerful demonologist. He will protect you."

Renee sank below the false water level of the coins, her eyes holding immeasurable sadness. *"I hope he can."*

"I hope so, too," Anya whispered after her. She couldn't imagine what would happen when Ciro died— what would happen to DAGR, what would happen without all his knowledge to guide them. The thought was simply too much to bear, even for the dead.

At the top of the room, she heard a woman singing. The voice traveled up the stairs, and Anya hoped the lullaby would give Ciro sweet dreams.

CHAPTER SEVEN

"LET'S GET THIS PARTY STARTED."

Max grinned at Anya as she slid through the narrow hidden door on the back stair of the Devil's Bathtub. The basement had become DAGR's base of operations: a large oblong room full of computer equipment, barristers' bookcases bursting with Ciro's dusty tomes, and wooden crates of arcane technological and magickal supplies. Jules, Max, Brian, and Katie sat in folding chairs arranged around a banquet table. Ciro's place at the foot of the table was empty.

Anya looked away from Brian's sunburned face as she slid into a chair. "Hey, guys," she mumbled.

Jules slid a file folder across the table to her. "Thanks for coming, Anya." Anya couldn't tell if he really meant it. He sat at the head of the table, opening a folder of his own. "We've got a pretty serious case tonight, folks: a case of suspected demonic possession involving a teenage girl. A parasitic leech." His mouth was set in a tight line. Jules had little patience for ghosts, but had some sympathy for them. At least, to Jules's thinking, ghosts had once been human. He *despised* nonhuman entities. Sparky usually made himself scarce around Jules.

"Let me guess." Brian lifted his finger. "Bored teenage girl buys a Ouija board, summons up an uninvited guest. Parents are pissed at having a boarder that's moving their shit around, drinking their beer, and bumping around in the night. That about sum it up?"

Jules nodded. "Well, that's how it started. It would have been easy enough to nip in the bud at that stage, but now it's gotten entirely out of hand. The kid's pretty close to being involuntarily committed to a mental hospital. Apparently she's lost all grasp on reality and she's medicated out of her mind. Mom thinks that she's being harassed by a demon. Dad thinks she dropped too much ecstasy and isn't buying any spiritual explanations. Little sister is starting to hear voices. Mom wants this stopped before the little one goes around the bend like big sis."

Anya flipped through the file. Jules always took meticulous notes and photographs. The house looked like any other suburban house: privacy fence hemming in the small property, two cars in the driveway, toys in the yard. Jules included a picture of Mom, Dad, and Little Sis sitting on the couch. Mom looked like a soccer mom: dark, curly hair pulled back in a ponytail. Dad worked in some environment where he had contact with the public—sales, perhaps. He wore a loosened tie over a dress shirt rolled up at the sleeves. A look of irritation creased his ebony brow. Above the couch, Anya saw framed military photographs, guessed that he'd been a serviceman. Marines, from the look of it.

The littlest girl sat on the floor at her parents' feet, playing with a sticky Barbie doll. She looked like a shy six-year-old, not looking up at the camera, absorbed in play. Her thick black hair was held back in pigtails and she wore pink pajamas with cartoon cats covering them. She reminded Anya of the little girl from the pop machine. She swallowed hard.

Anya turned the page, finding a picture of the missing member of the family: the oldest daughter. She was captured on film with a sullen expression, sitting in the corner of her room on a beanbag chair. Her room was curiously stripped of the usual objects of the teenage years . . . no posters, books, CDs, or computer. No hard surfaces. Her thin arms were crossed over her T-shirt advertising a popular emo band. Her ears had been pierced several times and Anya guessed that, out of rebellion, she had many more piercings than met the eye. Her hair was caught up in a black head scarf covered with a pattern of winking skulls. The label *Chloe—Age 15* was penciled in at the bottom of the photograph. Not old enough to have the freedom of driving, but old enough to want it badly.

But the look in her eyes was what arrested Anya. She didn't have the look of a child struggling against parental authority. The look in those sloe eyes was much darker, much older . . . Anya had only seen an expression like that in statues. It looked ancient, unyielding as stone.

"Has she been evaluated by a psychiatrist?" Anya asked.

"Yeah," Jules said. "The school psychologist gave her a referral. She was initially diagnosed with bipolar disorder—the psychiatrist thought she was doing it for attention. Parents couldn't get her to take her lithium. She wound up in the hospital after she broke the glass in her window when her parents grounded her. The hospital amended the diagnosis to acute schizophrenia . . . she was hearing enough voices that they had to sedate her. Chloe's on a nice Haldol/Risperdal cocktail now. The parents are afraid to put her in a mental facility, afraid that something worse would happen."

Anya's fingers traced the border of the picture. Chloe was a pretty girl. If she were thrown into a state mental hospital with a bunch of unstable adults, something much worse *would* happen to her.

"She's cute," observed Max, holding her photo at arm's length. "In a faux-goth, mall chick kind of way."

"Down, boy," Jules growled. "No hitting on the subjects. Ever."

"Has she been violent to herself or other people?" Katie asked.

"So far she's just been busting up inanimate objects. Her parents boarded up the window in her room and lock her in at night. They say she paces all night long, like a caged animal. She's more subdued in the mornings. She won't eat, won't sleep."

"Does she say anything? Anything coherent?" With

cases like this, it could be a toss-up. The victim could be raving nonsense or she could be incredibly lucid, speaking treatises in another language. Sometimes clues about the entity haunting the victim could be gleaned from what the victim said, or didn't.

"She's threatening to burn the house down."

Anya pressed her hand to her forehead. "Can I just have *one* night without someone obsessing about burning shit? Please?"

"This is Detroit, baby." Max lounged back in his chair, put his feet on the table. "We've got a rep to uphold." Jules whacked him on the back of the head and the boy's feet landed quickly on the floor.

Anya made a face at him. "So what's the game plan, Jules?"

"Chloe doesn't know we're coming. We get Mom and the little girl out of the house; Dad's out of town at a sales meeting. If the demon gets loose, we don't want it glomming on to the little girl. We try to drive the demon out of the older girl."

Katie frowned, fidgeting with her bracelets. "Ciro usually does that part."

"Ciro's out of commission, so the containment ritual's up to you. Max and I will restrain the kid, if necessary. Brian's on tech. Anya . . ." He looked directly at her. "It'll be up to Anya to eat the demon."

Anya stared down at her hands. Spirits were relatively easy to consume; they went down like a cold beer on a summer afternoon, with a sting that faded quickly.

Demons could be trickier; they tended to be more power-ful, had sharper volition, and could put up a bigger fight. But Anya never felt guilty about swallowing a demon. De-mons had never been human, and she didn't feel the ethical conflict she did when she devoured a ghost. A demon was pure evil and the response was simple. Black-and-white. Destroy it before it destroys someone else.

But the simplicity of the task didn't make it any easier. Eating a demon was like drinking straight bleach. Anya had only done it three times before. Each time had left her ill enough to clean the local pharmacy out of heartburn medications.

Katie's hand brushed her back soothingly. "I'll clear your aura afterward. Promise."

Anya looked down at Chloe's photo, resigned. What-ever bad taste the demon might leave in her mouth, what the girl was experiencing was far, far worse. She couldn't imagine the terrible feeling of having another creature under her skin, controlling her movements like a pup-peteer. She knew that other mediums did it, but she could never bring herself to.

She smothered a shudder. Yes, that would be far, far worse. But she still felt a tiny seed of resentment at being the only person who could help. She felt guilted into it, with Ciro laid up in bed upstairs, and she'd promised Brian to go out with DAGR tonight, but . . .

Her fist clenched under the table. They needed her far more than she needed them. But she couldn't walk away from her role in this. Jules was the leader. Katie was the witch. Max was the gofer. Brian was the tech wizard. Her role was inescapable: to bat cleanup, to be the garbage disposal for lost souls.

It would take Herculean effort for a mother to leave her child in the hands of strangers. Anya could see the struggle on Chloe's mother's face as she loaded her smallest daughter into the back of her SUV, then stared back at the house.

Chloe's mother crossed the yard to speak with Jules. "She's in her bedroom. The key to her door's on the kitchen table."

Jules nodded reassuringly. "We'll call you right after we finish."

"Call me on my cell. My husband doesn't know that you're here . . . but something needs to be done."

"We will."

The mother stepped back to the SUV, wiping her nose with the back of her hand as she pulled out of the driveway. Two bumper stickers on the back of the car proclaimed that her girls were honor-roll students.

Anya stood in the yard with Max, Brian, Jules, and Katie. Night had fallen thickly over the neighborhood. Chloe's mother had left every light in the house on, as if the light would frighten away the interloper in their midst. Anya knew better. Demons could always find a scrap of darkness to cling to: whether in the back corner of a closet, under the eaves, or in the stain on a heart. They always knew how to find it, nurture it, and make it grow. Despite the mother's best efforts to bring light to the house, it still seemed the most shadowed home on the block, the entrance obscured by thick hedges.

Jules opened the front door. The living room was lit by floor lamps, showcasing a precisely neat house, always prepared for company. No photographs or pictures hung on the vanilla walls. Even the magazines on the coffee table were arranged with the corners flush to the edge of the table. The carpet bore vacuum tracks. Beyond, in the kitchen, no dirty dishes were left in the sink. The kitchen table, tile, and floors were spotless, the stainless-steel refrigerator and stove wiped clean of fingerprints.

Anya wondered how a mother this tidy dealt with the disorder of her daughter's condition. Probably not very well.

Anya felt the familiar warmth around her neck as Sparky shook himself awake. He glided to the floor, taking on his fearsome hellbender shape. He sniffed the air. Anya could smell nothing other than disinfectant and some insipid cherry plug-in air freshener, but she suspected that Sparky could sense far more.

"Is *it* here?" Jules demanded.

Anya blinked. "I don't feel the demon just yet—"

"Not the demon. Your . . . pet." Anya could see the sweat prickling over his tattoo. Jules must have sensed the change in temperature indicating Sparky's appearance.

Anya bristled. "Sparky's here, yeah."

"Is it really necessary to have *it* here?" Jules's eyes moved back and forth, not registering the invisible presence he knew was there.

Anya hated when Jules called Sparky *it*. Sparky waddled over to Jules and growled.

"You want me to work this case?" Anya parked her hands on her hips, glaring up at Jules. "Where I go, he goes. Period." She dared him to kick her off the team. Part of her had been spoiling for this fight, so she egged him on. "I'm here because you can't drive these ghosts and demons out yourself." She lifted her chin, challenging him. "You want me gone? Fine. But you'd better be prepared to take out your own trash, all by yourself."

The truth was as effective as a slap. Anya waited, staring Jules full in the face as he weighed Chloe's life against his principles, against pragmatism. When he spoke again, his voice was cold and quiet.

"Let's get set up," Jules ordered.

Katie opened a patchwork bag and set her tools out on the kitchen table: a jar of coarse sea salt, a crystal bell, an atomizer of salt water, and a bundle of sage. She lit the sage bundle on the family's spotless stove, breathed on it to nurture the ember. Meanwhile, Max opened the windows and closet doors. Brian plugged in voice recorders and tested his video camera. Jules set an ominous black duffel bag down on the couch. It clinked when he opened it and Anya saw him surreptitiously tuck a pair of handcuffs into his belt.

Jesus. She hoped this wouldn't be that bad.

Katie began in the living room. Walking counterclockwise through the rooms of the house, she cast handfuls of salt in the corners and blew sage smoke in every closet and cabinet. She uttered a house blessing in her small, clear voice: "Let darkness leave and brightness remain. Bless this house and all who live within. So shall it be."

Max dutifully followed behind her with the atomizer of salt water, spritzing the drapes. He held the bell solemnly in his other fist, ringing it as he walked. Anya could tell, now that he was given something to do, he was trying very hard to get it right. The crystalline voice of the bell seemed muffled in this close space. These things were meant to purify, to drive negativity out the open doors and windows. But even Anya could feel the energy sticking here, thick as molasses. Sparky's gills curled, and he wound closely around Anya's feet, on high alert.

Something thumped down the hall, loud as a gunshot against the hollow interior doors. Katie ignored the sound, continuing to cast salt on the spotless floor of the kitchen. The lights flickered, dimmed.

A voice rasped from down the hall: *"Mother won't like you making a mess of the floors."*

Katie didn't miss a beat. She cast salt down the hallway, blessed the bathroom and the parents' room. She crossed into the littlest girl's room, crowded with stuffed animals. Anya noticed that she used extra fistfuls of salt here, under the child's bed and behind her pink flannel pillow with a pattern of dancing cats on it.

At last, they faced the closed door. Chloe's room. Jules inserted the key into the brass doorknob, turned it . . .

. . . and all hell broke loose.

The door burst outward with the force of an explosion.

Chloe, eyes wild, plowed into the hallway. The girl rocketed into Jules's arms, knocking him to the floor. Max lunged to grab her legs, but she kicked him in the head, sending him reeling. Brian grabbed one of her flailing arms, and Anya snatched the other. Sparky bit down hard on her hand, and the demon in her howled at the ethereal wound.

By God, the girl was strong. She flailed in Anya's grip. Anya tried to sit on her chest to keep her still. Jules's handcuffs glittered in the air above her head; he wasn't able to make contact with her wrists.

Chloe arched her back and howled: *"You can't hold me!"*

"Wanna bet?" Nose dripping blood on the perfect beige carpet, Max grabbed for her ankles.

Overhead, the hall light went out, plunging the fracas into shadows.

"Get her in here," Katie shouted, holding the door of the bathroom open. The room was small and windowless; they stood a better chance of controlling her in a small space, where she'd have no room to run.

Arms around her waist, Jules dragged her to the doorway. The girl's arms and legs spread out to catch the doorframe, like a cat resisting being stuffed in a cage. The girl giggled, spittle dripping from the corner of her mouth. Her pupils had dilated, rendering her eyes black as obsidian. This was bad.

Max and Brian rushed the door. The girl's fingers dug into the wood doorframe, clawing white stripes in the finish, but her grip gave way, tumbling her backward into Jules. Anya and Sparky brought up the rear, and Katie slammed the door behind them.

The girl, tangled in the shower curtain, hissed. The house lights wavered, then came on at half power.

"Cuff her to the bathtub," Jules ordered, and the heap of ghost hunters piled onto the girl. Someone kicked the water on, and the shower sprayed into the clot of people. They succeeded in getting a bracelet around her right hand and the other bracelet ratcheted shut around the metal grab bar on the side of the tub. The family of green frog decals decorating the shower stall looked on, far too cheerfully for the scene playing out below them. Chloe flipped like a seal in the bathtub, twisting at near-impossible angles as Katie struck the stopper. The tub filled with cold water crawling up the side of Chloe's jeans.

"What do you think you're doing?" the demon demanded through Chloe's bitten lips. *"You can't drown me."*

Katie didn't answer, murmuring a blessing over and over: "Go home and leave this girl in peace. Evil has no place here. As I will, so shall it be."

She poured out the remnants of her jar of salt on the girl's chest. Chloe writhed in agony, the salt steaming where it struck and ran down into the water: a saltwater baptism. Her fist lashed out and cracked the tile of the shower surround. She kicked over a bottle of bubble bath into the rapidly filling tub. The plastic cap broke, and frothy bubbles began to rise.

"What now, Jules?" Max had jammed a towel to his bloody nose.

"We let Anya do her thing."

Anya advanced on the bathtub, Sparky surging ahead of her. Brian stood above her, on the closed toilet lid, filming.

"Shut it off, Brian," she ordered.

He looked down for an instant to find the power button, and that's when the demon struck.

With the terrible groan of steel, the demon ripped the grab bar free of the wall. The demon-possessed girl swung her arm around and struck Brian with the mass of metal in her fist. Brian fell off the toilet, his feet sliding out from under him. His head cracked and bounced on the edge of the bathroom counter, the video camera shattering on the tile.

"You're mine now," Anya snarled, launching herself at the girl. Sparky hit her first, pinning the demon inside her to the tub full of bubbles and frigid spewing water. He landed hard enough that her head submerged under the water for an instant. She bobbed up, gasping. Anya threw herself into the bathtub, straddling the girl, one foot crammed in the soap dish and the other underwater. Water blasted in an uncontrolled spray in her face.

She slapped her hand on the girl's head, forcing her below the water's surface. Her kicks and flailing arms ripped away the remains of the shower curtain and launched a loofah across the room. A child's bath toy had gotten wedged under their bodies, squeaking like an asthmatic frog. Anya's left hand pressed to her own chest, and she breathed in, wanting to choke the life out of this spirit and commit it to the void in her heart.

She felt the demon bristling beneath Chloe's skin, seething like a swarm of ants over potato salad. Anya felt her aura flare to life, felt Sparky at her back, growling, tail wrapped around the girl's soggy feet. The warmth flooded her, the hunger rose in her throat, and she breathed in the demon.

She expected to feel something like she did on those other rare occasions when she'd swallowed a demon: a slow burn traveling down her throat, like scalding soup. It had always been a different feeling than devouring the ghosts. Ghosts went down cold as ice, working into her chest like a milkshake sliding down.

But this wasn't the chill of ice. This demon *burned*, burned like lye. Tears sprang to her eyes as she struggled with it, trying to destroy this caustic thing that scorched like acid she'd sucked behind her lips . . .

She choked. The hot blackness of the demon crept down her throat in spidery tendrils. She coughed, trying to expel it, but the demon clung to her. She reeled back in the bubbles to the wall of the shower, clawing at her neck. The amber flame in her chest burned brighter, striving to consume this demon that was so much larger and more powerful than she'd expected.

Dimly, she was aware of her body convulsing, of Sparky curled tight around her waist, front feet splayed open against her chest, trying to claw the demon out of her. Bubbles and water lashed around her; she wrapped all that terrible heat of the forge in her chest around the demon and squeezed. The bright star of her aura surged, then quivered out.

The demon whispered to her: *"Sirrush is coming. And I will give you to him."*

Anya rolled over in the bathtub and threw up. She felt Katie's hands holding back her hair, felt the blessed coolness of the water spraying against her face. Sparky clutched her back like a koala hugging a tree; the tremors of his fear twitched through his skin. He licked the back of her neck with his tongue, making worried little growls in the back of his throat.

Anya lifted her head and pressed it to the cold tile. Through slitted eyes, she saw Jules pluck the limp girl out of the water.

"Jesus, did I drown her?" she cried.

"No." Katie shook her head. "She's gonna be okay."

"Brian!" Anya flopped in the bubbles. She remembered the sickening crack his head made when it had struck the counter.

Max crouched beside Brian's prone form. "He's breathing, but I can't wake him up." A red gash crossed Brian's brow, drizzling blood down his nose.

"Call the squad," Jules ordered.

Anya crept out of the tub on all fours, stumbling on the soaked bath mat. She shook Brian's tennis shoe, smearing bubbles on him. Her fingers tangled in his shoelaces. "Brian, wake up, c'mon . . ."

His head lolled limply on his shoulder, unresponsive.

Tears blurred her vision. This had all gone so terribly wrong.

"Katie," Jules muttered. "Get her out of here. Max and I will clean up."

Anya's knuckles whitened on Brian's shoe. Even Jules couldn't dislodge them. She was taken out of the house with one hand wrapped around Sparky's neck and the other knitted in the shoelaces of Brian's empty shoe.

Chapter Eight

No matter how hard she tried, she couldn't scrub the taste of demon from her mouth.

Anya stood before her bathroom mirror, brushing her teeth for the twelfth time in a row. Sparky sat on the floor, watching her. The salamander wouldn't so much as let her pee by herself. Her shower-damp hair hung straight and dripping over her shoulder. Sparky had supervised that, too; he'd chased his tail in circles at the bottom of the shower, tracking the water as it circled down the drain. She didn't want to go to the hospital reeking of demon and vomit. That was a surefire way to attract unwanted attention, both from the visible and invisible worlds. She'd had enough of that for tonight. Perhaps forever.

She spat out the toothpaste. In the sink, it still held some traces of black, as if she'd eaten too much licorice. She let the water run, washing the crud down the sink, down the pipes, and far away from her.

Her fingers traced over her bare chest, and she winced. A new burn spread beside the old one caused by the little girl's ghost. It stretched like a waxy butterfly across her collarbone, down across one breast, and ended just above the navel. The center of it glistened spotted red: a second-degree burn. When she touched the edges, her fingertips left white marks. Gingerly, she spread antibiotic ointment on the area. No matter what she did, it would leave an unforgettable scar, but the primary concern was avoiding infection.

"Anya." Katie's voice trickled under the closed bathroom door. "Jules called. We can see him now."

Anya grabbed a pair of jeans from the dryer and snatched a cotton button-down shirt from her closet. She fastened it carefully over the ointment, feeling the fabric stick to her skin. She wanted something—anything—on her body that didn't smell like fear and vomit and Mr. Bubble.

Katie stood in Anya's living room, subdued. The witch had done a final blessing on Chloe, scrubbing her aura clean of any remaining blemishes. She'd said that the demon was gone, and that had been some relief.

"How's Chloe?" Anya asked, grabbing her jacket. Her voice was scraped raw and hoarse, as if she'd been a three-pack-a-day smoker for life.

Katie nodded, seeming to be trying to convince herself as much as Anya. "She's physically unhurt. She's got no memory of the exorcism whatsoever. She said that her dad would go ballistic when he saw the bathroom trashed. Mom was not too happy about that, either."

The women walked down Anya's narrow driveway to

Katie's car, a white SUV with "Wicked Confections" and her phone number scripted on the windows in red. Her catering gear was scattered all over the interior, and Katie pulled aside a couple of cake boards to make room for Anya. The interior smelled sickly-sweet, like frosting left out in the sun too long.

Sparky insisted upon sitting on Anya's lap, like a child. She distantly wondered if she should consider buying him a car seat, or one of those baby slings that yuppie moms and dads wore to keep their hands free for texting on their cell phones. Maybe a leash. The thought of walking an invisible pet down the street on a taut leash made her smile in spite of herself. She just might need to make a trip to the pet store sometime soon.

Much as she bitched about it, Sparky's clinginess was reassuring tonight. She wrapped her arms around his warm little body and rested her chin on the top of his leathery head. Perhaps they both needed reassurance the world was whole and safe, that it would always go on, pretty much as it always had.

But tonight had made her doubt.

They'd nearly lost Brian.

Sparky seemed to sense that Anya was in no mood to deal with shenanigans at the hospital. He trotted along at her heels, not even veering away to nip at a temptingly lit IV pole dragged by an elderly woman walking in circles. Even the ghosts seemed to shy away from her, disappearing behind walls and melting into the floors at the first sound of Sparky's growling. She could sense the chill of their shadows as she passed them, but not one made an effort to accost her. Perhaps she hadn't managed to scrub all the traces of demon from her skin. Perhaps they could feel Sparky's hypervigilance as he stomped before her like a bulldog on parade. But they left her alone.

The ICU was painted pale pink, the color of old gum stuck to the bottom of a shoe. The central nurses' station provided a central view of a dozen cubbies divided up by pastel-colored curtains and glass partitions. At this early hour, the lights were still low enough to allow the patients to sleep, casting the unit in a shadowy, enforced serenity. Machines beeped in counterpoint to the low conversations of the staff behind the desk, punctuated by the clicking of nails on a keyboard. A cart holding covered dishes in metal pans rattled down the green-tiled hall. Shift change was taking place, and the hospital only allowed visitors at those times when more staff were available.

Anya spied Jules and Max in the perimeter hall, and she quickened her pace. "How is he?"

Jules rubbed the stubble forming on his chin and gestured to the drawn curtain before him "We just got here. The doctor on rounds is checking him out now."

"Did he—did he wake up?"

Jules stared down at the floor. "He got out of surgery an hour ago, but nothing's happened yet."

The white-coated doctor scraped the curtain aside and stepped into the hall. He was a young man of Middle-Eastern descent with serious eyes, a stethoscope draped around his neck. "Are you here for Brian McKinney?"

"Yes." Anya craned to see over the doctor's shoulder. "How is he?"

"He came in with a head injury that was causing high levels of intracranial pressure and bleeding . . . an acute epidural hematoma. We performed surgery to repair a broken artery and to place a stent in his brain to drain the fluid. The primary danger is swelling and brain damage."

"Is he awake?"

"No. Now he's only responding to specific, intense stimuli and not in an organized fashion."

"When will we know if he's going to be okay?"

"We're going to watch him over the next several days, see how his coma score improves. An epidural hematoma, like his, is rarely fatal, but the impact on the brain can't be known until he regains consciousness." The doctor's eyes wavered among them, bottomless sympathy in his expression. "You can see him now, though."

Anya pulled back the curtain and tears prickled her eyes.

Brian lay in a metal hospital bed, the upper part of his body elevated to show the breathing tube taped to his mouth. His head had been shaved of the thick hair Anya had run her hands through just a day before, an angry series of precise stitches marching like ants over the pale skin. A tube and an electronic device were implanted near his temple, draining and monitoring the intracranial pressure. His eyes were closed, hands arranged on his stomach. His wrist and arms were full of tubes and wires, an oxygen monitor clipped to his finger. His chest, covered in a blanket and green surgical gown, rose and fell with a mechanical hiss. The heart monitors stuck like stickers on his chest ticked out a rhythm like a metronome on a screen beside him.

Anya laid the back of her hand against his face, almost afraid to touch him. His skin felt cool and stubbly, not warm and smooth like the night in the computer lab. Sparky reached up through the bars of the bed to rest his head on the crook of Brian's elbow.

"Hey, Brian," she whispered.

Only the whir and beep of the machines answered her. She leaned down, brushing his cold ear with her mouth. "I know you're in there. You come out when you're ready. I'll be waiting, okay?"

She stepped back, letting Katie and Max crowd into the tiny space. Katie said a prayer over him and Max's lip quivered.

She stepped beyond the curtain to find Jules waiting. She wrapped her arms around her elbows. "I can't believe this is happening to him," she croaked.

Jules looked past the curtain. He tried to be reassuring, but she could hear the fear in his voice. "He's gonna be okay. Really. It'll just take time."

Anya bit her lip. "I hope you're right."

"How are you doing?" Jules shifted his gaze to her.

"I'm fine." She brushed off his concern. "It was just more . . ." She paused. The exorcism of the demon had been much more than she'd bargained for: more powerful, more unsettling, and a helluva lot more painful. She finally watered the thought down for Jules. "It was more involved than I thought it would be."

Jules nodded sympathetically and his expression infuriated her. He had no idea what he asked, time and time again.

"Look, about that case, Anya, when you have time, can you—"

"No," she snapped, and her voice crackled. "No, I will *not*, Jules. No more of this." Jules's face creased in shock and she stabbed a finger in his chest. "Brian's lying in a hospital bed, and all you can think about are the damn cases. You're going to keep screwing around with things you don't understand until someone gets killed."

Jules backed up a step.

"Don't ever ask anything of me again, you hear me? I'm not going to be part of this any longer. You're on your own."

She stomped down the tiled hallway, away from him, away from DAGR. Her shoes echoed very loudly in that shocked, silent space.

The funeral was on a perfectly clear blue day the Sunday after Neuman's death, a vivid autumn sky with nary a breeze to ruffle leaves from the few straggly trees on the street.

Anya stood on the sidewalk, dressed in her black wool dress uniform. It was the most formal appropriate outfit she owned. Gold stripes curled in bracelets around the wrists of the jacket, brass buttons gleaming in the sunshine. The wool seemed to creep fibers under her white dress shirt and black ascot, scraping her burnt skin with every breath she drew. Tendrils of her chestnut hair leaked from her starched white hat, tickling her collar. Her badge was shrouded by a thin strip of black electrical tape. Sparky lay wrapped tightly around her throat today, clutching his tail. The tip of his tail was lodged in his mouth; he'd developed a habit of sucking his tail. Anya was concerned about him as it seemed to be a stress reaction, analogous to a child sucking his thumb. She reached up and pressed her hand to the warm copper collar, trying to reassure him over the roar of the ache in her chest.

The intervening days had done little to numb the ache. Ordinarily, the scorch mark left by a spirit would have faded, but this one wouldn't heal. Between running down fruitless leads on paroled arsonists in the area and sleeping, Anya tried to block it out. But it felt too hollow. Twinges of pain and restlessness invaded her unusually heavy sleep and woke her with the sensation that something was sitting on her chest. She'd find Sparky curled around her hip, and nothing but air would be pressing against the stubborn wound.

As the funeral procession drove into view, Anya stood on her toes to see over the heads of the hundreds of people congregating. A fire engine draped in black bunting and lilies served as the flower car. The caisson crawled along behind it, a pump truck that had had the pump removed to hold the casket. The pump truck was from Neuman's home duty station, surrounded by the firefighters from his station walking beside it in formation. Glossy black limos with their headlights illuminated followed behind, carrying family, pallbearers, and honor guard. The fire chief's car followed behind, leading two ladder trucks. The line of private cars behind those trailed back down the block.

Behind her, the Cathedral of the Most Blessed Sacrament loomed over the pavement. The neo-Gothic limestone spires gleamed stark white against the sky and ground, saints in their niches gazing down sublimely at the throng of people gathered on the grounds.

The caisson stopped just beyond the steps and the first of the escort cars pulled beside it. The pallbearers stood in formation before the steps, with DFD members and the general public staged behind them in rows. The DFD chaplain stood at the curb, waiting. Neuman's parents emerged from the first car. Anya remembered them from the vigil at the funeral home earlier in the day; they had seemed suspended in shock, their hands pumping up and down and glassy eyes frozen. The chaplain met them at the curb, then walked them up the steps and into the cathedral. One by one, the limos disgorged their occupants, blinking, into the sunshine.

The pallbearers, all firefighters from Neuman's duty assignment, climbed out of their cars. As one unit, they marched to the caisson and lifted the coffin from the back of the pump truck.

"Present arms." The officer in charge ordered a hand salute, and all the DFD members lifted their right hands to their hat visors as the flag-draped coffin passed over the sidewalk and up the steps.

As it disappeared beyond the massive wood doors into the shade of the cathedral, the OIC ordered the rest of the DFD to follow: "Right face." The black-uniformed figures congealed into three columns. "March."

Surrounded in a wall of black, Anya slowly marched into the cathedral. She tried to remember to keep her steps at exactly thirty inches, and to keep the correct distance from the firefighters at her right and left.

The Cathedral of the Most Blessed Sacrament had its own gravity, one that could be felt as soon as she stepped through the threshold. The glare of sunshine dimmed and cooled. Far up on the walls, stained glass cast fragmented patterns of color on the floor. The turn-of-the-century Gothic arches reached upward like the ribcage of some great beast that swallowed a flock of blackbirds. Twenty-first-century renovations contrasted with the structure's nineteenth-century bones: the font, cathedral, tracery, and altar included geometric, modern slabs of limestone. It reminded Anya of the sharp contrast between the old and new downtown. A requiem played softly in the background, trickling upward to cantilevered ceilings. Wisps of incense smoke drifted lazily in striations in the light.

As the columns parted around the font, Anya surreptitiously reached to dip her fingers in the water. She hadn't been a practicing Catholic since her mother's death, but being in this place . . . she felt the resonance of her mother's influence. Her fingers brushed the water.

A spark of static electricity stung her. Startled, she brushed the water on the side of her uniform pants and fell into line behind the other uniforms standing at the back. The pews were filling rapidly. Anya genuflected, crossed herself, and slid into one of the last pews. On her right side was a man scribbling notes on a yellow legal pad; a journalist, she supposed. On her left was a freshly minted, buzz-cut firefighter who smelled like garlic. She wrinkled her nose and turned away. Three rows ahead of her, she thought she saw the back of Captain Marsh's head, seated beside his wife.

The coffin had been placed just below the flat limestone altar. Flowers were arranged in profusion in the nave, as if a garden had sprouted from the black-and-white tile floor. The flowers spilled over into the sanctuary, filling even the back rows where Anya sat with the cloying smell of roses, lilies, and chrysanthemums. From this distance, she could barely make out the line of relatives seated at the front right or the features of the large photo of Neuman held on an easel. From this distance, he looked very young. His ears stuck out a bit, but it was too far away for her to see expression in his eyes. The photo had been from his graduating class; Anya had posed before the same flag and the same blue wall, once upon a time.

The archbishop, a small man in a blindingly white robe and stole, seemed to blend in with the limestone interior, cut as sharply as the stone. His hands fluttered like moths over the gilt Easter candle, water, pall, cross, and Bible arranged on the altar and coffin as he spoke: "May the grace

of our Lord Jesus Christ, the love of God, and the fellowship of the Holy Spirit be with you all."

"Amen." Anya answered with the rest of the assembly.

"In the waters of baptism, Steven Neuman died with
Christ, and rose with Him to everlasting life. May he now
rise with Christ in eternal glory." The priest sprinkled
holy water on the casket, water droplets glittering in the
filtered sunlight.

Anya's attention drifted. It drifted from the stain of
light the rosette window cast on the floor to the assembled
congregation. In this crush of people, she felt uneasy.
Sweat prickled under her copper collar. She felt watched.
She wondered if beyond these hundreds of people, there
was some spirit, somewhere haunting these old and new
walls, a fly buried in amber glass that watched over time.
She looked down at her folded hands. If whatever was
watching would leave her alone, she would leave it alone.

Perhaps it was her own uneasiness. She hadn't been
inside a Catholic church since her mother's death. Her
mother's funeral mass had been much smaller, simpler;
a seemingly ordinary woman's death would not have
made the front page of the paper, much less summoned
the bishop to perform funerary rites before a thousand
people. There had been no honor guard, no salute with
rifles, no flag on the simple black casket. There had been
an unembellished white pall and a plain rosary with plastic
beads placed on the casket, and egg sandwiches at her aunt
and uncle's house. No, her mother's death hadn't warranted pageantry. It had simply been a dozen people in a

small chapel in Hamtramck: Anya, her aunt and uncle, the priest, and the parishioners who had come to see what had happened to the quiet woman whose house burned down. Her aunt kept telling her to cross her legs, but she couldn't: Sparky was sitting between her feet, his feathery gills drooping. Anya remembered sitting in the first pew, not listening to a word the priest said, staring at the closed box. She wondered if there had been some mistake, that perhaps her mother wasn't truly in there. Perhaps she had gotten up and walked out on her own.

Then she had listened, straining to hear her mother's spirit, the way she had heard the voices of spirits all her young life. She had refused to believe her mother would leave her, no matter how shiny and pretty the afterlife. But no voice whispered from the black box, no cold hand reached out to brush her cheek. Her mother was gone, without a word or a backward glance. Though Anya had later come to understand that this is how it should be, a spirit slipping quietly into the darkness without the drama of a haunting, it saddened her to think her mother didn't care enough to stick around, for at least a little while.

Instead of her mother's spirit or the cold plastic of her rosary beads in her hand, Anya had wound her fingers in the copper collar. Her aunt thought that it was a terribly inappropriate thing for a young girl to wear, but her uncle had told her to "shut up and let the kid grieve."

Around her, the practicing Catholics knelt, gave the required responses to the mass. Anya sat still, with her hands knotted in her lap, lips sealed shut as the mass and eulogies continued. She was no longer one of them. When the time came to take communion, she stayed in the pew, watched as the priests laid the communion wafers on the tongues of the faithful.

Not her. She hadn't confessed since she was a child. And what was there to confess to? Creating the fire that killed her mother? Interfering with God's inscrutable plan for the spirits that wandered the earth, devouring them and sending them to . . . to who knew where? Destroying them? No, those were sins the church wouldn't forgive. And she couldn't bring herself to ask.

She remembered the kindly parish priest trying to counsel her after her mother had died. Her aunt and uncle had no use for religion, but brought her out of a sense of worry. For weeks after her mother's death, Anya had not spoken to anyone but her imaginary friend. She was entirely too old for such fantasies, and Anya's aunt and uncle hoped that the priest would be able to wake her from her stupor of grief.

The priest had sat with her in his office, where she stared at the wooden cross hanging on the wall beside the window. As he spoke, she watched the dust motes drift in the sunlight, listened to the ghost of a long-dead priest tread the hallway outside. She wondered what the dead priest had done that had been so terrible as to cause him to be denied eternal light. There was not a single thing the living priest could say that would bring her mother back, that would alter her perception of reality. And her crime was too great to utter. Her lips remained stubbornly sealed for months, until her frustrated aunt slapped her out of sheer frustration.

Anya gasped. That sound seemed to bring the world rushing in, lit the fire of anger in her lungs.

She slapped her aunt back.

The next day, her aunt and uncle made an appointment with Children's Services. They couldn't handle her, they said. They wanted to put her in foster care, they said. The caseworker looked across her desk at them and told them to take a number. She had serious families with serious problems to take care of.

And so she stayed with her aunt and uncle. Her aunt rarely spoke to her, and her uncle was rarely home. The silence in her room, at mealtimes, in front of the television set, gave her too much time to think, but her thoughts rarely made their way past her lips. She was like a ghost living in their house, slipping through the hall in her stocking feet and burying her nose in library books and Sparky's neck. When she was old enough to leave their home—never *her* home—she spoke with them even less.

Some remembered portion of that silence welled up in her, now, glued her to her seat like a little girl in adult's clothes. It welled up like a broken pipe in a flooded basement, and she bit her lip to keep it from overtaking her. She wondered if Neuman's parents felt that silence, far away in the front row, feeling the meaningless words washing over them.

The density of the people in the pews shifted. DFD

was lining up by rank to do the final walk through, filing past the casket to pay their respects. Remembering the bars on her arms, Anya slipped down the pew and fell into line.

She approached the casket, brushed her fingers across the flag draping the top. She felt no cool shadow underneath it, no bewildered ghost hovering near. The casket was empty of everything but bones and a dress uniform. She felt a stab of relief at that. Her attention slipped back to his elderly parents. Wherever Neuman had gone, he wasn't here with them.

The priest's voice echoed above her. "Merciful God, hear our prayer: open the gates of heaven to your servant. Help those who remain to comfort one another with faith, until we are with you and our brother forever in the kingdom of heaven. We ask this through Christ, our Lord."

"Amen," she whispered.

Anya walked the two blocks back to her car. The church bells rang around her, signifying Neuman's last alarm. The pallbearers and the honor guard had loaded the casket back into the pump truck, to be taken to the Holy Sepulchre Cemetery for interment and the rite of committal. The procession had slowly pulled away down the street, headlights shining in the clear blue day. The hundreds of mourners and DFD members dispersed, as if a black dandelion had been blown, seeds drifting down the streets.

Anya paused at her car, anger bubbling in her. A piece of paper had been stuck to her windshield. She'd placed her official business parking placard in her front windshield . . . what kind of an asshole meter officer would give her a ticket for a funeral, to boot?

She stalked to the driver's side and snatched the piece of paper from the wiper blade. Her meeting with Vross and the detectives was enough law enforcement cheer to last her a good long time. Someone was going to get this ticket crammed up their ass. . .

It wasn't a ticket. The note, scrawled in jagged handwriting, fell open in her hand. It read:

LANTERN, LANTERN, BURNING BRIGHT
IN THE CORNER OF MY SIGHT. . .

Below the words, a charcoal sketch depicted Anya in exacting detail. She sat in the cathedral pew in her dress uniform, hands open in her lap. Her eyes were unfocused, staring into the distance, and the turn at the corner of her mouth was sad.

It was signed with the hieratic character from the crime scene, the Horned Viper. The linen paper smelled faintly of sulfur.

Anya spun on her heel, bristling. Her heart hammered in her chest, hard enough to drive more itchy wool fibers from her dress uniform into her burn. She scanned the stream of dark-clad mourners exiting the church, nearly indistinguishable from one another in their somber clothes, scattering in all directions on the sidewalk. Cars drove slowly past on busy Woodward Avenue, while others waited with their turn signals on for a break in traffic.

She'd been right . . . she *was* being watched in the church. But not by a ghost. By her arsonist.

An arsonist who knew who and what she was.

CHAPTER NINE

HE WAS SOMEWHERE CLOSE.

Anya's gaze drifted away from Neuman's interment. She stood on the edges of the gathering, Sparky sitting on her polished shoes, as the flag was folded by the pallbearers and handed to Neuman's parents. She was too far away to hear what the bishop said, to hear anything but the ratcheting of rifles as the salute was prepared.

The rolling grass of Holy Sepulchre Cemetery was still green, though the many trees had turned color and begun to drop their leaves. Anya scanned the crowd assembled here in the newest part of the cemetery, the fire engines parked beyond at the access road, back at the oldest part of the cemetery with its sinking, ornate tombstones and crypts. The new section was planned in symmetrical rows with sharp, geometric tombstones, rolling away in meadow and grass to the jagged, ornately wrought stones of the turn of the last century. Those stones had been blackened by pollution and time, much of their information erased by years and acid rain. The cemetery had been begun during the park cemetery movement at the turn of the twentieth century, when graveyards had been planned to be pleasant, tree-lined places for picnics and children to play. Then, the Victorian idea of death breathing close to the living still held sway. As society chose to have less and less to do with death, the tombstones became plainer, less elaborate, and less visited.

Today, there were too many figures for Anya to single out just one, to pick her arsonist out of the crowd. The hundreds of mourners at Neuman's interment spread over several rows. The press stood at a respectful distance, clicking a few pictures and shambling away back to the news trucks. Beyond them, mourners for dozens of other sites wandered among the stones, clutching flowers. A woman was busily clearing out the overgrown weeds on a plot fifty feet distant. A group of high-school-age students were making grave rubbings of the older stones with crayons and butcher paper. A man who might have been a historian or genealogist stepped among rows with a notebook and pen. And those were the living. The park cemetery movement would have been pleased.

The dead walked in the sun as well. In the afterlife, this place remained a park, by design. The ghost of a child sat on a stone, swinging his legs back and forth, while a girl the same age climbed a nearby walnut tree. The spirit of a young woman stretched in the shade of a pine tree, playing with her infant child. A middle-aged pudgy man sat on one half of a double tombstone, ball cap in his hand. There was no death date for his wife on the other half, and Anya wondered how long he would have to wait for company.

An elderly man's ghost walked his dog between the rows several yards away. Sparky scampered away to play with the dog. The old man chuckled as the salamander and dog sniffed under each other's tails and romped around a headstone.

"I'm sorry about that," Anya said, moving to retrieve Sparky. In the hundreds of mourners at the gravesite service, no one noticed that she was gone.

The ghost of the old man laughed. *"Let 'em play. Bones gets bored. It'll make his decade to play chase."*

The guns fired the salute, jolting Anya back to the commitment rite. The guns sounded twenty-one times. Anya thought that even the spirits turned their attention to the scene, to the parents with no living children clutching the flag, to the riflemen with the white braid over their shoulders turning the rifles with white gloves.

But one man did not turn to look. In the distance, in the old part of the cemetery, Anya saw a figure walking in the spaces between the trees. He wore a black jacket, pants, and sunglasses. His profile was indistinguishable from this distance, but there was something familiar about the way he moved, the way he favored his right leg as he walked. In his path, the ghost of a man in a suit and a bowler hat strolled, hands in his pockets. The man seemed to quicken his pace, walking toward the spirit.

Anya slipped away from the ghost with his dog, breaking into a sprint. Sparky tore himself away from the ghost-dog and surged beside her, loping like a giant squirrel. The cool October air burned in the back of her scraped and ruined throat, her lungs threatening to reject it.

The walking man ignored her, advancing toward the ghost drifting along the edges of the tombstones. The ghost's feet didn't touch the ground; he wandered as slowly as a cloud, drifting down the worn path between the stones.

She shouted for the man to stop, shouted a warning to the ghost, but she could only emit a hoarse rasp. She doubted that anyone from the graveside service could hear her, much less the distracted ghost.

Too late. The man walked briskly across the grass, into the ghost. As if he walked into a wall of smoke, the ghost dissolved. The ghost shredded into tendrils that faded into the crisp blue air. A thin sigh, like an exhalation into the vault of a shell, rolled over the grass.

He'd devoured the ghost, as easily as if he'd walked through a sheer curtain. The nonchalant ease with which he did so shocked her . . . and he kept on walking, never breaking stride, heading over the hill to the crypts.

She chased him and he disappeared around a stand of trees. Winded, she ran out into a clearing dominated by an Art Nouveau limestone mausoleum. A trio of walnut trees stood before it, their branches skimming toward the ground in graceful arches. Two black iron lions guarded the arched entrance, paws lifted. Past them, the pierced iron door was cracked open.

An invitation?

Sparky's gills bristled, and his nostrils flared. Anya unbuttoned her dress jacket, reaching for her gun. She pushed open the door, snatching her hand away at the heat still lingering in the metal. The lock had been melted away, leaving the elaborate iron piecework intact.

The daylight cast her shadow long before her. Geometric shapes from the door and high grates played on the marble floors and the tarnished brass plates on the walls. In the center of the mausoleum, a marble bench rose from the floor. A dark figure stood at the far wall, fingering a smear of graffiti paint on one of the brass plates. Sparky lowered his body to the ground in a fighting stance, growling.

"They don't build places like this anymore," he said. In calm profile, without the aura of fire, his face was handsome: square jaw, chiseled chin, deep-set eyes under a thick brow. His sunglasses hung on the collar of his shirt. He could have walked from the pages of a glossy magazine. "Such a shame to deface them."

Anya laughed, a short, rasping bark. "An arsonist who's a historical preservationist."

He turned to look at her then, lifting an eyebrow. His left eye was a warm brown, the iris dilated in the half darkness. Over the other, a milky cataract spread over a frozen iris that didn't react to the light. The eyebrow over that eye was slightly twisted, as if scar tissue lay beneath the perfectly groomed eyebrow. He was blind in that eye, she realized.

"One has to remove the old to make room for the new," he said.

Anya kept her gun trained on him. "Is that why you're setting these fires? To make room for—"

"To make room for Sirrush." He broke into a brilliant smile, his teeth flashing white in the darkness.

"Who the hell are you?"

"I'm the Right Hand of Sirrush. Obviously."

"I don't care if you're the right hand of God. Put your hands up," Anya ordered.

"No," he said. "I'd much rather talk with you here, privately, than in the back of a police car."

Her eyes narrowed. "I'm not letting you out. You're coming with me, and I'm going to frog-march you down that hill."

He smiled. "I don't think that you can force me to do anything." His hand flamed brightly as a torch, and he delicately wiped away the graffiti from the brass with his fingers. He shook his hand out, as easily as if he doused a match. "You certainly aren't going to be able to get those cuffs around me."

Anya backed toward the door. She reached into her belt for her handcuffs. She fumbled them behind her back, wound them into the ironwork. She snapped them shut, securing the door, and tossed the key out into the grass.

"That's interesting," he said, crossing his arms.

She plucked her cell phone from her handbag, and dialed 911. "This is Lieutenant Kalinczyk from DFD . . . I need backup at Holy Sepulchre Cemetery . . ." She told them the location of the mausoleum, heart hammering in her chest. "Bring fire extinguishers. Lots of them." When she hung up, her arsonist hadn't moved.

"You've got about five minutes to talk before this place is swarming with cops."

He lifted a finger, limned in red fire. "I can burn through that door."

"Sure. Eventually. If it doesn't offend your artistic sensibilities. But I could probably shoot you a few times first." Sparky growled at her feet. "And you have to get through him, too."

His face split into a smile. On any other man, in any other place, she would have found it attractive. "How did you acquire a fire elemental? I confess to being . . . jealous." He reached his hand toward Sparky, and Sparky bared his teeth.

"Hands off the little guy."

"Indeed."

"What did you do with Virgil? And the ghost of the man here in the cemetery?" she demanded. Now was her moment to ask questions, before he was surrounded by the reality of Vross and his detectives at police HQ.

He shrugged. "I consumed them."

"Why? They weren't bothering you, or anyone else."

He looked back at her, as if puzzled by the question. "It's what we do."

She thinned her lips and decided to be obtuse. "I don't know what you're talking about."

"You. Me. We're Lanterns."

"I'm not anybody special, though at one point in time I was a Girl Scout."

He snorted. "You see them, every bit as I do." He approached her, and Anya leveled her gun at his dark, burning eye. "You're a Lantern. I can sense that hole in your chest, the heat from your skin . . ." He planed his hand in the air, inches from her. "You're like me. Burning from the inside out, like you've swallowed a star." His stare was black as obsidian and pale as quartz, taking her in from head to toe. "You've got no idea what you're capable of, what I could teach you to do . . ." He took another step toward her.

"Stay where you are." Her finger flexed on the trigger. "I don't know what you are, but nothing's immune to bullets."

He inclined his head. "True enough." When he moved to turn away, Anya saw the glimmer of white gauze peeking out from his right collar. She *had* struck him the other night. For all his power, he wasn't invincible. "I am what you could be, with the right teacher . . ."

"You're what I could be if I was completely, entirely insane. Who would want to summon Sirrush from his dirt nap? Why?"

His gaze glowed—with magick or avarice, she couldn't tell. "Sirrush is the city's last hope. You'll see . . ."

She heard footsteps racing up the grassy hill to the mausoleum, shouting. There had been enough cops at the firefighter's burial to take down a small army, and they were coming.

"In here," she called.

The arsonist laced his hands together. "You're wasting time, Lieutenant Kalinczyk."

"No. I'm keeping you from playing out your sick little fantasies."

He smiled, seeing the police crowding behind the pierced iron door. "We'll see whose fantasies are real."

She'd thought that the Right Hand of Sirrush would put up more of a fight.

The cops and firefighters cut open the door with bolt cutters. Anya warned them that the suspect likely had "flammable substances and an ignition source" on his person, but he let them cuff him without incident, fire extinguishers at the ready. The Right Hand of Sirrush smiled behind the glass of the police car, the same way he smiled at her now behind the one-way glass at police headquarters.

Vross and his cronies looked through the glass at the man in the interrogation room. "His ID says his name's Drake Ferrer."

"Why does that name sound familiar?" Anya asked.

"Used to be a big-shot architect trying to revitalize the city . . . tried to raise some grant and private monies to tear down the warehouse district and some of the worst neighborhoods. Wanted to build low-income housing, schools, that kind of crap in their places. Real do-gooder. Couldn't raise the money. He got the shit beaten out of him in a robbery several years back, and he dropped off the society pages. Hell, I'm surprised that he's still here."

Anya stared through the glass. He hadn't seemed like a typical, nervous fire-starter. He'd been too poised for that. "Maybe the failure drove him around the bend."

"Maybe, maybe not." Vross hitched his belt up over his considerable girth. "He says that he was minding his own business, looking at the design elements of the mausoleums when you took him prisoner. His lawyer's on his way, making noises about unlawful imprisonment."

Anya snorted. "You saw that note on my car."

"There are no prints on the note. And we don't know what the hell it means."

"The prints at the warehouse scene, on the window grate . . . they're his."

"There are twelve sets of distinguishable prints on that grate. That's assuming that the lab didn't fuck up. None of 'em are his . . . at least, none of the ones they can find now."

"Then he wore gloves. I've got his face on videotape at two of the scenes."

"That's circumstantial. He says he was at the school to pick up a teacher's aide volunteer form and he was on the beauty shop street to look at a rental."

Anya spun on him in frustration. "I shot him. Look at that wound on his shoulder." She stabbed the glass with a finger.

"All that's there is a burn. Could be a cauterization, could be who knows what. No record of him going to any emergency room that night."

"I saw him."

"Says you. It was dark. You also said that the arsonist had a blowtorch." Sarcasm dripped from Vross's voice. "You saw a guy that looked like him."

"Where was he the night of the warehouse fire, then?"

"The dude's got an alibi. He was at a high-society wedding. One of the commissioners was there. He's got alibis for the other nights, too."

She blew out her breath in frustration. "What are you saying to me, Vross? You working for the defense here?"

"I'm saying"—Vross crossed his arms over his stomach, and Anya could see the sweat stains in his armpits—"that we don't have enough to hold this guy. You jumped the gun, and we got nothing. I'm saying that you made an ass of yourself at Neuman's funeral, got his parents all riled up for no good reason. We're going to be turning him loose in twenty-four hours."

She slammed her fist on the wall. "How stupid are you? I just handed you this guy on a silver platter. There's more than enough to take to a grand jury."

"Watch your mouth with me, princess. There isn't a case until I say there is."

"The hell there isn't."

The door to the suspect observation area opened. Marsh stood in the doorway, still in his dress uniform.

"Call your bitch down, Marsh," Vross snarled.

"Shut the fuck up, Vross," Marsh told him.

Anya blinked. Marsh never swore.

"A word with you, please." Marsh gestured to the hallway. Anya followed him out.

"Captain, I——" she began.

Marsh held up a finger, and her protests died away. "You just stepped on some very big toes, Lieutenant," he said in a low voice.

"Vross isn't . . ."

"I'm not talking about Vross. Vross is useless. I'm talking about your suspect. He's got some friends in very high places."

Anya's cheeks burned. "But the evidence . . ."

"Does point in his general direction. But we need more. We need to be able to place him at the scene at the time of the fires. And we can't. The DA won't touch him in this case unless we've got a damn signed confession."

"This is the guy, Marsh, the guy who was in the warehouse the other night. I *saw* him."

"You and who else?"

Thinking of Brian lying in his hospital bed, Anya's heart dropped. "The other witness is no shape to talk."

"Get me more." Marsh's mouth was set in a hard line and he reopened the observation room door. "Get me enough to lock that son of a bitch up for the next fifty years. Put him at the scene."

Anya stared at the man behind the glass. He'd kicked back in his seat, staring at the one-way glass. She could swear that he could see her behind it.

"I want to talk to him," she said.

Vross began to protest, but Marsh held up his hand. "You didn't get anywhere with him, right?"

"He just keeps saying he wants his lawyer."

"Then, there's nothing to be lost by letting her try."

Vross crumpled his coffee cup in his hand and threw his electronic key card to the interrogation room door lock to her. It missed her head, and she plucked it from the air like a snake snapping up a bird. Her mouth quirked in amusement at him, but Anya could feel his glare on her back as she left the observation area.

Standing alone before the metal door to the interrogation room, she fingered the copper torque around her neck.

"Wake up, little dude," she murmured.

She felt Sparky stir. He stretched, yawned against her hair, and took his full shape as he clambered down her jacket sleeve and pant leg. He stretched up to her hand, licked the keycard. He made a face, as if he could taste Vross's fingerprints on it.

Anya swiped the card in the door lock slot. A green light flashed, and the door unlocked with a metallic thud. Anya let herself in, Sparky sidling beside her.

Ferrer leaned forward in interest. "Hello, again."

She pulled up a chair opposite him, then rested her elbows on the table. She didn't carry a notebook, a recorder, or have any deals on paper to offer him. But she knew he had been baiting her.

"Why are you here, Mr. Ferrer?" Conscious of the video camera over her head, she kept her tone civil.

"I think I already covered that with the police. You cornered me in the crypt, accused me of being a serial arsonist." Amusement glinted in his good eye. She watched as his attention drifted from her face downward, trickling down her neck. It was then that she was conscious of the fact that her dress uniform jacket was unbuttoned, that it flared open when she sat. She'd opened the collar of her dress shirt to allow her burns to breathe. She hadn't been able to stand the constriction of a bra on her charred skin, and she could feel the antibiotic ointment sticking her skin to the fabric. Her first impulse was to button her jacket, but she stubbornly refused to give him the satisfaction of knowing that she felt vulnerable under his scrutiny.

"Really, Mr. Ferrer. Why are you here? I don't imagine that a man of your power and standing goes anywhere he doesn't want to go."

From the corner of her eye, she saw Sparky reaching up the wall to lick the electronic door lock. She knew that Ferrer saw him, as his gaze twitched to the door. The light on the keycard reader changed from red to yellow. *Good boy,* Anya thought.

"I must admit that having the opportunity to talk with you again is a considerable inducement." Ferrer brought his eyes back to her face. "You're quite striking, in a very 1940s pinup girl kind of way. Maybe it's the uniform. You really should let me draw you sometime."

"Are you coming on to me, Mr. Ferrer?"

"Yes." His gaze was direct, unflinching. "I thought I was supposed to be honest under interrogation."

Sparky padded across the room, tail switching. He could smell the testosterone in the air, and wasn't about to let Drake Ferrer get away with hitting on his charge. He stomped up to Ferrer and savagely bit him in the knee.

Anya smiled as Ferrer gasped, tried to cover his reaction. She was certain that, to the bystanders in the observation room, it looked as if he'd had an unfortunate muscle spasm.

Anya put her elbows on the table, resting her chin in her palms to be extra solicitous for the camera. "Are you all right, Mr. Ferrer?"

"Perfectly fine."

"Good." Anya unfolded the drawing from her pocket. "It seems that you've already been busily sketching. Is this your work?"

Ferrer turned the page to face him and pretended to examine it with a critical eye. "It's good work. Your artist did a nice job of capturing that little moue at the corner of your mouth. The shape of your hands is quite delicate. Nice contrast to the severity of the uniform. And the gesture lines capture your posture quite well. The eyes are spot-on, shadowed and lovely." He turned the rumpled page back to her. "Sadly, it's not my work."

"You do realize that we'll be sending this to a hand-writing expert, don't you?"

"I'd expect nothing less of you. But the Detroit Crime Lab . . . well,"—he waved his hand negligently—"I'm sure that whatever analysis they come up with will be absolutely unimpeachable in court."

Her eyes narrowed. "What's your connection to these fires?"

"I don't have one. As I told the detective, I didn't have anything to do with them."

"You told me in the crypt you were setting these arsons to summon some mythical beast."

Ferrer laughed out loud. "That's a nice theory. I'm sure it goes over well with your superiors."

Anya flicked a glance at Sparky. The salamander reared up on his hind legs and took a bite out of Ferrer's elbow.

Ferrer stoically refused to cry out, tried to shake Sparky off. Anya was hoping to provoke him, to get him to burst into flame, as he had at the warehouse.

But he wasn't taking the bait. Not yet.

Anya had never hurt a suspect under interrogation before; it ran against her principles of the way an investigator should behave. That ideal clashed with the need to get him to confess, to stop the arsons. She paused, but for only a moment.

A hot voice in the back of her head hissed, *"No one will ever know."* The voice throbbed through her temples, squelched the pang of conscience she felt at Ferrer's discomfort. Ferrer was guilty. She had to get him to talk, whatever it took, before anyone else got hurt.

"A firefighter is dead, Mr. Ferrer."

"I read that in the paper. That's a terrible shame." His expression didn't betray the slightest twitch of remorse.

"I want you to tell me the truth. Why did you set those fires?"

"I told you. I didn't do it," he said through clenched teeth and a cold smile.

Anya nodded at Sparky. The salamander climbed up on the table. His nostrils flared, smelling blood. She admired the way the light played over his speckled body. Sparky wasn't burdened by the distinction between right and wrong—he just bit what didn't smell good. She envied him.

Ferrer watched him, not out of fear, but fascination.

"Do you have any pets, Miss Kalinczyk?" he asked. "I imagine that if you did, your pet would be very well trained. A fearsome foe, indeed."

"If I had a pet, you would be correct, Mr. Ferrer."

Sparky snarled and bit Ferrer in the right shoulder, where a bandage peeked out of his collar. Ferrer grunted and tried to fling the salamander off him, but it was like trying to loosen the jaws of a pit bull. Anya sat with her hands in full view on the table, watching Ferrer as he toppled out of the chair. She heard tapping on the glass, the signal for her to come out. She ignored it. She disregarded the rattling of the door handle. Sparky had jammed the lock. For all intents and purposes, she and Ferrer were alone.

Anya crossed around the edge of the table, keeping her hands and feet in full view while Ferrer wrestled with Sparky. She was certain that the videotape would show him struggling with air, perhaps a seizure. She crouched down, knowing it would give the impression that she was showing professional concern for the detainee. She called out for a medic to make sure that was recorded on tape.

"Mr. Ferrer. Tell me the truth. Tell me that you set those fires."

Ferrer succeeded in pulling Sparky off him. Blood rimmed the seam of his jacket sleeve and speckled the floor. Breathless, he looked her directly in the eye. Outside, she heard someone prying the electric door panel off the wall. Marsh and Vross would be inside in moments.

A beatific smile crossed his handsome face. "You have much to learn about being a muse in the service of fire."

He would say nothing else.

When Anya got home, there were flowers waiting on her doorstep.

She held the florist's paper gingerly and looked inside. White chrysanthemums. From somewhere in her memory, she remembered her mother saying that these flowers symbolized truth. They had been among her favorites.

Anya opened the plain white card. It said simply:

> THE THINGS YOU NEED TO KNOW ARE NOT
> THE ONES YOU'RE LOOKING FOR. —D

The edges of the card were sharp against her palm as she wadded it up and threw the flowers in the trash. That son of a bitch.

She let herself into the house, but didn't turn on the lights. Her answering machine blinked red: two messages from Katie, wanting to know if she was all right; a wrong number; and a salesman trying to peddle aluminum siding.

She felt incredibly heavy, exhausted from the weight of too much sorrow and frustration. Her clothes peeled off like a skin, and she climbed into the shower, letting the warm water rinse over her face and hair. The pirate rubber duck sailed in the shallow eddies at her feet. Careful to present her back to the spray, she tried to protect the tender burns on her chest. The demon-burn had begun to bubble and blister. Several of them had broken, seeping clear fluid. Her stomach turned when she looked at it, and she kept her gaze focused on the collection of rubber duckies canoodling in plastic joy on the shelf. At her feet, Sparky nipped at the spray of water.

It was then that Anya realized she was showering in the dark. She hadn't noticed the lack of light at all. It should have bothered her, but Anya couldn't summon up any additional anxiety from the recesses of her brain. It was all spent on Brian and on the case.

Anya brushed her teeth a half-dozen times, then gargled with mouthwash. She still tasted something sour in the back of her throat. Tying her rubber-duck bathrobe loosely around her, she climbed into bed. Sparky had left his Gloworm in the dead center, and he curled his body around it. He popped his tail in his mouth and she stroked his head. Poor little guy. Anya leaned over and kissed his leathery head. Though Sparky was assigned to be her guardian, she'd felt more like his caretaker in the past few days.

"It's gonna be okay, Sparky. We've gotten through much worse. We'll get through this."

The Gloworm cast a soothing light that seeped into her dreams like light under a door.

Once again, she dreamed of the ice cave.

At her right hand, Sparky paced in a circuit, glowing

amber. On her left, the little girl from the pop machine stood, her shoelaces untied. Ahead of her growled the unseen force that blasted heat down the slick walls.

But there was something else here. Something viscous and black as pitch, pooling on the white ice of the floor. It peeled itself up, swirling like ink in water, drawing itself into the shape of a human. It remained transparent, and she could see bits of the ice behind it. Ragged trails of ectoplasmic sludge trailed behind, as if it couldn't entirely gather itself into a fully formed outline.

Sparky snaked before her, hissing, his gills splayed. Anya shoved the little girl behind her. "What the hell are you?"

It undulated before her, like an eel in unseen current. *"We've already been introduced."*

That voice . . . she recognized it from the botched exorcism of the other night, and the voice in her head in the interrogation room. It was Chloe's demon.

"What's your name?" Anya demanded. She knew that if a demon was asked its name, it had to answer truthfully. And truth was the first step to control.

"Mimiveh."

"Great. Then, you won't mind if I call you Mimi."

The darkness lashed in irritation. *"Crass human."*

"What do you want, Mimi?"

The demon giggled. It swirled in the air, peering behind Anya's back. Sparky lunged at it and came back with a jawful of shredded black mist. *"I like to play with little girls."*

Anya lifted her right hand as a threat. She'd devoured this demon once; she could do it again. "Forget it. You're not playing with him. Or Chloe."

The demon reached inky tendrils toward her face. Its touch burned as surely as the blisters on her chest. *"Then I guess I'll have to play with you, instead."*

CHAPTER TEN

ANYA WAS DETERMINED TO FIND out everything about Drake Ferrer: who his high school English teacher was, where he bought his socks, whether he favored creamy or crunchy peanut butter. In knowing who he was, she would discover his weaknesses. It would only take a small weakness to cleave open and exploit, some small chink in the armor of his arrogance that she could use to trip him up.

She began with looking for large weaknesses by pulling his police file. Vross had said Ferrer had been the victim of a robbery. At her battered desk, Anya waited for the file to load over her slow connection to the city computers, drumming her pencil on the coffee-stained blotter. An arrogant fool like that might have been flashing cash he shouldn't have been. Maybe he'd been driving a shiny new car that someone else coveted. She expected that his flamboyance and self-assurance had caused someone to take him down a peg.

The police incident report popped up on her screen, a scanned image of a blurry fax from 1999. At that time, centralized computing for all fire and law enforcement agencies in Detroit hadn't been instituted yet. The best she could get would be whatever bits of legacy data could be manually scanned in and stored in a friendly format.

She scanned the report. Looked like Drake Ferrer had been leaving a fund-raiser for the American Historical Landmarks Committee when he'd been jumped walking back to his car. By the reporting officer's account, Ferrer said he had been confronted by three young men. He gave them his wallet and keys, but the boys weren't in a mood to be placated. They beat Ferrer into unconsciousness, stole his car, and emptied as much of his bank account as they could via an ATM. Ferrer's unconscious body was found beside a Dumpster by a garbage man some hours later, who radioed for help.

Anya clicked ahead to the next page. She leaned forward on her desk, steepling her fingers before her lips. A picture of Ferrer after the attack had been appended to the file. Both eyes were swollen shut, his face a mass of black and green bruises. A line of stitches crossed back into his hairline. Anya hadn't remembered a scar; perhaps Ferrer had been able to afford some good plastic surgery. Other photos of his broken ribs, mangled hands, and purple-stippled back had shown that the robbers intended to leave him for dead. Ferrer had ruptured a kidney and lost sight in one eye, as a result. Anya thought back to watching him walk in the park, the slight limp that she detected as he strode through the grass.

She clicked forward to the notes of the violent crimes

detective assigned to the case. The young men had been identified by ATM videotape. Two of the three were juveniles and served only six months in a juvenile institution until they legally became adults, then were released. The oldest perpetrator spent one year in state prison.

Anya clicked back to the unrecognizable photo of Ferrer. "I know what happened to you," she told the photo. "But that doesn't tell me who you *are*."

She could see his battered body clearly enough. That much of a person could be easily cataloged, photographed, and analyzed.

But what she really wanted was to get into his head.

The main branch of the Detroit Public Library had been constructed downtown in the early twentieth century with funds—like hundreds of libraries in the era—donated by Andrew Carnegie. One of the stately Italian Renaissance buildings that sat back from the street on Woodward Avenue, a series of terraces staggered up its steps, over which arched windows watched. The library was constructed from the same pale limestone from which so many of Detroit's enduring buildings had been hewn. In this day and age, Anya couldn't imagine that much effort being put into any place intended to hold man's endeavors. Quarrying seemed far too labor-intensive for a society preferring the polish of glass and steel.

But there was something to be said for old buildings, old ways, and old knowledge. Anya made her way into the great vaulted central hall of the library, supported by massive Doric columns. Above her, colorful mosaics of people and literary quotations stretched, depicting the River of Knowledge. A few homeless people sat asleep in the corners. Still, the atmosphere felt immediately soothing, tranquil. Anya tucked her notebook under her arm and passed through the turnstiles to the main stacks.

It had been years since Anya had been here. Her mother, a reference librarian, had taken her here every day in the summer when school was out. Her mother had been unable and unwilling to afford a babysitter to simply park Anya in front of a television for eight hours a day. At DPL, at least, her daughter would get some culture. Anya remembered sitting under the colorful murals in the children's section, whiling away summer afternoons reading Grimms' fairy tales or the adventures of Nancy Drew. She'd flipped through the picture books of dinosaurs, tracing around Sparky's silhouette on the pages with her finger, trying to imagine what kind of egg Sparky had hatched from. Back then, wooden card catalogs stood like apothecaries in the main stacks, holding index cards sorting every imaginable topic by subject, author, and title. Anya's mother had to hold her up to let her small fingers reach the drawers at the top. By the time she was in second grade, Anya knew the Dewey decimal system backward and forward.

But those days were long gone. The massive card catalog cabinets had disappeared, replaced by computer terminals on long tables. Anya slid behind a station. After brief navigation of the online catalog, she entered: Ferrer, Drake.

She received three hits in the stacks, mentions in architectural books. She jotted down the locations and climbed the great circular staircase to the upper floors to find them. She found all three on the shelves and lugged them to a reading carrel to page through the indices.

The first book was a *Who's Who in Architectural Design,* a 1997 edition. Ferrer had his own entry, extolling how the native Detroiter graduated at the top of his class at the University of Michigan, double majoring in urban design and architecture for his undergrad. He'd gone on to win a fellowship to complete his PhD in architecture, publishing his doctoral dissertation as a book: *Classical Architecture in Urban Islands.* He'd won several prestigious awards in drafting and design, and there was notation that he'd joined a downtown architectural firm in Detroit specializing in urban redevelopment.

The second book held a chapter Ferrer had authored on historic preservation. The tone of the author was surprisingly warm, speaking of great affection for downtown Detroit landmarks that were being threatened by careless renovation and the ravages of pollution on limestone. It was clear from his remarks that Ferrer disdained the use of modern architecture that didn't comport with the existing milieu.

In this town, any new construction had been considered to be a good thing, a sign of progress. Anya thought Ferrer's approach, while full of sentimental aesthetic appeal, was unrealistic. Perhaps it could even be interpreted as elitist. People needed functional places to live and work, and condemning those places for being ugly seemed useless.

A textbook on urban planning included one of Ferrer's sketches of a utopian mixed-use downtown space: a green park lay at the center of townhouses, shops, and office buildings. The elevations were pretty enough: brick and sandstone, calling for off-street parking and a police substation, modeled after mixed-use space in Japan. But Anya had never seen anything like it built in Detroit.

"Dreamer," she said aloud, louder than she'd intended.

A soft shushing echoed over the room. Anya started; she thought she'd been alone. She looked back to see the figure of a ghostly woman pushing a phantom book truck down the aisle. She was dressed in bell-bottoms and a flower-print shirt, her hair long enough to brush her hips, held back in a macramé headband. A fringed belt was slung around her slim hips.

"I'm sorry," Anya responded. She felt Sparky skim away from her collar to peer over her shoulder at the spirit.

The ghost of the librarian stopped in her tracks, then took a step back. Fear glittered through her wide eyes. "You heard me."

"Yes. But I don't mean you any harm." Anya lifted her hands up in a supplicating gesture.

"But you're—you're like him."

Anya was sure that spirits could sense something unusual about her. Perhaps they could sense the heat of the furnace that burned in her chest, knew that she could blow them out as easily as a child with a match.

"Like who?" Anya's thoughts raced back to her conversation with Renee: *"He supposedly ate all the ghosts in the library downtown in an afternoon."* "Was it a man, blind in one eye, with a limp?"

The hippie librarian cringed. "Yes. That's him. He took Stan and Marlo and the ghost of the homeless man outside . . . he even took the Viking guy from the archives, Sjorn." Her eyes were wide with terror. "I hid from him in the ladies' room. But now . . . but now, I'm all alone." Her shoulders sagged.

Anya wanted to reassure her, but if she touched her, she knew that her hand would pass straight through the stylized hibiscus flowers on her blouse. "I won't hurt you. I promise. What's your name?"

"I'm Felicity."

Of course it was. It was a perfect hippie name. If it wasn't Felicity, it would have been Meadow or Skye.

"I'm Anya. I think . . ." Anya's brow wrinkled. "I think I remember you from when I was a kid. My mom was in reference."

"The girl with the salamander!" Felicity grinned. "I remember you didn't want to talk to us, but this little guy would follow us around after you fell asleep in the window seats. He likes to play hide-and-seek."

Sparky oozed down to the floor and licked Felicity's outstretched fingers. His tail wagged.

"I wasn't allowed. My mom had a thing about talking to ghosts."

"Most parents do." Felicity stroked Sparky's back. "We

actually get a lot of kids in here who can see us . . . until the parents convince them otherwise, anyway."

"I, uh . . . I'm sorry he took away your friends," Anya said. It felt odd to be consoling the dead over a non-death. But she had sympathy for Felicity's aloneness.

Felicity's mouth quivered. "He just . . . he acted like it was nothing. He hunted them down like he was looking for candy in couch cushions. I saw him take Marlo . . . she ran from him. He pulled her apart, like she was taffy. And I heard Sjorn yelling at him downstairs, and Stan . . . it was just . . ." Insubstantial tears welled up in her eyes. "They were being killed and no one could hear them. It was horrible."

Anya swallowed. "He's doing the same thing in the outside world, too. He's setting fires. A firefighter got killed. I'm trying to catch him."

The hippie librarian's eyes were hard with grief. "What can I do to help?"

Spoken like a true librarian.

"Well . . . you could show me the way to the local periodicals section. I want to see what this guy's been doing in the society pages."

Felicity wrinkled her nose. "It figures a guy like that would be part of the Establishment. Follow me."

The ghost gestured to Anya to follow her down the stairs into the basement. The periodicals room opened to a huge reading area of current newspapers and magazines, dotted with overstuffed chairs and lounge furniture. Felicity led her around the reading area, back to the archives.

This room was lined with metal cabinets, with microfiche and microfilm reader stations parked on one side of the room. A layer of dust coated the machinery. Even Sparky had no interest in machinery that old. Only the PC beside them looked to have been recently used.

"Isn't that rather old-school for a world-class library?" Anya asked, only half kidding.

Felicity shrugged, her long dark hair sliding over her shoulder. "While it's true that many records are now created both in electronic and hard-copy formats, many older records have yet to be converted. Plus, formats change so often that data is lost. It helps to be able to go back to the originals."

Anya flipped open her notebook. "Our suspect's name is Drake Ferrer. He's an architect, a few years older than I am. Seems to have been quite the celebrated intellectual. I'm looking for anything you've got on him."

"I'm on it." Felicity walked into a cabinet, disappearing into its depths. Anya thought she detected a rustle of film and paper as she dug.

Anya pulled up a worn wooden chair at the computer terminal. This terminal was set up to do periodical searches. She searched for mentions of Ferrer in recent issues of the local newspapers. To her disappointment, the databases only ran from current issues back five years. She found a reference to him in an obituary three years ago, where he was named as his deceased mother's only surviving child. Beyond that, the only hit she received was a mention of a showing of some of his art at the Detroit

Institute of Arts. The article was a text-only blurb in the metro section, titled "Reclusive Architect Seeks Personal Renaissance." It mentioned that several of Ferrer's blueprints and sketches of Detroit city life would be shown at a charity auction. The article was from last week; the showing was scheduled for this Friday.

"I've got some goodies for you." Felicity carefully balanced a stack of microfiche in her palm.

"That's a nice trick," Anya said, impressed. "Most ghosts can't move substantial objects like that." The librarian's ghost was stronger than Anya had given her credit for.

Felicity smiled. "They're light. But you should take them before I drop them." She inclined her pointed chin at the microfilm machine. "You know how to use that antique?"

"You bet. I'll yell if I run into trouble."

"Shhh. Not too loudly." Felicity placed a finger beside her lips and ducked back into the cabinets. The contents rattled like baseball cards flapping in bicycle spokes.

Anya switched on the microfilm machine, then waited for the bulb to warm up. One by one, she looked through the sheets of film that Felicity deposited at her side. What she found was enough to piece together the fragments of a life.

From vital statistics reports in the paper, Anya learned that Drake Ferrer had been born in 1970, at Henry Ford Hospital. No father was listed on the birth certificate. Anya put her chin in her hand. That, at least, was something they had in common. Henry Ford Hospital was not a place where wealthy women went to have their babies in private suites. The address listed on the birth certificate was a tough neighborhood. Ferrer had not had an easy start.

School enrollment records showed he started first grade at age five, a full year before most students began. Ferrer had distinguished himself enough to be placed in an experimental magnet school for math and science by the fifth grade. A newspaper article describing the new school showed the first class. Ferrer was in the third row. He was a thin, serious kid with a wooden face in the grainy photo.

High school enrollment records showed Ferrer had skipped another couple of grades, graduating high school at age sixteen. He was easy to pick out: the shortest kid in his graduation photo, wan gaze focused on somewhere distant. He'd won a full-ride scholarship to the University of Michigan as a National Merit Scholar—his SAT and ACT scores had been near-perfect. He'd finished his undergraduate degree in short order, double majoring in architecture and urban planning. Anya found a couple of scattered mentions of him in the *Michgan Daily* . . . an op-ed piece railing about the lack of affordability of low-income housing, and a snapshot of him from the shoulders up in a sea of underclassmen running the annual spring tradition of the Naked Mile through campus.

The research archives showed a number of published papers from his graduate career. Anya skimmed the titles and abstracts, printing out the full papers for later reading: "Toward a New Paradigm of Affordable, Sustainable

Housing," "Art Deco Structural Preservation," "The Impact of Traffic Flow on Exploitation of Public-Use Landmarks." He'd given several talks in Chicago and Boston on gentrification of declining neighborhoods. He seemed to be a singly focused man, passionate in what he did.

When had that changed? Why hadn't he stayed in the ivory tower in Ann Arbor, away from the ills he'd surely know in Detroit? He could have easily won a tenure-track teaching position with his qualifications.

But that was not the road he took. He returned to Detroit. A press release from a local architectural firm welcomed Ferrer aboard. The blurb said that the firm was "enthusiastically looking for opportunities to work with Ferrer's fresh ideas."

Felicity had found some black-and-white slides, diagrams of plans filed with the Historic District Commission. Anya had to admit, his work was beautiful. He'd restored a number of run-down drug houses to their original visages. But such charity projects took money. She found that the money flooded in from grants, from larger projects like office buildings and banks. Even in these new designs, she saw a respect for the old designs, congruent with Detroit's early twentieth-century construction boom. Ferrer romanticized that, breathing new life into Deco and Nouveau.

But he breathed new life into more than that. Name registrations showed he created a nonprofit corporation, the Motor City Phoenix Foundation. The aim of the organization was to create a downtown renaissance. He intended to attract private investors and public grants to rehabilitate decaying residential and commercial space to attract new jobs and create affordable housing. She glanced at a local magazine photo of the ribbon-cutting at the foundation's headquarters. It was a local-boy-done-good piece, little of substance, but she could see the hope in Ferrer's smile.

Once upon a time, Ferrer had been a builder. A community leader. And then . . . and then, he disappeared. There were no mentions of his actions after 1999, after the attack that had nearly killed him. He'd been turned upon by the very people he'd been trying to help.

Anya chewed on her lower lip. Why did he stay? Why not begin again, somewhere else that would appreciate his efforts? What hope kept him in this place?

She stared at Ferrer's grainy picture, so glowing and young, so different from the broken creature she'd met. And she wondered . . .

Why did any of them stay? What kept all of them from abandoning this sinking city? Was it memory? Habit?

She had no answer.

Anya called ahead to make sure there were no other visitors for Brian at the hospital. She didn't relish the idea of another confrontation with Jules or seeing the hurt look in Max's eyes. She'd eventually try to smooth things over with Katie and Ciro when she had a moment to breathe. But she was done with DAGR for good. Nothing they said would make a difference.

She had expected to feel . . . lighter somehow, after

she'd given up DAGR. Instead, she felt heaviness dragging at her steps. Perhaps the weight of Brian's condition was too heavy; perhaps the dreams of Mimi and the unknown little girl were too tightly wound in her psyche; perhaps the burns on her skin would take time to fade. Whatever the reasons, the loss of DAGR made her feel very alone.

Slipping behind the curtain to Brian's bed, she pulled up a chair beside him. He lay motionless, the machines pressing his chest up and down. She saw Katie had been here. Though flowers weren't allowed in the ICU, she'd left him a small carved jade statue of Kwan Yin, the goddess of mercy, on the night table. A stack of magazines suggested the others had been here, too, keeping vigil over him.

But they were alone now. Anya stroked Brian's cheek. His stubble had grown on his face and on his head, prickly under her fingers. The stubble on his chin was lighter, redder than the hair on his head. She would have to tease him about growing a goatee if and when he woke up. . . .

When he woke up. Period. She kept that thought firm in her mind, would not consider any other alternative.

"I don't know if you can hear anything," she said, rubbing her thumb on the back of his hand. "But I want you to know I'm sorry. About everything. I'd give anything to have a do-over."

Sparky crawled up on the foot of the hospital bed, curling up on Brian's feet.

"You can't see him," she whispered, "but Sparky's keeping your feet warm. He's worried about you."

She dipped her head, holding her breath until she steadied. "There are a lot of things I'm sorry about. I'm sorry about some of the things I did as a kid . . . you don't know the whole story, but it's my fault my mom's gone." Some detached, observant part of her mind felt how much easier it was to confess to Brian, locked in his silence, than it ever had been to confess to a priest. "I left the Christmas tree lights on . . . and the house went up in flames. I guess . . . I guess I'm still doing penance for that. The firefighter gig and all.

"I'm sorry that I took the spirit of that little girl. Hell, I'm even sorry that my electric bill was late this month. But the thing I'm most sorry about"—she leaned forward, staring at him intently—"is pushing you away.

"I was afraid," she confessed. "I was afraid I would hurt you. I was afraid you'd see what I am—what I really, really am—and walk away. I just couldn't . . . risk that kind of hurt again."

Tears dripped down her nose and she rubbed them away. "If you give me the chance, I swear that I won't make that mistake again."

She rested her palms on his arm, between the tubes and wires, and listened with every fiber of her being. She listened for a ghost, for his confused spirit caged by the machines. Her breath brushed the tape holding his eyes closed. "Can you hear me?"

The machines bleeped and whistled in their artificial rhythms that pumped breath and life into Brian, not giving Anya any sign that the shell of the man heard her. In that silence, she sensed nothing. No chill of a ghost. Either Brian was well and truly rooted in this physical world, asleep, or he was already past it.

She stayed until the visiting hour was over and the charge nurse came to dim the lights. Sparky reluctantly climbed off the hospital bed and plodded behind Anya down the hospital hallways.

Anya stood before the elevator to the parking garage, waiting for the elevator car to come back to the floor. A ghost shambled down the corridor in their direction, dragging an IV pole. He was a bent elderly man, face covered in uneven stubble, eyes bleary with intoxication.

"*Hey, lady,*" the ghost slurred. "*You got a dollar?*"

Anya ignored the ghost and punched the elevator button again. Sparky coiled around her feet and hissed.

"*Hey. I said, you got a dollar?*"

Anya stared forward at the stainless-steel doors, willing them to open. The lighted number above the doorway indicated that the car was two floors away. Anya folded her arms, refusing to make eye contact. Irritation boiled in her chest. Why wouldn't the ghost just leave her alone?

The spirit grabbed her elbow. "*I'm talking to you, you uppity bitch—*"

Anya spun on her heel. Sparky launched himself forward, tearing into the ghost's knee with his sharp teeth. The ghost howled, flailing and kicking at Sparky.

An incensed, unreasoning rage washed over her. Anya cast out her hand, reaching for the ghost's throat. Her hand flamed amber, pure as sunlight, and black hunger growled in her throat. Her fingers tore into the ghost, and she felt the spirit pulling apart. It dissolved into a welcoming cold frost inside her throat, then sank into her belly. For that instant, the burn in her chest was quelled, smooth and unmarked as cool glass.

She staggered, leaning against the elevator. Her hands and forehead made steam marks against the polished surface. Sparky sat on her feet and stared up at her, crooning.

"Are you all right?"

A large woman in pink scrubs touched her elbow. Anya flinched. "I'm fine. I . . ." *I just devoured a ghost for no reason,* she thought, but her teeth clamped down on the thought.

"You don't look fine. Come sit down."

The woman in scrubs led her back to the nursing station and made her sit down. Anya sat with her head in her hands. The woman in pink scrubs gave her a bottled water. Anya's hand shook around it and she struggled with the cap.

"That's a bad burn you've got there," the woman remarked. Her scrubs were only pink from a distance; up close, they had a repeating pattern of fairies over them.

Anya glanced down. At this angle, her shirt gapped open, exposing her burns. The rest of her shirt had stuck to the antibiotic ointment she'd slathered on herself. She looked like a hot dog escaped from a rotisserie. "I'm fine, really," Anya said, waving her away.

"Honey, I've seen fine, and that's not it. You come with me." The woman in scrubs loomed over Anya, hands on her sizeable hips.

Anya hung her head in resignation. She might be able to take on homeless ghosts, but the woman in scrubs outweighed her by at least seventy-five pounds. Anya was pretty sure that she would lose in a fight with the pink pixie lady.

She shuffled along behind the woman, who took her to an exam room. Sparky swished along beside her, staring at the pattern of pixies on her ass. Sparky was in love. Anya made a mental note to get him a Tinkerbell doll the next time she got to the store.

Anya sat down on an exam table, and the pixie lady pulled up a stool. Her name tag read "Dr. Murdock." She pulled on a pair of latex gloves. "Now, let's see."

Anya unbuttoned her shirt. The fresh burn from the bum ghost had raised new welts on the mess of red and black she was already growing. She'd given up on wearing a bra with those burns, reluctant to imagine the hellish feeling of a bra strap digging into blisters.

Dr. Murdock clucked under her breath. "Girl, what happened to you?"

"I'm with the fire department," Anya said. That much was true. The doctor's eyes trailed down to her jacket, glimpsing the brass badge pinned to the inside. Anya pulled it out. "I swear I'm not an electrocution fetishist."

The doctor roared with laughter, slapping the exam table. The sudden sound startled Anya. "Honey, you wouldn't *believe* the weird shit I've seen here. That would be tame."

Anya smiled weakly. She wondered if the doc had any

sense of the unseen patients still wandering the halls . . . they were just as weird.

The doctor stuck a thermometer in her mouth. "I'll be right back. Don't go anywhere."

Anya sat obediently on the edge of the exam table, feeling foolish. Sparky climbed up on one of the stirrups used for gynecological exams and stared at the digital thermometer in her mouth. He batted at it. The temperature jumped and it beeped. Sparky squealed in delight.

The pixie doc returned with an armload of dressings and ointments. She snatched the thermometer from Anya's mouth and frowned. "You're running a low-grade fever. That's a sign of infection."

"Great." Anya sighed. "That's the last thing I need."

"*This* is what you need." Dr. Murdock held up a fistful of green blister packs. "These are antibiotics, two weeks' worth. You need to get in to see a doctor before they run out, to make sure that the infection's under control." She held up a tube. "Silvadene antibiotic ointment. Apply it twice a day, keep the burns covered."

Anya looked down. "Thank you."

"You're welcome. Now, raise your arms."

Anya did as she was told. The pixie doc began looping gauze around her chest.

"You have to keep those burns covered in the meantime. And, honey, if you aren't gonna be wearing a bra, you need a lot more gauze to keep those girls contained."

"I, uh, usually do. Wear a bra. Why?" Anya stared down. "Is there something wrong with them?"

The pixie doc laughed. "They're great, don't get me wrong. But if you're working with a bunch of men in the fire department, I'm sure that they don't need to see all your womanly charms spilling over, you know?"

"Yes, ma'am," Anya mumbled, feeling like a chastened teenager. "Thank you."

"You just keep doing the good work you're doing."

Funny. She didn't feel like she was doing good work.

Ten minutes later, Anya was walking out of the hospital with a bagful of samples and gauze, corseted up to her armpits in bandages. She sported a sticker of a fairy with glitter wings on her jacket collar. Sparky trotted along beside her, looking wistfully back at the place they'd left the pixie doc.

She didn't want to admit it to herself, but she felt better. It wasn't the new bandages, or the antibiotic cream. It was the cold chill in her chest soothing the heat of the burns. Taking the ghost had softened the pain. A stab of guilt rattled through her head, but it didn't disturb the cold humming in her heart.

She'd taken a ghost without real provocation.

Her grip on the bag of medicine tightened. She had never done that before, always adhering studiously to her principle: never take a spirit unless there's no other choice.

What kind of a monster did this make her?

A small voice bubbled up in her: *It makes you like him. Like Drake Ferrer.*

CHAPTER ELEVEN

WHATEVER DRAKE FERRER WAS, it couldn't be said that he wasn't well diversified.

Anya drummed her fingers on her desk at DFD the next day, scrolling through Drake Ferrer's property records in the city database. The city's real estate division showed numerous properties belonging to Ferrer. So far she'd found a former strip mall, a car lot, a gas station, six houses, and a lot on which a video store stood. They'd been purchased in the late 1990s, titled under Ferrer's name. She noticed they'd all been sold within the last six months, at well below market value, to his Motor City Phoenix Foundation. She'd love to see how the capital losses worked out on his tax returns.

"Are you finally planning to get out of Dodge? Or are you trying to raise money for other purposes?" she muttered.

She paused, her eyes sliding from the blue screen to her right hand. It gripped a pen, poised over a yellow legal pad. The skin between her shoulder blades prickled as she watched her hand scrawl across the page, without her conscious direction. Her meticulous notes on Ferrer's property acquisitions dribbled away to loopy scribbles that resolved into a childlike scrawl that read:

ME. ME. ME. ME.

Mimimimimimimimi. . .

She forced her hand to stop, clamping down on it with her left hand. With white knuckles, she slowly released her right hand. The pen began to move again, writing:

ME.

Mimi.

She'd heard of this before: automatic writing. Some mediums could communicate with spirits by allowing them use of their hands. Anya had never done it; she had seen it once, but it had given her the willies. She found her hoarse voice: "Mimi, is that you, you bitch?"

The scrawl paused: *Hello, Anya. No need to be confrontational.*

"What do you want?"

Actually, you could use some hand cream. Your cuticles are a mess.

"Thanks for the advice. Shouldn't you be boiling in some netherworld hell?"

Well, government offices are an institutional hell, of a sort. Does that count?

"Actually, I'm surprised you're literate, Mimi. Most demons of your ilk can't do much more than drag planchettes around Ouija boards."

That's fun. Especially at slumber parties. All those teenage girls with burning questions about their would-be beaux . . . delish. But that's not nearly as fun as looking over your shoulder.

"Was that you with me in the interrogation room?" She thought of the voice encouraging her to torture Ferrer.

He's cute. You should interrogate him more.

"No thanks. I don't touch suspects."

At least that one's conscious. Not like that atrophying bald guy in the hospital.

Rage bubbled up in Anya. "Go fuck yourself, Mimi."

Gladly. But you should try it. You might like it.

The pen stilled.

Anya reached deeply within herself for the burning core that devoured ghosts. The reactor inside her ignited, and she reached outward, searching for this irritating little demon that seemed to still have one foot in the physical world. She had never failed to entirely consume a demon before. She supposed it was possible, if the demon was stronger than she believed. She planed her hand through the air, searching for the demon to finish the job. She felt nothing, no acidic presence, no shadow of Mimi looming over her desk.

She returned her hand to the pen. "Where are you, Mimi?"

The pen didn't move.

"Mimi. Answer me. Where are you?"

The pen remained still. Either Mimi was gone or she didn't feel like talking.

Anya shuddered. Having the urge to scrub her hands, she stepped across the hall to the ladies' room. Green subway tile created a soothing, if somewhat institutional, ambiance. She emptied an entire soap pump of pink liquid in her hands, scrubbed until the hot water ran out and her right hand was pink and raw. To hell with her cuticles. She wanted to scrub the stink of demon off her, no matter how much soap and water it took.

She glanced up at the mirror. Her reflection startled her. She looked too drawn, wan. The antibiotics for the infection hadn't kicked in yet. She wanted nothing more than to go home and go to bed.

But she knew that she needed to get some help. Not from the pixie doc, but someone more well-versed in spiritual ills.

She had burnt her bridges with DAGR. There was no one left to ask . . . so she would have to figure this out on her own.

"Thank you for agreeing to meet me, Father."

The elderly priest sat beside Anya in a back pew at St. Florian Catholic Church in Hamtramck. This church possessed a much different grandeur than the Gothic-modern cathedral she'd attended days before. St. Florian remained in traditional Gothic form, warmed by red and gold carpets underfoot. The dark wooden pews had been polished to a deep sheen, and the stained-glass windows cast violet shadows on golden sandstone tiles on the walls. Colorful depictions of saints occupied the niches, wreathed with a riot of yellow and red flowers. Unlike the cathedral, this place felt warm and familiar. The irony that St. Florian was the patron saint of firefighters was not lost on Anya.

This had been the church her mother had taken Anya to when she was a child; this was the church that had overseen her burial, and this was the priest who had tried to counsel Anya after her mother's death. Anya was amazed to learn he was still in the parish, and even more shocked he still remembered her, and that he cleared his schedule to meet with her on such short notice. Anya had spent all night staring at the ceiling, too reluctant to sleep for fear that Mimi would invade her dreams. She'd been amazed that Father Mark himself answered the parish secretary's listed phone number at seven in the morning.

"Of course." Father Mark folded his gnarled hands on his knee. He was entirely bald, stooped with age, but his eye still held the level gleam of confidence. "I remember you. You were the girl who wouldn't speak after your mother's death."

Anya looked forward at the gilded altar, overlaid with red and orange flowers. She hoped the shadow of this holy place upon her would be able to lift the seed of darkness she felt growing in her chest. Perhaps the seed had been there a long time, but she felt it stirring, flowering, and needed someone to show her how to pull it out. "I have carried the guilt of her death with me for a long time, Father. I'm afraid it has tainted many aspects of my life, and I'm beginning to think that my life isn't really my own to control."

It was Father Mark's turn to be silent as she confessed what had happened with her mother, how her mother's death had been caused by Anya's disobedience. The guilt had left her heart fertile ground for so many tragedies: the careless stealing of spirits, rejecting love. Perhaps it even cracked open a door for Mimi to enter. She didn't tell Father Mark these things, but simply told him of the great and terrible darkness she felt weighing upon her. She told him of the arsonist, how he seemed untouchable, and that she feared he would continue unless stopped.

She even told him about DAGR, using a broad brush, and that she'd quit. Anya told him she had felt a most unpleasant presence since she had left, her fear that some bits of her former work clung to her.

Anya told him what she had told no one else: that she was afraid. Afraid that she couldn't stop the arsonist in time. Afraid that Brian wouldn't emerge from his coma. Afraid of being alone, of being unloved and unlovable.

High above in the vaulted arches, a bird had somehow found its way in. It flitted right and left, trying to find a way out, beating its wings against the impassible light of the glass. Anya watched it as she spoke.

Father Mark followed her gaze. "It will find its way out. They always do. And you will find your way out, too."

"Would it be too much to ask for a blessing, Father?" The words nearly stung her parched throat. She had not asked for such a thing, ever. She was sure the priest would send her away, tell her to come back for reindoctrination classes or come to the next mass.

"Though it may be out of the ordinary for a lapsed Catholic, I strongly feel it would be good for your soul to take communion, Anya," Father Mark told her. "You have a task ahead of you in bringing the arsonist to justice and many tasks before you in purifying your heart. I feel the Holy Spirit should be summoned to guide your hands and your heart."

If I don't manage to offend the Holy Spirit by nibbling on it, first, Anya thought. *And I'd much rather have the Holy Spirit guiding my hands than Mimi.*

Father Mark bustled away to prepare the communion. Anya sat alone in the pew, staring up at the bird. She felt a surprising measure of peace. She had hoped that being here might conjure up the smallest shred of belief to help guide her. After quitting DAGR, she felt very, very alone.

Except for Sparky. He laid at her feet, dozing. She leaned down and scratched his ear-gills. He chuffed happily in his slumber. He would always be with her. As long as she had Sparky, she could never be truly alone.

"Father Mark can't see it. But I can."

Anya turned in her pew at the voice behind her. She saw the ghost of a young priest in a black suit, sitting a row behind her. A worry mark was pressed into his brow. He seemed barely old enough to drive, much less to have completed the training. She remembered him from her childhood, pacing the halls outside Father Mark's office. When he lifted his hands to grip the back of the pew, Anya could see the thin white marks of scars circling his wrists like bracelets. A suicide. No wonder he was trapped here.

"See what?" Anya asked.

The young priest leaned forward. His eyes were wild and intense. *"The stain of the demon upon you."*

Anya's hands fluttered up to the bandages on her chest. "You can see that?"

"Yes. And I can see that the demon is taking root in you." His knuckles whitened to the point that they became translucent. *"I've been there. I know."*

"How do you know?" she asked, as dread twitched through her. She'd suspected, worried at it, but the priest had given the terrible thought shape and form. Anya had failed to entirely devour Mimi. The demon had moved from Chloe into her.

"It begins simply enough, as obsession. The demon feeds on it. For me, it was an obsession with a woman." He looked away, and she could see the pain in his eyes. *"But you can't let it take hold. Fight it."*

"How? How can I fight it?"

The priest's gaze was leaden. *"If you cannot defeat the demon through your own virtues, you must transfer it to someone else. Give the burden away."*

Anya leaned back, shocked. She couldn't imagine forcing Mimi on someone else, couldn't imagine a priest advising her to do that. The young priest was clearly mad, unhinged from the way he'd departed life. "I can't do that. This isn't a cold that I can give to someone by sneezing on them, that they'll eventually get over."

"You must. If you can't destroy it, you must pass it on." The young priest looked at her. *"You are needed for other tasks—to*

stop this arsonist, to keep Sirrush from waking. For the greater good, it has to happen. Don't let the demon sacrifice you."

"But, I—" she sputtered. It seemed that the entire underground spiritual world knew about Sirrush. Could they feel that much? Was he that close?

The young priest's ghost sank into the pew and disappeared into the floor. Anya heard the footsteps of the old priest approaching.

She turned. In one hand, he held a gold chalice. "Are you ready?"

"Yes, Father."

She knelt before the altar and recited the Lord's Prayer with Father Mark. She'd always said the Lord's Prayer in the company of others, and her voice seemed a tinny shadow compared to Father Mark's.

Father Mark said, "Deliver us from every evil, Lord, and grant us peace. In your mercy, keep us free from sin. Protect us from all anxiety as we await the coming of our Savior, Jesus Christ."

Anya responded, "For the kingdom, the power, and the glory are yours, now and forever."

"May the peace of the Lord be with you, always." Father Mark presented the transubstantiated body and blood of Christ to the empty church, then lowered the chalice to Anya. "Blood of Christ."

Anya pressed her lips to the cup. The wine scalded her throat and she struggled to swallow. "Amen," she croaked.

Father Mark placed the host on her tongue. "Body of Christ."

The wafer dissolved against the roof of her mouth and she felt it sizzling against her teeth, as if she'd swallowed a fistful of Pop Rocks.

"Amen," she gasped, lowering her head. She hoped that Father Mark thought her to be simply overcome with the power of prayer.

"Bless this child of yours, Lord. Relieve her of her suffering and assist her on her mission. Thanks be to God."

"Thanks be to God," she echoed, but she couldn't hear her own voice. She heard nothing but the sound of the trapped bird beating its wings futilely against the stained glass.

Anya lit a novena candle for Brian and said a prayer, hoping that wherever his spirit was locked away, it would have some small effect. She waited for the spirit of the young priest to return, but he didn't make an appearance. Ghosts were never particularly dependable creatures.

She left the church shortly after sunset. Autumn had reached into all the corners of Hamtramck, painting the leaves on the trees gold and red. The lawn around the ruddy stone of the church had stopped growing, splinters of yellow blades prickling into the carpet of grass. Cirrus clouds scarcely moved in the darkening sky, though a breeze rattled litter and leaves along the gutters. Sparky chased a paper cup rolling along the sidewalk.

She decided to walk home. The living priest and the dead one had given her much to ponder. Like it or not, she needed to face the fact she was being haunted by Mimi. Having seen a handful of these cases with DAGR, she knew the signs. Mimi had gained a toehold in her physical body. If she wasn't careful, she'd come down with a full-blown case of demonic possession like poor Chloe, flailing in her bathtub . . . and that would help no one.

The old priest's ritual had stung her. Anya hoped that meant it had worked, that the communion had driven Mimi away, at least for the time being. Passing Mimi on like a hand-me-down pair of jeans wasn't an option. It went against every last grain of ethics in her; she wouldn't visit the harm Mimi represented on an innocent. It simply wasn't going to happen.

She could go to DAGR. She'd thought about that. But her pride wouldn't allow her to go crawling back to them, to ask for the help that she'd been reluctant to give. No. There would be other solutions, solutions that wouldn't endanger them or her pride. That bridge was burned and she would find another way.

She opened her mailbox and rifled through her mail in the last of the sunshine. Bills. Junk mail. More offers for aluminum siding. Anya stood back and looked at her house. It didn't look that bad to her. Why did they keep bothering her? She fingered past three credit card solicitations before her fingers stilled on an ivory envelope. It was hand addressed to her. She recognized the scrawl from the flower card and the sketch Drake Ferrer had drawn of her in the cathedral.

She slit the envelope with a fingernail and pulled out

the message. It was an invitation to Drake's art opening Friday night at the Detroit Institute of Art. Her brows shot up. What the hell? Was he trying to date her or taunt her?

Her first impulse was to tear it up, but she paused. Why *shouldn't* she? Why shouldn't she take the opportunity to glare at him, to make him uncomfortable . . . to show him she wasn't afraid of him.

She looked down at her feet. "Sparky, do you want to go to a party Friday night?"

Sparky paused in his intense scrutiny of the electric meter. His tail kinked up.

"Yeah. A party. With wine and cheese, snotty art, and an opportunity to bite that nasty man from the graveyard again."

Sparky's tail wagged. He was on board.

Now, she just needed something to wear. Piss. She supposed it would be in poor taste to turn up in her firefighter's boots. She looked down at her hands. Maybe Mimi had been right. She could use a coat of nail polish.

She'd worry about that later. She chucked her mail and her keys on the kitchen table, beside the microwave she had yet to return. The light on her answering machine blinked furiously and she sighed.

She stabbed the button.

"Kalinczyk, this is Marsh. Turn on the news. Call me." That was Marsh: to the point. The time stamp on it was fifteen minutes ago. She hoped she hadn't missed whatever he was talking about.

Anya clicked on the television, an old set plugged into a scorched surge protector. The local evening news was still on, and the news anchors blathered in full-crisis mode. A newscaster in a hardhat was yelling above sirens that obliterated the sound feed. Behind him, she saw an apartment building going up in flames.

Anya put her head in her hands. "Oh, shit."

CHAPTER TWELVE

ANYA'S VISIT TO ST. FLORIAN had apparently done little to improve the karma of firefighters in the greater Detroit area.

By the time Anya arrived at the scene of the apartment fire on the northwest side of town, trucks from five different ladder companies were trying to keep the blaze under control. The fire had apparently begun in one building of twelve units and had spread to another. These were newer apartment buildings, built within the last ten years. Anya would never have considered living in such recent, cheap construction: the siding had melted and the firewalls only reached up to the roofline, allowing the fire to roar through the attic space from one unit to the next. There was a reason why firefighters called so many of the new builds *tinderboxes*. They were built to look good, with enough pretty details to impress the shallow eye, but not all the crown molding and walk-in closets in the world could protect you from a disaster the way solid metal doors and cinder-block firewalls could. There was definitely something to be said for old and ugly.

This fire was a bad one. Anya had passed two ambulances racing to the hospital on her way in. While this wasn't the worst time of day for a fire—most of the people who lived there would be awake—many of the occupants would be home from work and school.

Anya geared up and made her way to the perimeter of the scene. Five apartment buildings were tightly packed around a central parking lot, which was crammed with emergency vehicles. It looked as if a child had dumped out a box of toy cars on his sister's broken dollhouse. Residents wandered, dazed, in the lot. A woman somewhere was crying for her child. A man sat on the bumper of his car with his keys in his hand, watching his home burn. A teenage girl sat on the curb beside a police car, clutching her pet cat. A little boy holding a gerbil cage tagged along beside his mother, who was carrying a baby. The police were trying to keep the civilians out of the lot and behind the line, but more people kept pouring out of the buildings.

A patrolman was trying to hold back a wailing woman trying to cross the line. She was dressed in a waitress uniform, clearly just off work.

"You have to let me in!" she yelled. "My dogs are in there!"

Anya slipped on her helmet. "How many dogs?"

"Two dachshunds. Please get them!"

"Which apartment?"

"It's 1811 . . . A8 . . ." She pointed toward the next block of buildings to go.

"Give me your keys." Though Anya was a big fan of kicking in doors for fun and stress relief, there was no point in being inefficient.

Anya ran to the building, clumsy in her booted feet. The uniform scraped against her burns. She never remembered her uniform being this heavy before.

The waitress's unit was a ground-floor apartment. A plume of smoke drifted from two doors down, and the fire had spread to the roof shingles. She smelled burning tar. With clumsy gloved fingers, she jammed the key into the lock. She hoped with all her might that the woman had crate-trained her dogs, and that she would find a wire cage in the living room that she could simply pick up and carry out.

No such luck. The door opened to reveal a small apartment with a galley kitchen, a pretty decorative fireplace, chintz couch, and no dogs.

She tried whistling. "Here, doggies, c'mon!" She thunked through the apartment, hearing fire crackling in the units above her. There wasn't much time. She looked under the couch, under the desk, and finally under the bed in the bedroom. No dogs.

"Sparky, I need your help," Anya hissed.

Sparky unwound himself from the copper collar around her neck, then scrambled up from her fire-coat collar. His tongue coiled, tasting the smoke.

"We need to find those dogs."

Sparky slithered away, digging into laundry baskets. Anya opened the closets, rifled through the centipedes'

wardrobe of shoes she found at the bottom. No dogs.
Time was running out.

She heard Sparky mew from the bathroom. Anya
rounded the corner, shining her flashlight into the shower,
then behind the toilet. Four frightened eyes peered from
behind a toilet scrubber.

"C'mon, you guys." Anya got down on her hands and
knees to drag the dogs out by the scruffs of their necks.
They nipped and wailed, but there was little damage that
they could do to her gloves or coat. She jammed the dogs
unceremoniously in a laundry basket and backed out of the
bathroom.

"C'mon, Sparky. Let's go." The smoke had grown
thick enough to make her cough and obscure the path to
the door.

Sparky beat his little webbed feet ahead of her, incandescing brightly like a beacon. She followed him into fresh
air, stumbling out over the porch steps. Anya rushed back
over the grass behind the police line, carrying the laundry
basket, with the giant salamander loping beside her. A
woman's bra dangled from the laundry basket, and Sparky
was fascinated by the tassels dangling from it.

Anya ducked under the police tape and dropped the
laundry basket in front of the waitress. She was too out of
breath to speak, coughing against the back of her hand.
The waitress dove into the pile of laundry, pulling out two
squirming brown dogs. One was tangled up in black thong
underwear.

"Ketchup! Mustard! You're all right!" The lingerie-bedecked

dogs slobbered all over her neck, and the waitress started to cry. "Thank you!"

Anya fell back on her ass, bracing herself on her hands. She gave the waitress a sooty grin. Moments like this were when it was all worth it. Maybe St. Florian liked wiener dogs.

As she was catching her breath, she felt a tall, cool shadow fall over her. She looked up to see Captain Marsh tapping his foot.

"Kalinczyk. What the hell do you think you're doing?" His voice was harsh, but she detected a smile under his moustache.

"Um. Roasting wieners, sir." It popped out of her mouth before she'd had the chance to edit it.

"Quit loafing and get over here. I have some info for you."

Anya climbed to her feet. "Sorry, sir. May I ask"—her hand sketched the horizon line of the fire—"why you called me in? It's not cool yet."

"This one is the work of your firebug."

"How do you know?" Anya hoped he was wrong; there was no way any personnel could have gotten into the basements to look at the floors of the laundry rooms for Drake Ferrer's signature.

He pointed to the parking lot. "This is how I know."

A ladder truck pulled aside, exposing the striped center of the parking lot. There, dug into the asphalt, was the mark of the Horned Viper, carved large as the fire truck that just passed over it. It crossed over a dozen painted stripes, gouged into the black center as clearly as if it were painted on the fifty-yard line at the stadium.

Ferrer got around. And now he was just showing off.

The fire had cooled a day later. DFD found two bodies in the rubble: a guy doing laundry and reading porn in the basement who died of smoke inhalation, and a woman in a wheelchair who hadn't been able to get around the stacks of canned goods and bottled water she'd been hoarding for the apocalypse. One person was in the hospital in critical condition and there were a handful of minor injuries. The fire had spread to three apartment buildings, seeming to defy prevailing winds, fire hoses, and chemical foam. It moved like a living thing, surging through the buildings as it flashed over from rooftop to rooftop, until the decision was finally made to sacrifice one of the buildings and focus the entirety of the firefighting on preventing spread to further structures.

Anya had moved to cover the sign of the Horned Viper on the parking lot with a tarp as soon as she'd seen it, but had been too late. A news helicopter had gotten a nice aerial shot of it, and it was plastered all over the news outlets with the byline "Ritual Arsonist Torches Apartment Complex."

Vross held a press conference at DPD headquarters the following morning, once the bodies had been counted and his authority over the scene was made absolute by the administrative machine. He repeated the favor to the media twice a day, in the interest of "keeping the public informed of this serious public safety situation." He'd managed to find a jacket that actually buttoned over his belly, strutting like a chicken with his shiny badge pinned to his chest.

"There's been some suggestion that Satanism is involved. Is that true?" a reporter asked Vross.

Vross screwed up his pudgy face in thought. "There's been some discussion about ritual elements in the crime, yes."

"Are there other arsons connected to this case?"

"Tentatively, yes. DPD feels that there's a connection between some of the more recent crimes and the fire at the apartment complex."

"Which ones?"

"I'm not at liberty to discuss the details of a pending investigation. Suffice it to say, DPD is committing its full resources to find and apprehend the perpetrator—"

Anya killed the video feed on her computer. She'd watched each one of the press conferences he'd been giving for the past two days. Vross had no new information and would continue to mouth her results to the press, twisted with his own bent. Devil worshippers. Christ. She rolled her eyes to the stained ceiling. Vross was a media whore. He'd latch on to anything that would get him in the papers . . . and a story about fire-crazy devil-worshippers just days before Halloween would guarantee him several interviews. The national news might even give a shit.

She simply hoped the media feeding frenzy would keep Vross occupied and out of her hair. That would be the best that could be accomplished for now. Anya had been inundated with messages about whether there were other connected cases. She hadn't returned any of the calls and was avoiding her office. She'd set up a temporary office in the basement of the Detroit Public Library, next to the microfiche readers in the archives. Here, no one bothered her.

Sparky had finally mustered enough interest in the microfiche readers that Felicity had set him up with an old card of newspaper images of gangsters and flapper girls from the Prohibition era. He sat hunched on the desk, playing with the focus knob and horizontal and vertical adjustments. In deep concentration, his tongue curled out of his mouth, and he squealed in delight every so often when an image came into focus.

She studied the photographs she'd taken of the parking lot. A fragment of memory jarred loose. On this large scale, the Horned Viper symbol reminded her of a place she'd visited as a child: Serpent Mound. Built in rural Ohio by Fort Ancient Indians, the mound stretched over a thousand feet long, featuring a horned snake swallowing an egg. To her, the opening of its curved jaws around the egg was strongly reminiscent of the hieratic character of the Horned Viper.

"Hey, Felicity," she whispered.

The librarian's ghost peeked her head out of a cabinet. Anya had asked her to search for records that might tie Ferrer to the burned properties. She had a hunch that the targets, though intended to wake up Sirrush, weren't entirely random. She couldn't imagine any of his actions being less than deliberate.

"Check this out," Felicity said, brushing a long piece of hair behind her ear. "I pulled the addresses of your arsons and cross-checked them against known family members of the perpetrators of Ferrer's assault."

"I thought that the records of the juveniles were expunged."

Felicity rolled her eyes. "Yeah. Well, there's a difference between expungement and sealing. A juvenile's criminal record can be sealed automatically when the kid reaches the age of majority. Alternatively, the kid or his parents can petition the court for an expungement. The expungement requires nearly all traces of the criminal record to be destroyed. If the court isn't petitioned, then the records are simply sealed. Which means they're lying about in a file cabinet in records storage somewhere."

"You can get at those?" Anya asked, surprised.

"I know ghosts at the juvenile detention bureau. You probably can't use any of this in court, but it might point you in the right direction."

"What've you got?"

"The beauty shop that burned down, Hair Out There, was owned by one of the suspects' mothers."

"No kidding?"

"Yep. And the warehouse fire? One of the people leasing storage space from the owner was one of the suspects. Your firebug apparently managed to torch all of the possessions he left stateside before joining the military."

"Interesting." Anya leaned back in her chair. "Sounds like Ferrer is trying to cause a bit of misery to his perpetrators while he's at it."

"I'm going to keep looking for connections. I'll keep you posted." The hippie librarian made to duck back behind a wall, but Anya called out for her to wait.

"Felicity, can I ask you to switch gears for a moment?" Anya felt guilty about bugging the librarian, but the heart-shaped face seemed to brighten with each new question.

"Sure. You're the only customer I've had in decades. I'm all yours."

"Thanks. I appreciate it." Anya blew out her breath. "This may be a wild-goose chase, but can you find me anything on Serpent Mound in Ohio?"

"That's easy," Felicity chirped. "You'll have to come with me, though. Those books will be too heavy for me to carry."

Anya grabbed her gear and followed the spirit up the stairs to the second floor. Felicity drifted among the stacks and pointed to a shelf.

"Here you go."

Anya was impressed. "I can't believe you've memorized where everything is."

"I've read most everything in this section. Things get boring." She sighed. "But I have to say, if you ever get the choice to be a ghost, becoming one in a library is the way to go. Decades of entertainment await."

Anya crawled down on her hands and knees, brushing

her fingers over the titles. "I hope it's not too personal, but how did you come to be a library ghost?"

Felicity shrugged. "It's not a terribly exciting story. I was interning here during a remodel. A fifty-pound bucket of drywall patch fell off some scaffolding and hit me in the head. Not much to tell."

"But . . ." Anya tried to word it delicately. She had a lot of questions lately about what came *after*. " . . . There wasn't a bright light or anything that took you?"

"Nope. There was no big, glowing vacuum cleaner in the sky that sucked my soul up. I just remember making a decision: stay here or move on. Since there were books here I hadn't read and I couldn't imagine not reading them, I stayed. I mean"—she stuffed her hands in her pockets—"I had just picked up *Jonathan Livingston Seagull* when the bucket hit me. I couldn't live with myself if I didn't find out how it ended."

"Do you think you'll always stay?"

Felicity's eyes roved over the stacks. "As the afterlife goes, I'm quite content. I may consider moving on after I've read every book here . . . and if there aren't going to be any new ones I'm interested in." Her eye twinkled when she spoke. "So I guess I'm going to be here a very, very long time."

Anya smiled. "It sounds like a very pleasant eternity." Much more pleasant than the ones she imagined for the spirits she'd devoured.

She opened a book on her lap and flipped to the color plates of Serpent Mound in the center. These were aerial photos of the effigy, faded a bit with time. Indeed, the curve of its open mouth seemed almost identical to the horns on Ferrer's symbol. The pictures were as she remembered it: a shallow mound covered in closely mowed grass with lawnmower tracks in it, surrounded by forest.

She remembered her mother taking her there when she'd been on summer vacation. It was one of the rare times her mother had taken her out of the city for a trip, and Anya had watched the flat farmland of Michigan and northwestern Ohio give way to the rolling, forested hills of southern Ohio. It was a completely different world than the one Anya had grown up in. Here, hawks perched on power lines, buzzards circled overhead, and jet contrails barely interrupted the blue of the sky. Grass, honeysuckle, and trees grew wild, untamed by sidewalks or yards.

Anya recalled walking around the edges of the mound with her mother. She hadn't been impressed at the time. The mound wasn't more than three feet high and it seemed to melt into the grass, like a sea serpent sleeping. Sparky had thoroughly enjoyed himself, gamboling over the giant serpent's body and chasing chipmunks through the grass.

Anya's mother had stood over the serpent in an attitude of reverence. She had only seen her mother's face that pensive in church.

"What is it, Mom?" she asked.

Anya's mother pointed from the nose to the tail of the effigy. "This is the sleeping place of a great serpent. They all sleep underground."

Anya wrinkled her brow. "The museum said that people

once thought Native Americans were buried here. But they haven't found anything, so they don't think so anymore."

"They were, aboveground, to guard the serpent," her mother said with certainty. "But below it, the serpent sleeps."

Anya looked sidelong at her mother. No matter what the museum placard said, her mother would tell her the truth. Her mother wasn't given to flights of fancy, and she seemed to be serious in the fairy tale she was spinning now.

"Is it a salamander, like Sparky?"

Sparky had given up on the chipmunks and had turned his attention to a cabbage butterfly. The butterfly seemed blissfully unaware that the salamander was chasing it, twisting his body in the air like a dog after a Frisbee.

She shook her head. "No. It's related to Sparky, though. There are much larger serpents in the world than Sparky, my dear. And ones much larger than this one."

Anya shuddered. "I hope I never see one bigger than Sparky."

Anya's mother put her arm around her. "I hope that you don't, either."

It had seemed to be a very innocent educational field trip, like going to the Henry Ford Museum or the zoo. But it had also felt like a pilgrimage, and Anya hadn't really understood what she was supposed to learn from it. This wasn't a grand, glorious place like the Detroit Historical Museum or the Science Center. There wasn't anything to *do*. It was just dirt and grass. Nothing special.

But perhaps it had been something special after all.

Anya opened a chapter on the site's geology, and her hand stilled on the page:

> . . . the underlying bedrock on which the mound sits displays a rare cryptoexplosion structure. Microscopic shattering and melting in the bedrock suggests that this geologic anomaly is the result of an explosive force, such as magma and volcanic gases or the impact of a meteor. The source of the anomaly is up for debate, but it is clear that great pressure and heat affected this area, possibly dating back to the Permian period.

The page showed a photograph of striated rock that was identical to the melting patterns the crime lab had shown her in the concrete at the crime scene.

"Felicity," Anya asked. "Can you get me driving directions to Serpent Mound?"

While the librarian ghost disappeared to get the information, Anya's fingers splayed over the glossy page. Though she hadn't felt it when she was a little girl, she now felt this place was special. And perhaps it would hold a clue to Sirrush and his slumber.

She glanced at her watch. The library was getting ready to close. Much as she wanted to drive down to Serpent Mound this afternoon, it would be impossible. Drake Ferrer's exhibit opening was tonight and she wanted to make him as uncomfortable as possible.

Even if that meant wearing a dress.

CHAPTER THIRTEEN

SACRIFICES WERE ALWAYS MADE IN the name of good investigative work.

This was one of the worst ones Anya had ever made.

Anya stood in a three-way mirror at a dress boutique entirely too devoted to the color pink. Her socks drooped around her ankles, her legs were unshaven, and she was trying to convince the saleswoman to sell her a dress that would cover bandages up to her armpits. She was currently stuffed into an orange dress with a fabric corsage on the shoulder that looked like a traffic cone had regurgitated on her. Sparky stood beside her in the mirror, watching how his tail was displayed when he wiggled it from three perspectives.

"Look," Anya said. "I'm not interested in a prom dress. I want a plain, adult dress. Something in black."

The saleswoman folded her arms and pursed her lips. She was a prune of a woman with short hair and entirely too much eyeliner. "I don't really have anything else that will fit you, dear."

Anya's brows shot up. "What the hell does that mean?"

"That means," the saleswoman said, "that we don't have anything else in season in your size."

"I wear a size eight," Anya said frostily.

"Of course you do, dear." The saleswoman's mouth turned upward in a patronizing smile.

"You can have this monstrosity back." Anya yanked the dress over her head, heedless of the sequins. She dumped it in the saleswoman's arms and stalked back to the dressing room for her clothes. She gave the saleswoman a good view of her black-panty-clad ass and bandage bra as she stormed away. The black menswear socks were a nice touch, too.

When she exited the dressing room, the saleswoman was plucking the orange dress back into shape on the hanger.

"There's no need to be huffy, dear," the saleswoman said.

Anya sneered at her. "And there's no need for you to be a complete and utter bitch."

She slammed the door behind her and stormed out on the sidewalk. Sparky waddled past her, confused. Her fuse was growing shorter and shorter lately, and she struggled to keep her snarkiness in check.

"I *am* a size eight," Anya muttered to him and a passerby gave her a strange look. "It says so on the inside of my pants."

Anya was fast running out of options. It was past five o'clock and downtown was shutting down. She needed to get a damn dress, and quick. How hard could it possibly be? Christ, it wasn't like she was looking for a swimsuit.

She paused before a shop window full of exotic lingerie. Mannequins posed inside the window before a velvet curtain wore peek-a-boo bustiers, miniskirts, and fishnet stockings. A line of high-heeled fuck-me pumps dangled from ribbons at the ceiling. But the lights were still on inside.

Anya looked up at the sign. The store was called Wild Walt's Leather 'n' Lace.

What the hell.

She opened the door and was immediately struck by the smell of patchouli and oiled leather. Boxes of thigh-high boots and biker boots lined the walls, and racks of garments made almost entirely of strings and buckles jingled near the front. A salesgirl looked up from the counter. Her long black hair was gathered in ponytails on the sides of her head, and her lip was pierced with a chain that reached back to her ear. She was the polar opposite of the prune in the dress shop.

"May I help you?" she asked.

"Yes, please. I need a dress."

"Sure. What kind of dress?"

"Something black. Something that will cover this." Anya shrugged her blouse to show her bandages peeking out from her neckline.

"New tat?" the salesgirl asked.

"Um. Yeah. New tattoo gone wrong."

"No problem." The salesgirl hopped over the counter.

She clunked in her combat boots over to a rack, started plucking out hangers. A girl who wore combat boots was much better qualified to dress her than the pastel-clad biddy in the pink shop, Anya decided.

She shooed Sparky from a display of edible body paint. He skittered away and began batting at a shirt made of chain mail.

"Are you looking for a dance dress or a bedroom dress?"

"Um. Dance." Anya had no idea what that meant, but figured that *dance* sounded like a safer option than *bedroom*.

"Try these." The salesgirl popped her gum and led her back to the dressing area. She pulled out a few discarded bras that looked to be made of snakeskin. Anya assumed that these had been rejected by the previous customer in favor of the edible bras made of candy. The salesgirl hung the dresses on the hook and left Anya to her own devices.

Anya pulled the first dress on. It was made of a matte satin, very low-gloss. It hit her at the knee, very demurely, but the top was a corset that perfectly covered her bandages. Anya fumbled with the cords in the back until the salesgirl came in to check on her.

"Put your hands on your hips like a superhero," the salesgirl commanded. "Turn around."

Anya obeyed, shooting Sparky a worried look. The salesgirl laced her into the corset, tugging the laces so that the boning gripped tightly around her ribs. She felt a stab of panic, as if she were being trapped in the viselike fist of some fearsome beast from the 1800s. But the panic dissolved as the corset seemed to mold around her in a re-assuring embrace.

The salesgirl stepped back. "Take a look."

"Holy shit," Anya blurted. "I look like a girl."

The dress fit her like a glove, perfectly hugging every curve. It was long enough to require a kick-pleat in the back, and the built-in corset emphasized her narrow waist and the swell of her breasts.

Sparky wagged his tail.

"You like?" she asked Sparky, but the salesclerk answered instead, as if it were an entirely ordinary question.

"You're a smokin' hot dungeon mistress," the salesclerk said.

"What size is it?" Anya asked.

The salesgirl looked at the tag in the back. "It's a six."

"I'll take it."

"Do you have shoes?" the clerk asked.

Anya stared down at her black flats. "Um. No." She pointed at a pair of stilettos on the wall. "Those scare me."

"Those are bedroom shoes." She waved dismissively at them. "You need a dance shoe."

"But I'm not doing any dancing . . ."

The clerk didn't treat her like she was an idiot. She patiently explained the difference between dance shoes and bedroom shoes—dance shoes were apparently the ones used by girls onstage, that were designed to actually be walked in.

"That's an industry secret," the salesgirl said. "Department-store shoes hurt like hell. You can run a marathon in dance shoes. Hell, men wear these things. And even men dressing like women wouldn't put up with bad shoes."

Anya picked a pair of rounded-toe ankle-strap dance shoes that the clerk said were "very retro." Anya was shocked that they felt no more uncomfortable than flats. Her weight was perfectly balanced between the heel and her toes.

"I'm impressed. These actually feel really good."

"Just don't tell the soccer moms. We want them to suffer." The salesgirl winked.

Fifteen minutes later, Anya was walking out of the store with a bag in hand. She'd picked up a treat for Sparky: a tube of mysterious glitter gel that Sparky simply would not leave alone. Overjoyed, he gamboled at her heels, nosing at the bag. Glitter must contain some kind of elemental pheromone, she thought.

She'd opted to wear the dress home, doubtful of her ability to get in and out of it without the clerk's assistance. But it was worth it. Even under her jacket, she felt every bit as powerful as any dungeon mistress who ever shopped at Wild Walt's Leather 'n' Lace.

Armed with stripper shoes and a killer dress, she'd be more than ready for anything Drake Ferrer could throw at her.

Anya had never visited the Detroit Institute of Arts at night. All of her elementary-school field trips had been during the day, when the museum was crowded with kids in large groups ushered by teachers, by elderly people looking to while away the day, and by tourists repeatedly told by security to turn the flash off their cameras. Then, it had seemed like a haven for those escaping from the workaday world by virtue of age or geography.

After dark, it was entirely different. It was clearly a place for adults who would keep their grubby fingers off the canvases. Not just any adults—adults who appeared in glossy black cars, dripping with watches and pieces of jewelry that easily exceeded Anya's annual salary.

Anya climbed out of the cab, feeling rather intimidated at the elegant façade of the building lit for night with sweeping uplights. A cast of Rodin's *The Thinker* perched in the front plaza. When she had been seven or eight, he merely looked like a constipated man contemplating what he'd eaten for lunch. Now, with the benefit of time and artful lighting, he looked as if he were closely scrutinizing who would be permitted to enter the premises. The ultimate bouncer.

Anya's stripper shoes clicked softly on the concrete as she climbed the steps to hand her invitation to one of the white-gloved doormen. He nodded and opened the door for her, and she stepped into the Great Hall.

The vaulted, coffered ceilings of the Great Hall were strewn with chandeliers and mosaic-work. Thousands of strings of reflective silver disks hung from the ceiling, gleaming like stars in the half darkness. Voices, footfalls, and a breeze rattled through them as they turned. Suits of armor were stationed at regular intervals on the glossy floor, encased in glass and dwarfed by the display overhead. The reflections of the empty knights and artificial stars gleamed on the polished floors, as if reflected in a black pool.

One suit of armor caught her eye. Anya leaned closer, feeling Sparky's tail twitch against her collarbone. The thin skin of a ghost still occupied that shell of ancient armor, as inextricably entwined in it as a beetle in its carapace. All she could detect of it was its eyes glinting behind a slitted visor. Whatever kind of soldier the ghost had been, it now guarded this vault of stars and the treasure beyond it. Anya sensed no volition in it, no desire to speak, only to watch.

She left it alone. She hoped that Drake Ferrer would, too.

Anya followed the other invitees through a walkway of velvet ropes to the south wing, where the majority of the museum's twentieth-century art was held. The patrons walked through galleries open three floors to the ceiling, skylights casting paned shadows on the inlaid floors. Ferrer's exhibit was held in an airy, modern exhibit space with simple white walls and a dark floor. Coffered ceilings concealed down lights that highlighted a mixture of his blueprints and elevation sketches. The sign outside the door called the exhibition *Designs for a New Detroit*.

Anya melted into the crowd, feeling the chatter wash over her. She gazed at the first pictures in the series, blueprints showing an unfamiliar plan for downtown Detroit. Nearly all the buildings built within the last fifty years were gone, replaced by new structures that seemed to blend seamlessly with the 1920s architecture—a revival of Detroit's aesthetic heyday, its boom times come to life again. She didn't recognize all the features in Ferrer's skyline; some of the casinos were gone, replaced by what looked like apartment buildings rendered in bright colors.

Ferrer didn't stop with the architecture. Some of his casual drawings showed trees, meandering parks curving around existing and new buildings. Pedestrians milled on sidewalks lined with shops and restaurants. When she looked closely, she could see that Ferrer had costumed his people in clothes with lines speaking of Old Detroit . . . she even spotted some Jazz Age fringe peeking out from under a woman's skirt.

It was like looking at the old and new, all at once. Instead of warring with each other, the past and future melded seamlessly together. The elements of classical Art Deco were foremost in his designs: the geometric forms, the nod to ancient Egyptian stylized flowers and motifs. It was not hard to imagine how Ferrer would have discovered the symbol of the Horned Viper—his drawings were steeped in the memory of pyramids reaching to the sky, crowned with metallic caps in geometric patterns. His buildings opened onto gardens dotted with columnar statuary, the languorous steps of his public buildings spilling down into the streets

In his vision, he'd made the city a temple to a new age. And the view was breathtaking.

Anya bent down to examine the dates of his work. Most of these were not recent, dating from the late 1990s.

The only work she found of this year's vintage was at the end of the exhibit, a depiction of a park on the waterfront where warehouses now stood. It wasn't a blueprint, elevation, or a schematic. Instead, it was a simple sketch. The charcoal on this drawing was still fresh; Anya could smell the acetone of the fixative on the page as she bent near it.

The central figure in the park was a woman leaning on a railing, looking out at the water. The woman wore a long, dark coat, and her hair was pinned off her neck. A torque shaped like a salamander was wrapped around her throat . . . the throat of a woman who was an exact likeness of Anya.

Mimi's voice curdled up in the back of Anya's head. *"I think he likes you."*

Anya's fingers wound in her own necklace, feeling Sparky moving against her skin. Perhaps Sparky could feel Mimi moving within her.

"Do you like it?"

Anya started. Ferrer was at her elbow, looking over her shoulder. His breath disturbed a tendril of hair on the back of her neck. Anya stifled a shiver, and Sparky growled. He was dressed in a black suit and white dress shirt, eschewing a tie. Hands casually resting in his pockets, he looked every inch the dark, brooding artist.

Mimi's voice whispered in her ear: *"Yum. I think I like him."*

Anya ignored her and glanced at Ferrer. "Is this your vision of the new world? The world after fire?"

Ferrer laughed. "As it's clear that you're not wearing

a wire . . ." His gaze roved over her bare shoulders and arms, the laces of her corset. "I can tell you that, yes, it is. And you look . . . amazing." He took a step back to look her up and down, from the top of her head to the toes of her shoes. "That dress . . ."

She lifted an eyebrow and told him matter-of-factly, *"Thank you. It's from a fetish shop."* The voice that came out of her mouth wasn't hers; it was Mimi's. It tasted like charcoal. Anya bit down hard on her tongue to shut the demon up. It was a bad sign that the demon's control had extended from her hand to her mouth.

Ferrer smiled. "You continue to surprise me."

"Your drawings are lovely," she told him in her own voice, turning the subject away.

"Thank you. But it's clear you don't think much of the measures it would take to bring them into reality."

"I think you're a monster," she said coolly. "And I will catch you."

"I have no doubt that you'll try." He glanced at the crowd, busily murmuring over his work. His attention slid to the door. "Would you like for me to show you another monster? A relative of Sirrush?"

"How about you tell me where Sirrush is?"

"Nope. That's secret. But I'll show you his brother."

Anya leaned forward and backward on her stripper heels, deliberating. Ferrer was a monster, not to be trusted. For whatever reason, he'd fixated on her—for all she knew, he'd feed her to Sirrush for lunch. But . . . there was an undeniable aura of magnetism about him. He was the only other Lantern she'd met, and she wanted to learn more about him. He was a monster, but he was like her.

And surely that's worth something? She didn't know if the thought was her own, or Mimi's. Sparky slithered around her neck like a hot noose.

She swallowed, then decided. "Show me Sirrush's brother."

He took her hand. His skin fairly crackled against hers, and she smothered a gasp. He glanced back at her, and she was certain he felt it, too. Ferrer led her from the gallery, lifting a velvet rope up over the exit. She ducked under, allowing him to lead her into the darkness of a side corridor.

"Where are we going?" she asked.

"Ancient Babylon."

He led her into the light of a much larger gallery with ornate ceilings. Bits of ancient weapons, mosaics, and urns glimmered behind glass. Anya paused before a broken piece of frieze under glass. A figure of an armored woman stood beside a lion, holding a sword in one hand, and a lotus blossom in the other. Her hair was plaited in braids underneath her helmet, and her feet were the claws of an eagle.

Drake followed her gaze. "That's Ishtar, the Babylonian goddess of love, war, and sex. She was based on the Sumerian goddess Inanna. She wasn't a typical goddess of romantic love. All of her consorts wound up enslaved or dead."

"Charming," Anya murmured, but she couldn't tear herself away from Ishtar's stone face. There was something compelling about her image . . . the heat, the serenity, the fearlessness she sensed in her posture and the lift of her chin.

"There's a myth that I particularly like about her descent to the underworld." Drake unwound the ribbon of the tale under the stone goddess's glare. "Ishtar descended to the underworld to retrieve one of her lovers . . . or to conquer the underworld, depending on who's doing the telling. She passed through the seven gates of the underworld, surrendering a piece of her clothing in exchange for passage through each one. She arrived, naked and unarmed, before her sister, Ereshkigal, the goddess of the underworld.

"Ereshkigal wasn't happy to see her. She visited sixty plagues on Ishtar and strung her corpse up on a hook in her throne room. All romantic love died on earth in her absence—even the beasts of the fields stopped mating.

"The gods made a bargain to retrieve Ishtar, in order to save the future of civilization. Ishtar was revived and escorted out of the underworld by Ereshkigal's demons. But the demons wouldn't permit her to be freed unless someone else took her place in the underworld."

"I imagine that demons were much the same then as they are now," Anya observed, unconsciously lifting her hand to her burnt sternum. "Mercenary."

"Yes." Drake's eyes followed her hand, but he didn't comment on it. "The demons followed her as she wandered the earth. Ishtar rejected each human who they suggested be sent in her place, for she saw good in each one she met and couldn't bear the thought of exiling them to the underworld.

"At last, Ishtar came up on her husband, Dumuzi, who hadn't been mourning in her absence. She told the demons to take him instead. And Dumuzi was hauled to the bottom of hell to be hung as a corpse on a hook for his lack of sympathy."

Anya lifted a brow. "A very unusual goddess."

"She was quite ruthless, in her way." An inscrutable smile played upon Drake's mouth. "But she is not what I meant to show you."

He led Anya to a case holding a blue mosaic tile. "This is part of the Ishtar Gate from the walls of Ancient Babylon, the eighth gate to the inner city. It was built by Nebuchadnezzar II about six hundred years before Christ. The Processional Way, the path of Ishtar's priestesses, passed through this gate. It was decorated with symbols of creatures sacred to the goddess Ishtar: lions, dragons, and bulls. This is one of the Sirrush, the dragons, from the gate. There were originally more than three hundred dragons, one to represent each one of the ancient world.

"There is an old story called 'Bel and the Dragon,' describing one of these great serpents in a temple that Nebuchadnezzar built. The story goes that the Sirrush had been worshipped as a god."

Anya leaned forward to stare at the glazed blue tile. A border of red and white flowers surrounded the figure of a golden dragon, with a long tail, four clawed legs, and a sinewy body. Its forelegs were feline paws, and the hind legs tapered into an eagle's talons. Horns crowned its head, like the Horned Viper sigil. Even in miniature tile, the Sirrush had a spidery, poisonous grace about it.

"This is the type of creature you hope to summon? A Sirrush?"

"Only a creature with that kind of power could scour this place clean of the decay." His fists were balled together.

Anya touched his sleeve. "I know what those kids did to you. But this isn't the answer."

He shook his head. "You don't understand. I gave everything to this city. Everything. They took my sight . . . I can't see perspective anymore. I can't draw even the simplest building plans with one eye. All I have are the old plans you saw tonight, the ones I drew before the attack." Pain laced his voice, and Anya could not imagine what it had cost him to lose his vision, his livelihood, his passion . . . She guessed it would be like losing her own arm. "Now, I can only draw in two dimensions . . . like a child.

"It's time for me to start taking back," he told her. His free hand was pressed to the glass over the tile. The heat from his skin condensed water droplets on the surface.

She felt sympathy for him, for his terrible isolation. She understood. Her hand, unbidden, reached toward his, laced in his fingers against the glass case. His fingers knit in hers, knuckles whitening. A fine spiderweb of scars laced over his hand.

She drew back. She could feel Mimi's darkness coiling in her gut, feeding on her visceral attraction to Ferrer.

Like a worm, she could feel Mimi burrowing into the cold soil in which she'd buried her physical desire for so many years. She felt it welling in her chest like groundwater, suffusing her with an unreasoning need to feel his skin hot against hers.

Ferrer caught her, one hand slipping behind her neck and the other pulling her trapped hand to his chest. Sparky growled around her throat. Ferrer's breath scalded her cheek, and his mouth dipped toward hers.

She tried to turn away, but the darkness in her gut and her chest reached out for him, for the burning light of another Lantern. The kiss was powerful enough to bruise her lips, it stole the breath from her lungs. She felt her body leaning into his, drinking in the raw power she sensed shimmering beneath his skin. She felt his aura flare red, seeping into the surge of amber light she felt filling her throat.

It felt . . . God, help her . . . it felt like the purest sense of belonging she'd ever known.

She reached her hands up to his face, fingers trailing over the scars on his brow. Under her palms, she felt his pulse quickening, humming through his blood vessels. She could feel it, now: the irresistible force of nature that burned everything in its path. His body pressed her against the glass case, and she felt the heat of the fire before her and the ancient spirit of the dragon behind her.

Underneath her own skin, she felt blackness sidling toward him, pressing her chest to his. Tangled in her own desire, the tendrils of darkness wanted to feel that fire pressing against every inch of her body, wanted to feel it burning away her fear and her sense of aloneness.

She gasped, breaking away from the kiss.

Sparky lashed out, biting Ferrer on the shoulder like a striking snake. Ferrer stumbled back, startled, as Anya slid away from the cabinet. Sparky pooled around her feet, growling.

Ferrer's hand clasped his shoulder, but he smiled.

Anya walked away as fast as her stripper shoes would carry her, clicking on the marble in time with her pulse. In her head, she heard Mimi giggling.

Ferrer called after her, "You're a part of this now, Anya. You can't walk away from it."

She forced herself to put one foot in front of the other. She might not be able to walk away from the case, but she could sure as hell walk away from him.

"For now," Mimi whispered in her ear. *"Only for now."*

CHAPTER FOURTEEN

ANYA'S DREAMS WERE CROWDED that night.

She dreamed she was running in the vault of the ice cave, searching for Sirrush. Sparky ran beside her and the little girl from the pop machine was far ahead of her, braids flying. No matter how hard Anya ran, she couldn't catch up with her, to hold her back from running into the darkness where she knew Sirrush waited.

Behind her, she felt Mimi's fetid breath on her neck. Without turning, she could feel the demon overtaking her, feel the acidic tongues of the demon's filaments snatching at her skin. Still unable to fully draw human shape, its amorphous shadow was hot at her back, shifting and oozing as it pursued.

She slipped on the ice, her hands and elbows crashing down to the cave floor. The demon reached out and grabbed Anya's ankle with a black tendril spiraling around her leg. Where it touched, it burned like acid. Mimi dragged her back, howling. Splinters of ice dug into her forearms and knees as she kicked and struggled in Mimi's grip.

"You won't escape me, little Lantern. I've been waiting a long time for someone like you."

She had thought Mimi to be nothing more than a nuisance, a childlike trickster. But now she felt the full magnitude of the demon's hunger.

Sparky skidded, turning to attack the demon. Mimi lashed out, knocking Sparky ass over teakettle. He yelped as if he'd been hit by a car, and tumbled out of her periphery.

"What the hell do you want with me?" Anya growled.

"I want . . ." The diaphanous black shadow loomed over her. *"I want to wear your skin like a dress, little Lantern. I want to feel every skip and beat of that glowing heart."* Mimi reached into Anya's chest and squeezed, bringing tears to Anya's eyes. *"I want to taste your tears and know the flavor of your blood. I want to experience every ache and yearning in your pathetic little body.*

"And when I'm through with you, when I've used up every last bit of blood and bone, every shred of sensation . . . I'm going to feed you to Sirrush. I'm sure he'll look kindly on such a gift—and give me a fine place in his new order."

The darkness washed over her like the cloak of night, a night with no stars.

Anya awoke, gasping. She bolted upright in bed, knocking Sparky over and flinging his Gloworm to the floor.

She pressed her hands to her burnt chest and tried to steady her heart pounding behind her ribs. Sparky crawled into her lap and licked her face with his warm tongue. Anya put her arms around him and sobbed. The sobs racked her chest so hard she felt her skin split and blisters break. Sparky wound around her tightly, resting his head in the crook of her neck.

She reached down to grab his Gloworm, which had rolled underneath the bed. Wearing Sparky like a stole, she leaned down at an awkward angle, reaching farther under the bed for Sparky's toy. Something hot scraped across her fingers.

She snatched her hand back, skin crawling. Slowly, deliberately, she climbed out of bed, put one foot on the floor and then the other. She bent to peer underneath the bed. She could see the Gloworm, its smiling face looking toward her. Steeling herself, she reached into the darkness . . .

And the darkness reached back. The darkness wrapped around her wrist as surely as it had in her dream, dragging her under the bed. Anya wrested her arm back.

Sparky, teeth gnashing, dove underneath the bed.

Anya kicked the futon. The frame bounced against the wall, scraping against the hardwood floor. She kicked it again, and it bounced against the opposite wall, exposing the darkness beneath the bed.

But there was only Sparky, hunched over his toy, growling at the air.

"Mimi." Anya stood, turning on her heel. "Mimi, get the fuck out of here."

"I'm quite comfortable here, thank you."

It took Anya a moment to realize that Mimi had answered in her own voice. Anya clapped her hand over her mouth. The bitch had seized control of her voice, and was manipulating her waking reality. Anya dreaded imagining what else Mimi was capable of.

She glanced at her bedside clock, which read three thirty-five. Oddly, the date on the digital clock was wrong. It should be Saturday morning . . . but the clock read SUN. Anya squinted at it, rubbed her eyes. She flipped open her cell phone, confirmed that it was indeed Sunday.

The tiny scrap of dream controlled by Mimi had ballooned, had taken over. She'd been asleep for twenty-four hours.

Only then did she glance down at herself. Her forearms were scratched and bleeding. Underneath her fingernails, she could see bits of her own skin from where she'd clawed at herself in her sleep . . . perhaps struggling with Mimi, or with herself.

This had to stop. She'd been lucky Mimi hadn't mustered up enough volition to force Anya to scrape her own eyes out.

She picked up the phone and punched the buttons with a finger that shook.

"Hey, Katie. It's Anya. Can . . . can I come over?"

Katie opened the door, took a step back. It was as if a draft struck her, and she blinked. She looked like a character from a Regency romance, loose Pre-Raphaelite hair flowing over her ruffled, organic cotton nightgown. She was just missing a candlestick in one hand and a crush on a guy with a name like Heathcliff.

Anya stood on Katie's doorstep, her hands jammed in her pockets. She was certain that she looked a mess: hair wild over her shoulders, dressed in jeans, an old T-shirt, and a salamander draped around her shoulders, sucking his tail.

"I'm really sorry to bother you."

"Come in and sit down." She pulled back the screen door, ushering Anya in without touching her. Her bare feet curled against the concrete step.

Though the living room lamps were lit, Katie turned on the overhead light, and the kitchen light. She lit all the candles on the coffee table before she turned her full attention to Anya. Anya sat on the couch, her arms around her elbows, tangled in her jacket and Sparky. The cats were nowhere to be seen.

"You said on the phone that you were seeing things, hearing voices."

"Yeah. I think that I screwed up the exorcism of the girl, Chloe . . . I think the demon's attached itself to me."

"What makes you think that?" Katie perched at the opposite end of the couch. She was treating Anya as she would any other client, like any good investigator.

"I've had an incident of automatic writing. I hear the demon's voice—its name is Mimiveh, by the way—in my head. It's taken control of my voice on a number of occasions. It was in my dreams again last night, and I felt like it was manifesting under the bed. And . . . I slept through a full twenty-four hours, though it felt like just two. And Mimi's starting to leave marks." Anya rolled up her sleeve to show Katie the scratches.

"What have you done about it so far?"

Anya's mouth quirked upward. "I took communion."

Katie lifted her eyebrows. "Wow. This *is* serious."

Anya shrugged. "Yeah, well. Any port in a storm, and all that."

"Let me take a look." Katie closed her eyes, brushed her hand in an outline around Anya's aura. Her hands stilled above Anya's chest, and she withdrew them.

"Well?" Anya asked, dreading the answer.

Katie rubbed her hands, as if trying to brush some invisible dirt away. "You've got problems."

"How big?"

"Elephantine." Katie frowned. "The demon's anchored itself in your aura, feeding off of it. I recognize some of the elements of it from when it was in Chloe . . . the way it moves, the way it vibrates. But your aura is much stronger than hers, and it's become much, much more powerful."

"I thought most possession cases required the victim to open some sort of door to the demon."

"My best guess is there was something about your emotional state that made you vulnerable. You might just have been having a shitty day. That and the effort to try and devour the demon might have given it a foothold."

"How do I get rid of it?"

Katie shook her head. "I've never seen a demon of this magnitude before. I'm going to have to figure something out with Ciro. This is his area."

"Ciro's sick. He's got enough to worry about."

Bothering Katie was bad enough. Bugging Ciro after she'd given DAGR the metaphorical finger wasn't good form.

"And so are you." Katie's voluptuous mouth pressed into a thin slash. "This isn't something you can play around with. This demon is stronger than your power. I know you've never run across this before, but you can't take this lightly."

"I'm running into a lot of things more powerful than me lately. It's a great lesson in humility." She told Katie the Cliffs Notes version of her adventures with Drake Ferrer, omitting the kiss and the irresistible pull she felt toward him. "Can't you tranquilize this thing for a while?"

"Anya, you know this is serious. Why else would you be here in the middle of the night?"

The guilt barb hit home. Anya hung her head. "Look, nailing Drake Ferrer is my top priority. This thing with the demon is secondary."

"'Nailing Drake Ferrer'?" Katie gave her an arch glance.

Anya shook her head. "Mimi—that's what I've been calling the demon—is attracted to him."

"And you're not?"

"Not enough to act on it." She pressed the heels of her hands to her eyes. "I think. I don't know." She peeked over the tops of her fingers. "Okay, you're right. I'm fucked up."

"You are." Katie nodded sagely. "Acknowledging that you're fucked up is the first step toward sanity."

Anya felt like a drug addict begging for pills. "But

don't you have something that can get me through today . . . ?"

Katie rolled her eyes. "Hang on. I'll see what I have." She climbed off the couch and headed down the hallway. Anya noticed that she turned all the lights on as she went. The demon Anya was incubating must truly be a badass, she mused.

Sparky lifted his head. His tail was gooey with salamander spit, and his eyes brimmed with anxiety. Anya stroked the divot in his skull between his eyes. He jammed his head into her armpit, sighing. She held him like he was a child, rocking him, wishing that she could do more to reassure him. "It's gonna be okay. I'm not going to leave you."

Katie returned, holding something behind her back. "This is your spiritual Band-Aid."

Anya reached toward her.

Katie danced away. "Ah-ah. You can't have it until you agree to my conditions."

"Mercenary witch. What are your conditions?"

Katie lifted a finger. "You can't sleep alone."

Anya blinked. "Excuse me?"

"If Mimi has enough control over you to exercise volition while you sleep . . . you could wake up next time someplace you might not want to be, with no recollection of how you got there."

Anya frowned. Mimi seemed just sadistic enough to make her perform a striptease at the sex offender registration desk at the sheriff's office. Reluctantly, she caved. "Okay."

Katie continued to wag her finger before Anya's nose. "You have to follow my instructions and Ciro's instructions. Witch's orders. Or else you're grounded."

"Yes, mama witch. Now, what's in the box?"

Katie showed her a jar with a flourish. It was about the size of a chip-dip jar, labeled GINO'S GARLIC BUTTER.

"You're going to feed me?" Anya brightened.

"No. It's bespelled garlic butter. Use it as an ointment. Apply liberally to the affected area, twice a day. In your case, I'd slather it all over."

Anya's nose wrinkled. "I thought you were a modern witch. That sounds medieval."

"Tough noogies. Sometimes the old ways are the best." She handed the jar to Anya.

"That's a very commercial-looking label." Anya was suspicious. "I thought you said it was bespelled?"

"Excuuuuuuse me for not dragging out my velvet robe and silver athame for this procedure. I assure you, it's quite blessed."

"Blessed by who?"

"It doesn't really matter under what system of belief it was blessed. Despite what Jules thinks, a spell is a ritual of directed intent. It's a wish, united with imagination, to manifest a change in physical reality. A spell is a spell, whether it's conducted by a priest at mass or a witch in her kitchen."

"I don't think Jules believes he's a magician when he's quoting 1 John 4:4 and chasing a demon with a water pistol full of holy water."

"Maybe that's part of the problem why his techniques aren't working as well as they used to." Katie pursed her lips. "I mean, evil seems to be gaining more and more of a toehold here every day, and we're being challenged to increase our commitment and our imagination to fight it."

Anya was silent for a moment, digesting. "So . . . who bespelled the garlic butter?"

"I did, just now. And it's been blessed by the rabbi at the end of the kosher assembly line that made it."

Anya read the jar label. It was, indeed, kosher. She opened it and flinched. "Ugh. It smells like roadkill."

"You're overly sensitive to the odor because you have a demonic hitchhiker."

"Riiiiiight."

"C'mon and get buttered up with garlic love." Katie pursed her lips. "And look at the bright side . . . it'll keep Mimi from successfully hitting on Drake Ferrer."

The only things in danger of hitting on Anya were the bomb-sniffing dogs at fire headquarters Monday morning.

Anya slunk across the lobby, attempting to make it to the back stair without running into anyone she knew. She hated to admit it, but the blessed garlic butter had seemed to calm Mimi down. The demon hadn't uttered a peep since she'd slathered it on. She could feel the demon curled tightly in a ball in the pit of her stomach, but Mimi wasn't moving. Perhaps it was simply disgust. Or Mimi had been up too late and decided to take a nap.

Anya had the ill fortune to cross the path of two

massive Labrador retrievers in the HQ lobby. Their handler lost control of them the instant they caught the smell of garlic butter. The dogs ripped their harnesses away from their handler, their claws scraping across the black-and-white tile floors.

Anya looked over her shoulder in terror as the dogs plowed into her. Snouts slobbered in her hair and her collar, paws climbing all over her. Instinctively, she curled into a ball and covered her face. But the dogs were determined: they drooled on her face, licked every last speck of makeup and garlic butter from her face and neck before the handler dragged them off. Sparky squirmed around her neck in disgust.

"Are you all right?" the handler shouted at her, wrestling with more than two hundred pounds of determined dog.

Anya picked herself up off the floor. "I'm good."

The handler looked sidelong at her, then reached for his firearm around the leashes. "Ma'am, keep your hands in view, please."

Great. He thought she was carrying explosives. He shouted for the security guard at the station, who approached with his hand on his gun belt.

She lifted her hands. "Can I get my badge?"

He nodded. "Slowly."

She pulled her badge out of her jacket pocket and flipped it open. The handler nodded. "Sorry about that. I know that you wouldn't believe that these guys passed their training, but . . ." Only then did he get downwind of the garlic. "Ah. You smell like my wife's lasagna. The dogs go berserk over lasagna night."

The guard wrinkled his nose. "I think she smells more like bruschetta."

Anya smiled weakly. "Can I go now?"

"Have a nice day, ma'am."

Anya slunk to the stairwell door and clattered down the steps to her office. She ignored the phone messages from the press and punched in the dispatch number to patch her into the radios at the apartment fire site. DFD hadn't released the scene yet. As long as at least one firefighter remained at the location, DFD could claim total dominion over the damage area. They could control who came, who left . . . and detain anyone who trespassed.

"Hey, this is Lieutenant Kalinczyk. Can you post at least two DFD uniforms there for the next forty-eight hours?"

The scene commander's voice crackled back. "We're ready to clear out as soon as the gas company finishes up capping the pipes. What gives?"

"I'm pretty sure that our arsonist is going to show up." Anya gave him a description of Ferrer.

"I can leave two guys down here, but will Investigations eat the overtime costs? My budget's shot."

"Sure. I'll bring over the forms. Just don't leave that scene alone without calling me first."

"It's your dime, lady."

She'd no sooner hung up the phone than a knock rattled the loose frosted glass in her office door. She kicked her chair back, and the wheels rattled across the cracked tiles. She snagged the doorknob and pulled the door open.

Marsh filled the doorway. And he did not look happy.

"Good morning, Captain."

Marsh looked down at her. Anya followed his gaze. Her hair was straggly, makeup licked off by voracious dogs. Yellow Labrador hair covered her suit. She reeked of garlic butter. And it wasn't even nine a.m.

"Rough night, Kalinczyk?"

"Um. No, sir."

His nose wrinkled. "You smell like pizza."

Her mind raced. "I'm taking garlic tablets. For my blood pressure."

"Well, stop."

"Yes, sir."

Marsh crossed his arms over his barrel chest. "We've got a problem."

"Sir, I promise, the garlic—"

"We're past the garlic." He gestured out to the hallway, and Vross fairly bounced into the room. His pasty face was covered with a shit-eating grin. That couldn't be good. "Do you have anything to report to Detective Vross and myself about the arson case?"

"I just got off the phone with the scene commander to have the apartment complex put under surveillance. I'm certain that Ferrer will be back, just like all the other scenes."

"Yeah, well, we've had Ferrer under surveillance ourselves." Vross opened a manila envelope and dumped a half-dozen black-and-white photos on her desk. "These are pictures from the Detroit Museum of Arts surveillance cameras."

Marsh cast Vross a look that could have scraped paint off a wall. "Detective Vross took the initiative to conduct surveillance without bothering to let us know."

Anya swallowed. She paged through the photographs. They showed Ferrer holding her hand. Ferrer kissing her. Ferrer with his arms around her back, fingers buried in her corset laces. She laid them carefully back on the desk, leaving greasy garlic-butter fingerprints on the margins. "Ferrer sent me an invitation to his art opening. I've been trying to get him to talk."

"So, playing tonsil hockey with the chief suspect is your idea of interrogation?" Vross sneered. "Or did you make some quid pro quo arrangement? A little piece on the side for a piece of evidence?"

Anya stood up, knocking the chair back. She could feel Mimi uncoiling in her gut, awakened by her rage. She stabbed her finger into Vross's pudgy chest. "I didn't sleep with the suspect."

"Yeah, well, you look real familiar with him from here." Vross looked back at Marsh. "This is why you should never let broads out of the typing pool. They can't control themselves around men."

Anya reached back and slugged him. She didn't know if it was her own anger or Mimi's influence, but it felt damn good to feel her knuckles splitting open Vross's nose. He stumbled backward, hands clutching his face. Blood gushed between his fingers.

"I guess we can't," she growled at him.

"Lieutenant Kalinczyk," Marsh barked. He put himself between Anya and Vross. "Stand down."

Vross stabbed a bloody finger at her. "Bitch, I'm gonna charge you with assault on a police officer."

Anya crossed her arms, concealing her bloody knuckles in the crease of her elbow. It hurt like a son of a bitch, but it had been worth it. "Really? You going to fess up to the boys that you let a little girl hit you? I doubt it."

Vross came across the desk at her. Marsh blocked him with an elbow to the chest, shoving him back to the ground. Marsh stood over him in his perfectly starched shirt and loosened his tie. "Don't make me mess up my shirt, Vross."

Vross climbed to his feet and shoved past Marsh. He gave Anya a poisonous look and slammed out the door.

Anya righted her chair, then sank into it. She felt deflated and anxious, now that the wrath and adrenaline were draining away. She looked up at Marsh. It hurt her to disappoint him, because he'd always believed in her. "I'm sorry, Captain."

Marsh looked at her the way a father looks at a daughter who failed algebra. "Look. I know that no one's perfect in our line of work. We've got more than our fair share of addicts, drunks, psych cases, bullies, and sadists." His eyes softened. "I don't want to see you go through any of that. I don't want to see you become a monster like Vross. You're a good investigator. But you need to get your head screwed back on straight."

He opened his hand. "Give me your badge and your gun, Kalinczyk. You're off this case, on administrative leave until further notice."

Her face burned in humiliation, and her hands were balled into fists so tight her nails cut into her palms. She handed her badge and gun over to him, mumbled another apology as she slipped out the door.

"And for Christ's sake, stay away from Drake Ferrer," Marsh called after her.

Anya pretended not to hear him.

Anya sat at the bar in the Devil's Bathtub, staring forlornly into her orange juice. Sparky paced up and down the length of the polished bar like a caged tiger.

"Katie, I would really like to have something more powerful than this."

Behind the bar, Katie shook her head. Her long blonde hair was braided into a series of complicated knots, the overall effect resembling a macramé pith helmet. It was very Viking. "No. No booze for the demonically possessed. That's just giving Mimi a bigger opening to mess with your head. And your body."

Renee sat on the stool beside her, nodding. *"It's true. I once saw a guy with a demon infection drink 'til he passed out . . . and then the demon took over. It wasn't pretty."*

"What happened?"

Renee shrugged, rattling the beaded fringe of her dress. *"The demon thought it would be fun to confess to the feds the names of every rumrunner the guy knew. The mob had him rubbed out in less than a day. Poor sap didn't know what hit him."*

The back door to the bar scraped open, and Anya heard the squeak of wheelchair wheels on the scarred wooden floor. Max pushed Ciro's wheelchair across the room. The old man looked fragile as a husk, but at least he was sitting up. His eyes clouded when he saw Anya.

"Katie told me what happened. I'm so sorry . . ."

She slid off the bar stool and knelt beside the chair. Anya shook her head. "It's okay, Ciro. And I'm sorry to bother you about this." She bit her lip. This should be something she could take care of on her own, without having to ask others for help. She hated the feeling of being beholden to others, the vulnerability in the asking.

"Hush, child." The old man's hand brushed her face. "We're going to take care of you."

Tears sprang to her eyes, and she brushed them away. In the face of Ciro's kindness, she couldn't help but feel exhausted and humbled. "Thank you."

In the doorway, Jules watched. His hands were jammed in his pockets and Anya could see the wrinkle in his brow. "It's our fault that this happened, after all. I was . . . I was too busy looking out for the goals of the team, rather than the team itself. Now Brian's in the hospital, and you've picked up a hitchhiker." He looked away, and his voice was barely audible. "I pushed you guys too far, and I'm sorry."

"It's okay, Jules. Really." She was surprised at his declaration. Hell, she was startled at his presence here at all.

She figured she'd burned her last bridge with Jules at the hospital.

Jules frowned. "I can listen to ghosts on tape, hear the smallest whispers of what they're saying, but . . . I don't hear live people so well. And I wasn't listening very well to you, when you said you couldn't do these things I asked."

"We're good, Jules, really." Anya squirmed. "Can I at least buy you a beer?"

"Sure." Jules climbed onto a bar stool. Max scrambled up beside him. Katie handed Jules a Detroit Lager from a microbrewery across town. She handed Max a can of pop. Max sulked.

"And as for you, young lady." Ciro faced Anya. "Go get some rest while we plan."

Anya blinked. "Are you putting me down for a nap, Ciro?"

"You'll need the energy. Besides which, you know as well as we do that whatever you hear, the demon hears. We need to keep our strategy hidden from the demon, so it must be kept from you as well."

Sparky climbed off the bar into Anya's lap. His gill-fronds looked a little droopy. And, she had to admit, a nap sounded mighty appealing.

"I'll tuck you in Ciro's guest room." Katie wiped her hands on a towel and came out from behind the bar. She led Anya up the creaky back stairs to Ciro's apartments. She opened the door to a sunshine-filled room with an-tique wallpaper and a twin bed covered in a multicolored afghan. A window seat overlooked the street. Sunshine poured through the glass to a square on the bed.

Katie moved to draw the blinds, but Anya said, "That's okay. I think Sparky and I would like to sleep in the sunshine."

"That's probably for the best. I'll be downstairs if you need me." Katie quietly shut the door.

Anya crawled under the covers, which smelled like mothballs and cedar. Sparky stretched his full length out beside her, his pale, speckled belly raised to the sunshine. Within moments, snores tickled his gill-fronds.

From the corner of one half-shuttered eye, Anya spied Renee sitting in the window seat. The spirit of the singer hummed a dusky lullaby.

"Thank you, Renee." For the first time in many years, Anya felt inexplicably *cared for*.

"I'll watch over you, while the others prepare," the ghost said. *"Now, sleep."*

Renee returned to her humming and Anya closed her eyes. The sunshine filtering behind her eyelids rendered her not into darkness, but the warm, red glow of sleep behind her eyes.

Anya dreamed she was sitting in the last pew at St. Florian's church. No service was being held this late at night. Votive candles flickered near the altar, casting warm, moving light up to the darkness of the nave. She had the sense that this far back in the darkness, no one could see her. Not even God.

Ahead, in the first row, a woman sat before the votives. Her hair was coiffed in a 1950s-style back-combed bouffant with a wide headband. From the edge of the pew, Anya glimpsed the hem of a polka-dotted skirt. When the woman lifted her hands to the back of the pew before her to pray, her hands were covered in white gloves.

A figure entered through the back door. Anya watched as the priest walked through the aisle, toward the woman. She recognized him as the young priest from the church, the one whose ghost had frantically warned her to give up the demon. But now he was solid and real, his shoes making sounds on the floor. This was what he had been, when he had been alive.

Anya followed him up the aisle. She noticed her feet didn't touch the ground, that her presence was unknown to the priest and the woman.

The priest sat down beside the woman in the pew, at a respectful distance. He spoke to her, but Anya couldn't make out what he was saying over the sound of blood pounding. Anya realized it wasn't her pulse, but the priest's. She could feel the itch of the collar around his neck, as if it were her own. The woman looked shyly away, then back again, her gloved hands gripping the pew in front of her. Anya could feel the priest's hands sweating. In the back of his head, she could hear him reciting the rosary. Anya felt a twinge of panic, caged in the body of the priest. She couldn't move, couldn't breathe . . . could only watch.

"We have to stop this," the woman said. "My husband is beginning to suspect."

Anya could feel the priest reaching for the woman. His fingers tangled in her perfectly coiffed hair and his mouth pressed against the woman's. She yielded slowly, reluctantly, coiling her arms around his neck. She broke away moments later, her eyes dark and confused.

"We'll be more discreet," the priest promised, reaching for her hand.

"No." She shook her head. "It has to stop. This will destroy him."

"What if I left the church?" he said suddenly, desperately. "What if . . . ?"

She lifted her head and looked at the priest. "But I can't leave *him*. And I would not see you destroyed, either." She stood, breaking free of the priest's grasp on her wrist. She pressed her hand to his cheek in a moment of what looked like pity and walked away down the aisle of pews.

The priest sat alone, stunned and silent. Anya could feel the hollowness of his yearning, the aloneness settling over him like a fever. He rested his head against the back of the pew in front of him, but he couldn't make his hands fit together to pray. Each time he tried, his fingers failed to lace together, like the south and north poles of a magnet. There were no prayers to resolve this. Anya felt the acid tang of that obsession rising in his throat. He couldn't live without her.

And he *wouldn't* live without her. The priest stumbled out of the pew, through the back hallways and into his office. Anya could feel the bile rising in him, the rage and despondency as he rifled through the desk drawer. His fingers closed around the cool blades of a pair of scissors.

Anya tried to shout out to stop him, but her words were as ephemeral as her presence. She was forced to watch, helpless, as the priest cut his wrists with the scissors. Only then was he able to hold his hands in prayer over his desk, red spiraling down his sleeves like a red rosary. A dark giggle rattled through the priest's chest, expelled into the air like condensation.

It was then that she realized that the dream wasn't her own imagination, idly filling in the blanks of the history of St. Florian's ghost.

It was one of Mimi's memories, one of her most treasured ones: the time she drove a priest to suicide.

CHAPTER FIFTEEN

WHEN ANYA AWOKE, THE SUNSHINE had drained away, though she could still feel its heat on her face. The sun had set behind the buildings to the west, leaving a violet sky speckled with the tatters of clouds. Anya stretched in the half darkness. The motion disturbed Sparky, who put his feet over his eyes. Anya rubbed his belly vigorously, until he squirmed fully awake and stretched out on her lap.

As promised, Renee remained in the window seat, her arms wrapped around her knees. "You were talking in your sleep," she said.

Anya rubbed her eyes, and the memory of the dream of the priest flooded back to her. "What did I say?"

"It sounded like a Catholic Mass . . . in Latin."

A knock echoed on the bedroom door, which then squeaked open. Katie thrust her head into the room. "Anya, we're ready for you."

Anya swung her legs over the bed. "Can I go pee first?"

Katie nodded. "I'll wait for you on the stairs."

Anya crossed the hall to the tiny bathroom. She washed her hands and splashed water on her face, while Sparky circled underfoot. She could feel Mimi tightly coiled in her stomach, like a snake in a basket, waiting to strike when the lid was removed. The demon knew that the game was up and was biding her time.

Anya pulled her hair back in a ponytail with an elastic band, staring at her face in the mirror. She had the look of a drug addict: Her eyes were darkly circled and bloodshot, and her face was too pale. No wonder Marsh had ordered her off the case. She chewed her bottom lip, vowing not to think about that now. She needed to focus on helping herself, to help DAGR in whatever way she could to get Mimi untangled from her aura and kicked to the curb.

Anya took off her shoes and set them neatly beside the bathtub. She removed her belt, earrings, and watch. She emptied her pockets of loose change and hung her garlic-smelling suit jacket on the back doorknob. This was standard procedure for an exorcism: never leave anything on the victim that could be used as a weapon. She deliberately left the salamander torque around her neck. She hadn't taken it off since she was a child, and wasn't going to start, now.

She took a deep breath, then opened the bathroom door. Katie took her arm, and Sparky flowed down the steps behind them into the bar.

Anya stood at the bottom of the stairs as she emitted a low whistle. "Fancy."

The bar was decked out for a serious party. A chalk

circle wrapped around the bar, with candles placed in the cardinal directions. When Anya looked more closely, the circle was drawn in the likeness of Ouroboros, the world-eating serpent. A gap had been left open in the eastern edge for Anya, Sparky, and Katie to enter. The bar had been covered in multicolored chalk marks: runes, pentagrams, and angelic script for the archangels corresponding to each of the elemental directions. At the center, she thought she recognized the Kabbalistic tree of life. It was as if a mystical sidewalk artist had been on the loose, and had been doodling for hours. The mirrors behind the bar were covered in black trash bags. The air hung thick with incense; Anya could smell eucalyptus and cedar most strongly. The overall effect was one of cough-and-congestion-clearing cold medicine. Jules and Max stood near a strange assortment of equipment at the foot of the bar. Anya thought she spied an ice bucket with an egg beater in the collection.

These were the big guns, not the simple, natural magick blessings they used in DAGR's usual procedures to drive out simple spirits. That magick was born mostly of intention—spontaneous and effective in most situations. It was the kind of magick Anya used unconsciously when she drove out spirits and the kind of power that animated Sparky. It was derived from the environment, from the basic elements, operating without formulae or complex recipes.

Heavy ceremonial magick was for special occasions; it had to be designed carefully and followed to the syllable. Its power derived from hidden things, from the caster's innate skill and fortitude. Where natural magick could be considered an art, ceremonial magick was a science. Rules had to be followed, prescriptions memorized. Ritual magick was for real magicians, people like Katie and Ciro, who understood the history and implications of each utterance and gesture.

Ciro sat in his wheelchair, his finger holding a place in a very large, thick book jammed full with dog-eared recipe cards. The title was a tongue-twister: *Sefer Raziel HaMalach*. "Did you sleep well?" he asked Anya.

"That depends on who you ask," she responded. "I think I dreamed one of Mimi's memories."

Ciro frowned. "Then we should get started."

Katie kicked off her shoes and pulled an embroidered navy velvet robe over her street clothes. Wielding a silver athame, she looked a bit like a visitor to a Renaissance Faire preparing to peel potatoes, and Anya felt underdressed. She had to hand it to the Catholics and the Wiccans: they had a sense of ceremony.

"Where do you want me?" she asked.

"Up here." Jules patted the bar top.

Anya hopped up on the bar. "I don't have to dance on it, do I?"

"Just lie back. Think of it as the magickal examination table."

Anya fidgeted in nervousness as she leaned back against the bar top. This was weird, even for DAGR. She was conscious that her butt was smudging two of the stations on the Kabbalistic tree of life.

Jules was using the voice he used when explaining hauntings to frightened homeowners. "We're going to tie you to the bar rails."

Anya bit her lip. Her skin crawled at the idea, but she nodded. Jules and Max broke out a package of zip ties and lashed her right hand and both feet to the customer bar rail. Her left hand got tied to the top of a beer keg. She wiggled her fingers in her bonds. They weren't tight enough to cut off circulation, but she wasn't going anywhere unless and until someone cut her loose. Sparky clambered to the bar top and sat on her stomach. Good thing she'd emptied her bladder before the procedure, she thought. Jules turned his head away from Sparky's heat, but he didn't say anything about the warmth.

Out of the corner of her eye, she saw Katie preparing to close the circle. Renee paused at the edge. A spirit wouldn't be able to cross over after it had been sealed. Renee stepped over the circle and let Katie fill in behind. She came to Anya's side and smiled like a nurse calming a frightened patient before surgery.

"You don't have to be here, you know," Anya told her. An exorcism could be hazardous to ordinary house spirits.

Renee shook her head, her bob swinging along her jaw line. *Wouldn't miss it for the world. This is the most excitement this joint has seen since the Jazz Age.*

"Circle's closed," Katie announced. Standing at the eastern edge of the circle, she lifted her silver athame and made the sign of the pentacle in the air, uttering the name "Yee-ho-vah." She turned to the south, repeating the gesture. "Ah-doh-nae." Then, west: "Eh-hey-ah." Then, north: "Ah-gell-ah."

She returned to the east, lifting her arms to call the archangels. "Before me, Raphael. Behind me, Gabriel. To my right hand, Michael. To my left hand, Auriel. About me flame the pentagrams and upon me shines the six-rayed star."

She looked back at the bar, then nodded. The ritual she'd used, the Lesser Ritual of the Pentagram, had been around in different variations since the Gardnerian era of magick. Anya had only seen it performed a couple of times, but it was still impressive.

"Let's begin." Ciro turned the page in his book. "The first step is to call the spirit out of hiding."

Jules dipped an old-fashioned, crank-style eggbeater in an ice bucket. He lifted it out, turned the handle. Droplets of holy water splashed on Anya, fizzling like hydrogen peroxide on her skin. Max dipped a cocktail whisk into the bucket, then shook it on Anya in his best impression of a Catholic priest.

"Jules," she hissed. "I thought you guys had a special tool for that, or something."

Jules hushed her. "My mama always told me to make do with what you've got."

Ciro wheeled over to the bar, reached up, and laid a bread knife on Anya's shoulder. Anya supposed it had been consecrated: the poor man's athame. "By the sword of Michael, I command the demon Mimiveh to appear."

Anya could feel Mimi uncoiling in her gut. In horror,

she watched as her belly rolled like a belly dancer's stage trick, and the acidic burning rushed up her throat. Sparky adjusted his footing to the shifting terrain, turning his head right and left to watch the churning that gurgled behind her sternum.

Mimi's voice boiled out of her mouth, a full octave higher than Anya's natural contralto. *"You raaaaang?"*

"Tell us all your names, demon."

Anya felt her mouth twist. Sparky crouched low on her chest, growling at the foreign voice emerging from her mouth. *"I've been around the block a few times, old man. Lilitu, Zepara, Jezebel, Circe, Succubus . . . take your pick."*

Anya couldn't see the look that passed between Ciro and Katie, but she felt an extra dash of holy water flung on her face from Jules's quarter. Sparky climbed off her chest to circle her body. She could hear his claws clacking around the bar top.

"How old are you?"

"A lady never tells her age," Mimi answered coyly. *"I'd like to think I'm young at heart."*

Jules shook more holy water at her, and Anya could feel blisters rising on her lips.

"Again, how old are you?"

"I'm older than Babylon. You can consider me to be a contemporary of your friend, Sirrush. Of course, back then, creatures like Sirrush were as common as cattle. But don't call him common. His ego is rather delicate."

"Mimiveh, Lilitu, Zepara, Jezebel, Circe, Succubus . . . I order you and all your incarnations to leave this body."

Laughter bubbled from her lips. *"It will take much more than orders from an old man to give her up."*

Overhead, the bar lights shattered, one by one. Max shielded his head with his arm as he stepped back.

"Don't break the circle," Jules shouted at him. He yanked the young man back before he tripped over the magickal border.

Ciro began reading aloud from a recipe card and writing in Hebrew on her arms with a blue magic marker. The marks itched on her skin like poison ivy. She squirmed, trying to scratch them against her bonds. " 'Jehovah stands in judgment of all above and below. In purity, He destroys and divides every devil and demon, breaks every binding, unravels every enchantment and sorcery . . .' "

Glassware stacked on the bar shattered as if an unseen hand had pulled a cornerstone piece from the bottom. Renee yelped, ducking behind the bathtub full of coins.

Anya felt her head turning toward the ghost of the flapper. *"Come here, little songbird. Let the Lantern devour you. You would make lovely food for Sirrush."*

Anya forced her head away, trying to quell the darkness expanding in her chest. She wouldn't allow Mimi to force her to take Renee. She wouldn't. She could feel her fingernails scraping deep into the bar with the effort to stay present enough to keep the demon from unlocking her dark heart and destroying Renee.

The bathtub in the center of the floor cracked open with the sound of lightning striking a tree. Twenty years' worth of loose change rolled over the floor in a seething, shimmering mass.

Katie stepped forward. She touched her gleaming athame to Anya's body, sketching a pentacle on her body: forehead, right breast, left shoulder, right shoulder, right breast, and her forehead. The point of the athame burned into her skin, and she felt herself snarling.

"In the name of the archangels, I cast you out, Mimi-veh." Her voice rang sharp, clear.

And too brittle.

The mirror behind the bar exploded into fragments, as if a hurricane tore through the brick wall. Anya felt Sparky's body on her chest, trying to shield her from the glittering shards, but the will of Mimiveh was too strong. The blast ripped through the bar, shattering the remaining glass. Liqueur and rum bottles smashed on the floor; a bottle of vodka hit too close to one of Katie's candles and burst into an exhalation of blue and yellow flame.

Max, acting on impulse, threw the ice bucket of holy water on it. It doused the fire, but washed away the eastern rim of Katie's chalk circle, breaking the spell.

"No!" Katie fell on her hands in the debris, trying to redraw it with pink sidewalk chalk, but it was too late. The energy had already escaped, and the chalk wouldn't stick to the wet floor.

Anya felt Mimi's giggle escape her lips before the demon retracted into the pit of her stomach. Sticky with water, booze, and glass, Anya stared up at the tin ceiling of the bar, blinking back tears. Sparky put his head on her shoulder, sighing, as the mirror shards and coins rattled to a rest.

The remaining silence, the sigh of failure, was deafening.

Anya sat in the bottom of Ciro's shower, cold water pelting her skin. She shivered—from cold, from dread, from the pain of the water on her burns. Sparky paced in front of her, making small mewling noises. She knew he felt as helpless as she did, powerless. Powerless to do her job, to stop Ferrer and his arson. Powerless to help Brian, who seemed to linger in limbo. Powerless against Mimi, who'd invaded her body. Now Mimi had trashed the Devil's Bathtub, and she was no closer to any of those goals. It was a small blessing that Ciro's heart hadn't given out right there. Poor Renee had been finally coaxed out from beneath the floorboards with promises that Ciro would add to his already formidable Jazz Age record collection, to give her something "new" to dance to.

Anya scrubbed futilely at the Hebrew characters on her arms. Ciro had used permanent marker, and they weren't coming off anytime soon. If she had enough of her wits about her by the time Halloween rolled around, she could go as a dreidel. If . . . Devil's Night was only two days away. She was running out of time to stop Ferrer from waking Sirrush. Hell, two days from now, it might not matter a bit to her . . . she might be locked up in the psych ward, completely unaware of the world spinning outside her own skull.

She reached forward to shut off the water. As soon as she did so, tiny glass cuts on her arms, face, and hands began to bleed again. She reached out of the shower for tissue to stanch the bleeding, feeling like she had when her mother caught her attempting to shave her legs for the first time. She was eleven and hadn't realized that soap was part of the procedure. The red marks had taken days to fade from her legs.

She reached for a blue towel that wouldn't show blood and dried off. She wiped steam from the mirror to inspect the burns on her chest. The red had faded to a sickly pink color, and the texture of her skin felt too soft, like skin that had wrinkled under a Band-Aid for too many days. Dutifully, she slathered more antibiotic cream on the wound, though it honestly seemed the least of her worries. She dimly wondered if it would ever heal, as long as Mimi was infecting her.

Katie had left a jar of something more potent than garlic butter for her as demon tranquilizer. It was a blatant reminder that the exorcism hadn't worked. Anya screwed open the lid of the mason jar and sniffed. Beeswax suspended leaves of unidentifiable herbs and flowers, but the most overwhelming top notes smelled of mint and basil. She rubbed it into her skin, which seemed to absorb it much more readily than the garlic butter that had lain atop it all day in a sweaty mess.

Katie had brought her a change of clothes, for which she was grateful; Anya didn't want to imagine trying to shimmy back into wet pants studded with glass splinters.

Katie's clothes smelled like lavender: the linen poet shirt was cut loose and blessedly cool on her burns. Katie was shorter than Anya, and the crinkled black skirt hit Anya at mid-calf, when it would have brushed Katie's ankles. Katie had laid out a black brocade vest for her: perhaps out of a sense of whimsy, perhaps out of modesty. As Katie had collected Anya's original clothes to run laundry, she might have noted the missing bra.

Hair dripping over her shoulder, Anya shrugged into the vest. She slipped on some black ballerina-type slippers Katie had provided and padded out of the steamy bathroom. Sparky followed close on her heels, curling around her ankles like a cat as she navigated the back steps to the bar.

Conversation collapsed when she reached the last creaking step. Jules and Max were chucking large pieces of glass into a plastic trash can, while Katie swept. Ciro was scrubbing down the bar with something that smelled like ammonia. Renee stood over the remains of the bathtub like a child gazing upon a broken piggy bank. Windows were cracked open to let the air come through, to disperse some of Mimi's influence. Salt gritted in the glass under their steps, grinding into the spaces between the floorboards.

Anya hugged her elbows, guilty in the wake of all her destruction. "Hey, guys."

A chorus of wary greetings met her.

She gestured at the trashed bar, the ruined bathtub. "I'm sorry about all of this . . . I'll pay for it, really." Anya had no idea how she was going to accomplish this without any income, but she supposed that selling the Dart might be a start.

Ciro wheeled up to her. "I won't hear of it, child. That's what insurance is for."

"You've got insurance for Mimi's tantrums?"

"I've got insurance for acts of God. It'll cover acts of the Devil, too . . . just as long as I tell the adjuster that the damage was done by persons unknown." Ciro shrugged. "It's just stuff."

Anya's gaze flickered to a particularly bad cut on Max's face and the way that Renee shied back a few steps when she came into the room. The physical damage was the least of her worries. Strange that she'd been so eager to drive DAGR away and how bad she felt now that she really had.

"Let me help you guys pick up." Anya reached for a bucket to scoop the pennies and ruined porcelain.

"No." Jules firmly set his hand on her shoulder. "We've gotta talk."

The ghost-hunters righted bar stools and climbed up into them. Renee moved to melt into the floor.

"Renee, I'm really sorry," Anya began.

Renee paused, looking over her shoulder. "Sweetie, it's not your fault. I don't take it personally. But . . . neither should you when I say that you're scaring me right now. I know that you would never hurt me. But that thing inside you would." Her kohl-rimmed eyes were wide with nervousness and she played with her beads. "So . . . I'm gonna keep a low profile for now, okay?"

Anya nodded, mouth dry. "I understand. It's for the best."

Renee gave her a sad smile and faded into the floor.

Sparky put his feet up on the bar stool, gazing up at Anya with limpid eyes. She leaned over, picked him up, and parked him in her lap. He wrapped himself around her shoulders like Miss America's sash, his head buried inside her vest and his butt spilling off her lap. His tail curled around the legs of the bar stool. It was an awkwardly uncomfortable position from her perspective, but she knew that no one else could see it.

"Sparky's spooked," she explained. "He gets cuddly when he's scared."

"We're all spooked," Max confirmed.

Ciro folded his hands in his lap. "Though the exorcism failed, we did glean some useful information about your parasite."

"Parasite? That's an apt term."

"The names it says it's used are troubling me." Ciro's brow was knotted in concentration. "One of them was 'Lilitu.' That's a Sumerian cognate for 'Lilith.' "

"Wasn't she Adam's first wife?" Anya's knowledge of Bible Apocrypha was limited. The Catholic church hadn't been too fond of extra books beyond the Old and New Testaments.

"Depends on whose mythology you follow. According to the Sumerians, the Lilitu—there were more than one—were beautiful, succubilike creatures who fed on men's erotic dreams."

"That's hot," Max said.

Jules slapped him on the back of the head. "That is *not* hot."

Ciro continued, ignoring the squabble. "The Babylonians mythologized her as the prostitute of the goddess Ishtar. Other traditions tie her to the serpent in the garden of Eden, to storm-goddesses, and to the bearer of Adam's demon children. In the Kabbalah, Lilith is represented as a Qliphoth, a shell of impurity dealing with the temptations of seduction."

Anya sat very still, thinking back to her dream of the priest. "It tracks with one of her memories that came up in a dream . . . she drove a priest to suicide through obsession with a woman."

Ciro frowned and rubbed his beard. "She's very powerful. And ancient. And she may be well beyond all our powers to drive her out."

"Then what are we going to do?" Jules said. "We can't just leave it in her."

Ciro nodded. "We won't. I need to do more research, see if there's a specific weakness we can exploit. I have some friends to call for advice—a rabbi here in Detroit, and a voodoo priestess in New Orleans. Among the three of us, we should be able to come up with a solution. In the meantime, practical preparations need to be made."

Anya leaned forward, cradling the salamander. "What preparations?"

"Rest assured, we will find a way to drive her out. But it may take some time. In the meantime, you should not be left alone. And . . . you should consider drawing up some legal documents to protect you, in the event that you manage to slip out of our capable supervision."

"Like a durable power of attorney in case I wind up in the nut ward?" Anya was half kidding, but her voice stuck in her throat when Ciro nodded.

"I've seen what happens to people in psychiatric care without anyone to make decisions for them. I would not have that happen to you. Much as I like to think of you, of all of you, as family, there's no legal standing for any of us to see that you get the spiritual treatment you need."

Anya's grip on Sparky whitened. As bad as it was, being under the spell of a demon, she still had some measure of control over her life. If she were to wind up in a mental institution, no part of her life would be hers. None of it. She'd be at the mercy of a psychiatric nurse feeding her Haldol three times a day. The prospect of not only being unable to protect others, but unable to look out for herself, frightened her more than the prospect of Mimi chewing away at her soul, whatever remained of it.

"I have no way of peering into the future," Ciro told her. "And I hope I'm wrong. But please see to it, while you still can."

When she found her voice again, it tasted hollow. "I'll contact someone in the morning to get the papers drawn up."

CHAPTER SIXTEEN

THERE WAS ONE PERSON WHO she knew could get rid of Mimi.

And she knew that he would be glad to see her.

Anya waited until the house was asleep. Jules and Max had left hours ago. She listened to Ciro snoring like a freight train in his bedroom. The old man worried her; he would snore vigorously for about ten minutes, then snort and stop. When she was on the verge of leaping out of the guest bed to resuscitate him, he would begin again. This pattern had continued for hours. Anya didn't know how Max had been able to stand it.

Katie slept beside Anya in the guest bed. At least, Anya assumed that she slept by the steady rise and fall of her chest. The witch had wrapped a pillow around her head with both fists, and had wadded most of the comforter edge around her ears to block out the sound.

Stealthily, Anya slipped out of bed and gathered her clothes from the floor. In bare feet, she crept down the staircase. She tried to keep at the edges of the stairs, where squeaks would be less likely, but it sounded like she was murdering mice under high-heeled shoes. She heard no interruption in Ciro's snoring, no creak in the bed upstairs to suggest that Katie had been disturbed enough by her absence or the creaking to even turn over.

She dressed in the ruins of the bar in Katie's clothes, then pulled her coat and purse from the cloakroom. Holding her shoes in her hand and feeling like a teenager creeping out of her parents' house, she padded to the front door of the bar.

"Where are you going?"

The whisper caught her off guard. Anya looked back to see Renee sitting on the edge of the bar, swinging her bare feet into darkness.

"I'm going to try to find someone who can help me. Another Lantern," she said. That much was the truth. She hoped she wouldn't have to elaborate, that Renee wouldn't wake Katie and Ciro.

Renee fixed her with a knowing look. She'd seen decades of this same old story playing out within these walls. *"Be careful, sweetie. Any man that can devour that demon can ruin you, too . . . as easily as crushing out a cigarette."*

"I will, Renee. Thanks." Anya let herself out of the bar, car keys in hand.

As much as the thought boiled her conflicting emotions, as much as it stung her pride and mangled her ethics, she'd have to do it.

She would have to ask Drake Ferrer to take Mimi off her hands.

Drake had built himself a nice little fortress of solitude in Oakland County, northwest of the city. According to real estate records, it sat on Lake Angelus, a rich area where the few hundred residents jealously guarded their privacy. Unlike the McMansions in most of Detroit's suburbs, the people in Lake Angelus didn't park huge houses on tiny lots. Most of the Angelus houses were built on substantial acreage, hidden from prying eyes. The wealthy here had nothing to prove to their neighbors. Drake Ferrer's house was no exception to local habit.

Anya cruised down the winding lane to the lake, headlights shut off. Under the waxing moon, Lake Angelus shone like a flat obsidian mirror. This far out, away from the glowing light of Detroit on the horizon, Anya could see stars. Every so often, she would crane her head under the windshield to see them. She'd met little other traffic on the way here and most of the distant house lights she passed were doused. Everything was still and asleep.

Anya hoped the fact that Drake's house was out of DPD's jurisdiction would work in her favor. Vross and his men couldn't cross into Oakland County and do surveillance on Drake without an order from a judge. Given that remote possibility, the best that they'd be able to accomplish would be to ask the Lake Angelus Police Department to keep an eye on Drake for them. Given the high price people here paid for their privacy, Anya hoped that the cooperation they displayed would be lip service.

And she was not to be disappointed. The Dart passed a

Lake Angelus patrol car pulled off by the side of the road. Inside the car, the patrolman dozed, a newspaper on his chest disturbed by his breath. Anya drove on, counting the number of drives until she found Drake's.

She didn't blame him for moving from the city. After what he'd experienced, she could well understand the need to be insulated from the violence, the desire to withdraw to someplace safe. Someplace that could be controlled. But she found it odd for a man who had ducked out of public life to remain living at its fringes. The behavior reminded her of that of a voyeur . . . watching from afar, but not touching.

The property was tastefully overgrown. A wall of trees and shrubs obscured an iron gate. Beyond the gate, she could see nothing but acres of foliage, enough leaves still remaining to obscure the view. Anya pulled into the drive beside the intercom mounted on a gatepost. Above it, she could see the red eye of a video camera. She rolled down the window, reached out to press the buzzer, then hesitated. It was nearly three in the morning. What would she say that would make sense at this hour? *Mr. Ferrer, I have a favor to ask you, before I lock you up for the rest of your natural life.*

She blew out her breath and punched the button. There was a pause of nearly thirty seconds and Anya considered both pressing it again and driving away. She heard a small whir from the video camera above, and she glanced up at her reflection in its black lens as it turned toward her.

Without comment, the iron gates reeled back with the

clink of automated chain. Anya pulled the Dart through them and they slid shut behind her with the same clunk that she'd heard in similar gates at the county jail. She felt a bump as she drove over a strip of tire shredders.

Getting in had been easy. Getting out might be a great deal harder.

A gravel lane wound before her, disappearing into the wooded lot. Anya proceeded slowly, hearing the gravel thunk and pop against the inside of the car's wheel wells. This place must have been beautiful by day, she thought, but in the colorless stillness of night, the shape of the trees against the sky was all she could make out.

The lane widened after a quarter mile, spilling out in a turnaround before an English cottage—though "cottage" seemed too small a word for the structure. The façade was gray stone, pierced with dark windows that reflected the light of the moon in dips and warbles of leaded glass. A slate roof capped the two-story structure. Not a single light burned inside.

Anya shut off the ignition, listening to the engine plink as it cooled. With all the courage she could muster, she pulled open the door. She'd no sooner stepped out into the gravel than two dark shapes hurtled toward her, snarling.

Dogs. She scurried back into the Dart and slammed the door. The dogs lunged against the heavy door, their claws scraping against the Dart's paint.

She felt Sparky unfurl from her neck, fling himself against the glass. His toes and mouth spread wide, displaying the sharpness of his back teeth. His hissing breath condensed on the glass, and his tongue scraped fog away as he snarled.

The dogs must have been able to see him. They yelped and scrambled back, barking at the creature making faces behind the glass.

"Cerberus, Orthrus. Down, boys."

The dogs slid obediently to the ground, sitting upright with their tails slapping the gravel. They were gray and black speckled, with ears of foxes; Anya guessed that they were mutts. They would have been cute if they hadn't been trying to tear her face off moments before.

Drake Ferrer stood before her car. He was dressed in jeans and a dress shirt with the sleeves rolled up, walking barefoot on the gravel. "You can come out now."

Anya screwed up her courage then popped open the door. Sparky flowed out before her and waddled over to the dogs. His gill-fronds were flared in an impressive display, and he hissed.

"Sparky," Anya snapped.

The dogs bristled, and the two dogs and salamander circled each other. Anya braced herself for all-out war, but the display merely degenerated to an embarrassing round of butt-sniffing.

Anya looked at Drake. "Sorry about that . . . and for waking you."

Drake shrugged. Up close, she could see that his clothes were spattered with something. Paint. His hands at his sides were shaded in colors of charcoal and white. "I wasn't asleep."

He didn't ask her what she was doing here. It was as if he already knew, or wanted her to think he knew. He inclined his head. "C'mon back to the studio. I have to finish up a couple of things before the gesso sets."

And he walked behind the house, as casually as if he was well accustomed to nighttime visitors, and her being here was the most natural thing in the world. That bothered her.

She followed, and Sparky and the dogs fell into line behind her. He led her to what must have been stables in an earlier era, now converted to a garage. A light shone in the upper floor. Drake climbed the stairs to the light and motioned for her to follow him inside.

This must have been the hayloft in an earlier time. Now it had been entirely gutted and covered with spotty, unfinished plaster. Pine boards creaked underfoot, stained and damaged by years of paint and careless use of tools. Drake's work perched on easels set up throughout the space and tacked to the walls. His tools, paints, pencils, and brushes were scattered on a decrepit farmhouse table. The drop cloths wadded into corners smelled like turpentine. The light came from a system of shop lights strung overhead, casting a broad-spectrum glow with a bluish cast.

As chaotic as the space was, his work was breathtaking. Anya saw none of the precisely lettered blueprints she'd seen at the gallery. These works were abstracts and still lifes, paint sprawling large across canvas, in colors not permitted under the strict rules of architecture. The majority of the abstract works glowed in shades of orange and red, exhalations from corners of darkness. She saw curves of land that suggested deserts with the glisten of glass and sand mixed into the paint.

"These are gorgeous," she said.

"Thanks. I'm experimenting with adding minerals to the paint for texture." He crossed to the half-finished canvas he was working on, a broad sweep of reds and pinks. It reminded Anya of a bloody sunset she'd seen on a newsreel after Chernobyl. He dipped a broad brush into a paper cup, and curled a black line across the bottom perimeter. Using his forearm, he smudged the black into the red. The black carbon feathered into the substrate he'd applied to the canvas. "I'm using carbon tonight. It tends to melt right into the medium, so it has to be used up fast."

Anya examined a piece of watercolor paper at his table. A frosty pattern laced across the page, incredibly intricate and organic, as it laced into the green. "What did you use for this? It's amazing."

"That was salt. The salt drives out the color and purifies the tint. Each thing I use has its own chemistry, its own magic."

"Why didn't you display any of these?"

Drake didn't answer for a moment. When he did, he said, "These are personal. Without being able to see in three dimensions, this is all I can do . . . and I just don't feel like putting that out to the world for critique by some jackass writing columns for the arts section."

"These are for you."

"Entirely. And . . . well, now that you've seen them, they're for you, too."

She paused before a smaller piece of canvas, stretched on a complicated-looking cantilevered frame. It was a one-quarter profile of a woman, only the pale edge of her face visible. Her back was presented to the viewer, dressed in a laced corset, ribbons dripping off into space. Her hair was pinned up, and the luminously pale curve of her neck contrasted sharply with the glow of black behind it. On close inspection, the black was slightly crazed, like the alligator skin effect that Anya had seen on charred wood in fires. When viewed from the right angle, she detected the blush of smoke on the woman's cheek. The contrast between the seen and unseen was striking.

She swallowed. The painting was unmistakably of her, but to mention it seemed invasive. "What did you use here?"

He answered her without turning around, focused on his current work. "That's mica applied to the black paint. The white paint has a sheen of quartz in it. And parts were smoked with a candle."

"It's a beautiful effect," she said.

"I had an inspiring subject. It's called *Ishtar*."

She blushed, looking down and away. The dogs were busy showing Sparky the collection of tennis balls they'd squirreled away in a corner. He seemed distracted for the moment.

"What are you calling the painting you're working on now?" she asked.

Drake stood back from the orange and charcoal, taking its measure. "You won't like it."

"I think I already *do* like it."

"The working title is *Sirrush*."

Strange how he could do that: how he could make her feel at ease and then turn that off with a single word or glance.

He turned to look at her, one corner of his mouth upturned. "I will refrain from telling you that I told you so."

Questions rose in her throat, and she gave them voice, awkwardly: "If you summon Sirrush . . . what then? How could you convince a god to leave?" She couldn't even get rid of a minor demon—how could a mere human like Ferrer hope to control the king of salamanders?

"These creatures have existed since the beginning of time, Anya. In ancient times, in the time of Bel's temple, sacrifices were made to them. When well fed, Sirrush can be a benevolent god."

"What sacrifices?" she asked.

"Sacrifices of flesh and spirit." He dipped his brush into the carbon and began to work it into a new section of paint.

It dawned upon her. "The people you're killing in these fires . . . the fireman. The people in the apartment complex. You consider them to be sacrifices to Sirrush."

"Flesh is a potent sacrifice. But there are less visible ones."

"Virgil. The ghosts in the library." Anya's brow knitted. "You devoured them."

Drake turned to face her. "You don't wonder what happens to the ghosts you devour?"

She stared down at her hands. "I've never known."

He balanced the paintbrush on the top of his cup. "A spirit that's devoured by a Lantern, a human that's killed in a fire . . . these are offerings to Sirrush, and those like him. They are, to put it bluntly, food. Honored food, but still food."

She shook her head, refusing to believe, her hands balled into fists at her side. She refused to contemplate the idea that the ghosts she'd destroyed, that Neuman, that her mother . . . that all of them had gone to feed Sirrush. Sensing her distress, Sparky left his new dog pals and leaned against her side, casting a dirty look at Drake.

"That's not true," she said. "There's no way you could know that."

Drake's good eye burned black and intense. "After I was nearly killed in that armpit of a city that you're bent on protecting, I did some wandering. I didn't spend all that time on the shores of a bucolic lake in Oakland County.

"I spent some time trying to make heads or tails of it all. Creation. Destruction. They seemed terribly out of balance and I wanted to learn why. I went to Egypt, to Iran, to Jordan. I met many magickal masters who taught me a great many things: how to manipulate fire, where Sirrush and his kind sleep. I learned how to make glass out of sand with just my hands and my breath.

"But the most valuable lesson I learned was from an old man in Petra. He made me realize that nothing is ever destroyed. Just because you swallow a ghost, doesn't mean it stops existing. It has to go somewhere."

"That doesn't mean they go to feed Sirrush," she argued. "There could be any number of afterlives—"

"Anya." He set his cup down on the floor. "Everything must be fed, even things that sleep. In ancient Babylon, Lanterns like us were the priests and priestesses of Sirrush and his siblings. It was up to us to keep them warm, safe, and fed." He gestured to the salamander winding around Anya's knees. "Like you do with Sparky."

"Sirrush isn't a larger version of Sparky."

"No, he's not. But he's been around since there was fire and he's required food since then. Every time, since the beginning of time, that man has died in a brush fire, that man built a house or temple that burned . . . Sirrush and his kind have not allowed the sacrifice to go to waste. They're part of the natural world, and there's nothing evil about that cycle."

Anya leaned against the table, her heart churning with the possibilities. She quailed away from them. "No. I choose not to participate in this . . . and I choose not to believe what you're telling me." She couldn't imagine her mother in the belly of a dragon and she would not accept the explanation. She turned away, wrapping her hands around her elbows.

"If you didn't believe that I know some bits of arcane lore that you don't, why did you come?"

Her breath froze in her throat. "I came to talk to you."

She heard his steps behind her. He put his hands on her shoulders, and Sparky growled below her. "You came because you want me to devour that demon that's chewing a hole in your gut."

She turned in his arms, startled. "How did you know?"

His mouth curved up, but the smile was rimmed with bitterness. "I can feel it in you. Here." He touched the hollow of her throat. "And here." His hand brushed below her sternum, lingered. Anya's heart hammered and she was certain he could feel it. Under his touch, she could feel Mimi turn over and stretch. Acidity burned between her ribs, and she gasped.

"But I can't take it from you. Not now."

"Why not?" Her brows drew together.

His gaze on her was heavy. "I want to help you. I do. But that demon you've got inside you is older than most diamonds. I've got to conserve my power for Sirrush."

Anya turned her face away, cheeks burning. She didn't know why she'd come, why she thought he'd help her. He was a stranger, a liar, and a monster. What could he possibly do to help her? And why would he want to?

She jerked away from his grasp and started toward the door.

He reached out and caught her wrist. "Wait."

She looked back at him, feeling Mimi surge like bile in her throat.

"I will take the demon from you, but after. After I've summoned Sirrush. Please understand that . . . no matter what I feel, that must come first." The look on his face was resigned, lonely. She understood that look, that feeling of apartness.

And she was tired of it, tired of always being on the outside looking in. Tired of being different, tired of feeling used, tired of no one understanding what she felt or why she just couldn't allow anyone to be close to her. She was tired of everything she cared for breaking, and having it be her fault.

Drake was the only unbreakable person she'd ever met, the only other Lantern. He didn't want anything from her, but her. And she didn't want to let go of him. She would hold fast to this one thing.

His fingers laced in hers, and she heard Mimi laughing in the back of her head.

She tipped her face up to his. His fingers wound in her hair as he kissed her, scalding her mouth with his. His fingers scraped up through her hair, sending a shiver from her scalp to the base of her spine. She splayed her fingers on his chest, feeling the heart that beat so quickly there, and the void beyond it. His lips slid from the corner of her mouth down to her neck, leaving a molten trail of heat from her jaw to her collar. She pressed her body to his, feeling the tense warmth beneath his clothes.

Anya felt Sparky tugging at her skirt, heard his warning growl. For an instant, her breath and her hands faltered. She felt Sparky pulling her in one direction, Mimi in the other. The demon roiled underneath her skin, eager to vicariously feel the pleasures of Drake's touch.

Drake snatched her hands, stared at her full in the face. His expression was guarded. "Is this you or is this the demon? What do *you* want?"

"I . . ." She swallowed. She wanted him to fill this dark void in her chest, wanted to feel something other than this damnable standing at a distance from the world.

"I want you," she answered. "Maybe not for the right reasons, but I do want you."

The tension in his face fractured into a dark smile. He laid his fingers on her lips. "Stay right there."

He backed two steps away from her, reached for a can of spray paint on the table, and shook it. He sprayed a circle on the floor, nine feet in diameter, surrounding her, Sparky, and the table. He left a three-foot break in the circle open beside Anya. He threw a handful of salt that scattered across the floor like insects.

Drake picked up one of the dogs' tennis balls. "Sparky." He bounced the ball through the circle and to the opposite side of the studio.

Instinct got the better of Sparky. He lunged through the break after the ball, with the two dogs. After he realized he couldn't grasp it with his elemental jaws, he turned back to Anya and Drake—only to find that he couldn't cross the circle Drake had finished painting on the floor. The salamander paced at the perimeter, whining.

Drake advanced on Anya, backed her into the edge of the table, and laced his fingers in hers. His thumbs rubbed circles against the backs of her hands. His paint-stained hands left smears of gold on her skin.

"How did you do that?" she breathed.

"It won't hurt him. Just a plain old magic circle that will hold just about any magickal creature—symbol and intent." He nibbled at her earlobe. "And very delicious intent, it is. Is that mint?"

"Mmm." She felt the muscles of his chest moving and slid her fingers under the collar of his shirt. She reached up on her tiptoes to kiss the scar above his blind eye, the bridge of his nose. He sighed and grasped her tighter, circling her ribs with his hands.

She flinched. He softened his grip immediately.

She cast her eyes down, dropping her hands. "The demon, ah . . . left me with some grill marks." She couldn't imagine how his artist's eye would be revulsed by seeing the ugly burn on her chest. The overhead light suddenly seemed very bright.

Drake unbuttoned his shirt. "I've got a few scars of my own."

His chest was crisscrossed with a spiderweb of raised white scars running across his ribs and curling around his back. Anya tentatively brushed them with her fingers, how they bumped over his ribcage and crossed over his spine in jagged tracks. It reminded her of the frost patterns made by the salt on his watercolors, strangely beautiful in their asymmetry, speaking of untold reactions beneath the surface, beyond what the eye could see. Her hands slid up to the cauterized, angry burn on his shoulder, where she'd shot him.

She lowered her mouth to a scar scraping just below his nipple, heard the hiss of his indrawn breath.

He picked her up, setting her on the edge of the table. She wrapped her legs around his waist, feeling his tongue thrusting in her mouth and his desire pressing against her belly.

His hands moved up from her hips to her breasts, teasing her nipples through the fabric. Plucking open her buttons, he pushed the blouse from her shoulders and kissed the first Hebrew character in blue permanent marker he found there.

"Your exorcist can't spell," he murmured against her skin.

"I thought intention was all that counted."

"Not always." He peeled the shirt from her chest, to her waist, stroked the burn crossing her chest with the back of his hand. He leaned forward to whisper in her ear: "Now, that's the effect I've been looking for with carbon in my painting."

He smiled against her hair, kissed her from her jaw to the hip bone jutting out over the waist of her skirt. His hand slid up under her skirt, stroking the inside of her thigh before sliding between her legs. She moaned and arched her back, pressing her breasts against his bare chest. She reached for his belt buckle, drawing it out of the belt loops and casting it aside on the floor. When she reached for him, he moaned, thrusting against her hand.

Drake pushed her back on the table. Bottles of paint and ink rolled away, clattering on the floor. Something shattered, but Drake ignored it as he drew open the drawstring of her skirt and slid it over her hips. He shucked his jeans on the floor and climbed up on the table.

She ached for him, craved the sizzle of his hot skin on hers. Taking his weight on his elbows, he pressed his body to hers. She moaned as he thrust inside her, wrapped her legs around him as he drove them both to an oblivion that rattled the last of his drawing pencils to the floor.

Somewhere in that sweetness of not being alone, something in her broke. It wasn't the demon. It was something deep within her heart, behind the black void of the Lantern. It cracked and welled up, leaking from the corner of her eye in the form of a tear that she brushed away before Drake noticed.

It was a crack in the façade of fear.

Afterward, she lay drowsing on the floor in the enemy's arms, wrapped in a clean muslin drop cloth. She lay with her head on Drake's chest, watching the sky lighten to the east. Sparky lay piled with the dogs in the corner, his head tightly tucked under his tail. After this, she figured that the tail-sucking would be the least of her worries.

She rose and dressed in the thin gray light of morning. As soon as she stepped out of the circle, Sparky attached himself to her knee. She turned back and looked at Drake, stretched in the makeshift circle on the floor and the glitter of salt.

"Stay," he said.

"I can't."

"Why fight what you are?" There was no accusation or anger in his voice, only a genuine wanting to know.

"Because I am what I am." She bent down to kiss the scar on his eyebrow. "And I am not what you are."

"I think," he said, smiling sadly, "that you are not quite certain of that yet. But you will be."

She left the studio when pink dawn began to stain the sky, his words ringing in her ears.

CHAPTER SEVENTEEN

"Look, I told you I couldn't sleep with Ciro snoring like a chainsaw, so I left."

Anya gripped the steering wheel and stared at the road ahead, not meeting Katie's eyes. She still felt the witch's disapproval heavy upon her. Between them, Sparky lay on the bench seat of the Dart. He was making a show of ignoring Anya by sitting this close to her with his back turned, thumping his tail on the seat.

"Yeah, well, it's where you were afterward that bothers me." Katie frowned. "You smell like enough fire magick to cook a steak."

Anya rolled her eyes. "You're not my mom, Katie."

"Actually, since we got those forms notarized this morning, I *am* your mom. If you become mentally incapacitated, I get to decide which nursing home to stick you in." Katie crossed her arms.

"I am not mentally incapacitated. Not yet, anyway," Anya grumbled. "Are you navigating, or are you here solely to bust my ass?"

Katie smoothed the map over her knees. "The next turn is just ahead. Left. And I will bust your ass whenever you're deserving of it."

Anya made a face and switched on the turn signal. She'd been stuck in the car with Katie for the last five hours, including two bathroom runs at gas stations with very interesting assortments of entertainment available from the machines on the wall. Katie had bought her a fistful of glow-in-the-dark French ticklers, and stuffed them in the Dart's glove box.

This far south in Ohio, the flat glacial plane had given way to rolling hills and woods. Autumn's breath was more evident here than in the cities, the brilliant fiery foliage speckling the landscape in a riot of reds and gold. The straight, wide freeways of the north yielded to winding two-lane roads bent back with blind hairpin turns. The gray sky overhead spat occasional raindrops on the windshield. The Dart growled up the hills and valleys in third gear, making progress irritatingly slow. Or perhaps it was just the company.

"Remind me what we're doing here again?" Katie grumbled, looking greener than the Wicked Witch of the West. She popped another peppermint into her mouth. Anya hoped that if Katie barfed, she would give enough warning for Anya to pull over. The smell of vomit would be nearly impossible to clean from the Dart's interior. Anya had been under the impression that getting back to nature was supposed to be good for witches. Apparently, the ride there wasn't so agreeable.

"I'm not really sure," she admitted. "My mother brought me to Serpent Mound when I was a kid. The shape of it reminds me of the Horned Viper symbol. The research that Felicity did for me indicates that there are some abnormalities in the bedrock here, melt marks consistent with the marks left around the arson scenes . . . it's just a hunch, really."

"At least it'll keep you out of Drake Ferrer's backyard."

Anya gave her a dirty look as she pulled into the parking lot of the Serpent Mound Museum. The park perched on a plateau overlooking two branches of creek and surrounding forest. This far south, the grass was still green as summertime, curving around the small blacktop parking lot.

Katie had wrenched the door open before Anya had even shut off the ignition. She took two mincing steps to the grass at the edge of the parking lot and heaved out the remains of a gas station hot dog. Sparky looked balefully up at Anya, the first time he'd looked her full in the face all day.

Sighing, Anya crossed to the front of the car to rub Katie's shoulders and hold her hair back. She hit the dry heaves pretty quickly, then sat down hard on the curb.

"I'm driving on the way back," she announced.

"Okay," Anya agreed, stroking the top of her head.

When Katie wobbled to her feet, the women made their way to the Serpent Mound Museum, a log cabin flanked by two pop machines. They were in luck—the Ohio

Historical Society was promoting Ohio's Haunted Places for October, and the museum was open. Anya bought Katie a bottled water, which she sipped at gingerly. Now that her feet were on solid ground, color had begun to return to her face.

The modest museum exhibited maps of the mound and aerial photos. From the sky, the mound looked like a squiggle of a horned snake opening its jaws around an egg, its spiraling tail curving away. The exhibit information described how, in the late 1880s, a Harvard University researcher had excavated the mound and attributed its construction to the Adena Indians as early as 800 years BC. Later researchers attributed the formation to the Fort Ancient Indians, who built it between 900 and 1550 AD. The exact reason for its construction and its meaning was lost in history, though some speculated that the effigy mirrored the constellation Draco, the dragon.

"Like the old magickal rule goes: 'As above, so below,' " Katie murmured.

The head was measured to be aligned with the summer solstice sunset, but no concrete purpose beyond that could be found. Some historians speculated that the snake symbolized the creature known as the Uktena by the Cherokee people, a horned snake who was charged with the mission to destroy the sun.

A display case showing a chunk of ruddy, striated stone confirmed Felicity's research: that the site of the effigy showed geologic signs of volcanic or meteoric explosion. The exhibit further noted that the effigy was built at the intersection of three fault lines, suggesting unusual geologic activity in the meteor crater overgrown with vegetation.

The myth surrounding the mound was that it had been a burial site, a memorial to fallen Adena. The mound had been partially excavated in the late 1880s, but no human remains had yet been found. Still, the speculation continued about what could be found, if one just dug deeply enough.

"I want to see it," said Katie. Her voice sounded stronger.

"You up to it?"

"Yup. I've exorcised the demon chili dog." She raised a triumphant arm and pointed to the horizon. "Onward."

A blacktop path led from the museum around the perimeter of the serpent. No more than three feet high, the Serpent Mound coiled across the top of the plateau for a quarter of a mile. It was the same as Anya had remembered: freshly mown grass clippings blowing over the rills in the earth. No other visitors walked the path; Anya, Katie, and Sparky were alone with the snake.

"Wow," said Katie. She knelt and brushed her hands over the grass. "This place . . . it's like it hums."

Anya stepped off the path into the grass. She could feel it, too, as if some deep underwater current roiled beneath the surface. She climbed up the short hill of one of the serpent's coils and sat down, surveying the land spread out below her. The land was foreign to her, but the taste of isolation was familiar.

Katie perched beside her, still combing the grass with her fingers. She arranged herself in a meditation posture, wrapped herself in silence. Sparky sniffed and snorted around the curls of the snake's body, like a dog seeking out a buried bone.

Anya's eyes slipped shut. She reached out with her mind, down the length of the serpent's spine, reaching for some answer, for some fragment of knowledge that would help her understand the Horned Viper and its kind, some key that would help her find and keep Sirrush away from Drake Ferrer.

Her senses slipped below the ground, below the shorn grass, below the sediments built up over centuries. Her mind circled around something deep below the fault lines, far below the excavations of men. Deep in the bedrock, she saw the shape of a massive, serpentine creature, suspended in rock and silt, like Draco in the blackness of the sky. She sensed a heartbeat, slow as tides, thrumming in the hibernating creature. It had been here for thousands of years, content to listen to the seasons and the burning of stars overhead. As above, so below, indeed.

Why did it sleep? What kept it there, peacefully bound to earth? Her brow wrinkled as her thoughts smoothed over the mound, paused on a collection of delicate bones near the serpent's head, fathoms and fathoms below the symbol of the sun above its horns.

Anya heard the ghost sigh, and she opened her eyes. The ghost paced the length of the serpent's spine, from head to tail. Anya watched the spirit as she walked, barefoot, the grass prickling up between her toes. She was dressed in a white deerskin robe adorned with beads.

Long, straight black hair was swept off her coppery face with braids pierced with hawk feathers. In one hand, she held a steady flame that didn't burn the flesh of her palm. In her other hand, she held a staff, ribboned with snakeskin and beads, with the skull of a serpent perched atop it. She traced and retraced her steps in a circuit, watching the ground, her beads rattling as she moved.

"Do you see her?" she asked Katie.

Katie lifted her head, and nodded.

The ghost paused before Anya. She gestured for the women to follow her. Anya rose and followed her on her path, lit by the light from her hand.

"Anya." Katie gripped her elbow. "I think she's a Lantern. Her aura . . . it's not amber like yours, but orange, like a sunset."

Anya squinted at her. She could see a warm orange churning behind her chest. It wasn't the black void Anya kept feeding with the shells of spirits, or the red burning chasm that pounded behind Drake's chest. Her heart glowed with a warm orange light . . . and it was full. Not hungry. Anya sensed the stillness of glass, a transparent and peaceful love. The need to know prickled over her—how had the Indian woman found that balance, that perfect equilibrium? And, feeling that peace radiating from her, why was she still an earthbound spirit? Why had she not wandered to a bright hereafter?

"Why are you still here?" Anya asked her. She had no idea if the woman could understand her, if she could hear the question behind her foreign speech.

The woman turned, smiling radiantly. By now the three women had reached the head of the Horned Viper. She reached down to touch the head of the serpent effigy with a sense of reverence. Anya saw she wore a beaded necklace with a fetish of a winged serpent dangling on it, carved in bone.

"*Uktena,*" she said. She pressed her hand to her chest. "*Nina.*"

Anya pressed her hand to her own chest. "Anya." She crouched down beside the woman. Sparky waddled through the grass behind her, drawn by the irresistible scent of ghosts and magick. She touched the salamander's head. "Sparky."

The Native American woman smiled and extended her hand. "*Sparky.*"

Sparky licked her hand and she stroked behind his gill-frond. Sparky made happy contorted faces of pleasure, scratching at his neck with his back paw.

Anya looked at the circular mound crowning the Horned Viper. Beyond it, she could sense Nina's bones, arranged in meticulous order, in a hidden chamber beneath the earth. Her body was surrounded by urns, bits of pottery, the remains of a beaded belt. She had been placed here, with honor. Perhaps Nina had been a priestess to Uktena . . . or a sacrifice to him.

"Nina," she said. "Are you guarding Uktena?"

Nina nodded, rubbing Sparky's chin.

"Is it you who's keeping Uktena here, underground?"

Nina pointed behind her, at her bones in the earth. She

nodded. She pressed her right hand to her chest, the hand that flamed with unending fire. *"Nina."* She placed the other on the ground. *"Uktena."* She knit both of her hands together, then pressed her hands to the earth.

Nina placed her right hand on Anya's chest. She didn't feel the burn of fire where Nina touched her. Instead, she felt a swelling of peace that reached deep into her lungs, softening the hard edge of her fear and isolation. *"Anya."* Nina reached her other hand to the north, grasping something too far for her to reach. *"Sirrush,"* she said. She knit both of her hands together, pressed them to the clay soil.

"I think I understand," Anya said slowly.

The spirit brushed her cheek as tenderly as a mother might touch a child. In that gesture, Anya thought she detected that the spirit pitied her a bit, pitied her for her fears and struggles.

Nina climbed to her feet and walked away, continuing her patrol on the green grass. Her beads rattled softly and she hummed to herself in a melody that was quickly snatched up by the wind.

Her meaning was clear. Anya could see how Nina was rooted in place, bound to Uktena, patrolling the land while he slept. On a visceral level, she understood what would need to happen to keep Sirrush buried.

It would take the sacrifice of a Lantern.

The ride back stretched out long and gray as the road and rain before Anya, Katie, and Sparky. As soon as they'd climbed back into the Dart, rain began to strike the hood in earnest, drumming on the roof of the car and causing the windshield wipers to thunk in a slow, mesmerizing rhythm.

Anya curled up in the passenger seat, jacket wrapped around her shoulders and a salamander's ass in her lap. Sparky still ignored her, but not as fiercely as before. She dozed somewhere between the pearliness of the sky and the charcoal of the road, in the gray rain-spangled space between the shift of gears and the hum of the engine.

And she dreamed.

She dreamed of the shimmering darkness of the underground ice cave, a darkness that seethed and glistened in the heat like a living thing. She was swallowed in the dark, swallowed like the bones of Nina's grave, forever underground with Uktena.

But she knew, deep down, that this was also her destiny . . . that she would have to watch over Sirrush's sleep, pacing the perimeter of his grave until the end of time. She'd watch as the world above fed him, in fire, but she would feed him no more.

But she wasn't alone in this strange afterworld. She felt Mimi, boiling behind her.

"Leave me alone," Anya told it. "Do you want to spend eternity in this darkness, with me?"

Mimi giggled. *"Don't be so optimistic. You won't succeed. You and I will be in Sirrush's service, the servants of chaos, at Sirrush's left hand. And we won't be alone."*

Anya squinted further into the darkness. She saw the pale yellow dress of the girl from the soda machine, floating like a butterfly in the haze. She saw her among hundreds of dead victims, walking through the cave to the growling blackness at the back. Food. She saw her mother, walking in her charred pink nightgown, and Neuman heavy in his firefighter's gear. All dead from the hands of fire, nourishing Sirrush.

She shouted at them, tried to elbow through the crowd. But Mimi had ruined her voice, scraped it clean of her throat like an oyster from its shell. She reached out, caught an elbow, and turned a figure around to face her.

"Brian," she whispered.

His head was shaved and stubbly, a tube dangling from his temple to his shoulder, dripping a leak on the shoulder of his hospital gown when she shook him. A tangle of wires and tubes followed him like the severed strings of a marionette.

"Brian . . . Brian, you shouldn't be here," she insisted. "You're alive."

He stared at her with glassy, blank eyes, his attention turning back toward the gaping maw of darkness.

"Do you hear me?" Tears streamed down her cheek, and she gripped him fiercely. "You're alive. You shouldn't be here."

He looked beyond her, past her, at the growing darkness.

Anya awoke in darkness, with a jerk that slammed her burnt chest against the seat belt. Sparky tumbled from her lap to the floorboard.

Katie slammed on the brakes. "What? What's wrong?"

Anya clutched the seat belt that cut into her chest, pain lancing across her skin. Deep in her gut, she could feel Mimi giggling.

"It's Brian," she gasped. "I dreamed that Brian was dead."

Katie set her mouth in a grim line, and wordlessly stepped on the gas. The Dart growled down the highway, toward the light of Detroit on the far horizon.

Anya pressed the heels of her hands to her eyes. If she lost Brian . . . She'd promised him that everything would be different. That she would learn to open her heart to him.

"*You lied,*" Mimi hissed at her. "*You lied to him. If you loved him, you wouldn't have screwed Drake Ferrer.*"

Anya pressed her fists to her ears. "Shut the fuck up, Mimi."

"*You've got a funny way of showing love, Anya. Leave the one you love all alone in a hospital bed. He probably died all alone . . . just about as alone as you'll end up.*"

Katie looked sidelong at her. "Do I need to use that power of attorney?"

Anya slid her hands down the side of her face. She took a deep breath. "No. I've got it under control."

Mimi snickered. "*If she only knew that you were long out of control . . . she'd have you locked up in a rubber room.*"

Anya dug her fingernails into her palms. She stared out the window, trying to tune Mimi out. She wondered what collection of stars up there were Draco, if any of them could be seen under the city's relentless halo, that miasma of man-made light.

Katie sped to Detroit without stopping, drove until they pulled into the hospital parking garage with the gas gauge an eyelash above the big *E*. Anya had raced out of the car to the walkway into the hospital before Katie had locked up. Sparky scrambled to catch up, his short legs churning across the litter-strewn concrete like Godzilla stomping Tokyo.

Anya sprinted through the corridors, her dream fresh as upturned earth in her head, tasting like ash in her mouth. She ignored a warning from a nurse to slow down, dodged around a meal cart, and sidestepped the ghost of a woman pacing down the hallway with a stuffed animal in her arms. The ghost ignored her, slowly drawing a thread out of the teddy bear's foot and pulling the stuffing out of it.

Anya reached the ICU, skidding to a stop when she saw Jules and Max in the common area. Panic washed over her.

Jules raised his hand. "Anya. Don't go back there. You don't want to see that . . ."

She made a strangled noise and lunged past him. Heart in her mouth, she ripped aside the curtain . . .

. . . to see a full-moon flash of Brian's ass and a nurse's assistant removing a bedpan. Brian twisted his gown around and glared over his shoulder.

"Jesus Christ, Anya. I haven't taken a piss in days. Some privacy, please!"

She burst into tears, jostled the nurse's assistant aside, and flung her arms around him. His stubbly cheek felt warm against hers, and he felt joyously, perfectly alive.

Bewildered, Brian stroked her hair. "I'm glad to see you, too."

She sat down on the edge of his bed, wiping tears from her eyes. "I thought you were a goner."

Sparky launched himself into Brian's bed. Brian's heart monitor skipped a few beats as Sparky scrambled up to lick his face, tail wagging.

"Pfffbbbt. I had a nice nap with some trippy dreams. Jules tells me that I whacked my head on the sink. Not a glorious wound for a ghost-hunter." Brian reached out to turn her chin to the light. "You, you look like hell."

She smiled through the gloss of tears, as she patted his hand. "Don't worry about me. Tell me about your trippy dreams."

Brian blinked up at the ceiling. "I dreamed you and I went out for ice cream."

"That sounds like a nice, non-trippy dream."

"Yeah. It was. Until the Great Pumpkin drove up on a Harley and offered us pumpkin seeds he scooped out of my head." He rubbed his stubbly head. "Damn. I'm bald. That's gonna take some getting used to."

Anya rubbed his scalp. "It's kind of hot. Feels like Velcro."

Brian shrugged. "Meh. I'll figure out a way to work it. Maybe get some sunglasses."

Anya shook her head. "I love you just as you are. Without the shades." She paused, realizing what she'd just blurted out.

Brian grinned. "Well, *that* was worth waking up to." He reached for her hand. "What brought that on?"

She swallowed. "No time like the present."

There's no knowing how much time any of us has, she thought.

Mimi snorted at her: *"Keep marking those minutes, Anya. They're going to keep slipping through your fingers, until they're all mine."*

Mimi's grip on Anya's dreams tightened.

Anya tried to stay awake as late as she could, watching infomercials for dozens of arcane devices that variously promised to remove Jack the Ripper's laundry stains, flatten out unflattering panty lines and arm bulges, and both curl and straighten hair. Katie snored on the other end of Anya's couch, having given in to the impulse to purchase an item resembling a cheese grater to exfoliate her feet. She rationalized the purchase by deciding to use it to grate nutmeg if it didn't work on human flesh.

Anya stared at the ends of her hair, seriously contemplating if her hair could be steam-pressed into the attractive flip the spokesmodel shook before the camera. About the time she decided it wasn't worth the effort or the twenty to buy another gizmo that Sparky would enjoy nibbling on, she nodded off . . .

And fell into the centuries-old well of Mimi's memory.

She surfaced at night, a thick, warm darkness that clung to the skin like sand. Like the dream of the priest,

Anya was a spectator, able only to watch Mimi's memory unfurl and stain the water of her dreams like ink.

She watched as a woman walked through the darkness of ancient dirt streets. The bracelets on her arms and bells sewn into the fringe of her garments clinked with the sway of her hips. The bells had been intended to drive away evil spirits, but there was no use in such petty charms. Anya could feel Mimi moving through her, luxuriating in the breeze moving through her clothes and the languid warmth of a recent sexual encounter on her skin.

The woman's black hair gleamed in the darkness, bound up with bits of metal and wire and set with beeswax. Sausage-thick curls wrought of horsehair brushed over her back. The blue of her ankle-length tunic and her belted shawl was paler than the azure of the tiles of the massive Ishtar gates she passed through, reaching up in all their splendor to the starry night.

The low skyline of Babylon was jagged, pierced by the geometric edges of ziggurats, the king's palaces, and the sharp crenellations of the Ishtar gate. Beyond the defensive walls surrounding the city, palm trees nodded on the banks of the river, leaves whispering in the arid breeze. To the west, she could hear the soothing rush of the black waters of the River Euphrates. The city had a deceptively safe, sleepy feel about it, as if no one knew about the monsters behind the gates.

A voice curled down from the top of the gate, like smoke: *"Where is a priestess of Ishtar wandering to at this late hour?"*

The woman turned her beautiful rouged face up to the source of the voice, a massive shadow on the wall. From the ground, Anya could only see a shimmer of gold and the harsh red burning of a pair of eyes above. She smelled something burnt, like warm carbon. The dark shape was beyond the reach of the guttering torchlight, but it was large enough to blot out the light of the moon.

"Sirrush." The woman sketched a deep bow. She looked up at him through fringed lashes. "I am merely searching for tribute for Ishtar."

A rustling above sounded like silk over dry leaves. *"Food for your goddess?"*

"Yes. Food for the goddess." Her smile curved upward. "A sacrifice."

The creature pacing the top of the wall snorted. From the ground, Anya could see the dark ripple of what might be a tail or the curve of a spine, the shimmer of refracted light. *"Lilitu. Your goddess requires strange sacrifices."*

Lilitu lifted her eyebrows in mock surprise. "They are no different than the ones required in your temple, Sirrush. Flesh is flesh."

A summoning bell tolled in the distance. The creature on the wall above stilled, listening.

"Your temple is calling you to feed, Sirrush."

Massive claws scraped the stone as the creature walked away, following the sounds of the bell. *"May all the gods and goddesses eat well tonight, Lilitu."*

Lilitu bowed her head, smiling a predatory grin. Anya could feel the grip of the demon tight around her throat.

She prowled through the darkness of the streets. Her kohled eyes roved over the few citizens of Babylon still awake at this hour: the guards, the carousers, the holy men taking out the dead. None of them were what she sought. She needed something special to sate Ishtar's taste for flesh. Something new.

She found it beside the inn, a traveler handing the reins of his horse to the quartermaster. She admired the way his body moved beneath his dusty traveler's shawl, the thickness of his curly hair and beard, the broadness of his shoulder. He wore a tunic richly dyed in shades of red and violet, the sparkle of jeweled rings glinting as he gestured to the quartermaster. His beard was knotted with bits of wire and gems, and the embroidery of his cap glinted with gilt. The traveler had more than a little coin. He would make a nice offering to Ishtar.

She sidled up to him as his horse was led away, looking up at him through her eyelashes. "The temple of Ishtar welcomes you to Babylon."

The foreigner smiled at her, his eyes scraping her from the top of her head to her sandaled feet. "I'm pleased to be so richly welcomed."

Lilitu bowed her head, dipping to display the bronze flesh of the tops of her breasts. "My name is Lilitu. I'm a priestess."

The foreigner tipped his head. "I am Darius. When you say that you are a priestess, does that mean . . . ?" He trailed off, not wishing to insult her. It was clear that Darius didn't understand their customs. Like many travelers, he'd heard rumors about the beautiful priestesses of Ishtar, but never experienced them firsthand.

Lilitu grasped his arm, smiling. "Aye, I am one of Ishtar's sacred prostitutes, an incarnation of her flesh. And I invite you to partake of the goddess's hospitality."

The foreigner's broad face broke into a grin. "I would be honored to follow the customs of my host city," he murmured as Lilitu led him away down the dirt streets.

He followed her up the steps of a temple of smooth, sand-colored rock, between the sculptures of two roaring lions. The temple smelled of incense, rich and musty. Inside, vaulted ceilings reached up to darkness, lit by guttering torches. Priestesses carried serving trays, plucked the strings of lutes, flitting like butterflies against the glazed brickwork interior.

The back of the temple held a massive altar, overhung with flowers and lit with the glow of a multitude of lamps. A life-sized gilded statue of Ishtar stood on a pedestal, surveying her dominion. The goddess bore some characteristics of the eagle, wings tucked behind her, and her clawed feet balancing her on the pedestal. Her golden armor gleamed in the candlelight, which cast undulating shadows across her eyes, inset with lapis lazuli. Jewelry and garlands of flowers draped her outstretched arms.

"This way." Lilitu led Darius on a room to the right, concealed from the main area by curtains. It was one of six rooms splitting off from the great hall; giggles and sighs of pleasure could be heard from the others.

Grinning in anticipation, Darius let Lilitu draw the

curtain behind them. He reclined on a pile of cushions, watching the priestess move near. She bent over him, tickling his chest with her hair. His gaze roved over her voluptuous body, his hands reaching to grasp her buttocks as she straddled him. Slowly, she drew out the laces of her golden girdle, exposing her breasts to the dim light.

In his ear, she whispered. "My flesh is the flesh of Ishtar. Feel the blessing of her skin upon yours."

He shivered in pleasure.

Lilitu smiled at him. She lifted the hem of her dress, rubbed her hand over her exposed coppery skin. She reached for her sandals, for the small, jeweled dagger she'd tied in the laces. Darius' attention was focused on her breasts, and he never saw it. She smiled, leaned forward to cradle his head in the crook of her elbow, and covered his mouth with hers.

Pulling the dagger free of its sheath, she raised it behind her head and plunged it between his ribs. He screamed against her mouth, but the demon held him fast, locking his head to hers with superhuman strength. Her mouth muffled his cries as the demon twisted the blade, scraped it against bone. The foreigner's lung deflated, and he rolled back against the pillows.

Mimi smiled with Lilitu's lips. "A sacrifice of flesh for flesh."

Anya awoke, her palm feeling hot and slick from the sensation of the knife in her grip. Instead of guttering torchlight in the temple, the television in her living room showed a man doing push-ups with a nasty piece of exercise equipment. Beside her, Katie slept, curled up in a ball and drooling on the back of the couch.

Sparky shifted in Anya's lap. He leaned into her chest and Anya imagined he could feel her heart hammering. Anya rubbed her grainy eyes, as if she could drive some of Mimi's murderous influence away. But she could still feel the warmth of Lilitu's victim underneath Mimi's hands, the scrape of metal drawing out against bone and the sigh of a collapsing lung.

How long would it be before Mimi would drive her to such acts? How long could she fend Mimi off with beeswax ointment and holy water, before the demon seized control and hurt someone with Anya's own hands?

Anya pressed the heel of her palm against her forehead. The irony of Mimi's demonic possession pressed thickly upon her: As lonely as Anya had always been, no matter what terrible things she did, she would never be alone again.

Mimi whispered at her, gentle as a desert breeze: *"Never."*

CHAPTER EIGHTEEN

"IF SIRRUSH IS ANYTHING LIKE Uktena, he'll have a nest somewhere."

Anya flipped through a street atlas of Detroit in the archival room at the library. The thick walls blocked out the clear morning sunshine. Anya missed it—she felt that, with Mimi's influence, she was slowly losing her grip on time.

She turned the pages of the atlas with one hand, while the other held a pen scratching on a notebook. Mimi had seized the opportunity to compose a sonnet about the virtues of lust.

Katie peeked over Anya's shoulder. "Ugh. That's disgusting. I didn't think that you could do that with a spatula."

Anya made a face. "Trust me, I'm not that creative. You've seen my kitchen."

Katie peered into Anya's face. "Mimi. You're one nasty-ass demon."

Anya couldn't stop Mimi's voice before it escaped her

lips: *"I go both ways, dear. Want to play?"* Anya clapped her hand over her mouth. "Sorry," she said.

Katie wrinkled her nose. "I can't wait until you get rid of that bitch."

Felicity popped her head cautiously through a cabinet. *"Is it safe to come in?"* Mimi had threatened to consume Felicity with a side of tofu an hour earlier, and the ghost of the librarian had made herself scarce.

"It's safe, as long as you're not a spatula."

Felicity stepped over Sparky, who was taking a nap on the floor. *"I've got that list of underground parking garages for you that predate 1950."* A scrap of paper floated to Anya's right hand. Her left hand snatched it before her right had the chance to scribble more obscenities involving kitchen utensils on it.

"Thanks, Felicity."

"I was thinking . . ." The ghost kept well out of reach of Anya's right arm. *"What about the Detroit Salt Mine?"*

Anya's hand stilled. "Talk to me, Felicity."

"Well . . . it's closed down now. Has been since the 1980s. But, if memory serves, the Detroit Salt Mine spreads under a large portion of the southwestern part of the city."

Anya hopped over to the computer terminal to search for information on the salt mine. Unfortunately, Mimi wouldn't cooperate well enough to type, and she hit three pornographic sites before an automated message threatened to kick her off the computer. She surrendered the chair to Katie before a flesh-and-blood librarian turned up to ask her to leave.

"I shudder in pleasure to imagine what I could have managed with the internet in ancient Babylon." Mimi sighed under Anya's breath.

Katie closed down dozens of pop-up windows describing a variety of flavors of online services directed to aficionados of webcam voyeurism. She searched for the Detroit Salt Company, and opened up a page displaying a grainy black-and-white image of a cave larger than an airplane hangar.

Anya's breath snagged in her throat. "That's the cave from my dream. I'm sure of it." It hadn't been ice, after all . . . the cave had been hewn of salt. "Felicity, you're brilliant."

"I try," the ghost said modestly.

"It says here that the mines cover more than one thousand five hundred acres under the city . . . that's a lot of ground to cover," Katie said.

"I'll pull the maps from the archive." Felicity popped out of sight.

Anya's cell phone chirped, and her right hand reached for the phone. She slapped it back with her left, snatching the phone and pressing it to her ear.

"Kalinczyk."

"This is Marsh. Merry early Christmas, Lieutenant. You were right . . . Drake Ferrer returned to the scene of the apartment fire. DFD caught him last night carving a number one in the pavement. He surrendered without a fight. He just finished intake in the county lockup."

Anya sat in the visitation area of the Wayne County Jail, waiting on her side of a Plexiglas partition for Drake to be brought to her. The room was painted a sickly yellow, illuminated by buzzing fluorescent light. Even this far away from the cellblocks, it smelled like sweat and stale piss. Anya wished she'd brought a bottle of disinfectant with her; she wondered whether or not pressing the visitation phone to her ear would give her head lice.

She'd been lucky to get in at all. Mimi had thought it would be funny to sign her in on the visitor log as Captain Kangaroo. Anya had caught it in time to scratch it out with her left hand and scribble her real name on the next line. The visitation officer glared skeptically, as her signature didn't match the one on her driver's license, but Anya had convinced him that she was suffering from a bad case of carpal tunnel syndrome.

Jails were not among Anya's favorite places. Like hospitals, they tended to be haunted, only with a less pleasant clientele of ghosts. At the moment, she was trying very hard to ignore the ghost of the orange jumpsuited man sitting on the plastic chair beside her. The inmate's ghost sat with his feet drawn up on the chair and his hands wrapped around his knees. Around his neck, he bore a ligature mark. Hanging, definitely. The question was whether or not it was his own idea. Sparky sat in Anya's lap and growled at the ghost, daring him to come within reach of his teeth.

The ghost stared at her, unblinking, with a look of thirsty malice that gave her the willies. Mimi kept twitching toward him. Anya considered devouring him, but was reluctant—if Ferrer was right, she didn't want to keep feeding the monster.

But if that piece of ectoplasmic shit touched her, all bets were off.

The deputy supervising visitation finally brought Ferrer back to the other side of the Plexiglas. Anya drew in her breath. He looked like hell. Dressed in an ill-fitting orange jumpsuit, his hands were folded in front of him, wrists braceleted in handcuffs. His good eye was blackened with a shiner, and small cuts covered his left arm. She had a visceral sense of him not belonging here, not in the harsh brutality of this place that smelled like sweat.

Anya picked up the phone. "What happened to you?"

Drake shrugged. "The other inmates don't like me much." His focus slid from her to the ghost of the inmate. He lifted his hand, threatening the ghost.

Anya tried to distract him, speaking quickly. "I hear you got caught at the apartment scene. Is that true?"

"That's what the police say." His smile was enigmatic, serene. His hand fell back down on the desk.

Anya's eyes narrowed. She knew there was nothing that could hold him; she'd seen him walk in fire, knew he could cut through concrete with his bare hands. Those handcuffs would be like butter to him.

"Why are you here, Drake?" She leaned forward, pressed her fingers to the Plexiglas. "Where's your lawyer? You could have bonded out before you even hit a holding cell."

"Isn't this what you wanted?"

Her gaze flickered to the ugly bruise on his face. "Yes . . . no. Not like this." She watched him watching her through the plastic. "You wouldn't take Mimi from me, because it would interfere with your plans. Will you take it now?" Hope flared within her at the thought of getting rid of the demon.

He shook his head. "Not yet, regretfully."

Mimi giggled. *"I think he's afraid that I'm a better lover than you are. He's right."*

Anya ignored the demon's voice in the back of her head, and concentrated on Drake. "You're not here because I want you to be here." She leaned back in her creaky plastic chair. It wasn't over. "You're here because you want to be."

He smiled enigmatically. "Architects are planners. Wait and see."

The ghost leaned forward, so close to Anya that she could feel the chill radiating from him. He didn't speak, couldn't harm her, but that sense of intimidation still hung in the air. Anya stared through him. Sparky growled deep in his throat, but Anya kept her fingers tightly wound in the loose skin of his neck. She could feel Sparky's muscles tensing to leap.

Drake tapped on the glass, and both the ghost and Anya turned to face him.

"Hey, buddy," Ferrer said. "I have something to tell you."

The ghost leaned toward the plastic.

"Come closer. I have something I want to give you."

"No, don't," Anya said.

The ghost took a step, then two, toward the desk. Anya let Sparky go, in hopes that the salamander would tear him down and away from Drake's grip, but too late.

As soon as the spirit of the inmate passed through the Plexiglas, Drake had him. The ghost disappeared in a wisp of smoke that blew away. Sparky landed on the floor, shaking his head in disorientation.

Drake leaned toward the Plexiglas. "Don't worry. I've got everything under control."

"He's in jail for a reason." Anya drummed her fingers on the surface of Ciro's bar. The chalk sigils had all been washed away. Jules and Max were busy installing new mirror tiles above the bar. The bar was closed to patrons and Ciro liked it that way on Devil's Night. Too many crowds had gotten out of hand over the years. At least this gave him an excuse not to open his doors in the first place. Every once in a while, a group of drunken revelers would thump on the plywood boards as they walked by, giving the Devil's Bathtub denizens a jolt.

In the background, the television droned. The Lions were losing to the Steelers at home on Ford Field and it seemed like that bit of normal noise drove out some of the thick atmosphere still clinging to the bar from the exorcism. Sparky sat on the bar top, his head craned to watch the images on the screen over the bar. Every so often, he would reach up and lick the screen, eliciting an instant of static. Max and Jules would yell for him to sit down and the picture would resolve itself.

"Well, yeah. He's a felon. He got caught." Katie looked up from the cake she was demolishing in a booth with Ciro. To celebrate Brian getting sprung from the hospital, she'd baked a cake in the shape of a Detroit Lions football helmet. DAGR had also pitched in to buy Brian a real Detroit Lions helmet, as safety equipment for his next encounter with the paranormal. Given the Lions' dismal record, it was an appropriate gift for a guy unlucky enough to give himself a brain injury falling off a toilet.

"No. His bond's been set, and he hasn't made any effort whatsoever to make it. According to Marsh, he pretty much handed himself over on a silver platter at the scene." Anya pushed her cake around her paper plate with a fork. Food didn't have much taste anymore. Drake's behavior stymied her. Her conversation with him suggested that his plans were still in motion, but how? He had no accomplices and Devil's Night was tonight. He was cooling his heels in the lockup, probably getting his ass kicked. It made no sense. "There are plenty of ghosts there for him to devour, but that can't be the only appeal. He could find as many walking around a graveyard or a nursing home."

Beside her, Brian was busily scarfing down his third serving of cake. He paused to thumb the keys on his web-enabled cell phone. "According to the sheriff's online inmate database, Ferrer's been there for nearly a day now. I'm sure he's enjoying his time locked up with all the other inmates." He shrugged. "The food's probably pretty on par with hospital food, anyway."

Max turned around. "That's pretty cool. You can tell who's in jail just by checking the Web site?"

"Yeah. It's all public record info. I imagine that it's great fun for people who wonder where their spouses are at three in the morning."

"With all the other inmates . . ." Anya echoed, stuck on Brian's earlier statement. The glimmer of an idea lit in her thoughts. "Brian, can you check the database to see if Martin Carr is in jail?"

Brian's thumbs flew across the text keypad of his phone. "Nope."

"How about Joseph Lindsey?"

"No. Got a John and a James, but no Joseph."

"Anthony Sellers?"

Brian's thumbs skittered across the keyboard. "Yup. DOB is November 29, 1987. He's been locked up for three days for a domestic violence charge. Hasn't made bail. He's at Correction Center 1, downtown." Brian glanced at Anya. "You know that guy?"

Anya's mouth pressed into a grim slash. "Those are the guys who attacked Drake Ferrer years ago. Felicity and I were able to connect some of the arsons to them and the members of their families. If this guy was arrested and taken to jail before Ferrer, it's no coincidence." Dread prickled over her. "Can I use your phone?"

"Sure."

Anya punched in Marsh's number, careful to use her

left hand, lest Mimi choose a random 1-900 number. She slid off her barstool and snatched her jacket. "Captain Marsh, this is Kalinczyk."

"Shouldn't you be taking it easy on a beach somewhere?"

"I need you to get Drake Ferrer transferred out of CC1 to CC2 or CC3. One of his assailants from his 1998 attack is in jail with him."

"So?"

"I think that Ferrer is going to try to get back at him. I've been able to trace some of Ferrer's previous fires to his attackers: the beauty shop was run by one of his assailants' mothers and one of his assailants stored property at the warehouse. It's circumstantial, but . . ."

She could hear the gears whirring in Marsh's head. "I'll ask them for a keep-separate order, but they may not transfer him to another facility. The best we may be able to accomplish might be to keep them in separate cell blocks."

Anya bit her lip. "Marsh, if this guy's as crazy as I think he is, that might not be good enough."

She heard Marsh's pager go off on the other end of his line. A chorus of other pagers chirped in the background. It sounded like an aviary of electronic birds.

"Gotta go," he said curtly, and hung up.

Anya headed toward the door, sidestepping the sad remains of the cracked bathtub in the center of the floor. Maybe if she went down to the jail in person, she could convince the duty sergeant to move Ferrer if she brought a pizza. . . .

"Anya," Jules said. "Come see this." He turned up the volume on the television set.

The Lions game had been preempted by an image of a reporter clutching a microphone. "This is Paul Phillips, reporting from downtown Detroit. The Wayne County Jail Corrections Center 1 is on fire. Police and sheriff's deputies are on the scene, while the Detroit Fire Department is trying to contain the blaze . . ."

The camera swung behind the reporter to the gray concrete jail, sandwiched between Ford Field and Greektown. The structure was nearly entirely engulfed in flames. Glass had broken out of the slitted windows, but there wasn't enough room for inmates to escape through the bars. Hands and feet reached through the slits, clawing for fresh air. On the ground, fire trucks surrounded the building, and riot police had formed an armed perimeter, aiming their guns at the windows.

Anya pressed her hand to her mouth. "Oh my God. There are a thousand people in there. Drake's going to sacrifice them all to Sirrush."

It was even worse in person than on the television hanging above Ciro's bar.

The Lions game had been evacuated, and the outflow of traffic pouring from Detroit Field hampered the efforts to get fire trucks and emergency vehicles to the scene. News helicopters hovering over the scene reported on the radio that the chaos downtown had inspired other smaller fires in outlying areas. The state police and National

Guard were reportedly on the way, but Anya bet that they wouldn't make an appearance until tomorrow morning.

Traffic going downtown had been rerouted, causing Anya to double back with the Dart several times. She was finally successful in skipping past a barricade in Greektown by waving to a distracted officer while she was wearing her firefighter's coat. She pulled into an alley beside a restaurant. A man with a moustache in a white apron patrolled the bistro, carrying a shotgun.

"No parking," the swarthy man in the apron announced, brandishing his weapon.

"I'm a fire investigator," she said, raising her hands and lifting her hat. She gestured to the shotgun with her chin. "Will you watch my car for me?"

The man with the moustache grinned. "Lady, I'll watch your car for the price of ammo. You just make sure those thieves and rapists don't get out and screw with my restaurant."

"I'll do my best." She handed him a fifty and sprinted through the alley toward the orange blaze in the sky. Ash from the fire charred her throat and she had to struggle to breathe. It seemed that both Mimi and the smoke pooled low in her chest, giving her the lung capacity of a child. Coughing, she sprinted into view of the burning jail.

The scene was an unmitigated clusterfuck.

Incredible heat radiated from the concrete like fire from a blast furnace. Ladder trucks were having difficulty getting ladders to the shatterproof windows and breaking them out. The metal slats in the frames meant cutting tools had to be used, wasting precious time to get the inmates and deputies out. Hands thrust into the openings, making it nearly impossible to work without cutting arms off. Firefighters kept shouting for the people at the windows to "get back," but the warnings went unheeded in the crush of panic.

Deputies and SWAT teams led handcuffed groups of inmates in daisy-chain strings out on the ground floor, but controlling them was nearly impossible. The jail deputies weren't armed, and many inmates took this opportunity to try and make a break for it. SWAT launched canisters of tear gas into the doorways of the vestibule and the gas ignited under the intense heat. Someone had commandeered a school bus, and the bright yellow cheesewagon was already ripe to bursting with orange-suited inmates.

Anya stared up at the jail. The jail was haunted before, and it was sure as hell going to be even more haunted after this. She sensed new ghosts flaring whitely inside, like matches, as the air grew too thick to breathe and the heat blistered through the walls.

Anya raced with other firefighters to try to open another hydrant. Half the hydrants on this block were broken and spurting weakly, left too long without inspections. She dragged the mouth of heavy hose to a nozzle, and fitted it, while another firefighter tried to wrench it open. The hose inflated with water, coursing back to the source of the fire.

She squinted in the doorway of the vestibule. Something was seething through the flames, rolling toward the door. The crews, thinking a gas main had blown a fireball, backed away.

But it was not a fireball. It was a man, burning, his silhouette as red as an eclipsed sun. He incandesced serenely in the chaos, bits of ash floating down around him like autumn leaves. He walked with an unmistakable limp.

"Drake," she breathed.

The fireman at the nozzle of the hose Anya was holding aimed a blast of water at the burning man, out of pure instinct. The water hissed and steamed, evaporating before it touched his skin, curling around him in an arc of mist. The figure walked slowly through the wall of water, down the steps of the jail. Where he stepped, his feet melted into the concrete, leaving fiery footprints in his wake.

Over the wail of the sirens, Anya could hear shouting:

"What the hell is that?"

"Drop him!"

"No!" she yelled, running forward, but she was too late. She heard the sharp report of bullets fired, saw the burning man stumble . . . but he continued walking forward, a fiery juggernaut.

Above, the structure groaned. Both cops and firefighters focused their attention on the metal roof. The internal support structure had burned away, and it caved inward with a metallic groan. A ladder truck parked close to the building was forced to pull away, a firefighter still clinging to a swinging, extended ladder.

But Anya's attention was transfixed by the burning man. He walked across the street. The heat he generated was so powerful that windshields cracked as he passed by and paint bubbled up from the hoods of the police cars. She chased him on foot down the street, shouting, "Drake!"

He turned, perhaps recognizing her. But in this inhuman form, she did not know what he felt.

"Stay away." His voice was scraped raw, like rust. He reached out and punched the side of the school bus full of inmates.

Anya dove for cover behind a Dumpster as the gas tank ignited and the school bus exploded. The impact knocked over the Dumpster and threw her under a police car. The explosion rattled the cruiser on its tires, and she smelled scorching rubber. Through burning garbage and tearing eyes, she watched, horrified, as the flares of white ghosts howled through the flames and windows of the bus.

Aching, she crawled out from under the car on her elbows, torn between wanting to help the victims and catching Drake. She was the only one who had any hope of stopping Drake before he brought this fate down upon the entire city. She knew it, but she felt like a failure as she pulled herself to her feet and ran down the street, scanning the burning debris for a figure that shone brighter than the rest.

"Drake!" she yelled into the chaos.

But he was already gone.

CHAPTER NINETEEN

"DRAKE'S ESCAPED."

Anya clomped into Ciro's bar with her helmet under her arm, coat covered in ash and reeking of gasoline.

The members of DAGR were huddled around the bar, poring over Felicity's maps.

"Are the police going to chase him down? Or will a bounty hunter go find him, like on that show, *Dog the Bounty Hunter*?" Max asked. "That would be cool."

Jules slapped him in the back of the head. "Haven't you been watching what's going on on the TV? There are fires all over town. It's Devil's Night. The cops have got bigger problems than looking for a rich white boy. And anybody else with any sense is home sleeping with a shotgun."

"It's gonna be up to us to find him," said Brian. "No cops."

Anya shook her head. "No, I don't want any of you guys getting hurt. Drake is my problem."

Jules shook his head. "Nope. Not gonna happen. We're going with you."

"Absolutely not."

"This isn't a discussion," Jules said. He leaned against the bar and crossed his arms. "Like it or not, we're a family. A weird, fucked-up family, but family, nonetheless. And you aren't going after that monster alone."

Anya opened her mouth to protest. "But—"

Katie waved an envelope in the air. "Lest you forget, I have power of attorney over your ass. Unless you want to spend Devil's Night in the psych ward with twelve guys who think they're all Jesus, you'd better play ball with us."

Anya looked at their resolute faces. She slumped in a chair. "Look. I don't even know where Ferrer is exactly. If he's going to the salt mine to pull Sirrush's tail, that's a whole lot of ground to cover."

Brian lifted the map. "The oldest part of the mine is the deepest . . . hasn't been touched since the 1920s." He stabbed a vein at the back of the mine, outlined in black ink. "If I were a sleeping dragon, I'd want to be back there, where no one would bother me. And I bet that's where Ferrer will go."

"But what do we do when we get there?" Max asked.

Anya chewed her lower lip. "I think he's wounded. He may be moving slowly. And, actually . . ." Her fingers traced the lines of the mineshaft on the map. "This terrain might give us an advantage. There's nothing flammable down there for Drake to set fire to."

Jules pulled a shotgun and a box of shells out from underneath the bar. "There's not much that can outrun buckshot."

"You got any more where that came from?" Max spun on his bar stool, fascinated.

Anya showed him her empty hands. "The Department took my gun."

Ciro harrumphed. "I've got all of you covered. Don't worry." He gestured to Renee, who was floating by the stairs. "Renee, take Jules, Max, Brian, and Katie down to the basement. There'a a stash of old guns wrapped up in oilcloth under the floor in the wine cellar."

"Gotcha, boss." Renee led the team down the stairs to the basement.

Anya sat alone with Ciro. She looked down at her shoes.

"Anya, let me see your hands."

She stripped off her thick Nomex gloves and presented her hands to Ciro. They had begun to blacken from the fingertips, stretching up her arms. His quavering fingers danced over them, and his face crumpled in a frown.

"I can't feel my fingers, or much of my toes," Anya said. "It feels like frostbite. Is this . . . is this from the demon?"

"Yes." Ciro nodded. "I'm afraid that you have little time left until Mimiveh takes over."

"I can't let that happen, Ciro."

The old man leaned forward in his wheelchair. "Katie told me about what happened at Serpent Mound. About Nina . . . that her sacrifice kept the Uktena underground, sleeping."

"Yes." Her eyes glistened. "Ciro, she was the most

beautiful spirit I've ever met—pure of heart, pure of purpose. I envied her that . . . that sense of peace. That love."

Ciro brushed a tear from her eye. "Dear child, if you and the others fail in stopping Drake Ferrer, are you willing to follow in her footsteps to keep Sirrush underground?"

Anya nodded. "Yes." Her nose dripped and she wiped it with numb fingers. For the first time in her life, she didn't feel that there were things left undone. It seemed right to do this thing, even though no one would ever know.

Sparky put his paw in her lap and gazed up at her. The little guy had always been with her, and would never leave her. From somewhere down below, Anya heard Renee warbling "Somebody Loves Me."

"Remember that you're going into a salt mine," Ciro told her. "Salt absorbs magick and binds it to its own structure. It's like fire in its purifying properties . . . the oldest spells known to man involved making a wish on a handful of salt. Realize that any action you take in that place may have unintended results."

"I will, Ciro." She kissed the old man on the forehead.

The clomping of shoes on the stairs heralded DAGR's well-armed return to the bar. The team looked as if it had been antique shopping in the Prohibition era: Katie held a tiny pearl-handled Derringer .22 caliber between two fingers, as if terrified it might spontaneously go off. Jules brandished a tommy gun, grinning. Max looked at the machine gun in lust, but made do with stuffing a six-shot .38

Colt revolver in his belt. Jules slapped him on the back of the head.

"Ow."

"You aren't cool enough to be a gangster. Never stuff a gun in your pants. It's a great way to lose a nut."

Brian held a pair of M1911 Browning semiautomatic .45 pistols. Anya held her hand out.

He shook his head. "These are mine. No way I'm trusting you with guns."

"You're not going," she insisted. "You just got out of the hospital."

"There's no way I'd miss this." He gave her a lopsided grin.

Anya spun to appeal to Jules. "Jules, don't let him go. He's not in any shape to fight Sirrush," she pleaded. She didn't want to be responsible for hurting him again. He needed to be kept away from the fight, away from Mimi, and away from Drake.

Jules's gaze roved over Brian's bald head, laced with stitches. "Humpty Dumpty can go." He picked the Lions helmet off the counter and extended it to Brian. "But he has to wear his helmet."

"Fuck you, Jules."

"I have more bullets than you do. Be a winner. Wear the damn helmet."

Brian snatched the helmet. "If I was a winner, I'd be wearing a Steelers helmet."

The lights in the bar winked out, and the television fizzled to black.

Renee summoned a weak ball of ghost light, a will-o'-the-wisp that allowed Jules to dig around the bar to find flashlights and a box of fuses.

Anya stood on tiptoe to peer out the narrow window at the top of the bar door. As far as she could see, blocks upon blocks, the streets were dark. "Guys, I don't think it's the fuse box. I think that the electricity's gone." In the distance, she could already hear the sirens beginning to wail and the breaking of glass.

Jules swore. "Every thug, ghoul, and demon in the city is going to be out on the prowl. It's gonna be a helluva night."

As the Dart growled down the darkened streets, chaos had grown thick and palpable. Traffic lights swung dark from their cables, their red, yellow, and green eyes shut against the packs of looters breaking shop windows and tripping car alarm systems. Power was hit or miss; some blocks were lit up bright as Christmas, while others were plunged into darkness. Sirens wailed from all directions, but too distant to deter a group of young men in the process of boosting an ATM. They'd wrapped a length of chain around the machine, tied the other end to a pickup truck axle, and were determinedly rending it from the side of a convenience store. Headlights and the yellow blaze of fire were the only illumination in this part of the city. Anya watched as a fast-food restaurant burned, the cartoon character mascot engulfed in flames. She thought she smelled french fries, but suspected it was only the last of the fryer oil burning.

Katie reached forward from the backseat and pushed down the manual door lock. Max and Jules chortled at her attempt to keep the big green tank of the Dart secure.

On the radio, the deejay warned that the governor had called in the National Guard, and martial law had been declared in Wayne County. A curfew had been imposed; any nonemergency personnel found out on the streets were subject to being detained. Anya wasn't quite sure how that was going to be accomplished, but it made it sound as if *someone* was doing *something*. She glanced back in the rearview mirror. If they got pulled over, they'd have a lot of explaining to do. The Dart was bristling with guns, and Jules was passing out ammo in the backseat like it was Pez. Katie's silver pentacle necklace gleamed in the light of Jules's flashlight, and she was nervously organizing a backpack full of holy water. Max bounced up and down in the backseat like an excited poodle on meth. In the front seat, Brian, wearing his football helmet, was solemnly reading the map and fiddling with a video camera he'd duct taped to his facemask. Sparky sat on the front bench seat, alternately playing with the radio knobs and tweaking Brian's wires, setting off a bout of colorful swearing.

Anya was certain that they'd be arrested on first glance. Do not pass Go, do not collect $200. Go directly to jail.

"What's with the camera?" Max slapped Brian's sleeve.

Brian sighed. "Yeah. Need I remind you that this has the potential to be the largest paranormal event in history caught on tape?" He tapped the red light taped to the side of his helmet. "This is our retirement fund, ladies and gents."

Anya stared down at her hands on the steering wheel. Even in the darkness, they felt numb, swollen. Monstrous. In the back of her head, she heard Mimi humming Sting's "I Burn for You." When Brian gave her a sidelong glance, she realized that Mimi had been singing aloud, and that the sound buzzed through her lips.

Katie flipped some holy water on her from the backseat. "Down, Mimi."

That pissed Mimi off. The steering wheel swerved in Anya's hands, out of her control. The Dart plunged straight toward a mailbox. Brian wrested the wheel back, and the Dart slewed back on the street.

"No more driving for you."

"I've got it," she said through gritted teeth.

Brian slammed the parking brake back, and the Dart lurched forward with a jerk and a hiccup. Anya's head snapped forward, barely missing the steering wheel. As a stream of invectives filled her mouth, Brian popped the car into neutral and tried to climb over her into the driver's seat.

Anya felt her mouth curl back over her teeth in Mimi's lascivious smile. *"Not in front of the children, lover."* She wrapped Anya's arms around Brian's neck and purred, *"Though, I suppose if the kids don't mind, I don't, either."*

Brian hauled her over to the passenger seat and disentangled himself while Katie and Max grabbed her arms from the backseat. In the flailing mass of arms, Anya found herself wrapped in a seatbelt with a salamander pinning her in place.

"Settle down, Mimi." Jules's voice growled from the backseat. His hand snaked into view, holding a glass bottle of holy water. He flipped the cap off with his thumb, held it over Anya's chest. "You can sit quietly or take a shower. Your choice."

Anya could feel her lungs contracting around Mimi's hiss. *"Go fuck yourself."*

Jules made good on his threat. He threw the bottle in Anya's face. The water sizzled against her skin, stinging like ammonia on a wound. Where the water slapped her chest, she howled, as the water seared into the raw wounds on her chest. She wrapped her hands around her arms, bent double, and screamed. She called Jules every filthy name known to man, some in languages she didn't recognize. Spittle rattled against the window glass under the force of her invectives.

"Are you through? Or do you need a second application?" Jules's hand appeared again, with another full bottle.

Anya felt Mimi shrink back, and she regained control of her voice. "I'm okay, Jules." With a shaking hand, she pushed the bottle away. Sparky licked the fizzling water off her face, making sympathetic little mewls.

Jules watched her with a wary eye as Brian restarted the ignition and put the Dart into gear. Like a big green tank, it tooled through the streets of the industrial area south of Fort Street until it pulled up before the entrance to the Detroit Salt Company. Railroad tracks spidered in and out of the site, overgrown with weeds behind a chain-link fence. Behind it, an industrial elevator hulked against the sky.

Anya climbed out of the Dart and walked to the fence. The Dart's headlights cast her shadow long over the rusted links. The chain had already been severed, and the fence swung open with a rasp that scraped the cracked macadam beneath. She fingered the melted edges of the chain.

"Drake's been here," she announced. The metal still felt lukewarm to the touch.

"Goody." Mimi giggled in the back of her head.

She climbed back into the car. The Dart nosed through the overgrown weeds to the mouth of the tallest building on the site, a black tower overlooking the ruins of industrial buildings that held the rusting carapaces of trucks. Saplings split the pavement with their roots and weeds filled the gutters of the elevator building.

DAGR's flashlights seemed like puny pinpricks of light within the hulk of the elevator building. The sheet-metal walls blotted out nearly all the light from without, except where rust had burned through, opening pieces of the roof to the night. The industrial elevator was suspended by a series of massive, rusted pulleys, cables, and counterweights that angled far overhead. The structure had been open to the sky for some time. Doves warbled from their nests overhead, disturbed by the flashlights of the trespassers.

"How long did you say it's been since anyone's been down here?" Max asked.

"At least twenty years," Katie confirmed. "That's the only way in or out."

"I don't suppose we could just wait for Ferrer to come out on his own?" Max scratched the back of his cap.

"If there's no electricity, we might just have to do that." Jules shined his flashlight on the control panel for the elevator. "Let's hope that there's juice." He punched the button to recall the car.

The machine drives and sheaves overhead squealed and rumbled. The cables drew taut, and the counter-weights descended into the mine shaft. Anya could hear a sloughing, ticking sound from below, as the car was laboriously hauled up the mine shaft.

"How far is it down there?" Max asked.

"About twelve hundred feet," Brian answered.

"Shit."

Jules cuffed the back of his head. "Language, young man."

The elevator car reeled to the top, and the doors creaked open. The cavernous car, caged in perforated metal, was large enough to trap a large truck. Jules took the first step on the car, which seemed solid enough. The rest of DAGR crept in behind him, craned their necks as he punched the grimy buttons inside the elevator. Dim red hazard lights lit up the panel and cast warped shadows on the ceiling of the cage.

"Here goes," he said.

The car lurched and clanged.

"Oh, shit!" Max squealed.

Jules gave the kid a murderous look, but let it slide.

The car steadied under their feet then began to glide downward like a stone on the end of a string. The car plummeted, faster and faster, and the counterweights flashed past them. Anya laced one of her hands in Sparky's tail, and squeezed her other around Brian's hand. Her heart lifted into her throat, and she heard Katie shriek.

The elevator car screeched to a halt at the bottom of the shaft, stopping a foot above the floor of the mine. The car creaked slowly, swaying back and forth, as its occupants clambered to the door.

All false bravado, Max lifted his hands, as if he was on a roller coaster. "Whoo! Let's do it again."

Jules slapped the back of his head, but too late. The whoop echoed above and below them, bleeding out in a milky-white glittering cavern. Salt crunched underfoot. Like the surface of snow in winter, tire tracks could be seen crisscrossing the surface, scattered with debris. Anya's flashlight picked out a boot, broken pieces of wood, discarded bent steel tubing. But it smelled pure, clean. Somewhere water dripped, tapping a slow, steady rhythm like a leaky faucet.

"Where do we go now?" Max whispered, mindful of Jules's hand hovering near his head.

"There are more than fifty miles of road," Brian said. He pointed toward a heap of rusted out vehicles and carts. "We'd better find one of those that runs."

It took several tries, but the engine on a Jeep finally turned over. A broken trailer hitch behind it hauled half of a shattered cart, and the rear wheel on the driver's side was flat. But it ran. DAGR piled in with its guns and holy water, and the Jeep thumped down the tracks of its predecessors, piercing the dark with its dim yellow headlights. Salt spewed like gravel under its tires.

Anya clutched the bottom of her seat, Sparky wound around her knee. In the shotgun seat, Brian juggled a compass, flashlight, and the map, trying to navigate the tunnels to the oldest part of the mine. Striations of dirt and salt gleamed on the walls, suggesting the waves of what had been a vast inland sea.

"Stop." She clamped her hand down on Jules's shoulder. He stomped on the brakes, sending the flat tire flopping and skidding against the road. She pointed ahead of her. "Look."

She didn't know if they could see what she did, but she saw her: the little girl from the pop machine. She stood at a split in the road, her shoelace loose over her sneaker. She stared at the truck for a moment, then disappeared into the darkness after the Jeep's headlights washed over her.

"Do you see her?" Anya demanded. "Go that way . . . left."

Brian and Jules traded glances, but Jules wrestled the Jeep left over the loose ground. This far into the mine, the fine sea-salt fragments of rock had given way to large chunks, pieces broken from the ceiling, left behind from the dynamite of eras past. The ceilings of the vast chambers they drove through were supported by salt pillars every twenty-five feet. The further they went in, the rougher-hewn they appeared, like chiseled sentinels standing guard in the dark.

"Lot's wife," Katie muttered. She shuddered, and Anya could well imagine human shapes in the bounce of light and glistening shadow.

Deep within the belly of the mine, something rumbled. At first, Anya thought it was the whine of the overstressed Jeep's engine, but the sound grew in intensity until it lifted the hair on her arms. Sparky sat up between her knees, craning his neck into the dark. It growled and yawned through the chamber, rumbling like thunder that rattled the crystals on the ground. Fragments of rock shook loose from the high ceiling, pelting the Jeep like hail.

"Sirrush," Anya whispered, feeling his call deep in her bones. "Sirrush is awake."

The Jeep skidded to avoid a piece of boulder crashing to the road. Jules wrenched the wheel, but the Jeep rocked back too far on the flat tire, catching the rim on a rut in the road. Anya lunged forward to catch Katie, to keep her from falling out the Jeep's shallow backseat, as Jules struggled to regain control. The Jeep sawed to a stop against a salt pillar with enough impact to spill Anya from the back of the Jeep.

She tumbled to the ground, salt scraping her hands and knees. She picked herself up and turned back to the Jeep.

Sirrush's roar rose, filling the cavern. As she had in her dreams, she clapped her hands over her ears. Her heart trembled, shifting in response to the bass of that terrible sound. That single note reached up into the salt overhead, and wrenched it down with the deafening sound of millions of years of crystal fracturing and raining down into the dead, dry sea of the mine.

Fire followed behind the roar. The blistering heat of Sirrush's breath yawned through the mine, simmering the air like heat mirages on pavement. Anya pressed her hands to the floor of the cave, felt her sweat mixing stickily with the salt as it dripped from her brow. Sparky scrambled beside her, his tail scraping the damp salt on the ground.

Her attention was transfixed on a tiny figure far in the distance, barely visible in the farthest reach of the Jeep's shattered headlight: the figure of the girl from the pop machine. She stood silent as a sentinel, waiting for Anya.

Mimi's voice rattled in her skull: *"Don't let her get away."*

Behind her, she could hear shouting from the Jeep, glimpse the wash of flashlights in her periphery. But she turned her attention back to the little girl. She climbed to her feet and followed the girl's ghost into the dark.

CHAPTER TWENTY

THE GHOST OF THE LITTLE girl led Anya through a side passage, away from the wrecked Jeep and the flashlights. Like a will-o'-the-wisp, the girl bobbed and weaved around broken boulders, around cracked and shattered columns. Anya followed slowly, the amber light of her aura burning sickly above her skin. Strings of darkness permeated it, churning within the light: Mimi's influence. Sparky struck out ahead, his clear golden light illuminating his intentional tracks in the sand-fine salt: the curving sidewinder trail, punctuated by the scrape of his toes. In the ghost-light, his tracks looked very much like the mark of the Horned Viper, marching toward Sirrush's lair. Sparky rarely left tracks, but now he was blazing a trail for Anya.

The further she walked, the more the heat increased. Anya's clothes stuck to her body, and she stripped off her jacket and cast it aside. The sweat and condensing salt of the mine ran down the burns on her chest, stinging her wounds. Her damp feet squished in her socks and boots.

Her breath grew fast and shallow, and she felt Mimi twisting in her gut, clawing at her lungs.

Finally, she could see light ahead, the surreal orange light of Drake's paintings. She clomped toward it, feeling the sweat sizzle on her skin. Her copper collar scalded her throat like a bruise. On some level, she understood that the heat was growing beyond human tolerances, but she was past human tolerance.

She had to stop Sirrush from rising. Nothing else mattered. Not pain, not her friends left back in the mine. Not Brian. Not Mimi. Not Drake. Only Sirrush.

The pathway spilled down into a chamber as smooth and round as an egg, polished glistening white by centuries of heat and light. Nearly blinded, she shaded her eyes with her hand. Her breath caught in her throat as she beheld him.

"Sirrush." She and Mimi breathed the word together.

He turned to look at her. She understood, in an instant, why men had worshipped him and his kind as gods and her heart broke, seeing his unforgiving beauty unfurling before her. He towered above her in boneless curves of flaming scales, his serpentine body churning in a display of copper and gold. Golden horns lifted from his head like a crescent moon, above eyes as clear and brilliant as noon. Diaphanous gill-wings fanned around his face, so pale a gold that she could see the traces of his arteries beneath them. His armored forepaws were thick, like a cat's, claws piercing the floor. His rear legs were terrible eagle talons, flexing against the salt, his glistening tail wrapping around them as bonelessly as fire itself.

He lifted his golden head to roar at the ceiling, displaying three rows of ivory teeth as tall as men. The sound rattled the salt around Anya's feet, and she fell to her knees beside Sparky.

"Ancient one," Mimi whispered with her voice. *"I have brought you a gift."* She opened Anya's arms wide, a gesture of surrender and supplication.

"No." The dissenting voice was Drake's. He stood at Sirrush's feet, dwarfed by the glory of the creature he'd summoned. He stood barefoot on the sizzling salt, shirtless, his scars gleaming in the light. Anya could see that he bled from a wound in his side. His blood stained the salt rust. He looked up at Sirrush. "Your sacrifices are above. A whole city is yours. Can you hear it?"

"Sssssacrifice." Sirrush cocked his head, his gills moving, as if listening. Anya had heard that voice many times before, in the heart of every burning building she'd run into. When he spoke, it was with the crackling hiss of fire

"Sirrush," Anya said, with her own voice. "Take me instead and sleep. Do not level the city. Please."

Sirrush looked down his long nose at her, at Sparky. *"Another Lantern."*

"She's not giving herself to you of her own free will," Drake shouted. "She's got a demon in her, compelling her."

Sirrush's tongue reached out, snaked over her cheek and neck. She felt it sizzle and burn, but she made no move to resist. His breath smelled like the ozone aftertang of lightning.

"Mimiveh." Sirrush wrinkled his nose as he withdrew his tongue. *"Filthy demon. You taste like rot."*

Anya clenched her fist. "I'm telling you the truth. I'm giving myself to you, of my own free will." She pointed at Drake. "He can take the demon from me. I will give you the same offer, then."

Sirrush turned his noonday eyes to Drake. *"I will not be deceived by demon nor by man. Take the demon."*

Drake made no move, staring at her with a leaden gaze.

"Lantern," Sirrush snarled. *"Take the demon."*

Drake crossed to her and cupped Anya's face in his hands. He bent his head to kiss her.

Anya felt Mimi surging up from her chest, struggling against him. Anya clawed at his hands, fighting. But she felt Drake's burning red aura reach deep into the pit of her chest and dig the writhing demon out like a splinter.

She screamed. She screamed as Drake pulled Mimi out through the infected burn in her chest, at the writhing roots wound deep in her bones and her skin. The roots pulled, snapped, and were sucked up in the red rain of light that dug through her.

She fell to the ground, gasping. Her body rattled around the void that Mimi had left, at the empty space in her heart. She stared up at Drake. She could see him wrestling with Mimi. She could sense his aura was weak, weak from summoning Sirrush. He pulled the demon's inky tendrils away from his skin, grasping, as Mimi fought for its unlife. One of Mimi's thirsty arms reached deep into his ribs, through the gunshot wound.

Mimi wore Drake's voice like a puppet: *"Even better. This one is stronger."*

Anya reached up, snagging one of Mimi's tendrils. She felt the void in her chest opening like a black hole, sucking at the demon. Between the gravity of her power and Drake's, she felt Mimi pulling apart, like a cloud tattered by wind. The demon ripped like worn velvet, dissolving into the blinding purity of the salt chamber.

Sirrush watched silently, his paws pressed together like a cat's, and his body undulating like a kite.

Anya turned to face him. "Take me. But don't harm the city."

Sirrush stared at her, burning. *"I sense filth and decay. Crime and evil. The other Lantern is right. Why should I not take it as a sacrifice? It would be in the service of purity to do so."*

Anya spread her hands. "Because there are good things in it. There's art . . . the tile of the Sirrush in the museum. There's loyalty . . . you should see the number of people who come out to see the Lions play even though they always lose." She was babbling in the heat, but what she said was true and she hoped Sirrush could hear it. "Because more than a thousand people showed up for one firefighter's funeral. Because of music: Aretha Franklin, the Temptations. Hell, we're even responsible for Eminem. Because there are people falling in love and helping strangers. Because there are people who aren't going to give up." As she spoke, the dark spot in her chest that devoured ghosts filled with something a little bit like light.

Sirrush turned toward Drake. *"And is there not one thing worth saving in this city you would have me destroy?"*

Drake looked at Anya with such a look of tenderness that Anya ached to reach out and touch him. "One thing. Her."

Sirrush inhaled. Anya could hear the air whistling through his nostrils before he exhaled through his mouth, and the chamber erupted into flame. Fire coursed from his lungs into the egg-smooth surface of the chamber, consuming it in a seething roil of yellow flame.

Anya put up her hands to protect her face. The fire washed over her, crisping and disintegrating her hair. Out of the corner of her eye, she saw Drake in his Burning Man form. The yellow fire washed over the red flames covering his body, and she saw him fall.

She felt the threads of her blouse singe. Her shoe leather melted, and she felt the salamander collar dissolving into her skin. The flames washed over her raw, bare skin, blackening it to a crisp. She turned her attention inward, focused on the amber light in her chest that shined like love, that shined with the same color Sparky did, with her mother's love. With her love for her city, her friends, for Brian, and even Drake. She felt that warm purity in her, reaching through her body, welling up in her skin. This must have been what Nina felt, before she gave herself over to her dragon.

She felt her aura settling into her skin, hardening into copper scales. Dimly, she was aware of stepping forward to protect Sparky, of holding her arms before her, now heavy as gauntlets with copper skin that deflected the heat. Her senses had closed down, as if she was locked within a shell, and she could hear only her breath rattling against her wrists.

The fire slowly sank into the floor, and Anya opened her eyes. She looked down to see Sparky unharmed on the ground.

She scooped him up, snuggled him in joy. "Sparky!"

Then, she realized that something was wrong with her. Her skin was covered in copper, as if she wore a suit of armor, articulated to the very last detail. She flexed her fingers, watching in amazement as the finger-joints of the armor slid together. She pressed them to her chest, feeling a molded breastplate over her skin, articulated to swell with her chest when she breathed. She touched her face, feeling her skin grown copper and solid under her hands.

"Drake." She turned on a copper heel, scanning the red-hot crystal for him, and her face crumpled in sadness when she saw him. She fell to her knees at his side.

He was ruined, a blackened husk. His burning skin had not been enough to withstand Sirrush's fire. Every inch of his body was blackened with carbon. His eyes moved slightly, sightlessly in their sockets.

"Drake," she whispered, her hands hovering over his chest.

The remnants of his lips pulled back in a smile, and when he spoke, it was around a ruined tongue: "Armored goddess. Like Ishtar."

And his chest simply stopped moving under her hands.

Anya watched as his ghost climbed out of his body. But it wasn't the ghost of the Drake she had known. This was the ghost of Drake before he'd been blinded and scarred: Drake as a young man, whole, walking without a limp toward Sirrush, with his hands in his pockets and a luminous smile on his face.

Sirrush looked down his nose at her and Anya could have sworn he smiled. *"You have done well, Lantern. Your city is safe. I will sleep."* He turned his gaze to Drake. *"I will sleep under the watchful eye of a Lantern."*

Anya covered her mouth with her hands, tears blistering over her metal cheek. "I don't understand . . ."

"You will," Sirrush said. He yawned and circled like a cat in his nest. The yawn rattled the ceiling, and Anya could hear stress fractures forming above her in the rock.

"I'd get out of here, if I were you," Drake told her. *"When Sirrush makes a nest, walls come down."*

Anya scooped up Sparky and bolted for the exit. When she looked back, she saw Drake beginning to pace around Sirrush, like Nina had done for Uktena at the mound.

And he did it with the same serenity and love that brought tears to her eyes.

CHAPTER TWENTY-ONE

ANYA DISCOVERED, ONCE SHE MADE it topside, that the copper skin was an unfortunately temporary situation. She was embarrassed as hell when DAGR found her, their flashlights trained on her nude body. Fortunately, her firefighters' gear was still in the trunk of the Dart, so she didn't have to ride around downtown Detroit naked—though the firefighter's coat was perfectly ridiculous with bare knees and boots. She drowsed in the backseat on the way, her head resting on Brian's arm.

Detroit had calmed down by dawn. The radio announcer said that the jail fire had been contained, but that the casualties and escapees had not been counted. There were a handful of other casualties around town due to the Devil's Night celebration, but the majority of crimes had been property offenses: looting, burnt cars, and the like.

Max and Jules found Ciro slumped in his wheelchair in the bar. They panicked until Renee emerged to tell them that she and Ciro had spent the night singing and drinking.

The old man woke up asking for some hair of the dog and Jules slapped Max for giving it to him.

Katie took Anya home and put her to bed. She slept for a full day, before climbing out of bed and stumbling into the bathroom. Her shriek woke Katie from the couch.

Anya ran her hands over her perfectly bald head. Sparky climbed up on the sink and craned up to give her skull a loving slurp. "What the hell?"

Katie looked in the mirror behind her and pinched the shelved pirate rubber duckie on the ass until he squeaked. "You're bald. Like him."

Anya touched her eyes. She had no eyelashes, either. Anya opened her robe to look at the burns on her chest that Mimi had left behind. Only smooth white flesh glowed under the fluorescent light. Her salamander collar was wrapped around her throat, as always. She touched it, wondering if the armor still lived underneath it, and if she would ever need it again.

"I think it's gonna grow back," Katie offered, rubbing the back of her head. "You've got some stubble going on here."

"What did I miss?" Anya asked, fingering the unfamiliar sharp and blunt planes of her skull. She didn't realize that she had a freckle above her temple. Weird.

"Bad news or good news first?"

Anya steeled herself. "Hit me with the bad stuff."

"Remember Brian's video setup of the salt mine? He got nothing useful on camera, except some nice footage of the Jeep wreck. He's really pissed about that, but he's thinking about selling it to one of those reality shows that runs footage of a lot of shit getting blown up."

"Is that all the bad news?"

"Depends on how you look at things. Jules got an update on the little girl from the pop machine. The police were able to identify her. Her name was Gloria Selby. She went missing in 1974, lived across the street from the pickle lady. The coroner ruled it an accidental death— probably a game of hide-and-seek gone wrong."

Anya frowned. It was a sad case, but at least the little girl would have a name and a proper burial.

"You've also got some mail and phone messages." Katie wandered out into the living room, ticking reminders off her fingers. "Your boss, Captain Marsh, wants you to—and I quote—'quit loafing and get back to work Monday.' Brian's coming by later today to bring you some groceries. Sparky's Gloworm is out of batteries. And you got this." Katie pointed to a package in the living room with her toe. A brown paper–wrapped box leaned against the living room wall.

Anya picked it up and turned it over. The return address was Drake's, and the postmark was two days ago. She gingerly opened the brown paper, which covered a wooden box. Using a butter knife, she dug enough nails out of it to pull the item out of the straw.

It was his painting of her, from the night at the gallery. *Ishtar*. A pang of regret lanced through her as she held it up to the light. Seeing herself as she had just been in the mirror minutes ago, the painting seemed part of another world . . . not the bald bare woman standing in her yellow duck-patterned bathrobe.

Katie gave a low whistle. "That's seriously hot."

Anya leaned it on the fireplace mantel.

It was a reminder of what she could become, if she allowed it to happen.

Anya sat in the front pew of St. Florian's, waiting. She'd been waiting all afternoon for the ghost of the priest to appear. She watched the shadows and light play through the stained-glass windows, watched the faithful come and go. Sparky had stretched out his full length along the pew to take a nap, only to get snappish if an unwary parishioner tried to sit on him. More than one person got a nasty chill, stood up, and moved.

Finally, at dusk, the ghost of the priest appeared. As he had in her dream, he walked up the aisle and sat in the front pew. The last of the daylight shone through him and his ghost seemed very thin.

"I want you to know," she told him, "that I know what happened. That the demon Mimiveh had you."

The young priest stared down at his hands. *"I should have been stronger."*

"So should I. But she took me over, just the same." Anya leaned forward, her fingers playing with the fringe at the edge of the scarf she'd wrapped around her head. Her hair was pixie short, but the air felt cool enough on the back of her neck to make her want to cover it up. "And I also want you to know that Mimiveh has been destroyed."

The priest smiled. The last of the sun shone through him, and his ghost vanished. Anya reached out, and felt no whisper of him, no chill or hint of his presence.

This had been the first time that Anya had dispelled a ghost without devouring it. She savored the sensation as she walked from the church, out into the sharp November evening.

Brian was waiting for her on the church steps. He had always been waiting for her, and she had never appreciated it much, before. But now . . . She reached out and linked her hand in his arm. "Hey, Captain Cue Ball."

"Hello, Bald Stuff." They were having a contest to see who could grow hair back the fastest. So far, Brian was winning. His reached the tops of his ears. "I got you something," he said. He handed her a plastic bag. "Well, it's actually something for Sparky."

She opened it to find a glittery nightlight inside with a fairy on it. "He's going to love it."

"I thought that it might work with your new décor."

Katie had helped Anya paint a stylized circle on the bedroom floor around the bed. It was very decorative . . . and Anya hoped to make use of it to Ferberize Sparky, as necessary. She hoped to get to use it, anyway.

She leaned up to kiss Brian on the cheek. "Thank you."

"Are we still going to that benefit thingy? For the Motor City Phoenix Foundation?"

Drake Ferrer's second disappearance had caused something of a stir in the art world, especially after his comeback showing. The newspapers had not let it go and some of the deep pockets in town still seemed to be willing to fund the project. With the discovery of the new art in his studio, it seemed that the charity auction would bring a good turnout.

"Yup," Anya said. "I've just got to go home and change." She thought about the little black corset dress in her closet. Even though she no longer had long hair, she wondered if she could rock it enough to get some good use out of the magick circle in her bedroom.

She looked up at the darkening sky, at the stars beginning to peek out of the firmament. "Hey," she asked suddenly. "Do you know where Draco is? Can we see it from here?"

Brian stared up at the sky. He reached up, and her gaze followed his pointing finger. "See those four stars in the west, low on the horizon? That's his head. His tail arches up and around . . . he winds around the North Star, between the Big Dipper and the Little Dipper. Draco is one of the constellations that doesn't set in this hemisphere."

"I see him," she said, her breath frosting the air, feeling very small under the dragon strewn against the blackness. She imagined Sirrush sleeping in the white underground, guarded by Drake's spirit. What was the old magickal saying? "As above, so below . . ."

They walked into the dim evening, and Anya smiled at the city. Her city to guard. Though the city didn't know it, it had been given a second chance. And she would help make sure that they made the most of it.